CAGED
LIGHTNING

A WYATT STRYKER *NOVEL*

Praise for
CAGED LIGHTNING

"Dr. Brent Russell's *Caged Lightning* reads exactly like its name suggests: fast and furious. Wyatt Stryker, a special op soldier turned doctor, launches the reader on an adventure rarely seen in this genre."

DR. DEBORAH ROBERTSON
DIRECTOR OF EMERGENCY SERVICES
ST LUKE'S WOOD RIVER

"*Caged Lightning,* by Dr. Brent Russell doesn't build to action- -the action starts at the beginning and never lets up. The story holds your attention while your inquiring facilities are asking, "Where does this gripping, curving literary road lead?" The first fiction from this medical mind has a seldom-seen perspective and is written with a use of the language that is fresh, clear and exciting."

DR. ROY RUBY, EMERITUS
VICE PRESIDENT FOR STUDENT AFFAIRS
MISSISSIPPI STATE UNIVERSITY

CAGED LIGHTNING

A WYATT STRYKER *NOVEL*

BRENT ROCK RUSSELL, MD

elevate
fiction

Editorial Work: Dave Troesh

Cover Design: Aaron Snethen

Interior Design: Aaron Snethen

This book may be purchased in bulk for educational, business, organizational or
promotional use. To do so, contact Elevate Publishing at info@elevatepub.com

ISBN-10: 9781943425372

ISBN-13: 9781943425686

"Like an arrow in the hand of a warrior, so are the sons of those who have been shaken. Hurl lightning bolts and scatter them. Shoot your arrows and rout them."

-KING **DAVID**, CIRCA 1000 BC

CHAPTER
ONE

I was about to take a bullet to the cranium. Not for a particularly noble reason, like foiling a terrorist attack or hurling my body in front of the President. Nothing remotely worth the risk of a skull peephole.

At the time, the day seemed as good as any. Actually, better than most. With my gorgeous wife at my side, the Mexican sun gazed deep and thoughtful as we traveled to Senator Ripp's beach home, a short clip south of Tijuana. My mission was to protect the health and safety of a dozen of California's biggest egos: influential politicians and gazillionaires.

I first met the senator in the ER. He'd crashed his bike, taking a header down a jagged ravine. The sticks and stones didn't break his bones but did quite a number on his hide.

While I picked gravel out of his abraded skin and sutured his lacerations, we hit it off while discussing our mutual enthusiasm for mountain biking. He was intrigued by my background as a Navy SEAL. Then he surprised me by asking if I'd consider being his personal doctor and security consultant, sort of a bodyguard-doctor combo. I jumped at the opportunity since I'd long admired him, a national icon. And I couldn't blame him for wanting to avoid a clinic, as busybody staff might gossip. Mark Ripp was a moderate and humble congressman, scarce as unicorn shit.

After passing Tijuana, we arrived in Rosarito, footloose and kid-free. We had a wide open afternoon since the Ripps and their guests were not scheduled to arrive until evening. Catherine dropped me 10 miles from the house so I could go for a run. She went shopping for ceramics, feeding her addiction to bright Mexican pottery, our overburdened shelves already sagging toward collapse.

I swam a couple of miles in the ocean then did push-ups on the sand. I ran along the beach until I arrived at the Ripp's magnificent hacienda-style home, roosting on a cape like a sea hawk's nest.

I climbed the umpteen steps from the shore. With nothing to do until the guests arrived, I strolled around their manicured yard and noticed a man inside, probably domestic help.

I cooled off on the flagstone patio as the sun drooped earthward, backlighting gulls as they floated on ethereal thermals. The untouched beach stretched between emerald palms and the ceaseless onslaught of corkscrew waves, like Redcoats on a dogged march.

I felt a pang of temptation, a hankering to rent a surfboard and hit the glassy curlers. Instead, I wisely decided it wasn't a brilliant idea to ditch Catherine on our anniversary weekend. I felt bad enough that I had agreed to work but I couldn't turn down the senator's request. I wasn't planning on doing much and my pay was, to say the least, outrageous. I would be available, mostly to make his guests feel safe. Rich folks be nervous about Mexican crime and germs and such.

I walked toward the house and glanced through a window; their large flat screen sat on the floor in front of the entertainment center, the man's head buried in the open cabinet. I ducked out of sight, wondering why he would move their TV.

I crouched below the window, thinking. He could either be a repairman, a housecleaner or a thief. I considered phoning Senator Ripp but I'd feel ridiculous if he said, "Oh, that's just José." I imagined him hanging up the phone and laughing, *Wyatt was about to assault José for dusting behind the television. He might be taking his security job a bit too seriously. He probably relives his glory days as a SEAL, leading his neighborhood watch in fatigues and camo face paint, sprinting between trees as he searches for nefarious criminals.*

I decided against calling.

I crouched behind a bush so I could see both exits. The safest play would be waiting for him to exit. Things might get rowdy if I confronted him inside. Or I could clatter noisily before entry. If he were a burglar, hopefully he'd drop the loot and bolt. My gun was in our vehicle with Catherine since I'd come by way of the beach.

After a few minutes, my inquisitiveness got the best of me. I crept around the house, like a cat about to get himself dead for his errant curiosity.

When I peered around a corner, the man was climbing out the window, his back to me. Rushing forward, I arrived as his boots sunk into the grass.

3

From the elevated patio above him, I announced my presence, "¿Que esta haciendo?" *What are you doing?* I spoke decent Spanish.

He startled but quickly recovered with a convincing smile, "Limpiando la casa." *Cleaning the house.* He had a thick mustache beneath a straw cowboy hat.

"¿Por que se sube por una ventana?" *Why did you climb out a window?*

He switched to English with a heavy accent, "I mop and no want to mess clean with shoes."

"Why did you place the television on the floor?"

"Clean behind. I do very, very work. Very cleaning!"

"Where's your car?"

"No car. Bus! I ride bus."

"Are you a thief?"

"No, mi amigo! No thief! I work very good. I no steal!"

"Please wait while I call the owner."

I pulled out my phone. I was on the elevated patio, four feet above the grass where he stood. I could jump down if he ran; he was much smaller than me. As I'm six-three and pushing two twenty, most folks are.

He leaned against the patio wall below my feet, seeming bored and unconcerned.

I pulled up my contacts, finding Mark Ripp's number. The man slowly turned around and rested his hands on the edge with his chest against the wall.

As I dialed, his hands flashed forward, grabbing both my ankles, his movements astonishingly quick.

I tried to kick him away but he yanked forward with brutish strength. My legs shot skyward. I was airborne, falling ass over teakettle.

My shoulders landed hard and my neck whipped back. My skull hammered into the flagstone. It felt like I'd been smacked with a crowbar. My vision blurred and my head throbbed. I desperately wanted to curl into a fetal position. That single blow nearly took the fight out of me.

It took a moment to muster the strength to sit. As I pushed up, I saw him tearing around the rear corner of the house, holding my phone. Somehow during the fall, I'd dropped my cell.

Forgetting my pain and furious enough to chew glass, I leapt down and sprinted after him.

There was no easy escape from the backyard due to the cliffs and the long flight of stairs down to the beach. I doubled back, hoping to cut him off, heading for the front driveway.

I raced across the front yard, hurtled a low wall and gained speed as I neared the end of the house.

We rounded the corner at the same time. He threw his arms out when he realized I wasn't slowing.

I dropped my shoulder, exploding into him like a linebacker protecting the goal line. His feet left the ground and he flew backwards, his hands clawing the air. He landed on his upper back and skittered across the damp grass.

In a hot rage, I scrambled on top of him, knees battering whatever was in the way. I threw a haymaker, landing a solid blow below his eye.

He yelped and covered his face. He didn't try to defend himself but lay still, defeated: a poverty-stricken thief caught in the act.

With my brain-splitting headache, I felt like repeatedly cracking his skull but resisted since he looked so pitiful. I tore the phone from his weak grip.

Looming over him, I barked, "I'm calling the police!"

He gingerly touched his swollen cheek, trembling. Seemed like he was about to cry. He closed his eyes and rolled on his side. He reached behind, rubbing his lower back and groaning miserably.

Pathetic.

I studied my phone, wondering if 911 worked in Mexico.

His hand swung back around and he trained a pistol on my face. His expression transformed from meek to malevolent. The bumbling tremble gone, his aim was deadly calm.

I backed away, hands up. His pistol was a rare and expensive Kimber 45, not the gun of a common burglar.

He stood. His broken English suddenly quite good, he spat, "Throw me the phone then get on your knees." He extended his free hand.

I tossed it then dropped to my knees. He pocketed the cell.

I had a horrible sinking feeling, but still hoped he would leave since he'd gained the upper hand.

Instead of escaping, he moved behind me then racked the slide, chambering a round with a snap like a teacher's ruler.

I stammered, "There's no need to kill me." My pulse drummed in my ears.

I heard a faint click then a screwing noise, but didn't interpret the sound fast enough. If I'd reacted, I might've had a chance to save myself. But I was out of training, out of the SEALs for too long. He'd attached a silencer to the pistol.

He planned to kill me.

I tried to think of a way out but came up with nothing. He stood several feet behind, too far.

My eyes clenched tight, waiting for the end. Cursed myself for being so stupid. I should've allowed him to escape. I'd stuck my nose into something that wasn't my business. I was hired to protect the guests, not to fight petty crime.

With my eyes shut, I was aware of everything, hyper-alert.

I felt my breathing, my heartbeat and the lawn beneath my knees. Damp from a recent watering, grass that didn't belong in this parched desert, the water-wasting, time-consuming suburban affliction. Water and fertilize and grow and cut, water and fertilize and grow and cut. Then repeat the preposterous cycle until the river runs dry.

I changed my thoughts, not wanting to die while mentally critiquing yard-culture.

I would face the end with my eyes open. Stared straight ahead at the ocean. A fitting view for my last moments.

I thought about my precious son and lovely wife, soon to be fatherless and widowed.

A seagull hovered then dove, sliding toward an unsuspecting fish, and then emerged with a beakful of prey.

I couldn't believe I'd die this way, slain by a random Mexican thug. The bullet would drill through scalp and bone then enter grey matter, disrupting my brain's electric currents with a short-circuited pop. My consciousness would instantly vanish. Lights out. Game over. Same as the hapless fish abruptly crushed in a beak.

7

I supposed he was particularly vile thief, as killing me served no purpose. I would pay for the Senator's television with my life. Fairly expensive.

I heard gravel crunching under tires, a car pulling into the driveway.

He straightened to listen.

Since his back was to the entrance, he moved to my left and jammed the suppressor hard against my temple, glancing toward the front. The driveway was out of sight. If he were going to kill me, he would have do it quickly. Now or never.

But he'd made three mistakes.

First, he should've stood on my other side, where there was more space. A large palm tree crowded him close. Within reach.

His second mistake was holding the gun in just one hand.

But his crucial mistake was pressing the pistol hard against my skull.

The car door slammed. While he was distracted, I dug my right hand into a bald patch beside my knee and scooped a fistful of damp earth. I slowly kneaded the fine gravel and sticky dirt, forming a ball, heavy and hard. I'd been a fairly decent baseball pitcher in my high school days. The game wasn't over just yet.

He pushed the muzzle against my scalp. Most victims would pull their head away from the muzzle.

But I leaned into the gun, adding to the pressure.

I'd used a Kimber. The trigger required five pounds of squeeze, more than most handguns.

I felt subtle movement as he began pulling the trigger.

Game on, bottom of the ninth.

I spun my neck hard, jerking to face him. The pistol was snug against my head, so the muzzle rotated back. The long silencer added to the fulcrum, making the gun pivot easier, as did his singlehanded grip.

The bullet exited with a bright flash and a muffled thump, lacerating my scalp. I smelled gunpowder and burnt hair.

If he'd held the barrel just an inch from my skull instead of pressed tight, no matter how much I herky-jerked, my bloody consciousness would've splattered the adobe wall.

I'd already spun my head toward the batter. Continuing my rotation, I swept with my left forearm, knocking his gun aside and exposing his face.

Now all my weight and momentum was channeled into my throwing arm, coming around like a wrecking ball.

The wad left my right hand, traveling well over the speed limit.

The heavy ball struck him square in the face. The perfect beanball. Then exploded in a wet cloud of dirty shrapnel, penetrating his skin with jagged gravel and needles of sand.

He stumbled backward, off balance.

I completed my rightward rotation by dropping my shoulder and rolling in a tight somersault behind the palm.

He fired blindly, rounds whistling and thumping against the earth. Even if he'd managed to close his eyelids before impact, his face was caked with wet, sticky sand.

I popped onto my feet, landing in a crouch. Keeping the tree between us, I sprinted toward the house. As I glanced back, I saw him clawing at his eyes with his free hand, chunks of bloody sand falling away. He swung his gun toward me.

A bullet struck the wall near my head. The stucco exploded, fragments peppering my face.

I circled the rear of the house and rounded the next corner, passing the window he'd climbed out. Thought about propelling myself through the open window but decided it would take too much time. I didn't want to lead him to the front yard, endangering the car's occupant. Leapt onto the retaining wall of the flagstone patio then slid on my hip, baseball style.

Rolled onto my belly and lay flat behind a gazebo. Through the vines on the gazebo's lattice, I'd be able to see him coming.

After several excruciatingly long minutes, I decided he'd escaped, probably down the stairs to the beach. I surged with adrenaline, simultaneously feeling like joyful cheering and breaking something.

I quietly stood instead and cautiously walked to the vehicle in the drive, my Ford Explorer. Catherine was already in the house.

I touched my scalp where the bullet grazed me, feeling burnt, frizzy hair from the muzzle flash. I palpated a two-inch laceration. Catherine, a nurse, could tie my hair together to close the wound, an old battlefield trick.

I leaned against the truck, thinking. Why would a burglar enter the house but not take anything? Perhaps he'd seen me outside and gotten spooked.

But why did he have a Kimber semiautomatic with a suppressor?

Maybe he wasn't a random thief. His skills were beyond that of a two-bit crook. Of course, he failed to kill me, but had no clue he was dealing with a former Special Ops soldier.

He seemed Mexican but the more I thought about it, he had vaguely Asian features. Iranian or Pakistani maybe. But not exactly.

I couldn't put my finger on it, but I doubted he was Mexican. His accent vanished when he was about to kill me, like he didn't need to continue the ruse since I was marked for death.

I wondered if he was a professional hit man. Senator Ripp or one of his elite dinner guests could plausibly be the target of a foreign assassin.

CHAPTER
TWO

Behram was a given name, but not by his parents. At Behram's birth, his devout parents gave him an honorable and pious name, Anwar, meaning devotee of God. Behram had unique and peculiar values, but neither honor nor piety was among them. He had many exceptional skills, but earned the name Behram because he could accomplish one task better than any peer.

He was brilliant, with interpersonal skills honed like a Machiavellian politician, interpreting others' motivations and imperfections to accomplish his goals. Behram's knowledge of culture and customs was the result of study, intuition and unending travel. His language skills were legendary. He had the strength of a Brahman bull combined with a viper's deadly reflexes. But none of these were the sole justification for his name.

Behram was given his name because he was unrivaled in his ability to expel surprised souls from their cozy ninety-eight degree vessels.

He studied the windows of a cedar shake house. He was a master of disguises and accents. He had an average build with light olive skin and black hair, neither ugly nor handsome, his vague features disguising his ethnicity. His pack contained surveillance equipment, a set of lock picks, weapons, restraints and vials of anesthetic. He had everything he needed to make sure the meddling doctor couldn't identify him. He carried his backpack like a duffel bag, slung casually over his shoulder, his right hand wrapped in an ace bandage, concealing a cheap .38 special.

He'd stolen the .38 from a local thug, Karl, and saved it for a rainy day. Karl's fingerprints remained on the gun. Behram wore a black leather coat and a ponytail wig, imitating Karl. The throw-away gun would soon disgorge the doctor's spirit: abruptly, prematurely and unexpectedly. The vehicle carrying his soul would spill its warmth, eventually cooling to an ambient temperature.

Behram did not believe in souls or the afterlife, but he liked to think of death this way, as it made him feel mystical, godlike, omnipotent. The rainy day had arrived as black rain, for both Dr. Stryker and Karl.

He mentally reviewed his plan. The .38 was wrapped in the ace bandage to disguise the gun and muffle the shot. When the man rolled into view, Behram would wave him down with a smile. Once the car stopped, or even if he didn't stop, the pistol would send a thunderbolt into his skull followed by a maroon drizzle. A rainy day indeed.

He'd been lurking since early morning, but still hadn't spotted the doctor. Behram was certain he was at the correct house, as the mailbox held letters addressed to Wyatt and Catherine Stryker. He could see the woman in the kitchen. He waited patiently.

Behram could blend into any crowd, making himself invisible even while in plain view. He never left a trail, unless it was a false one. He hadn't been injured in over ten years.

He got his name from the world's most prolific serial killer, the original Behram, who murdered nearly a thousand victims in the 18th century, as a member of the Hindu death cult, the Thuggee. The reincarnation of Behram worshipped the same way, although his only gods were money, power and himself.

This second Behram began hunting souls as a commando in his native Nepal, assassinating enemies of the state. As the body count mounted, so did his notoriety as the ultimate human predator. He eventually grew tired of his leaders' smug religiosity and patriotism. He was neither religious nor patriotic. Anwar faked his own death and was reincarnated as Berham. Then he began selling his services to the highest bidder. That's how he had landed in San Diego.

He looked at the house with mounting unease. He decided he couldn't wait any longer. If the doctor's wife was in the kitchen, he must be upstairs with the boy. Even if he weren't, his family's safety would provide sufficient motivation to rush home.

Behram walked quickly to a window screened by tall shrubbery. He unwrapped the ace bandage from his hand and stored the .38 in his pack. He popped the screen and unlocked the window, raising it noiselessly. He entered an unused bedroom.

He removed the wig then covered his head with a black balaclava. He gripped the Steyr semi-automatic pistol with a long suppressor. He clipped plastic restraints, duct tape and a hunting knife to his belt. He drew a vial of tranquilizer into a syringe. He activated the cell phone jammer and connected a pen-sized device to a vacant phone jack.

He cracked the door open and listened: the hallway was empty. He crept toward the kitchen.

The woman's back was to him, engrossed in a book, her golden hair past her shoulders. She wore sandals, jeans and a plaid flannel shirt.

She was beautiful.

He unsheathed the razor-edged knife as he stepped into the kitchen. She aimlessly fiddled with a dangling earring. He silently crept forward. He smelled her faint perfume and a familiar thrill surged.

He lifted the blade.

Inside the house, Blake searched his room, deciding his Lego battleship was the most impressive thing he could show her. He proudly admired his creation. The battleship had four cannons on the front and two in back, to defend an attack from the rear. She'd love it! Blake was ten and a half, the half important enough to mention whenever asked his age.

He headed out to rejoin his Aunt Susan. His mom's sister was baby-sitting while his parents were in Mexico. He carefully picked up his masterpiece and started down the hall, socks padding silently.

As he turned the corner to enter the den, he found Susan facing him from the kitchen. A man stood behind her, his arm around her neck. At the strange sight Blake froze. Was he one of her friends? What were they doing?

He looked closer. The man was holding a knife to Aunt Susan's throat!

Blake slowly backed into the hall. He set the battleship down before creeping to the corner to watch, his heart punching against his ribs.

The man's black mask covered everything but his eyes. He pushed her into a chair, facing Blake. He tied her hands behind the chair with plastic ties. Tears ran down her pretty face.

He had to help her. If he could sneak around them and grab the cordless phone in the kitchen, he could call the police and his parents. Dad was a SEAL and a college football player, a linebacker. He could easily beat the man up.

The man crouched, tying Susan's feet to the chair. Blake's gaze met Susan's frightened eyes, more scared than he'd ever seen a grown-up.

She moved her lips, saying something. He watched carefully. She mouthed again. What was she saying? Won? Gun?

Run! She was telling him to run! He backed into the hall, wondering if he should run. He could climb out his bedroom window and run for help.

He hurried softly to his room. Yet he didn't feel right about leaving Susan with the man. He spotted the prized bat his parents had gotten him for his birthday, perfectly balanced for his swing. Dad taught him how to swing with power, saying, "Swing with the force, like Luke Skywalker."

He picked up the heavy bat. Felt good in his hands.

He decided he couldn't leave Susan. The man might take her while Blake was gone. He might even kill her.

He picked up a batting practice weight, a heavy metal cylinder, and slid it down, resting on the bat's sweet spot. The cast-iron donut would make it hurt even worse. He'd spent countless hours swinging the weighted bat.

He crept down the hall, tightly gripping his bat with both hands. He noticed he was breathing hard. The man might hear it. He controlled his panting, forcing himself to slow down.

He crawled, peeking around the corner.

The man was facing his way.

He pulled back, wondering if the man had seen him. He stood; ready to run if the man came. Felt sweat trickle past his nose.

He felt fluttery inside, like he had before breakdancing in the talent show. His knee trembled. Breathed in and breathed out.

He would save Aunt Susan.

Once he was sure the man hadn't seen him, he peered around the corner. The man was whispering in Susan's ear, his back to Blake. He charged into the den, but his socks slipped on the hardwood floor. He nearly fell. He continued running, and then ducked behind the couch.

Susan was facing the couch. She'd seen him. She knew he was coming to help.

He pulled off his Spiderman socks so he wouldn't slip again. He held the bat in one hand as he crawled to the edge of the couch. The man was putting duct tape on Aunt Susan's mouth.

He squatted and scooted forward, peeking around the edge. The intruder knelt in front of Susan, searching for something inside a large bag.

Blake stood and ran forward, the bat cocked behind his head. He threw his full weight into the bat, swinging for the bleachers.

The bat cut a sharp arc toward the man's ear. At the last possible instant, the man ducked, throwing up his arm. The bat connected with a sound like a dry stick breaking. The man moaned a deep-throated grunting noise, his forearm bent at an angle never intended by nature.

The man rotated, ferociously kicking Blake in the chest. He flew backward and landed on his back, striking his blonde scalp against the floor. He rolled onto his face, trying to breathe. He groaned, his wind gone.

He slowly pushed up with his hands. He tasted metal, blood. A black arm hooked around his neck, squeezing, choking. Everything seemed blurry, like he was going to sleep.

His face felt swollen. His feet were hoisted off the ground, the man lifting him by his head with his uninjured arm. Crying out, Blake gripped the man's arm with both hands. He gagged as the man tightened. He helplessly kicked his bare heels against the man's legs. The man breathed noisily in his ear.

Blake bent his knee, hoping to kick the man in his privates. But the man swung Blake to the side, and then bent over, heaving Blake's body onto his back. Blake's head was upside down, his curved back arching over the man's shoulders, his soft little toes barely touching the floor. His neck was hyper-extended. He gagged and choked. Felt like his throat would be crushed. Blood bubbled from his mouth.

The man adjusted his arm, and during the moment of slackness Blake ducked his chin under the forearm and sucked in a breath.

The man had only one functioning arm, so he couldn't hold Blake's feet. Blake pulled his knees to his chest then threw his legs over his head in a slow backflip, landing hard on his feet. The man still held his neck.

The intruder moved slowly, gingerly protecting his wounded arm. Instead of dropping and pinning Blake, he remained standing.

Blake tried to pull his head loose, pushing the man's arm and backing away. He squirmed and kicked. The man bent forward, pulling Blake's head under his chest then tightened the headlock. He was too strong. Blake felt his brains squeezing out, like toothpaste.

Blake became weaker, his vision going black. He was underwater, drowning. He stopped struggling and fell limp, his arms dropping to his sides.

The man loosened his stranglehold.

Blake's eyes blinked open. He stared at the floor, his wits returning. He saw the man's bent arm dangling. He reached for it.

His little fingers caught the man's thumb and clenched tight. Pulling the hand toward him, he grabbed the man's wrist with his other hand.

The man jerked away but his arm bent in the middle of his forearm. He gasped and released Blake, dropping to his knees.

He swung but was off balance and landed only a glancing blow to Blake's shoulder. Still holding his hand, Blake stepped behind the man, the untethered forearm moving helplessly. Twisted as hard as he could, turning the hand in a circle, and then viciously yanked it side to side, like a dog with a toy.

With a prolonged crackle like wood splintering, jagged bones punched through his black shirtsleeve, bright red blood spattering Blake's Star Wars pajamas. The man screamed like a feral animal. Blake released the hand and ran.

He was free!

He raced to the kitchen and grabbed the cordless phone. He sprinted in an arc around the kneeling man. The man barely glanced up, sweat dripping from his mask as he cradled his destroyed arm.

Blake slammed his bedroom door, locking it behind. He turned on the phone, but there was no dial tone. He entered 9-1-1. Nothing. He tried again. Still nothing. He yelled into the phone, "Hello? Hello? I need the police! Hello?"

The phone wasn't working.

He dropped the phone then pushed his twin bed against the door with a screech.

He heard footsteps in the hall.

He ran to the window and rapidly turned the handle, cranking it open. In his panic he couldn't figure out how to remove the screen.

He heard the man kick his prized battleship, Lego pieces scattering down the hall.

He grabbed a chair from his desk. Standing on the chair, he threw his shoulder into the screen. The screen ripped.

The doorknob rattled.

He tried to fit through the split, but the hole was too small. The man kicked the door. Wood splintered.

Blake screamed, "Leave us alone! Leave us alone!" He threw his shoulder against the screen again, the tear growing.

The man struck the door again and the doorknob broke through the frame. Blake stared in horror as he pushed it open, easily moving the bed.

Lurching, Blake thrust his head through the screen, but his shoulder got caught. He pulled back in.

The man kicked the chair under Blake's feet. His head struck a cabinet as he fell, landing on his back. The man crushed his chest with a boot. With his good arm, he removed a syringe from his belt, removing the needle sheath with his teeth. He stabbed Blake's leg through his thin pajamas.

Everything started going fuzzy all at once. Blake felt warm and comfortable. His room looked shimmery, like a dream. He stared at the man's hurt arm, wondering why the bent arm looked so weird.

His world faded to black.

CHAPTER
THREE

Monday morning, Catherine and I drove back across the border, travelling home from Mexico. We'd spent Saturday at the Ripp's house then Sunday night in a swanky beachside hotel, an anniversary splurge.

Catherine said, "What a whacked-out, crazy weekend! First, you almost got yourself killed playing Strike Em Stryker." My baseball nickname. I grinned at her lighthearted jab, mostly because she was right.

I said, "Then we had dinner with some of the most powerful people in California. I was expecting a bunch of rich stuck-ups, but most of them were pretty cool."

I fingered the small braid Catherine made to close my scalp wound, "That prim woman who droned on about her art foundation kept sneaking glances at my weave, like I was rocking a terrible new do."

Catherine laughed, "I know, right? The mono-braid!" She wore shorts, sandals and a hooded cobalt sweatshirt, matching her eyes. Her long tan legs looked as great as they did in college. I felt lucky to have her by my side. If she knew she was beautiful, it didn't seem important.

I said, "But my favorite part of the weekend was the reenactment of our honeymoon last night."

She smiled. "Me too. We gotta get away more often. I wonder how Susan's holding up. I bet Blake's giving her a run for her money."

"He's a wild man. But he seems to be doing a little better."

"You wish! I got a note from school; he put chalk in Mrs. Brown's drink." She frowned comically.

I burst out laughing but made a mental note to discuss such shenanigans with him, man-to-man. Blake was fun loving and sweet but pushed every boundary, a chip off the ol' blockhead.

I thought about my conversation with the Ripps about the burglar, or whatever he was. After hearing the entire story, the Ripps looked aghast.

"Wyatt, I'm so sorry," said Beth Ripp. "We've never had a burglary. The neighborhood's gated with twenty-four-hour security. We remotely deactivated our alarm so you could enter."

Mark added, "I grew up coming here, my parents' home. In the old days, Tijuana was a dusty, colorful town, the Mexicans riding donkeys and wearing sombreros. Rosarito was tiny, just a few houses on the beach. The crime rate's soared since the cartels moved in but we stubbornly continue to visit. I hate that happened to you, Wyatt."

"Don't worry about it. Should we call the police?"

"The locals don't know I'm a senator and we don't want attention. If you want to report the assault and phone theft, you could say you're guests of my parents. They still own the place."

"I don't think it'd do any good. He probably didn't leave prints since he wore gloves."

I told them of my suspicions. They tried to act concerned and polite but I thought I detected a hint of skeptical bemusement, like I had an overactive imagination. I hoped they were right.

I'd been a fan of Senator Ripp long before he was a client and a friend. He was a national figure with presidential aspirations, a highly respected U.S. Senator for nearly twenty years, one of the clearest thinkers in U.S. politics. Almost every time I listened to him speak or read his opinions, I agreed with his logic, a remarkable man with a nuanced grasp of facts. He seemed like a genuinely well-meaning person who used his remarkable talents to improve life for others. His approval ratings were through the roof.

Distance wise, Rosarito wasn't far from San Diego but the noontime border crossing was a huge time-suck due to increased security. I found it bizarre that U.S. tanks patrolled the border.

I remembered what Senator Ripp had said about Operation Cartel to his dinner guests, "For years, U.S. law-enforcement chafed that they were merely advising their Mexican counterparts in the battle against the cartels. Many wanted American armed forces to have wide operational latitude on the ground, as they had once had in Colombia. But the prospect of an overbearing American law-enforcement presence offended many Mexicans' sense of sovereignty, since we've invaded Mexico multiple times in our history. The current Mexican administration finally relented and allowed our troops to aid in select operations. Since then, there's been considerable mission-creep." The Senator had raised his hand, as though holding off an objection.

"Don't get me wrong. Admiral Landfair has my utmost respect. No one's more capable than Landfair and the president picked the right man to run Operation Cartel. But it's done nothing to stem the tsunami of drugs entering the U.S."

We soon were approaching our neighborhood. I eagerly anticipated Blake bursting from the door looking for a family hug. He'd tell us about their adventures in great detail. He'd beam in our presence. It had been less than three days since I'd seen him but seemed like an eternity. I loved that blond-headed rascal.

Being a father was different than anything I'd ever experienced. In some ways, raising a child was the most challenging task I'd ever faced, more than SEAL training or med school. In his first year, he was a poor sleeper and everyone suffered from sleep deprivation. I was in the throes of residency and worked long hours, often gone for days. I sometimes felt like my affectionate wife had been lost to the new baby. During his infancy, we argued more than the rest of our relationship combined.

As a toddler, he wanted to be the boss, almost never doing what we asked, usually the opposite. Even at ten, he was still pushing Catherine's buttons and arguing with both of us.

But no question, being Blake's daddy was the most rewarding thing I'd ever done. I loved he and Catherine more than life itself. He was a bundle of loveable childish energy. He made us laugh as much as our most entertaining adult friends. Already, Blake was a giant compared to his peers and a stellar athlete. He was an interesting mix of the two of us and I thought he had the best qualities of both.

I pulled into the drive behind Susan's car. Blake would be eager to see his mom's response to her anniversary gift, a painting of Mount Hood near my parents' home in Oregon. I could tell by Catherine's response that he hadn't told her and I was proud of him for keeping the secret.

I carefully carried the painting. She opened the door and yelled, "We're home!"

The TV was blaring. Catherine turned it off. I called, "Come out, come out wherever you are!" No answer. I set the painting on the couch.

Blake loved to hide then jump out to scare us. Usually, we pretended to be scared, but sometimes he scared the bejeezus out of us. Once Catherine dropped a bag full of groceries, breaking a jar of spaghetti sauce. She made him clean the mess and sent him to his room. But I'm sure he thought the crime was worth the time.

They were hiding somewhere. I smiled at Catherine knowingly and she grinned. I walked to his room. Looked like a cyclone had struck. His door was broken and his bed in the wrong place. The cordless phone lay on the floor. The window was agape, the screen dented and torn. I frowned.

I yelled again. Maybe they were out walking in the neighborhood. We were back a little early.

Catherine screamed, a blood curdling, horrified scream. My adrenaline surging, I ran into the kitchen. Susan was bound to a chair, gagged with duct tape. Catherine removed a blindfold from her eyes, tears streaming silently down. I grabbed scissors, cutting the duct tape. A cloth ball fell from her mouth.

She spoke in a whispering croak, "He took Blake!"

Catherine was immediately hysterical, "Who? Who took Blake?" She gripped Susan's shoulders, "Who took my baby?"

Before Susan could answer, Catherine bolted from the room, yelling, "Blake! Blake!" She entered his bedroom and screamed.

Susan's hands and feet were secured with plastic ties to the chair, the plastic cutting into her skin. I cut them loose.

I asked, "Who took Blake?"

"A man. A man came," stammered Susan, her voice hoarse. She stood but buckled, her legs cramping. I helped her to the couch and got her a glass of water.

Catherine ran back into the room, her face a mask of horror. Her voice was unnatural, guttural, inhuman, "Where's Blake? Where is he?"

Susan wept, "A stranger took him." She threw her arms around Catherine, sobbing, unable to speak.

Catherine asked, "Did he hurt you? Did he do anything to you? Oh, my baby!" She pulled back but kept her hands on Susan's shoulders, searching her face for answers.

Susan's voice quavered, "A man came yesterday. He tied me up and took Blake. He made me write a ransom note. I've been tied up for nearly a day."

"Oh my God," whispered Catherine.

"I was reading and suddenly there was hand on my mouth and a knife to my throat. He said, 'If you make a noise, I'll kill your family. Cooperate and you'll both be fine. This is a robbery.' I thought he was a rapist."

She covered her mouth, sobbed loudly for a moment then recovered. After she told us the initial details, she said, "Blake grabbed the phone and ran to his room. I prayed he was climbing out the window. The man clamped his hand over his bleeding arm and said, 'I'll kill him if you're not here when I return or if you make a noise.' The man broke the door open and must've put Blake to sleep. He was unconscious when they returned. He looked like a sleeping angel. He seemed so little." She began to sob uncontrollably.

Catherine waited in agony, her face contorted. Susan finally controlled her crying then whispered hoarsely, "I've been thinking about it ever since. The man didn't seem rushed so he must've cut the phone lines. He removed my gag and asked where Wyatt Stryker was. I said you were out of town. I begged him to take me instead. He bandaged the arm that Blake injured with one of your towels. He closed the shades then turned on the TV at full volume. He chained the chair to this post. He made me write that note." She pointed at the table.

I read the note, the writing shaky and spattered with tears. *Bring $20,000 in small, unmarked bills in a duffel bag to Tidelands Park on Coronado at 10 PM, October 16. Wear your yellow parka and sit on an isolated park bench. If you contact the authorities, you'll never see your son again.*

My yellow parka lay beside the note. We only had a few hours.

"He wiped up his blood then blindfolded and handcuffed me. I think he put Blake inside his bag." She burst into near hysterical sobbing.

Catherine cried, "Call the police!"

"Let's take a few minutes to think," I said. "If we call the police and the kidnapper finds out, we won't get Blake back."

"We can't waste time!" They can put out an Amber Alert!" She pulled her phone from her purse.

"Hold on. We should just pay the ransom." I held my finger to my mouth in a hush gesture. I wrote a note. *They could be listening. Hidden mics.*

Catherine nodded and gathered her composure, "Okay. Let's not call." Susan touched her arm.

We embraced but my mind raced, eerily calm. My SEAL background and emergency medical education trained me to have crystal-clear thoughts during stress. My thinking shifted into high gear. I said, "I'm going to get a few things from our bedroom."

I walked upstairs to think. I sat on the edge of our bed, staring at a blank wall. It didn't make sense. Only twenty thousand ransom?

Maybe it was a botched rape. Catherine and Susan were both beautiful; either could've caught the eye of a sadistic pervert. But that didn't explain why he'd take Blake.

Maybe it was a kidnapping racket. An excellent cat burglar could snatch children for relatively small demands and stay under the police radar, big business in some Latin American countries. If they kept the payout demands low, the families could pay quickly and might avoid going to the authorities.

Maybe it was personal, but as far as I knew, I had no enemies. Was it related to my SEAL career? Revenge? Military
secrets? Who wanted something from us? If the kidnapper
planned to hurt or abduct me, he would've waited until I was
home. Or he could've lured me by having Susan call.

There was the unthinkable possibility: a pedophile or a
child sex trafficking ring. The ransom demand could be a ruse
to throw off law enforcement. If the police thought it was a
hostage situation, they might not issue an Amber Alert.

If he was a child molester, he wasn't your typical greasy
loser. The man entered a locked home in broad daylight and
snatched Blake without leaving a single clue. He wouldn't go
on a pathetic road trip, stopping at truck stops, pretending
Blake was his nephew. Blake would already be locked in a
basement, never again to see the light of day. An Amber Alert
would be futile.

I wouldn't mention this possibility to Catherine and Susan.

I needed to bounce my thoughts off someone else. Someone
less emotionally involved than the three of us, someone wise
and logical. Someone used to solving difficult and dangerous
problems.

I hoped he was available.

I wrote on a piece of paper. *We need to leave to speak freely.
We won't return until this is over. Get whatever you need for a
few days. Remove all private information and files. He might
come back.* I walked downstairs and showed them the note.
They nodded.

I said, "Let's go to Susan's house then I'll get money from
the bank."

"Okay."

I returned upstairs, studying the street and yard. I was confident they weren't watching the house, too risky to have a person on scene. Cameras would be easy to detect. On the other hand, a pro could wire the house in minutes. Only an FBI team with specialized equipment could locate microscopic listening devices.

I jumped our backyard fence into my neighbor's yard. They were out of town. I knew where they kept a key: the same place everyone does, under the floor mat.

I called Javier Alcaraz from their phone. I prayed he'd answer, since he wouldn't recognize the number. After three rings, he answered, "Hello."

"It's Wyatt."

"Riot Wyatt, the surf is up!" He exclaimed with his normal enthusiasm. "Let's go! Black's Beach is going off! I was about to call you."

"Blake's been kidnapped by a stranger. I'm not joking."

He shouted, "What?"

"I'll explain later. Can you meet now?"

"Of course. Where?"

"Meet us at the Target on Balboa in an hour."

"I'll be there."

I returned to the house and scribbled another note. They were upstairs in our bedroom, throwing clothes in a suitcase, both crying. They wiped their eyes to read. *Let's take my SUV and leave the other cars here. They might have tracking devices. Javier will meet us. Leave your cell phones. They can be traced.* They nodded in understanding.

I spoke aloud, "Let's go to Susan's house. She needs to clean up."

Javier and I had been through a lot. He was unbelievably intelligent and had a quiet strength, both physically and mentally. He was the best soldier I'd ever known and the best friend I'd ever had. I could always count on him to have my back. If anyone could save Blake, it was Javier.

CHAPTER FOUR

After leaving the house, I circled the block, watching the rearview mirror. I drove evasively, stopping at green lights and running red ones. I doubled back twice.

I withdrew the money from our bank then went to Target. I bought four pre-paid cell phones with cash. When I returned to the parking lot, Javier's black double-cab pickup was parked next to my SUV.

Javier was visibly shaken. He embraced me in a bear hug. "I'm so sorry. We'll get Blake back, I promise."

I tried to answer but the words didn't come.

He gave me time to recover then asked, "Let's go to my house on the base."

I asked, "Can one of you drive and follow us to Javier's house on Coronado? I need to discuss the situation with him."

"Sure," said Susan. She wiped her eyes.

I climbed in Javier's truck. He listened impassively as I told him about Blake's abduction, his dark eyes furrowed in deep concentration, occasionally asking pertinent questions. He was in information-gathering mode, his brilliant mind considering every angle.

Javier and I went through SEAL training together. Basic Underwater Demolition/SEAL development, known as BUD/S, is the harsh proving grounds for potential SEALs. Only one out of five accepted into BUD/S successfully complete the grueling ordeal and become SEALs.

During the first few days of BUD/S, his frequent grin got on my nerves as I wondered how he could smile while the instructors did their best to break us with screamed insults, extreme sleep deprivation and brutal physical training. After a few days, I realized Javier's impish grin was sincere. I began to draw strength from his positive attitude and we became fast friends.

We were assigned to SEAL Team Three. After I got out, Javier progressed to SEAL Team Six, the elite of the elite, and then became Commanding Officer of Team Three, his current position.

His family was from Peru and spoke Spanish at home. Javier was born in Lima but went to high school in the U.S. then graduated from Annapolis Naval Academy. I loved learning about his Peruvian roots. Javier embraced my curiosity, teaching me about Hispanic traditions and culture. We spoke Spanish, Javier patiently helping me improve.

When not deployed, he ate dinner at our house at least once a week. As he was unmarried with no family close, we were his surrogate family. We both liked to surf and toss the football. He often took Blake to sporting events and movies. I'm sure he did it partially to return the favor for all the meals Catherine fed him but he seemed to truly enjoy Blake's company even if it meant enduring Toy Story 3. Between Javier and Susan, we almost never hired a sitter.

When I finished, I asked, "What do you think about going to the police?"

Turning it back on me, he asked, "What do you think?"

"I'd rather not, but I don't want to be foolish. The police'll surround the park and grab whoever picks up the ransom. But we might lose Blake. Win the battle and lose the war."

"The park will just be the starting point. There's no way the kidnapper's going to saunter out with the moneybag slung over his shoulder. They'll use every precaution. But I think you should at least discuss it with the police. You can decide how much information to give them."

I called 911. A woman with a harsh smoker's voice answered. "Nine-one-one, what's your emergency?"

"I want to report a child abduction."

"When did the abduction occur?"

"My son was taken yesterday."

"Name please." Her phlegmy voice grated on my frayed nerves.

"Blake Stryker."

"How are you related to the alleged victim?"

Irritated by the word "alleged," I snapped, "I just said he's my son."

"Please calm down sir." She paused dramatically then continued, "What's your son's name?"

"Blake Stryker."

"You have the same name?"

"No, my name is Wyatt Stryker."

She had a coughing spell. "Why did you say your name was Blake?"

"I thought you were asking for his name."

"Please listen carefully and answer my questions honestly and to the best of your ability."

"May I speak with the police?"

"Not until I gather the pertinent information. Why was there a delay in reporting the incident?"

"We were out of town."

"When did you return?"

"An hour ago."

"Where?"

"Our house, 214 Willow Drive."

"When I'm ready for your address, I'll ask for it. Where were you when your son was taken?"

"We were in Mexico. In Rosarito."

"I'm sorry, sir, but Mexico's just a wee bit out of our jurisdiction. You should report to the Mexican police." She continued with a mocking, syrupy tone, "If you haven't already done so, I can connect you."

My knuckles whitened on the phone. "May I tell you the story rather than answer questions?"

"Again, why are you just now reporting? This line is for emergencies only."

"My son's been kidnapped. Isn't that an emergency?"

"Most emergencies are reported immediately. Not the next day." She coughed up a hairball.

"Could I speak with a detective?"

"A little patience, sir. Who is we?"

"I don't understand."

"You just said, 'We were in Mexico.' Who is we?"

"Could I have the phone number for a detective?"

"You called me, not the other way around."

I hung up. Javier grimaced, "That went well."

I seethed. "Classic bureaucracy." She called back but I turned off the ringer.

"Maybe we should just handle it. We know how to control a scene and defend ourselves. We're experts in surveillance. We can do this."

"I don't know. We're talking about Blake's life."

"We're better than the cops. We have to give Blake the best chance."

We drove to Coronado Island, an affluent town across the bay from San Diego. Tourists and locals flock to Coronado for the Mediterranean climate, perfect waves and quaint seafood restaurants. The Naval Base Coronado occupies the northern half of the island, the location of the SEAL training center and headquarters. Javier lived on base.

At the entrance, a soldier checked his ID, saluted sharply and waved us in. Javier parked his truck next to the house. Catherine was crying so hard she was incoherent. As I helped her out, her knees buckled. We supported her, leading her into the house. Catherine collapsed on the bed, sobbing.

When Catherine recovered, I said, "I tried to call the police but got the runaround. But we have the money."

Catherine said, "If you think that's best...but I still think we should call the police." I knew that some of her fear was concern for my safety.

"I promise I won't put myself in harm's way."

"Wyatt, don't try to be a hero. Please."

Javier left us at his house, a three-bedroom bachelor pad a stone's throw from the beach. He went to gather supplies and scout the park, located on the other end of Coronado. Two hours later, he returned.

He said, "I took plenty of photos in the park. Check it out." He pointed at a button on his short sleeve polo shirt. I leaned over and inspected it. Hidden in the button was a camera lens, about two millimeters in diameter.

"How did you get that?"

"A benefit of being commander. I said I wanted to try out the new equipment."

We drove the short distance back to the park. This time I took his truck while he used his motorcycle, a powerful Italian Ducati 1199. As we parked, my nerves started surging like they were connected to jumper cables.

Tidelands Park, the largest park on San Diego Bay, sat near an enormous bridge, the primary exit from the island. Tidelands had a beach, picnic areas and plenty of open space. A scenic path wound along the water, connecting to other beaches on the peninsula.

Carrying the duffel bag, I walked along the beach, hyper-focused, painstakingly observing every object and shadow. Well past dusk, the park was nearly vacant, except sporadic joggers and walkers. I carefully studied each person. I circled back to the park bench, near an outdoor bathroom.

I entered the concrete restroom, empty except a gaunt man leaning on a sink. He was about my height, but junky thin. His greasy hair hung in unhealthy strands, his face littered with pockmarks and raw sores, a meth-freak version of Ichabod Crane.

I washed my hands in an adjacent basin. The man was supposed to wear blue jeans but wore green cargo pants instead. He had a beer can in each hand, double fisting. A few empties lay in the sink. He glared.

I asked, "Wayne?"

"Yep. Show me the money." I opened the duffel bag and handed him two hundred dollars.

He smiled, displaying a square yard of meth-infested teeth. At some point, his mouth must've sprouted entirely too many teeth. And he'd clearly never paid a visit to an orthodontist. Or a dentist, for that matter. Or even a toothbrush. The result looked like a Crayola box crammed with broken and worn crayons jutting at odd angles, all in the unfortunate yellow-brown-black spectrum.

Years earlier, Wayne sold meth to a teenager that Javier knew. Javier confronted him in a parking lot, warning him to stop selling poison to kids. Wayne wasn't very polite. But he quickly changed his tune after Javier ground black asphalt onto his teeth, and black from Wayne's teeth onto the pavement.

Wayne cried and said he had no other way to make money. Javier took pity on him, occasionally hiring him for odd jobs. I called him once but, knowing I was a physician, he asked me to pay for his work with narcotic prescriptions. I refused, so I never actually met him.

"You were supposed to wear jeans." He was my substitute and needed to look like me.

He sneered, "Yo, since when do they have a dress code to buy some smack? My jeans was dirty." I almost pointed out the filthy condition of his pants, but held my tongue.

"These guys are very particular."

"All they gonna care about is the color of the stuff in the bag…" He smirked, waiting for his punch line. He bugged his eyes triumphantly and said, "Green!"

I pulled the yellow parka from the bag. "You'll have to wear my jeans and this jacket."

"Whassup wit asking me to drop my pants? Is you a rest-stop pervert? Wayne don't play that way."

"Put these on if you want the money."

He glared menacingly, "Maybe I'll just take the money. All of it."

I suppressed a laugh, fairly certain even Catherine could thrash his skeletal ass. "Should I call Javier?"

"Yo, this is wacked! You's a freaking amateur, scared to buy your own dope."

"Do you want the money or not? Ten seconds before I walk. Javier won't be happy."

"Whatever, smether."

I pulled off my jeans, wearing charcoal running tights underneath. I held out the jeans but he didn't take them.

"Yo, nice panty hose, perv," he sneered.

"Put these on. Now."

He grudgingly took the jeans and dropped his pants, unfortunately wearing no underwear. His flat buttocks were scarred with needle tracks. He'd destroyed his veins, so he skin-popped, hurtling fast down a dead-end road.

"Follow these directions if you want the rest of the money. Follow them exactly."

"Exactly, shmacktly."

I wanted to backhand the smirk off his face but took a deep breath and continued, "Sit on the bench nearest this bathroom. Stare straight ahead and keep the parka hood up. Someone will take the bag. They might give you a message. Follow them if they ask, but don't get into a car or leave the park. For your own safety."

"I ain't getting in no car wit' no dirty rider. Yo, I been doing this shit my whole life."

"I know you're street smart. Javier speaks highly of you. That's why we asked for your help."

"Me and Javier get each other. We cool." His icky mouth curled into a grin. I made a mental note to use flattery if I ever had the misfortune to deal with him again.

"They'll be here in about thirty minutes."

He smiled earnestly, like we were suddenly bestest buddies. "This is the easiest money I ever made. Yo, I won't even be haulin' dope, so I ain't worried about pigs. Javier said you's his doctor friend. I called you today but it went to voicemail."

"My phone got stolen. Why'd you call?"

"Since I'm doing this favor for you, I was thinking you could pony up some Oxycontin prescriptions."

I started to refuse, but we were supposedly making a drug deal. "We can talk about that later. Javier will call you to discuss and deliver the rest of your money. Don't return to this bathroom or look for me."

He held an outstretched hand in the air. I gave him an awkward high five.

He put on my parka and raised the hood, stuck the two hundred dollars down his pants then sauntered out, carrying the ransom bag.

I entered a stall and replaced my shirt with a tight dark-grey hoodie then pulled on gloves. Inserted a tiny two-way earpiece, strapped on a chest holster and pulled a dark balaclava over my head.

Javier had disabled the outside lights. I put on night vision optics and slipped out on my belly, shielded by surrounding bushes. The goggles automatically adjusted to the near-total darkness. I soldier crawled toward a mesh fence under the bridge. Javier had snipped a hole in the fence. I pulled the gap open then entered the neglected area, thick with underbrush.

Zooming the goggles, I saw Wayne like I was just ten feet behind him, although he was over three hundred feet away. The duffel held a tiny transmitter; I heard him mumbling.

Scattered people strolled the beach, maybe two dozen. A family on a picnic packed up to leave. A boom box thumped as a group of guys took turns rapping. A jogger ran behind Wayne, but kept going. As instructed, Wayne stared straight ahead, his hood up.

From the beach, a man walked directly toward him. I held my breath. The man veered then entered the bathroom. Moments later, he exited and walked away.

A woman walking a dog stopped right in front of him. The dog did its business and the owner scooped it up. Wayne muttered, "Wayne don't touch no dog shit, yo."

It was well past ten. They were late.

A transient wandered aimlessly; disguising as a homeless person would be a viable ploy. He lay in the sand near Wayne. I zoomed in. He faced the water, away from Wayne.

I spoke to Javier, using my ear bud. "See the bum near Wayne?"

"Yeah. Could be our man."

Another jogger. A few drunken college students laughed and ran barefoot on the sand. Two lovers smooched on the water's edge. The rappers left.

A jogger with his hood cinched entered the scene, running along the beach. His right arm appeared bulky under his coat, like a splint or cast. I inhaled sharply.

I whispered, "Here he comes."

"Copy. I see him."

The man jogged behind Wayne. Without breaking stride or even seeming to notice Wayne, he angled his left hand at the back of the yellow hood. I heard a muffled thump as a faint flash leapt from the man's sleeve.

Wayne's forehead spat a fistful of brains.

CHAPTER
FIVE

It took me a moment to interpret what had just happened. They wanted to kill me, not collect ransom money. But I had no time to think, just react.

Wayne slumped forward. The jogger pulled his shoulders back, into a semi-seated position, his head lolling to the side. The man unzipped Wayne's bag and placed something inside.

I burst through the hole in the fence, sprinting parallel to him. I said, "He killed Wayne. He's moving south."

"Copy."

On the GPS monitor screen in the periphery of the goggles, I saw Javier's signal rapidly moving toward the beach from the ocean. He'd been monitoring the scene using a tiny periscope from underwater in scuba gear. Through the mic, I heard the water splash as he climbed onto the beach then his heavy breathing as he ran to his motorcycle.

I raced, keeping the killer in view. Tore across uneven ground, struggling to keep up as he was at a fast jog on the paved path, running as fast as he could without drawing attention. He moved with feline precision.

I heard Javier's moto crank and accelerate. His helmet visor had a translucent display with GPS navigation and tracking so he knew my location.

The assassin crossed onto a sidewalk paralleling the street. An SUV pulled beside him and slowed. He jumped into the passenger seat then sped off.

I said, "He's in a dark green Escalade, heading east onto Baker Street."

"I'm close."

As they pulled out of sight, I saw Javier's moto pull into the line of traffic behind the Cadillac.

I ran back toward Wayne. I felt terrible he'd been killed. No one noticed him yet.

I laid him on his side in a fetal position then cinched the hood tight around his streaked face and cratered forehead. Scooped sand and threw it on the pool of blood below the bench. Grabbed the duffel bag and sprinted to Javier's truck.

I ran through a group of young skateboarders. One yelled, "Lookout! It's a crazy ninja!" A black clad commando wearing space goggles was a bit unusual. I gave them a thumbs-up as I raced away, hoping they wouldn't call the police.

I arrived at the truck and clambered in. I radioed, "I'm driving. I've got you on GPS. Where are they?"

"I'm behind them."

I stomped the accelerator and barreled out of the parking lot. They were several miles away. I stripped off my goggles and balaclava, replacing them with a baseball cap and sunglasses.

"They're heading onto the Coronado Bridge," said Javier. "I can't stick the magnet now. I probably can't follow for much longer without them noticing but they aren't driving to elude me. They just turned north onto the interstate."

"I'm on the bridge." I couldn't pass due to oncoming traffic, so I moved frustratingly slow.

A few minutes later he said, "They're off the freeway, heading east toward the bay."

I took the exit onto the interstate at seventy miles an hour. The tires shrieked and the truck shuddered. On the interstate, I weaved between lanes, the top-heavy truck rocking wildly. The Ram topped out at one-thirty, rattling toward dilapidation.

Javier said, "They're coming back south, toward you. Probably making sure they aren't being tailed."

I exited the interstate, sailing through red lights.

Javier reported, "They're stopped at the red light on Ash and Pacific Highway."

"I'm close!" I turned onto Pacific Highway, a busy six-lane road. Javier needed to place the magnet tracer without detection. I had to simultaneously make them stop while creating a diversion.

"They're heading south on Pacific."

"On it," I said. "I'm heading north on Pacific."

"You'll see them soon. They're in the center lane about a mile from you."

I slowed and moved into the center lane.

He said, "They're the second car at a red light, I'm five cars back."

I saw Javier's GPS blip, two blocks ahead. I was traveling toward them as his blip moved, the light green. I examined each oncoming car, finally spotting the Escalade. "I see them. I'll crash into the car in front of them. Place the magnet in the chaos."

"Copy. I'm pretty far behind but I'll get there." I heard the deep-throated roar as he twisted the throttle.

The motorcycle jumped into view. Javier was an expert, racing both dirt and street bikes.

He crouched with his elbows tucked, his chest touching the gas tank and his helmet barely above the handlebars. He careened forward, his red sport bike leaning deeply as he weaved between cars, closing the gap.

They were a block away, a large space between the Escalade and the car they followed. I couldn't crash into the car in front. The Escalade could easily stop. They'd probably notice Javier if he placed the tracer.

They remained in the center lane. I held my cell like I was texting, blocking my face. I crossed the centerline then turned sharply into the driver's door of the Escalade.

The driver adroitly swerved but my bumper caught the rear door with the howl of metal on metal. With my head turned away, I mashed the accelerator and bulldozed their rear axle sideways. He locked his brakes, attempting to regain control. The Escalade was completely sideways, the front pointing at the centerline. On both sides of the road, cars squealed to a stop. I kept light pressure on the gas, maintaining contact with their vehicle.

Javier pierced the line of stopped vehicles like a javelin. Hooked a smooth turn around the front bumper of my truck and the rear of the Escalade, leaning so his knee brushed the pavement. Extended his arm, sliding his hand under their rear bumper.

He righted the bike then glided away. I slammed the truck in reverse, backing into my original lane. The Escalade reversed to straighten then ground the gears into drive. It sped off with a deep scrape, and, hopefully, a magnetized passenger.

Driving off, I radioed, "Did you place it?"

"Yeah. It stuck."

I breathed a sigh of relief. The tracer moved in the opposite direction. The GPS was about the size of a deck of cards and would last for three weeks without recharge. As with cell phones and laptops, the battery size is the limiting factor for surveillance equipment size.

"We shouldn't tail them anymore," I said. "We should remove Wayne's body. We don't want them to know they killed the wrong guy."

"Agreed."

The signal was being recorded so we could retrace their movements. They probably didn't notice Javier, since they were both looking forward when we crashed. The commotion from my bumper grinding muted the sound of the magnet hitting their vehicle.

I stopped near the park and opened Wayne's duffel bag. The money was untouched. The plastic bag placed by the assassin contained prescription injectable narcotics: Dilaudid and morphine, as well as pills: Oxycontin and Xanax. They wanted me to seem like a dirty doctor, trafficking stolen hospital narcotics. My death would be chalked up to a dispute between criminals.

I put on my shirt, removed my tights and squeezed into Wayne's nasty cargo pants. I radioed, "I'm at the park. He put a bag of drugs in Wayne's duffel."

"Stay put. I'll see if the body's been noticed."

Ten minutes later he radioed, "Wayne looks like he's asleep on the bench. No one's paying attention to him."

"Is that bum still there?"

"No."

"He might've been a lookout. If so, he saw you exiting the water and me grabbing Wayne's bag."

"There's nothing we can do. There are even more here now. Don't these people need to sleep? Should we wait?"

"Gotta move him now. The police keep homeless people from sleeping in waterfront parks."

"How are we gonna carry a dead body down the beach without notice?"

"We could move him into the brush and return later."

"We could also screw around and get arrested for murder. Maybe we should leave him."

"I'm walking your way."

Javier was standing about a hundred feet from the blood-stained bench that held the wretched remains of Wayne, like a Transylvanian church pew visited by the Count.

The place was crawling with people. The families had deserted, replaced by the younger, nightlife crowd. We'd have to carry him for nearly half a mile. If anyone noticed blood dripping from the forehead cavity, the gig would be up.

Hiding him in the bushes was an option, but police presence would increase after midnight.

I had a thought and pointed at the ocean. "That's where we put the body. Deliver him to Davy Jones' Locker." The waterline was only about a hundred feet away.

"Good idea. Let's buy some chains, weights and padlocks. There's a Wal-Mart nearby."

I drove into San Diego. Parked on a cross-street and walked to the Wal-Mart, avoiding parking lot cameras. I wore leather gloves, dark glasses and kept my hood pulled up. If his body was found, I didn't want the materials traced to me. I kept my face away from security cameras. I paid cash for heavy fishing line, sewing needles, beer, chain, padlocks, a cooler, a beach wagon, a black wool beanie, aviator sunglasses with ear hooks, snorkeling gear and two 50-pound, cast-iron kettlebell exercise weights.

After parking, I set the cooler on the wagon then loaded the cooler. Placed the kettlebell weights and chain in the bottom and covered them with beer cans. I pocketed a few beers then rolled the wagon down the bike path.

I radioed, "I'm on my way. Still clear?"

"I don't think anyone's noticed Wayne. But there's still lotsa people here. Too many."

I walked down. Someone passed by every minute or so. I removed Wayne's beer cans from the bathroom, holding them gingerly to avoid disturbing his fingerprints. I placed them in a zip lock bag. Evidence might come in handy.

"Distract anyone who comes near," I said. "I'll get Wayne ready."

Javier took the cooler to the water's edge. I knelt next to Wayne. He had a three-inch gaping hole of bone splinters, shredded skin, brains and blood. Wiped his face with a towel then snugged the black beanie over the cavity. I hooked mirrored aviator sunglasses behind his ears, covering his deserted eyes.

His shirt was blood-soaked so I cut it off with my knife and zipped up the parka. I placed his shirt and cell phone in another zip lock bag. Then poured beer on his parka, washing away blood and giving him a zesty party odor.

His mouth gaped. Drunks don't open their mouths wide. Corpses do.

I inserted the curved sewing needle into the inside of his bottom lip and threaded stout fishing line internally through both lips. Inside his mouth, I tied his jaw shut.

I called Javier over and handed him a beer. We waited for a break in the pedestrian traffic then we slung Wayne's arms over our shoulders. I grabbed a handful of Wayne's hair through the hood, holding his head off his chest. We lifted his feet, so they wouldn't dig sea turtle troughs in the soft sand.

Halfway there, a couple approached, strolling along the water's edge. I whispered, "Sit."

We dropped to the sand, Wayne between us. I slurred, "Remember when Karen caught Dave in the act?" We laughed stupidly, like frat boys too blitzed to walk.

The couple seemed uncomfortable and hurried past. We lifted him again.

As we neared the water's edge, I looked back. A man was walking directly toward us. I whispered, "Down!"

We plopped down and launched into the whole drunk bit, snorting and carrying on. Javier sat between the man and Wayne, his arm around Wayne's shoulder. I watched the guy in my peripheral vision.

About thirty feet away, the man stopped and looked toward us. I couldn't tell if he was staring at us or the ocean.

"That's what she said!" Javier laughed at his own joke. I drained the can and flung it.

The man took three rapid steps toward us then stopped. I reached inside my jacket, gripping my Glock. I looked directly at the man. He looked away.

I whispered. "If he's homeless, we'll shoo him off. If he's a gangbanger, we should get the drop on him."

"What if he's with the guys who killed Wayne?"

He took another step toward the ocean. Toward us.

"Cover me."

Javier nodded and brought the tip of his pistol into view, peeking from his jacket.

I moved my Glock into my coat pocket and kept my hand on it, pointing forward. I walked toward him, looping so Javier had a direct line of sight. The man's hands were buried in his coat pockets.

I slurred, "Yo, man. Got a light?"

He turned toward me and asked, "What?" He looked Hispanic.

"You got a light?"

"A light?" He didn't smile. He looked up and down the beach, then behind him, toward the bench and restroom.

My hand tightened on the pistol. Behind my sunglasses, my eyes were glued to his hands.

"What kind of light?"

"A lighter. A flame."

"What you need it for?"

"A cigarette."

"Those are bad for your health."

I blurted, "So's drinking and we did too much of that."

He studied Javier and Wayne then asked, "Why you smoke cigarettes?"

"I was just asking for a light. Don't worry about it."

"Those guys with you?"

"Yeah."

"That one guy don't look so good."

"Yeah, he hit the hard stuff tonight."

"Looks bad fo' his health. Real bad. Dude looks dead."

"Naw, he just passed out."

"He ain't moving."

"Gets like that sometimes."

"What was you doing to him on the bench? Looked like you was pulling his teeth."

Where had he been? Had he been inside the bathroom, peeking out? Or maybe he'd used electronic surveillance. I wondered if he was the bum.

"He fell down and busted his nose."

"Looks like it killed him. You carried his ass a long way."

"He's fine."

"It ain't good to be so messed up in a place like this. There's thugs around. Gots to keep yo' wits in this city."

I stared at him, hard. "We can take care of ourselves."

I studied his pockets. If he had a gun, it was a small one. I wasn't sure.

He said, "I got something you might wanna smoke. You interested?"

"Naw, I only smoke cigarettes."

"Cigarettes cause cancer. My smokes don't cause cancer. What about your friends?" He took a step toward them but I stepped in his way, cutting him off.

"They only smoke cigars."

"Chill, hombre. That's what I was talking about. Cigars." He turned and sauntered down the beach.

I backed toward Javier, keeping the man in view. We watched until he was out of sight. I stripped off my street clothes then pulled a diving mask and snorkel from my pocket. Lifted the cooler, my fins attached to the handle. Javier duct taped the lid, sealing air inside so it'd be easier to carry underwater.

Javier quickly changed back into his dive gear and entered the bay. Wayne's body was tied to Javier and trailed below, his lungs now full of water. We connected a rope between us since I didn't have a night vision dive mask. He stopped frequently, allowing me to use his oxygen. About a mile into the bay we removed Wayne's clothes and chained the kettlebells to his ankles.

We released him, strands of hair floating above his upturned hollow face. He sank into the inky depths like Poseidon, defeated.

Walking back to the truck, I said, "We ain't dealing with novices. These guys are shrewd. The only physical evidence was the note that Susan wrote. It'd be hard to convince the police that a kidnapping caused the murder. Easier to believe

I was a drug-dealing physician and if anyone snatched Blake, it was the competition."

He nodded grimly. "Yeah. They've probably turned your house into a drug lab by now."

"What next?"

"We wait. We track the beacon and react accordingly. One thing's clear: they wanted you dead and Blake was the bait."

"I feel shitty about Wayne."

"Don't feel bad. He's scum of the earth. He spent time in the big house for beating a hooker within an inch of her life."

My conscience wouldn't let me off the hook that easy. "But we lied. And now he's dead."

"We had no idea they meant to kill anyone. It surprised the hell out of me. We can't unring that bell."

"I guess you're right."

Sensing my ambivalence, he launched into a pep talk. "Better to be alive to find Blake. If I were snatched, I'd rather have you hunting for me than anyone else. I really mean that, Stryker. As much as I hate to admit it, you're brilliant. Plus, you have a deviously clever imagination. And you're the best athlete I've ever known, an All-Conference college linebacker. All-State in high school baseball *and* football."

"Okay, enough already." He'd read my SEAL application and loved to bring this shit up. He usually did it to harass me, but tonight, he was trying to make me feel better. Regardless, I felt awkward.

"I'm serious Wyatt. You claim your skills are rusty but you did a damn fine job today. Whoever has Blake should be afraid, very afraid."

I felt a little better. I knew I'd sacrifice anything to keep Blake alive, including myself. Wayne was an unintended casualty but we'd lived to hunt again.

But I was also shell shocked. If my little dude didn't make it to eleven, I'd be forever broken. Like Humpty, just a shell.

CHAPTER
SIX

Blake opened his eyes but the world was still black. He blinked them open and closed, back and forth, trying to decide if he was asleep or awake, dead or alive. He groped until he found a lamp. When he turned it on, the brightness was shocking. He looked away, squinting, slowly realizing his nightmare wasn't a dream.

A sandwich and water sat on the bedside table. He was parched and he guzzled the water; his throat ached with each swallow.

The bedroom had two doors but no windows. He gradually stood, his muscles shrieking in protest. He tried the first door. Locked. Behind the second, he was relieved to find a bathroom. He peed like Seabiscuit, but didn't flush, trying to stay quiet.

He looked in the mirror. The boy staring back was a wreck. His neck was covered with purple blotches, he gingerly felt along the edges of the boot-sized bruise tattooed on his chest. His nose was swollen, dried blood peeling like old paint.

He turned on the water and scrubbed his face and neck. The black flakes colored the sink bloody. Hobbled to the bed and sat on the edge, debating. If he yelled, the evil guy might come. He wondered if he should stay quiet, or if the water splashing in the sink had already alerted his captors.

He had to find a way out.

He pondered the fate of his family, his chin trembling. His drug-induced sleep had been fitful, partly because his body ached, especially his neck where the man strangled him. But mostly, his sleep was full of sorrow and danger: the monster in black with fish eyes, Susan tied to the chair, the bad man entering his room, blood spurting from the destroyed arm. Actually, the broken arm was the only good thing he could remember.

He couldn't stop thinking about his parents, especially his sweet, kind mom. She always smiled, the prettiest mom at his school. She focused on the happy side of life; making jokes, snow skiing and riding horses. On horseback, she didn't plod slowly like most people, but barrel raced in rodeos. She was the bomb.

He heard approaching footsteps outside on the tile floor. He quickly turned off the lamp and slipped under the bed. The door opened.

He heard muttering as someone searched the bathroom. He saw boots coming toward the bed. A man's face appeared inches from Blake's. "*¡Hola, chico!* Why sleep on the floor? The mattress is soft."

The man grinned, totally getting on Blake's nerves. He wanted to spit in the man's face.

Blake crawled out and noticed the man's gun, glad he hadn't spit on him. An overweight man in fancy clothes hulked in the doorway. He looked like some of his dad's football buddies, broad chested with a feed-sack belly, an ex-athlete gone to seed.

The heavy man smiled. His teeth glittered against his cinnamon skin. Blake thought the smile seemed fake. His eyes didn't smile; they burned. He had eyes of fire.

He spoke with a Spanish accent, "Hello, little boy. What's your name?"

"None of your business." The man smelled like he'd bathed in cologne.

"How old are you?"

"Ten and a half."

"Do you know why you're here?"

"No."

"Your father was a drug dealer."

"That's not true! My dad's a doctor. You're a liar!"

The guard interjected, "Easy, *chico!*" He looked more alarmed than angry.

The big man continued, "He stole drugs from the hospital to sell. He also stole money."

Blake's eyes flashed. "I don't believe you! Dad's a good person. What happened to Aunt Susan?"

"A man went to your house to get the stolen money. After you hurt him, he killed your aunt. Your parents returned and he had to kill them also. I'm sorry."

Blake's world suddenly vanished, any remnant of hope instantly replaced by sorrow and anger. He burst into tears and screamed, "I hate you!"

Blake cried uncontrollably, shaking. The men stood silently, watching him sob. Finally Blake controlled himself enough to yell, "Get out! Leave!"

"I understand you're upset. I will take care of you and find a nice home for you." He stepped forward to put his hand on Blake's shoulder.

Blake knocked the hand away and shouted, "Don't touch me! I don't want your help, *you fat ass piece of shit!*"

The guard startled. The overweight man's smile faded. "I want to protect you. If you don't accept my help, the man who killed your parents will kill you."

The sobering words rang in Blake's ears. *Kill me?* Confusion wracked his brain. He'd never cooperate with the people who killed his parents.

But he didn't want to die either. He decided that he could pretend, buying time until he could escape.

He knew he was a pretty good liar. He felt a little guilty about it sometimes, but it was true. Once, he blamed a broken window on the neighbors' dog and his parents bought it. He hoped these men were as easily fooled.

Mustering his acting skills, he said, "I don't ever want to see that man again. I'll be good from now on."

The guard exhaled, looking relieved.

The man returned his hand to Blake's shoulder. Blake stiffened, detesting his touch. It felt foul and heavy. He ached to kick the man in his shin.

He forced a contrite look. "I'm sorry for calling you fat."

"Most people wouldn't live to insult me again."

Blake swallowed hard.

The man smiled, "But I like you. Cooperate and I'll help you."

"I will, sir. I promise."

They left, dead-bolting the solid metal door behind them. Blake returned to the bed and stared at the ceiling. He would find a way out.

Alfredo Rodriguez was known as El Jefe: The Boss. At that moment, the boss was in a foul mood. The boy called him a fat piece of shit. And the insult stung. He wondered if the guards had laughed about it afterward. The thought made his blood boil.

He made a mental note to ask his informer. If so, it would be the last time they laughed about anything. He'd kill them himself, carving away their fat as they screamed for mercy. He'd done it before. He didn't consider himself particularly cruel but he never showed mercy, a weakness. Fear was a tool that El Jefe used to his advantage.

He knew his body was heavy from fine food and excellent wine, the spoils from his victories. But his mind was lean. His intellect was his weapon. Besides he had plenty of loyal, robust men to carry out physical tasks, their brute strength enforcing his brutality. He decided his girth added to his mystique, like a medieval king.

Sitting in his grandiose living room, he poured another glass of wine and thought about the future. His brilliant plan was working; he just needed a little more time to completely obliterate his competition. El Jefe would soon become almighty, unchallenged, the boss of all bosses. The others would bow before him. Or die.

The phone rang at the prearranged time. He answered, "Hello, my friend, how are you progressing?"

Behram spoke with vocal distortion, his voice deep and robotic. "Now that the doctor's dead, I'm ready. I've placed surveillance throughout the house."

"When will you do it?"

"Within a few days."

"Excellent. It *must* seem like an accident. If you have doubts, abort and wait for a better opportunity. The stakes are very, very high."

"I understand."

"Is there anything else to discuss?"

"What are your plans for the boy?"

"I haven't decided. Why?"

"I'd like to kill him."

Jefe almost laughed out loud at almighty Behram's humiliation. The proud assassin met his match, a boy who still cried for his mama. He took a moment to compose himself then continued, "My advisors say we should dispose of him, as he serves no purpose. I hadn't considered that you'd want to pull the trigger."

"This is the first time I've asked you for anything. Please keep this in mind when considering my request."

"What's your request?"

"I will come to the house and take him. I plan to exact my revenge by breaking his arms and legs, but I will eventually dispose of him. There will be no trace."

Jefe startled. "Behram, he's just a child! I will consider killing him out of necessity, but not torturing him."

Even with the electronic voice modulation, the fury in Behram's voice was apparent. "He's not just a child. He's fierce beyond his years. He twisted my broken arm until bones thrust through my skin. My arm will be forever crippled, like a pathetic beggar. Your assassin has been diminished. Forever."

"He was protecting his family."

"If I am not allowed to exact my revenge, my reputation will suffer."

"If you accomplish the mission, your fame will grow. The boy is a distraction. Focus on the prize."

Jefe waited for a response that never came. He continued, "You killed the boy's father. That seems like adequate vengeance."

"If you let him live, he will be a man soon. Do you want a relentless, ferocious man avenging his father?"

"I agree he has great potential. Maybe we should consider grooming him. A fierce gringo working for El Poder would be quite an asset. He's young enough to be malleable."

"If he's allowed to live, I will no longer work for El Poder."

Jefe paused, considering the ultimatum. He was conflicted. The blonde child was stunningly handsome, his face glowing like a noble prince. He admired the boy's spunk, his fighting spirit. Killing him seemed like a waste of moldable talent.

On the other hand, he was still somewhat irked at the boy's disrespectful insult. The boy might eventually be beneficial, but Behram was the best assassin in the world, irreplaceable.

His advisors were probably right. He should kill the boy. What did it matter if Behram hurt him first? Allowing Behram's request would increase his fealty, making him indebted to Jefe.

"When you complete the task, I will grant your request."

CHAPTER
SEVEN

We arrived at Javier's house after the attempted ransom drop. Catherine was heartbroken to hear we were further from finding Blake. She wept as I told the story.

My voice cracked as I saw her agony. With my pain exposed, she cried harder. I realized we were playing into each other's fears, adding fuel to the twin fires of pity and hopelessness.

She mumbled, "Please call the police."

"Let me tell the whole story. Then I'll call, if you still think I should."

"Please call the police! This has gone too far!" She seemed panicked.

"You should hear what happened first."

Tears streamed down, her mouth trembling. "Please, please, *please* call them now." She wiped her eyes and drew a ragged breath. "Wyatt, I'm begging you!"

I was on my heels. Going worse than expected. I didn't know what to tell the police. I couldn't mention Wayne. We'd tampered with a crime scene and stolen from the military. We'd probably broken twenty laws. I wanted to think about my narrative so I didn't get tripped up.

But she was unraveling. And her pain felt like a garrote strangling me. I'd do anything to make it stop.

Susan softly interjected, "I don't see what it could hurt, Wyatt."

Javier remained silent. Wisely.

Against my better judgment, I relented. "Okay. I'll give them another try."

I called information for the direct line to the bureau and put the phone on speaker.

"Detective Brikell here."

"I'd like to report a child abduction."

"Jumpin' Jehosephat! You're the third person to report a kidnapping in the last two days! Let me find something to write with."

The phone clattered. I waited for nearly a minute but it seemed like ten. Finally he returned, "Okay. I found a pen. What's your name?"

"Wyatt Stryker."

"Dammit. My pen's out of ink. Cheap Chinese junk! Hold on."

Silence.

I stared blankly at Javier. He shrugged.

"All righty then, I'm back. Is this the initial report?"

"I called 911 earlier."

"Good. That'll save time. Let's pull it up." He spelled my name as he typed, like he was pecking with one finger.

"Got it. Let's see here...looks like your son was kidnapped in Rosarito, Mexico, two days ago. You were in Mexico with some other people but...uhhh...refused to say who they were. This says you were evasive. Even sez here you hung up on the operator. She called back but you didn't answer. From an unregistered phone...the same one you're using now."

"My phone was stolen in Mexico. I bought a new one."

"Why the new number?"

"I bought an untraceable phone so my movements can't be followed."

"By whom?"

"The kidnappers."

There was a long, dramatic pause. "Right." He sighed loudly. "Well, this is better than my last call. The lady said a spaceship from Pluto snatched her child. I'm guessing the kid's burned up from the Sun's heat by now!" He snickered. In the most annoying way possible.

I spat, "I'm not in a joking mood." I hoped Detective Brikell knew more about solving crimes than he knew about the Solar System.

"Easy fella. Just trying to lighten the mood. Why don't we start from the beginning? What happened in Mexico?"

"That's unrelated. I was robbed in Mexico but my son was kidnapped from my home in San Diego." I briefly told the story, omitting the events of the last few hours.

"Could you issue an Amber Alert?" I asked.

"Hold your horses. Lemme see if I got this straight. What we've got here is a young couple hobnobbing with a famous

U.S. Senator. You left your son in San Diego and a black clad man kidnapped him, a ninja type so-to-speak. Your ten-year-old bloodied him up real good but there's no evidence except a note written by your sister."

"My sister-in-law."

"Whatever. Irrelevant. You discovered his kidnapping six hours ago and just got around to letting us know. And you're calling at one thirty in the morning? From an untraceable phone since nefarious people could be monitoring every move. That about right?"

Catherine wiped her eyes angrily and shook her head in disbelief.

I said, "That's basically correct but I don't appreciate being mocked."

"Lets all calm down and take a deep breath. Why doncha come on down to the station so we can sort this out?"

"I'll be there in an hour."

"I won't be here. My shift ends at two."

"If you won't be there could I speak with another detective?" Maybe that was the solution.

"Listen, you don't get to pick and choose investigators. That's not how it works. You called me so I'm in charge of your case. If your claim seems credible, I'll pass you off to the juvenile branch but honestly, you got some work to do. Most of our so-called missing children lose track of time while playing video games with buddies. We also get runaways, the parents convinced little Johnny just happened do get snatched after running from the house crying and screaming about the divorce. Then you got your quacks pretending to be someone else, calling from pay phones or untraceable lines."

My teeth could crush a diamond. "I'm not pretending to be someone else. My son didn't run away. A man entered our home and *took my child!*"

"Just for you, I'll work late. What say we meet at the scene of the crime?"

"I don't want to return to our house. The kidnapper appears professional. They might have surveillance."

He sighed loudly. "It keeps getting better. Howsabout we let the experts be the judge of all that?"

Catherine crossed her arms and glared at the phone.

I tried to sound conciliatory, "Could you at least give me the benefit of the doubt?"

"Tough to do since you told 911 a completely different story. Now that I think about it, this ain't a whole lot better than the Martian abduction."

I hung up and tossed the phone over my head. "How can we trust that idiot?"

Catherine muttered, "*That* didn't inspire much confidence."

"The 911 operator was even worse."

She looked genuinely surprised, like she couldn't believe there were bad cops. I knew better since I'd dealt with the police scores of times in the ER. Like any profession, some are great but others are terrible. We'd drawn a short straw. Brikell was a perfect combination: jaded and incompetent.

Catherine had faults but wasn't particularly stubborn. She was capable of changing her mind. If she realized she was wrong, she usually admitted it. She shook her head in disgust and said, "Maybe you're right. I can't imagine trusting Blake's life to that idiot." She smiled sadly then started to cry.

I hugged her. As I felt her tremble, I made an abrupt decision to play the strong guy for Catherine's sake. She needed faith and strength, not doubt and fear. Time to pivot, to play aggressive offense instead of defense. I wanted her to see me as a fierce soldier, as Blake's protector.

I put my hands on her shoulders and gently pushed, holding her at arms length. My eyes narrowing, I said, "We put a GPS transmitter on their car. And they have no idea. Those bastards will die and Blake will live. I'm sure of that." I said it with total conviction and unquestioning certainty. I wanted to project total invincibility.

She brushed her tears aside. "Really? You think you'll find him?"

I gave it everything I had. "No question. Javier and I battled and defeated every force dumb enough to try us: the Iranian Special Ops, the Taliban and even Al Qaeda. A bunch of amateur crooks have no chance. They're dead men walking. With the shitstorm we bring, we'll turn the rain brown."

A faint smile flickered. She seemed to turn a corner, mirroring my emotions. The GPS beacon was our beacon of hope.

Moments after I busted headstrong into this world, the doctor yanked me upside down and spanked my backside. But I didn't cry. Instead I frowned like I was spoiling for a fight. My little hands became twin pistols, thumbs cocked and pointers aimed. My arms swung around and the surprised doc found himself staring down the business end of each

Derringer. *Reckon you should think twice before you do that again, Pardner.*

My parents jettisoned their selected name and christened me Wyatt Earp Stryker, after the legendary gunslinger. During medical school I learned newborn hands make all sorts of random, involuntary movements. But my parents' interpretation of my little six-shooters was nearly prophetic. I've mellowed but during my youth I had more testosterone than sense.

My dad was a small town doctor. Growing up, I said I wanted to become a doctor but secretly hoped to play NFL football. I studied pre-med in college but dreamed of pro ball. I played middle linebacker at Boise State, leading my team in tackles three years in a row. I tried to pack on the pounds by lifting weights and ingesting an astronomical amount of calories. But I stalled at two-twenty, too small for a middle linebacker in the big leagues. My senior year I came to the disappointing realization that I wasn't NFL material.

I was accepted into med school but felt skittish about committing. My dad's patients called him at obscene hours and would even show up at our house unannounced, often bringing a home-baked sticky blob wrapped in tinfoil. Then they'd ask about their high blood pressure, hemorrhoids or the intermittent ringing in their ears.

My gregarious father exacerbated the problem in my mother's opinion. Whenever the doorbell shattered the peace, she'd groan, "Dr. Stryker, your patients are testing my patience."

I wasn't enthused about hemorrhoids on a Sunday evening and wanted to examine all options. I investigated fishing in

Alaska, working at a ski resort and the Peace Corp. All seemed interesting but lacked the adrenaline punch I craved.

A guy from my high school bragged about being accepted into the SEAL training-program. He plied us with stories of SEAL heroics and bad-assery.

He lasted less than two weeks in training. He returned with a feeble excuse about asthma, previously undiagnosed.

I was fairly certain I was tougher than Corporal Fake Asthma but I wondered if I could make it. My parents weren't enthusiastic about deferring med school. They probably thought being a SEAL was another game, a substitute for my dashed fantasy of playing pro ball.

I met several SEALs. They seemed intelligent, discussing complex topics with ease and nuance. Most were grounded and confident, not cocky like Corporal Wheezy Pants. They were paid to do things I'd spend well-earned money to do in pursuit of adventure: parachuting, scuba diving, learning to use top-secret technology to fight terrorists intent on killing civilians. I could be a part of a team of intelligent problem solvers, working for the common good.

I was accepted into the SEAL program in San Diego: cue the national anthem and Fourth of July fireworks, a bald eagle soaring overhead.

I met Catherine at Boise State. At first I was a little intimidated by her beauty, but she was grounded, more interested in fun than being a glamor queen.

Catherine was supportive. We were both wide-eyed youngsters, neither ready to commit. We parted ways after graduation but the cliché rang true, absence definitely made my heart grow fonder.

Halfway through my term, Bin Laden's brain-scrubbed disciples punched the Twin Towers. It got real serious, real quick like.

I deployed to Afghanistan and took part in the assault on Tora Bora. During my deployment I killed two Al-Qaeda fighters, one at Tora Bora. The other attacked a UN convoy.

When I joined, I wondered how I would feel taking a life. I was sad for their mothers but I believed in our mission. They chose to attack America, not the other way around.

I considered lengthening my commitment as we were fighting the worst madman since Hitler. At that time, it wasn't clear which side would prevail. And the adventure was intoxicating.

But when I mentioned reenlisting, Catherine grew sullen. She made it clear she wouldn't wait forever. I decided marriage and medicine would provide plenty of excitement and adventure.

We were married shortly after I began med school. Blake, the blond tornado, exploded on the scene my first year of residency. After finishing my training, I accepted a job at the Naval Hospital in San Diego. I was no longer in the Navy and worked as a civilian doctor but liked the connection. Emergency medicine fit me well, the adrenaline punch of the ER reminiscent of my SEAL days.

I found Javier tracking the beacon in his office. I asked, "Did you get a look at the guys in the Cadillac?"

"Yeah, they had black hair and olive skin."

"Hmm…could be Iranian."

"Yeah, the Qud Force is sophisticated enough to pull this off. But why?"

"They probably don't like us too much."

"Why would they come after you now? It's been a long time."

"You know how the Iranians are about revenge. That old Farsi proverb: *Beware the fury of a patient man.*"

"They'd probably just off you with a car bomb rather than kidnap Blake and the rest of it." He focused on the tracking software. "Here they are. The beacon's at a hotel in El Cajon. I'll run their route." We paused while it came up on the screen.

"Looks like they zig-zagged all over hell's half acre," he remarked. "But they've been stationary for a few hours. I doubt the men are there. An abandoned car will be noticed, so they'll probably return. Gotta sit tight. It'll chime when the beacon moves. If so, I'll wake you. Get some sleep. Like I tell my team, rest is a weapon."

A few hours later Javier shook my shoulder, waking me. The clock said 5 a.m.

I followed him to his office. He said, "The beacon moved. It's in Rancho Santa Fe. Run the address on my laptop using that CIA site. I'll track their route."

I entered the address: 1244 Camino de Arriba, Rancho Santa Fe.

The database searched, then resulted:

Private, single family home

Owner: Blue Chip Investment LLC

Square feet: Largest dwelling: 21,800. Other buildings: Three guest houses: 2700, 1250, 4400

Lot size: 24.2 acres

Real estate value: 32.3 million dollars

I clicked on Blue Chip Investment LLC.

Blue Chip Investment LLC is a multinational private equity corporation with private anonymous investors. Accounts are in tax haven areas, such as the Cayman Islands, the Netherlands Antilles and Panama. Investments are highly secretive, but have real estate holdings in Mexico, Columbia and Venezuela.

I said, "Looks like a swanky home owned by money launderers. Let's go."

"I'll borrow my buddy's old Chevy. We need surveillance equipment and guns. I'll grab them from the depot."

A few hours later, I placed two M4 machineguns in the trunk. I chambered a round in my pistol and locked the safety. I shoved it in a crossdraw holster: cocked, locked and ready to rock.

CHAPTER
EIGHT

We drove to Rancho Santa Fe, one of the highest income communities in the U.S. I wore a grey wig with a mustache. Javier was sporting curly black hair. We were both well trained in disguise.

Stucco mansions sprawled on enormous lots set back from the winding roads. We were several miles inland but the hills afforded jaw-dropping views of the shimmering ocean. We passed perfect golf fairways, horse clubs and ostentatious estates. The smell of recently cut grass mixed with the salty ocean air.

As I cruised past the address, we saw the enormous Tuscan style house crowning a manicured hilltop. A white equine fence surrounded the property. Behind the fence loomed a twenty-foot rock wall, buffered by eucalyptus trees. A guardhouse monitored a formidable entrance gate.

I continued past then dropped Javier a mile from the address. He wore running clothes, wired with a camera. He jogged down the road then stopped to tie his shoe at the entrance gate, searching for a location to leave the spy camera. He moved on, running twenty more minutes then returned past the compound for further inspection.

He arrived at the car. "The place is protected like a fortress. But it's subtle. That white fence is laced with high-voltage wires. Men with dogs patrol the perimeter between the fence and the wall. Cameras are mounted every fifty feet."

He changed into work clothes and removed his wig, replacing it with a wide brimmed hat like a lawn maintenance man. He grabbed hedge shears from the trunk of the land yacht then walked a few blocks to a neighbor's palatial spread.

Stopping at the front gate, he spoke into their intercom with an exaggerated accent, "Ees Pablo heeere to trim the busheees."

"Who?"

"Pablo! For treem the shubs. If you no want, I leeeeve."

The electric gate swung open. He strolled around the yard, hacking randomly, totally screwing up their flawless hedge. He worked his way to the area nearest the fortress, leaving a path of shrubbery destruction.

He removed a battery-powered drill from his pack then bored into a tree trunk. Screwed in a pencil-sized cylinder, a tiny camera with a view of the compound's main gate. He placed a repeater disguised as a rock, boosting the signal.

On the way to a nearby coffee shop, we left two more repeaters. At the café, we logged onto their wireless, synching the repeaters' signals, enabling us to access our surveillance equipment through the Internet.

We headed to Coronado. A few hours later we returned to Rancho Santa Fe with a large blue van and a new toy, the DragonFlier. Javier had surreptitiously borrowed the four-inch drone, a top-secret prototype shaped like a real dragonfly.

Javier didn't want to keep the unmanned aerial vehicle, or UAV, for long. The DragonFlier was years ahead of other nations' technology and access was strictly guarded. If discovered, he'd be sent to prison. He'd pulled it off, but he still had to return the multi-million dollar device.

The van didn't contain top-secret technology so Javier could sign it out at will. The UAV flight tracking equipment inside the vehicle was standard, compatible with most U.S. military drones.

There was no public parking near the compound. Due to the tiny size, the drone could only fly for twenty-minutes before needing to recharge, so we parked the van on the road-side. From the outside, it looked like a nondescript van driven by overeager parents, including a decal of a cartoon stick-family labeled: *Dad, Mom, Kathy, Austin, Mark, & Baby Jeffrey,* and a bumper sticker: *I ♥ My Kids!*

Two types of cars passed, luxury sedans and rattletraps long overdue to kick the bucket, maintained with Rust-Oleum and desperate prayer. The homeowners and the workers.

We entered the rear compartment of the van, closing a thick partition disguised as a curtain, blocking the view from the front windows. Packed with high tech gizmos, the interior looked like a spaceship.

Javier pushed a button and an overhead door slid open. He sent the DragonFlier through the roof. The drone climbed three hundred feet. He wore a fully enclosed video helmet and steered from a pilot's chair using a helicopter joystick. He flew at max speed, eleven mph, toward the house. I watched on a high-def video screen.

The UAV sailed over the cutesy white fence and the not-so-cutesy rock wall, like a dainty teen with her glowering boyfriend lurking behind. There were several garages and outbuildings as well as four houses. After getting the bird's eye view, he dove quickly toward the gigantic home, stopping above the gently sloping terracotta roof. Armed guards stood on each corner. Avoiding them, he peered into several rooms, each beautiful, luxurious, and empty.

He careened around a corner then approached a forty-foot tall bay window. He zoomed down, peering into a grandiose room appointed with sculptures and paintings. The center-piece was an Italian marble replica of Rome's Trevi Fountain.

Javier said, "Holy Mary, mother of God! Look at that!"

"I wonder what that cost."

"More than we'll ever have."

There was a cleaning woman in the room, dusting a gigan-tic statue of a sombreroed Pancho Villa on horseback, holding a rifle above his head. A perfect reproduction of Michelangelo's David stood beside the Mexican folk-hero. The owner seemed prone to garish displays of wealth. Poncho Villa didn't really fit with the Italian sculpture. Classic new money, gaudy and clueless.

"Gotta keep moving. Not much time left."

He climbed, circling the main house until he came to an expansive balcony that opened into a cavernous bedroom suite with travertine flooring and cherry paneled walls. A magnificent chandelier hovered above a canopied bed. A stunning young woman in silk underwear stood behind an older, heavyset man in a robe. She massaged his shoulders while kissing his neck.

Javier said, "Pay dirt."

"Yeah, looks like the boss."

"Should we bug the master bedroom?"

"Who has meetings in their bedroom? We ain't making porn."

We had five minutes until the drone needed to recharge. He zoomed around the compound, filming, and then brought the DragonFlier home.

While the drone recharged for three hours, we studied the video. The place was secured like they expected marauding zombies. A twenty-foot wide dirt path, raked smooth to show footprints, sat between the perimeter rock wall and an inner electric fence with elevated guard posts on every corner: Alcatraz.

Whoever lived there was incredibly paranoid and obscenely wealthy. We didn't see the Escalade, but there were multiple garages.

A few hours later, he attached the new load to the UAV then sent her flying. He flew about fifty feet off the ground and entered the compound at maximum speed over the perimeter wall, varying the entry pattern.

He moved toward a guardhouse and saw two men heading toward the main house. He slowed the drone to listen, following slightly behind. One man said, "No puedo esperar hasta el fin de este dia. Tengo una cita con The Flamingo." *I can't wait until the end of this day. I have a date with The Flamingo.*

The other laughed, "Tonto! Vas a perder todo tu dinero en esas strippers!" *You idiot! You're gonna waste all your money on those strippers.* They both laughed.

I said, "Focus on the garages. Let's see if the get-away car is there."

He careened over to the garages but they had no windows, so no dice. I had a nagging doubt that the GPS tracer could've been discovered and moved to a random vehicle. We'd be monitoring the wrong location. But probably not, since this looked like a den of thieves.

He zoomed around the main house, looking in. We found a dark, cozy den with oversized leather chairs and a wet bar. A man's hangout. The chairs were near the window, and the room looked well used. We decided to leave the mic there.

He perched the drone on the windowsill. The pressure of the landing released a spring-loaded clip, leaving the microphone, disguised as a bird dropping.

"Look for signs of Blake," I said.

He moved to the guesthouses. We saw no signs of a child. I was sorely disappointed.

He lifted off and flew the drone to the van. We left another stone-encased repeater. Now we had eyes and ears.

Javier dropped me at his house. He returned the equipment then went to his office to catch up on work. I watched the live-stream of their front gate while listening to the mic, fervently hoping for clues.

I was scheduled for an ER night shift that evening but Catherine was working the phone, calling my partners to find a replacement. I couldn't bear to think about anything but finding Blake.

After excruciating hours of nothing but ambient noise and meaningless conversations, a quiet panic crept up on me. Our only child was in their evil clutches.

My thoughts swam into unfriendly waters. The kidnappers believed I was dead, so they had no use for Blake anymore. He was just human bait. They had no reason to keep him alive. I shuddered and felt like crying.

Catherine interrupted my internal misery, "I've called everyone. No one can work your shift tonight."

I faked a smile. "Thanks for trying." She left.

I wondered if I'd ever be able to return to regular life. For unknown reasons, I was a marked man. I couldn't leave the ER unmanned, but working in a public place was fraught with peril. The kidnappers might discover they'd killed the wrong man.

My eyes narrowed as I pushed away my concerns. Let them come for me. They'll expect a meek lamb but find a lion.

We'd win or die trying. Maybe it was the denial phase of grief, but I felt like he was alive. And I could never rest until I knew. I vowed to find him, whether dead or alive. If dead, I would avenge his death. We would defeat our enemies then spit on their graves.

Then uproot the graves and spit on their rotting corpses.

CHAPTER
NINE

Behram looked out the hotel window as the rising sun caught fire, casting a hellish glow like the red eye of Kali, the goddess of the Thugee. He opened his laptop, clicking on a surveillance camera. He saw Senator Ripp's wife exiting the shower.

After dressing, she lit a prayer candle and made the sign of the cross, as she'd done the previous three mornings. Behram felt a surge of pleasure, knowing her pathetic faith would soon be tested like never before.

As she walked downstairs, he selected a different camera. She prepared breakfast, humming a familiar tune. He'd noticed she seemed oddly content no matter what she was doing.

The senator entered and kissed her, "Good morning, beautiful."

She smiled wryly, "Back atcha, handsome."

She set the breakfast tray on an outdoor patio table. The senator inhaled the brisk ocean air and threw a ball to their frisky beagle.

"Who'll be at today's meeting?" Beth asked.

"Mostly senators but the guest of honor is Admiral Landfair. He's top notch but his job is impossible. Operation Cartel is a total quagmire. Vietnam mixed with Iraq with a jalapeño on top."

"What will you say?"

"Same thing I've said before. American police should enforce our laws and the Mexican police theirs, but the U.S. military should do neither. As long as the U.S. is buying, the cartels will keep selling. Like Whac-A-Mole, knock one down and another pops up."

"Do you think you'll persuade them?"

"Half of 'em already agree. Soon, very soon, I'm going call for a congressional vote. It's time to end that failed experiment."

"What about tonight?"

"We're invited to a hoity-toity party but I'd love to spend the evening with my gorgeous wife. I'll grill my famous ribs."

"I'll be here with bells on."

"And I'm ready to ring those bells." She returned his grin and winked.

Behram closed the computer. Perfect. A quiet evening at home with the wife. And a surprise guest.

He wiped down the hotel room then left, never to return. He had no permanent home, moving at least twice a week. Using public transportation whenever possible, he limited potential witnesses, like taxi drivers. As he walked to a bus stop, he considered his mission. This would be his ninth assassination in his current job and the most important. The death would make headlines, but more importantly, it would make him rich beyond belief and quench his new thirst for vengeance.

He got off the bus near the Senator's home. After spending weeks scouting, he knew every nook and cranny in the neighborhood. He slowly worked his way up the road, ducking out of view whenever a car approached.

He settled in a neighbor's enormous backyard, waiting in a grove with a view of Senator Ripp's house. The homeowner was an ancient widow, so he could probably hold a rave in her yard without notice.

At dusk, the senator returned home. Unlike most powerful men, he drove himself. His sedan was nice but not particularly expensive or showy. Behram thought it was probably a thinly veiled attempt to get votes, trying to seem like the commoners.

Behram changed into black clothes with difficulty since his right arm was wrecked. A surgeon employed by El Poder had pinned his shattered bones but was unable to fix the nerve injury. His forearm hurt constantly, sometimes horribly. He detested his crippled arm but would soon avenge the pain, tenfold.

The sun disappeared over the horizon. With his handheld viewer, Behram watched her hug the senator from behind and kiss his cheek as he manned the grill, like they were really in love. He guessed they were so used to pretending in public, the charade bled over to their home life. But he enjoyed watching them, knowing it would be their final meal together. The Last Supper.

After dinner, Senator Ripp retired early, neglecting to ring any bells. Behram knew they usually did that sort of thing in the morning since he usually went to bed before his wife.

He clicked through his cameras, searching for their dog, relieved to find him sleeping by the fireplace. He thought about his boyhood pastime, butchering any drooling mutt dumb enough to cross his path. Unfortunately he couldn't kill the animal, as there could be no signs of an intruder.

He pulled on a black mask then snugged his night optical goggles. He carefully taped the fingertips of his right hand, since a glove wouldn't fit over his cast. Weeks before, he'd placed a camera zoomed on their alarm keypad, the code allowing him to enter at will. With so much surveillance equipment hidden in the house, the task would be ridiculously easy.

Death was raising his fist to knock on the door.

As she did most nights, Beth poured herself a nightcap. She turned on the television and settled in. Striking before she went to bed was crucial.

He slinked to the rear of the house then punched in the code. No need to pick the lock since he'd copied their key. He stepped inside then walked silently down a long hall. He entered an unused bedroom, down the hall from the senator's wife.

A few minutes later, she stood and walked into the hallway. Behram stiffened as she neared his location, but she entered a bathroom. He saw his opportunity and crept into the hall, quietly passing the restroom.

Her martini sat on an end table, next to her recliner. He emptied a vial of powdered Ambien into her drink. With profound amnestic qualities, the sleeping pills would erase any memories of the evening. While stirring the vodka, he heard the restroom door open. He grimaced, his only exit blocked.

Footsteps neared. He jumped over the end table and landed silently, catlike. As she entered, he ducked behind her chair. The oversized recliner was in a corner, the table and a couch blocking his exits.

She sat with a loud sigh. He was tucked behind her, his back to the wall. There was a little space behind the sofa but he might make noise if he moved. He unholstered his silenced pistol, hoping she'd drink the martini soon. He could hear her breath clearly but wasn't concerned about his. He was adept at silence, a quiet wraith. He was an undead spirit from the Thugee death cult.

With his pistol in his left hand, he held the viewer with his casted hand, carefully concealing the glow. The surveillance camera was hidden on the television; he watched her face on his screen. She lifted her glass and took a few sips while watching a comedy sitcom. He would never understand the awful television Americans found humorous.

A few minutes passed but she didn't seem drowsy. The talc probably settled in the bottom since he hadn't finish stirring.

He waited, his thoughts wandering. Stealing the ultimate possession made him feel like a capricious deity. He grudgingly admitted to himself that he was addicted, sometimes aching to murder random strangers like his namesake, Thug Behram.

The Thugee were devoted to the Hindu goddess Kali, who demanded endless human blood to satisfy her cravings. The word 'Thug' originates from these ancient killers who slaughtered over two million innocents in a reign of terror.

But he was an emotionless professional and thrill killings were counterproductive. He had plenty of opportunities to murder and occasionally torture. His intelligence kept a lid on the indwelling sadistic beast, creating one of the most efficient killers lurking the earth.

She made a sudden movement, jolting him to the present. She pulled the handle to recline, the chair bumping hard against Behram. He felt a moment of panic as the viewer dropped from his maimed hand. But he deftly caught it with his other, inches from the floor. There was a click as it hit his pistol grip.

He froze. If she discovered him, Behram would be forced to kill her. But Jefe was adamant: the senator's death must appear unintentional.

She pushed out of the chair and stood, probably wondering what was blocking the recliner. He had to make a split-second decision whether to hide or shoot. If detected, she might escape since he'd be wedged behind the enormous couch. But if he killed her, Jefe would be furious.

She pulled the weighty end table out of the way, the legs grinding across the pinewood floor. The noisy task distracting her, he seized his chance, slithering behind the couch.

Suddenly she stopped moving. He wondered if she'd seen him, jammed awkwardly on his side. He couldn't see her since the monitor was in his hand against the floor. He waited in anguished limbo.

Then his stomach lurched as he heard paws scratching in the hall. The dog would smell him and go berserk.

She spoke softly, "Hey, Chewie. Did you have a good nap? You wanna go outside? Okay, let's go."

She walked into the hall. He wondered if she was using the dog as an excuse to flee and quickly moved the monitor into his good hand. She seemed hurried as she walked to the rear door. He considered following to ensure she didn't run or make a phone call. But, again, the filthy mongrel might detect him.

She might notice the alarm was off. With her cell, she could call 911 before he reached her.

Behram had a horrible sinking feeling, the possibility of failure very real. His meticulous plan would be ruined. She went outside, disappearing from view.

If she called, dozens of police and search dogs would arrive in minutes. On foot, his capture would be inevitable.

The blaring television grating on his last nerve, he tried to think logically. If she'd noticed the alarm, she probably thought they'd forgotten or hit the wrong buttons. If she'd seen him, she would've screamed and run. She wasn't an icy professional, able to nonchalantly conceal her fears. She was an uppity housewife who tranquilized her privileged con-science by working with ridiculous charities.

But he was nervous. As time passed, the more anxious he became. She'd been out of sight for nearly five minutes. The police could roar in to rescue her at any moment. He felt the fringes of panic, an unfamiliar feeling.

He had to admit that his plan was in shambles. She'd been gone too long. Something was up. Time to abort.

As he prepared to flee, she strolled into view, the slobbery animal at her heels. Behram relaxed slightly. They entered the house. He felt better. They walked toward the television room.

He felt like rejoicing. She hadn't seen him. His mission would be accomplished.

But a sudden thought destroyed his brief joy: when the yapping cur entered the room, he'd be discovered. He heard the dog panting as they neared.

The reality settled in like humidity. He'd failed.

He decided to make it seem like a robbery gone wrong. He unscrewed his suppressor, as the senator needed to hear the shot, completing the illusion of a violent thief.

He seethed. As much as he hated to ruin his perfect streak, he was more anguished to lose his reward. Jefe wouldn't allow him to rain his wicked revenge on the boy.

But she entered without the dog, closing the door behind.

Behram's face broke into a perverse smile. The goal was still within reach.

She sat and drank half her martini. As canned laughter howled from the TV, her face relaxed into a flabby smile. As she gulped down the rest, she chuckled at every lame joke. Behram lay still as a corpse.

Her head began to bob, her eyes blinking slowly. Her head drooped. She jerked and shook her head. Then her eyes closed, the remote slipping from her hand as she entered the dream world.

She would awake to a nightmare.

Behram scanned the cameras until he found the dog asleep by their hearth. Changing views, he saw Senator Ripp sleeping soundly.

He pushed out then crept upstairs to their bedroom door. He unpocketed a cellphone. He entered a number and the screen went translucent, revealing three fluid-filled chambers inside. Behram was impressed; Jefe had serious connections. The device came from military sources or an intelligence agency, probably Russian.

He entered another code and the three glass rectangles emptied into a mixing chamber, creating ViXen gas. Standard VX nerve gas can be detected on autopsy but ViXen rapidly degrades to harmless, undetectable compounds.

He snaked a thin hose under their bedroom door to the bedside. He plugged the other end into the jack of the mock phone. After entering a third code, the odorless venom flowed out, reminding him of the Naja, the spitting Nepalese serpent.

He retreated to the spare bedroom, watching. The Senator's breathing became raspy and labored. Then it slowed to a few breaths a minute. Then stopped. Forever.

Behram had taken another soul.

His task was nearly complete. Entering their pantry, he removed a bottle of vodka and a glass. He pulled a gasmask from his pack and snugged it tight over his face.

He entered the bedroom, checking the senator's pulse. Finding none, he gingerly placed a gastric tube down Ripp's throat, filling his stomach with vodka and crushed pain pills.

He filled the martini glass with vodka and pressed it to the senator's hands and lips. Then he placed the fifth of vodka and a pill bottle against the cadaver's fingers.

He removed the surveillance gear from the house. He left, locking the door behind and turning the alarm on. He'd left no trace. He was euphoric.

He would celebrate his ninth assassination by killing the tenth, the child who'd broken his arm. The boy's cries would be music to his ears.

CHAPTER
TEN

Catherine and Susan grew up in Ketchum, a ski town in the heart of Idaho's Rocky Mountains. Catherine, five years older, made time for her little sister. They often skied together and both ripped, earning the nicknames Mama Bear Ripper and Goldilocks Ripper, as in "Hey Catherine! Where's Goldilocks Ripper?"

To hear Susan tell it, every guy wanted to date Catherine and every girl wanted her friendship. She said Catherine paved the way for her. Both raced rodeo barrels, skied for the varsity ski team and were crowned homecoming queen.

As adults they were best friends. Catherine was more assertive and outgoing but otherwise they were very similar: kind, intelligent and fun.

Susan moved to San Diego a few years earlier and we were stoked to have her around. She was like Blake's second mother.

She still seemed traumatized, not surprising since she was restrained for over a day, wondering if Blake was being tortured or killed. She appeared frail and skittish. I hoped she didn't blame herself.

But Catherine had morphed from a traumatized victim into a steely-eyed hunter. She cried very little, instead spending her time brainstorming and offering ideas, many quite helpful. A calm anger replaced sadness. To twist the quote, hell hath no fury like a woman protecting her child. She was itching to fight, to bare her frothy teeth in a swarm of bloody claws, torn clothing and fur.

Mama Bear Ripper wanted her cub back.

We spent much of our time monitoring the mic, planning to call the FBI after discovering Blake's location. We caught a few significant conversations. The boss was called El Jefe. We heard about shipments of mangos from Mexico. Mango farmers weren't ridiculously wealthy, nor did they murder and kidnap. I suspected they were drug traffickers, but still had no idea why they'd snatch Blake or kill me.

My previous dealings with Hispanic cartels were limited to gangbangers I'd seen in the ER. But they would have nothing against me. I patched them up so they could live to fight again. Maybe I'd saved a key rival's life, marking me for death. Seemed unlikely. There was that guy in Mexico but I couldn't see how that could be connected.

I had an ER shift that night. I usually slept before night shifts but spent all day getting the surveillance set up and listening. The night before, I'd slept very little after the ransom fiasco.

So I started the shift tired. Not optimal.

I was concerned about being in public, so I entered the hospital through a utility door. Halfway through my shift, the radio sounded. Over wailing sirens, the paramedic shouted, "We are en route with a middle-aged man in cardiac arrest. Be there in ten minutes."

The charge nurse said, "Let's put him in room three."

I nodded then hurried to discharge room eight. I had a few minutes to spare so I ducked into another room. After a cursory exam, I thought the patient had gallstones. I ordered pain meds, labs and an abdominal ultrasound.

I hurried into room three to prepare. Checked the intubation equipment then moved the defibrillator closer to the bed. My phone rang, "The paramedics want to speak to you. They're on a land line since they don't want to broadcast sensitive info on the radio."

"Sure."

The paramedic said, "Dr. Stryker, the patient is Senator Mark Ripp."

The floor dropped out beneath me.

I tried to speak but the words wouldn't come. Finally I said, "Go ahead."

"His wife requested Balboa Naval Medical Center since you're his doctor."

My mouth sandpaper, I replied, "Yeah. Bring him here."

"She found him in cardiac arrest. He's in asystole. We're proceeding with CPR and have given him three rounds of epi. Be there in five."

"Copy."

I walked outside to the ambulance bay. The lights of San Diego glowed in the distance. Palm trees swayed in the breeze under the lidless eye of a full moon.

I wondered how many more surprises I could take. In the past three days, a weirdo tried to kill me in Mexico, Blake had been kidnapped, an assassin killed my stand-in, and now Senator Ripp was in cardiac arrest.

A haunting wail grew louder, closer.

Mark seemed fine in Rosarito. He was the picture of heath and vigor, running a marathon last month. I'd recently suggested he get a cardiac workup, just because he was over fifty. If he'd had chest pains, he would've called me. I wondered about an assassin.

I hated to think it but I knew our efforts would prove futile. A patient in asystole, complete absence of any cardiac activity, has a survival rate of about one in ten thousand.

The wail turned into a scream. Flashing lights colored the surrounding palm trees as the rig roared to the bay. The rear doors burst open. As they rolled him into the ER, one paramedic jogged beside, compressing his chest. His vacant eyes bulged with each violent thrust, his handsome face violet, distorted by an endotracheal tube hanging from his mouth like a snorkel.

The paramedic reported, "When we arrived, he had no pulse and no cardiac rhythm. He's intubated with an eight ET tube. I think he's been dead for a while. But we thought it'd be best to transport him, given who he is and all." The paramedics often bypass the ER, transporting an obviously dead patient directly to the morgue.

I studied Mark's flank. There was a bluish hue, caused by blood pooling after his heart ceased beating. He'd been dead for at least an hour.

I squirted ultrasound gel on his chest then ran the probe over his heart. I said, "Stop CPR."

We watched the screen in anticipation. Nothing, not even a quiver.

His chance of resuscitation was zero. Senator Mark Ripp was dead.

"I'm calling it now," I announced. "Time of death is 11:45 PM."

I felt empty and sad, wondering if I'd failed to detect something. I tried to hide my emotions as I asked the paramedics, "What happened?"

"His wife called 911 after she found him. She was slurring and crying hysterically. She seems totally loaded. A policeman is bringing her. There was an empty fifth of vodka by his bed."

I was surprised. The Ripps were moderate people. They drank socially but I'd never seen either of them drunk. Their blood tests never showed liver problems.

"Let's draw an alcohol level and tox screen. Any evidence of trauma?"

"No. He looked asleep."

I inspected his entire body, finding nothing unusual. I looked for blood behind the eardrums, a sign of skull fracture. Nothing.

I told the nurses, "Mrs. Ripp should arrive soon. Please prepare his body for viewing. I'm their doctor. I know her well."

I left to chart. Felt like I was in a nightmare. I'd tried to get out of working and it turned out worse than any shift I'd ever had. I'd never taken care of a dead friend in the ER. But not only a friend, Mark was a role model, a hero. I looked up to him more than any man besides my dad and Javier.

I studied the computer screen, fifteen patients in the waiting room. I was the only doc on after midnight. It was going to be a long night. Mark's death would take a lot of time to sort out, dealing with family, investigators and possibly the media. Rubbed my eyes with the heels of my hands. Then jolted.

The media! My thoughts lurched, panicked. If I made the morning news, the kidnappers would discover they'd killed the wrong man. They might conclude we'd tricked them, endangering our careful surveillance. And Blake. I seriously considered leaving but decided that would bring more attention.

When I looked up, a nurse was studying my face, concerned. She gently asked, "Are you okay?"

"Yeah, I'm fine. But he was a good friend."

Rattled, I went to see the sickest patient, an elderly man with severe abdominal pain. I had a hard time paying attention.

A nurse called my phone, "Mrs. Ripp's in the family room."

I checked Sen. Ripp's lab results. His alcohol level was over five times the legal limit. His tox screen showed opioids. Mark died from an accidental overdose. I couldn't believe it.

Was he a secret abuser, fooling everyone? Had he inadvertently overdone it? I'd seen overdoses where the patient had gotten buzzed then kept going, their judgment impaired.

But Mark was a measured, controlled person, doing nothing haphazardly.

I rubbed my eyebrow with a thumb. *What a way to go out.*

He was one of the most powerful men in the world. Many, including myself, hoped he'd eventually be the President.

One can never know the private ghosts that haunt others, even those you think you know well. One of my med school friends got caught stealing narcotics. I was floored. He'd fooled all of us.

I walked out, dreading the conversation. Delivering bad news is never easy but to relay that the great senator, her beloved husband and father of their children, died in such a sorry manner would be particularly painful. Beth Ripp was a wonderful person, a tireless worker for charity, leveraging her considerable fame and power to help others.

I heard weeping as I approached the family room. The bright sterility and noisy racket of the ER seemed grating, blasphemous. I gripped the cold doorknob, breathed deeply then entered.

She was alone and frail, her face submerged in damp hands.

Simple words work best. To avoid prolonging the uncertainty, I cut straight to the chase, "Beth, I'm very sorry, but Mark died. He couldn't be revived." Not *passed away, no longer with us* or *moved on.* He was dead.

Beth attempted to focus through spattered mascara. She slurred, "I know. I know."

I hugged her and caught a wiff of vodka.

"The paramedics did everything possible but couldn't bring him back."

She mumbled, "I'm sure they did, Wyatt. They seemed like good men." The intoxicated grande dame, attempting to be dignified.

"He was a great man and a good friend. I admired him."

She nodded but said nothing.

"What happened tonight? Was he ill?"

Her thick words plopped out slowly, "He was fine. He exercises daily and ran...what do you call it? He ran...a long thing for miles..."

"A marathon."

"Yes, that's it. He ran a marathon. We had a quiet night at home. He grilled ribs. Have you ever had them?"

"Yeah."

"He went to bed at his usual time. When I went to bed, he wasn't breathing."

"How much did he drink tonight?"

"He might've had a martini...maybe a beer. Don't really remember..." Her voice trailed off. She gazed vacantly at the wall.

"I thought he wasn't much of a drinker. Does he drink a lot?"

"No...not so much. He'll get tipsy...a few times a year."

"When did you notice he wasn't breathing?"

"What time is it?"

"Almost one."

"Must've dozed off in my chair. He probably went to bed around nine. He's an early riser, Mark is. Or he was." She sobbed quietly.

I waited for her to stop crying. After about a minute, she became very quiet, then slowly her head slipped from her hands. She jerked suddenly. "I'm sorry. I must've fallen asleep. Did you ask me something?"

It seemed odd that she could fall asleep in this situation, even being drunk. "Has he complained of anything, like chest pain or headache?"

"No. Nothing."

"Does he use recreational drugs?"

"Like what?"

"Illegal drugs, like cocaine."

"No! He's against all that."

"Sorry, I had to ask. What about pain pills?"

"No...maybe aspirin." She bobbed crazily like she might fall out of her chair. I reached to steady her.

"Has he been depressed or suicidal?"

"No. That man would be happy in hell." She wept again.

"Would you like to see him?"

"I'd rather wait until my friend arrives." She cried harder.

"I'm so sorry. Do you want to call your children or should I?"

"I should tell them."

"Would you like to see a chaplain?" She was a devout Catholic, living her faith by helping the less fortunate.

"Yes, I would." She stood then lurched sideways. I stepped forward but she caught herself on the wall. She sat down but missed, striking the chair arm with her hip. "Oh, I'm a bit unsteady." I helped her down.

I left. I asked a tech to sit with her until the chaplain arrived. I didn't want her to fall or, God forbid, have the same fate as Mark.

I thought about the man in Mexico. Rosarito seemed like years ago, but had only been a few days.

Maybe it was a professional hit. But Mark Ripp was beloved by all. He had no real enemies. Mark wasn't a dirty, ruthless politician. He won because he got things done and found the middle ground, not because he slung mud. His death wouldn't help any particular cause, at least none that I knew about.

And they both were drunk. I couldn't imagine how that could be faked. She'd tell me if they were forced at gunpoint to drink themselves to death. I'd ask about their drinking when she sobered up a bit.

Patients were stacking up in the waiting room. I worked as fast as possible, while trying to be safe with others' lives. After a few hours, I went to the locker room and splashed water on my face. I stared at the clock, willing it to move faster. I hadn't felt this exhausted since SEAL training, emotionally and physically.

My phone rang, an annoying interruption to my brief respite. "Hello, Dr. Stryker here."

"This is Karen Bitts, I'm in charge of public relations for the hospital. I understand you're the doctor who took care of Senator Ripp?"

"Yes. He's my private patient. His wife asked the medics to bring him here."

"As you can imagine, there will be a national feeding frenzy. It's imperative that all information comes from official channels. Do *not* speak to the media! Do I make myself clear?"

I was annoyed by her shrill tone, interrupting my busy shift to state the obvious. Basic medical ethics taught in all med schools preclude sharing private information without consent. Plus, I had ulterior motives for avoiding the media at all costs.

I paused, as I didn't want to say something I'd regret. After awkward silence, she said, "Dr. Stryker?"

"Yeah."

"Okay, I just wanted to make sure."

"Sure of what?"

"That you're still there."

"Am I supposed to say something?"

"No, I just want to be clear."

"Loud and clear. Clear and loud. Commanding me to follow clear medical protocol is clearly unnecessary. I clearly need to get back to work. Do I make myself clear?"

She sputtered, "I'm just doing my job!"

"I'm trying to do mine." I hung up.

I went to speak with Beth, planning to ask about the drinking.

She was snoring loudly in her chair, her mouth agape. The chaplain sat near, looking uncomfortable. I shook her shoulder gently, "Beth."

"Yes. Oh, I'm sorry. Can't seem to stay awake."

I asked, "Are you okay? Is there anything I can do?"

She sat up and looked with blurry eyes. "Will you come to his funeral? Mark thought a lot of you, Wyatt. So do I."

"Of course."

"Mark always said you could've accomplished anything you wanted, but you chose to serve others at every step. You've always reminded me of Mark, so talented yet so humble. I think you reminded him of his younger self. He really liked you, Wyatt."

I swallowed hard. I had no idea they'd ever thought much about me. I'd thought about him a lot, but he was famous and I wasn't. He was the only famous person I really knew, except a few pros I knew from college ball. I felt honored. And sad.

"Mark was a hero. He was one of the only politicians who seemed to truly care about others. Comparing him to me... that's one of the best compliments I've ever received. I really mean that."

She reached out and grabbed my hand, smiling sadly. Then drifted off to sleep.

I decided to wait until later to ask about the drinking. After returning to the ER, I called the paramedics and asked, "Did you see any signs of foul play? Any signs of a break in?"

"No, but we scooped and ran. Why?"

"He's not much of a drinker. I was wondering if he could've been murdered. But it seems unlikely, since his alcohol level was through the roof and he had narcotics in his system."

"Now that you mention it, there was an unlabeled pill bottle on his bedside table."

"Please keep it quiet. The press'll have a field day if they find out."

"Yeah. Of course."

Unlabeled. He'd bought them on the street. I couldn't believe it. My stomach felt sour.

I saw a few more patients. My fatigue worsened. My phone rang and the secretary said, "An FBI agent wants to speak with you about Senator Ripp."

"Okay. Put him through."

"Dr. Stryker, this is Agent Wachowski from the FBI. I have a few routine questions about Senator Ripp's death. Do you know the cause of death?"

"His alcohol level was very high and his tox screen showed narcotics, probably pain pills."

He said softly, "Whoa. That's not good."

"You're telling me. Of course, it could've been anything, heart attack, stroke, whatever. But I bet the autopsy will show he quit breathing from the combination. Why's the FBI involved?"

"He's a national figure and he's too young to die of natural causes. He has a very high security clearance, so we have to cover our bases. It sounds like an accident. There's no reason to think otherwise but we need to be certain."

I hung up and rubbed my forehead, feeling uneasy. I wondered if I should've told him about the guy in Mexico. I didn't like the idea of withholding pertinent info. The truth should be known and justice served.

But I wanted to think it through before getting involved in lengthy interviews and a complex investigation. I had to focus on Blake. I would decide after some sleep.

I went to see Beth a final time. Three hours had passed since our initial conversation. She was asleep on the couch, snoring softly. Her shirt was twisted awkwardly and one shoe lay in the middle of the floor.

The chaplain said, "Her friend came but we couldn't wake her, so she left to get coffee. Poor thing must be exhausted."

I shook her gently. "Beth, do you want to see Mark before he's taken to the morgue?"

She partially opened her eyes, "Wyatt, what're you doing here? Where am I?" She looked confused then closed her eyes and breathed noisily.

"Beth?" I shook her again.

"Stop kidding." She swatted the air but didn't open her eyes. The chaplain looked embarrassed. I shrugged my shoulders then left.

I finished up and prepared to leave. Worst-case scenario would be a television crew with cameras. If a reporter jammed a mic in my face, I'd chomp it like an ice cream cone.

The parking lot was quiet. I headed back to Javier's, too tired to think and too wired to rest. With my recent luck, I'd fall asleep at the wheel and massacre an innocent family.

It sunk in. I'd endangered every bit of progress we'd made to find Blake.

CHAPTER
ELEVEN

When I arrived at the house, everyone was asleep. I crawled in bed with Catherine and covered my eyes with a travel mask.

I awoke in the early afternoon. Susan and Catherine were out. I found Javier in his office. "Mark Ripp died last night. His wife asked the medics to bring him to my ER. I'm worried my name will show up in the news and blow our cover."

He whistled softly, "It's all over the news. What happened?"

I told him the story.

"Sure it was an accident?"

"Seemed like one. He crashed the pearly gates too drunk to tell Saint Peter his name."

"An assassin could've forced them to drink and take pills by threatening a loved one."

"Beth would've told us. She was too drunk to lie. Even in that absurd scenario, death wouldn't be guaranteed. More likely, he'd get drunk and puke."

"Let's see the news."

He opened his laptop and clicked on a brief obituary:

San Diego (AP) -Sen. Mark Ripp of California, who dominated public life in California the past two decades and became a voice of national conscience and moderation, died yesterday at his home. He was 54. He was transported to Balboa Naval Medical Center where he was pronounced dead on arrival. The cause of death was not released but sources say he died of natural causes.

Turning down lucrative offers from the country's top corporate law firms, Ripp began his career as a fearless prosecutor. He was elected LA's District Attorney at the age of 33. Two years later, he was elected Senator, making him the youngest member of the U.S. Senate.

The friendly, soft-spoken Senator Ripp often deferred publicly to his outspoken and ambitious colleagues, seemingly content to broker deals and legislation behind the scenes. He referred to himself as a "flaming moderate" and was popular on both sides of the aisle. Many hoped he would eventually run for President, although he never publically expressed any interest in running.

California Governor Peterson addressed reporters this morning, pausing to regain composure several times. "It's hard to think of anyone in recent history who has done more for mankind. He was loved by all." For fifteen minutes, the Governor eulogized Sen. Ripp then concluded, "Mark was a true renaissance man, tirelessly working for the betterment of others with a sunny outlook. I will miss my dear friend."

The President extended his condolences and hailed Ripp as, "one of the greatest thinkers of our time. He lived America's promise as a citizen and fought to keep that promise alive as a senator. His untimely death is a blow to our nation."

Javier clicked on several more articles. None mentioned me.

"So far, so good," I said. "But it's a matter of time until my name comes out. I don't feel good about being here. Any two-bit private detective could easily link you and I. What if we move to your house in Alpine?"

"Good idea. Hardly anyone knows about that place."

I called Catherine and we quickly threw our stuff together.

Javier bought the rural farmhouse under his sister's name. Many SEALs have secret get-away places. The paranoid edge that keeps us alive in the battlefield doesn't vanish when we return home. Maybe it's overkill, but we worry about a foreign group wanting revenge. A SEAL would be a prestigious kill for an Al Qaeda sympathizer, revenge for Bin Laden.

For almost twenty years, I'd avoided having my photo taken. I wasn't hiding, but I wasn't going to make it easy either. A web search of Wyatt Stryker came up with football articles but nothing since my SEAL days. There were no photos of me in our house.

And it had paid off. The kidnappers probably didn't know what I looked like.

We left, heading to his farmhouse. Riding with Javier, I said, "Who'd want to kill Mark? He was a moderate, a rare animal these days."

"Seems too bizarre for coincidence. You're his personal doctor. You spent the night at his house in Mexico and some weird guy tried to kill you."

"And the next day, Blake gets kidnapped. The following day, someone tried to kill me in the park. Then the day after, Ripp died. Got to be connected."

"Has he told you any confidential information?"

"No. We've never discussed anything remotely secret."

"Can you get the autopsy report?"

"It'll take a few days but I have a friend at the morgue. The FBI agent asked about foul play. I didn't tell him about that guy in Mexico."

"I vote we hold off until we know more."

After passing through the mountain town of Alpine, we stopped on a side road to make sure we weren't followed then continued past undeveloped forest and farmland, rural houses spaced widely apart. He turned into his steep long driveway.

The hilltop house, invisible from the road, was a 1930s four-bedroom farmhouse, surrounded by forty acres of rolling hills with mixed evergreen and hardwood forest. A barn sat between the house and his pond, a few hundred yards down a rolling slope.

Catherine called the director of the ER, telling him my best friend was suddenly diagnosed with terminal cancer. I'd flown to Australia to see him.

My director said it was imperative that I speak with the FBI immediately about Senator Ripp. He'd been flooded with calls; the hospital CEO was breathing down his neck. The director had been to my house, looking for me.

Catherine said I was overcome with grief and was not behaving rationally. She would tell me to call him.

Later, I sat outside, researching potential leads. Javier opened the front door and shouted, "I got something!"

He hit the button to play the message. A voice said, "Jefe, there's been nothing in the news about the child's father, the doctor. After he died, I sent men to the house to remove equipment. They planted narcotics and meth." The man sounded like he was from the Bronx.

The man called Jefe asked, "Why was his death unreported?"

"We don't know. Maybe there's an investigation into his involvement selling prescription drugs."

"Have the pigs been to his house?"

"We haven't seen them but we don't have continual surveillance. If the DEA or the feds get involved, they'd discover our wires."

"True. Well, it appears that the problem's solved. Even if the doctor spoke of his child's abduction or Behram, he's been discredited. Seagulls ate his educated brains. You'll be rewarded."

He chuckled, "*Gracias*, Jefe."

"God may be merciful, but El Jefe is not. We'll snatch your sweet Yanqui child. When you come groveling for the innocent's safe return, we'll blow your eyes from your skull, leaving the weeping mama a widow."

They both laughed like it was the best joke ever. The conversation ended.

I was shocked at his brutality. I stammered, "They think it's funny."

"He's a bastard, and an evil one at that."

My voice shook with rage, "He'll pay if it's the last thing I do."

Our eavesdropping led to a few other discoveries. The group referred to itself as El Poder, or The Power. Neither of us had heard of El Poder but Javier said he could find out more from Admiral Landfair, the commander of Operation Cartel.

El Jefe, the boss, left the compound infrequently, but bodyguards discussed El Jefe's dinner at an upscale French restaurant scheduled for the following night.

Javier made a reservation to Chateaubriand. We would see him up close and personal.

Javier needed to go to his office to catch up on work, I wanted to search for clues and check my home phone to see if anyone had called about Senator Ripp, since I'd cancelled my cell after it was stolen.

At dusk, I drove to a strip mall, three miles from our house. I'd attached a thick blonde beard and dyed my hair the same, as opposed to my normal sandy hair. I wore a puffy jacket and three pairs of sweat pants underneath the hooded jogging suit.

I plodded along, like an overweight suburban dad trying to shed a few pounds. Circled the block and saw nothing suspicious.

I walked to the front door. An envelope marked FBI was taped to the door as well as a note from the ER director asking me to call him immediately. I removed the FBI envelope then unlocked the door and stepped inside.

The house looked the same. The anniversary painting was propped on the couch. Blake's baseball bat leaned in a corner.

I picked it up, feeling perverse satisfaction. I swung it a few times, imagining Blake cracking the assassin's forearm. My little bruiser gave that son-of-a-bitch more than he'd bargained for. Compound fractures, when broken bone penetrates skin, often create permanent pain and disability.

I hoped so.

I hung my extra clothing and my pistol in a closet then boiled water on the stove, steaming the envelope. I carefully peeled it open. "Dr. Stryker, please contact the FBI as soon as possible regarding the death of Senator Ripp. Call this number 24 hours a day." I resealed the letter.

I checked the messages. There was one from my cheerful parents wishing us a happy anniversary. I shook my head sadly. If they only knew.

The next message: "Dr. Styker, this is Special Agent Wachowski from the FBI. We spoke briefly in the ER. Please call." There were similar messages from the hospital CEO, the coroner and the ER director.

I walked to Blake's room. The bed was still in the wrong place. The screen was dented outward and torn. I lifted a picture of he and Catherine on the beach. Blake was about three and wore orange arm floatation inflatables. Catherine was radiant. I hadn't seen that smile since Blake's abduction.

I studied his posters; Boise State football, Star Wars and a skier going off a cliff. I picked up his iPod and scrolled through: hip-hop and electronic dance music. We both loved funky tunes. Catherine didn't really share our taste so we turned it to eleven when she was gone. Blake won the talent show at his school with a mesmerizing break dance, a combination of fluid and robotic moves.

I opened his closet, filled with his brightly colored shirts, superhero jammies, well-worn athletic shoes and barely-worn dress clothes. As I held his little skateboard shoes to my chest, my face contorted.

I sank to my knees. Was he alive? If so, where? Was he being treated humanely? Did he wonder why we hadn't come for him? Did he cry for us at night?

Of course he cried. He was a lost little boy. Our little boy.

I had to leave. If I stayed any longer, the room would swallow me whole.

I plodded upstairs to our bedroom and stared at the bed. The pillows looked so soft. I reclined, staring at the ceiling. Thoughts of our little family rushed like muddy floodwaters. The deluge engulfed me: his birth, water gun battles, snow skiing, birthday parties, Blake jumping from behind a bush to give me a hug.

He asked us to read to him every night. Sometimes Blake fell asleep between us on our bed, this bed.

A Father's Day card hung on the wall. The cover displayed a Psalm, carefully handwritten by Blake, *"Like an arrow in the hand of a warrior, so are the sons of those who have been shaken. Hurl lightning bolts and scatter them. Shoot your arrows and rout them."* I smiled sadly, noticing the faint ruler lines below the words, keeping Blake's lines straight.

I removed the card from the frame and opened it. He'd painstakingly drawn two ancient fighters. The larger warrior aimed a longbow at unseen enemies. The other's arm was extended, giving an arrow to the bigger archer, his other hand gripping a small bow. Crayon lightning bolts flashed in the background. The large fighter was labeled *Dad* and the smaller *Blake*.

He made the card in kindergarten. When Catherine explained that I'd been a warrior in the Special Forces, he came up with the idea.

I put the card in my pocket.

Three thousand years ago, King David wrote about children supporting their parents during hardship. But the verse took on a new, tragic meaning.

I was a father without a son, a warrior without arrows.

I pulled a pillow over my face, drowning in my thoughts. I abruptly stood to clear my swamped mind. Time to finish and leave.

I stepped into our bathroom and checked the drawers. One held five Ziploc bags stuffed with narcotic pills and vials. Meth was hidden somewhere but I wasn't going to search.

I went to the kitchen to check the trash for the restraints but the chair distracted me. I stared at the horrible chair, where Susan was tormented. The chair seemed haunted, evil, possessed. I wondered how she felt with ties cutting into her hands and feet, wondering if Blake was being tortured, abused or killed. I wanted to smash the heinous chair, to burn it, to hurt it the way the chair hurt Susan.

Or maybe...maybe it was a holy place. I brushed my fingers across the top of the chair. A long hair lay across, Susan's hair, like a tiny thread of woven gold over a splintered crucifix.

I gingerly lifted the hair, holding it up to the light.

From behind, a harsh voice spoke, "Hello."

CHAPTER TWELVE

I jolted, dropped Susan's hair and spun. Flight or fight instincts surged.

A policeman stood in the living room. I asked, "Can I help you?"

"I hope. We got a call about a suspicious person. You the home owner?" He didn't smile. His hand rested near his gun.

My mind raced. A random jogger entering an unoccupied house was unusual. The FBI had probably questioned the neighbors. I should have come late at night, under cover of darkness. I mentally chastised myself.

If I admitted my identity, he might ask me to go in for questioning, especially if he knew the FBI was looking for me. If the Jefe had a police mole, I'd be marked. Better for them to believe my brains were mixed with sand. But if I denied being the homeowner, he might arrest me.

I said, "I'm Brian Peterson, a close friend of the family. No one's heard from them recently. I came to investigate."

"Where's your car?"

"I was jogging."

"Where do you live?"

I was painting myself into a corner. I didn't have a friend named Brian Peterson. I should've used the name of someone I knew. It'd be easy for the police to cross reference the name and address.

Susan's address popped into my head, "108 Camas Drive." I could pretend to be Susan's boyfriend. She didn't have one.

"You were on a run and you dropped by?"

"Yeah."

"Camas Drive is ten miles away."

I was on the ropes. Changing the subject, I attempted to put him on the defense, "Why didn't you knock or make your presence known? You nearly scared me to death."

"We don't usually alert burglars." He stared hard.

"Do you know anything about the family? Wyatt and Catherine Stryker?"

"Do you?"

"They're good friends."

"Really?" His eyes were dead.

"Yes. I've got a house key."

"You're on a twenty mile run and you drop in to search your friends' house?"

"I've come by several times. They haven't answered phone calls. We're worried."

"Do you have permission to be in their house? If not, you're trespassing."

"If you want to arrest me for being in my friend's house, go ahead. But entering a with a key they gave me isn't breaking and entry."

"Have you reported a missing family? How do I verify the owner gave you a key? How do you know the owner?"

I was flummoxed. I could say I lived with Catherine's sister, but he probably knew Susan was missing. He immediately knew Camas Drive was ten miles away.

I decided to call his bluff. "I'm a responsible citizen worried about my friend. You're behaving like a bully. What's your name?"

"What's yours?"

"I told you already. Isn't the first part of a conversation typically a mutual introduction? What's your name officer?"

"I'm asking the questions." His hand moved, resting on his gun.

I was missing something. This wasn't routine cop behavior. Maybe he was harshly interrogating me to determine if he should make an arrest. The FBI might have our house under surveillance due to Ripp's death. I was behaving suspiciously so he treated me as a suspect. I had to chill.

He pointed to the FBI letter, "What's that?"

I swallowed hard, my mind racing. "I got their mail, looking for clues."

He held out his hand, "Pass it to me."

He looked down at the envelope. "An FBI letter taped to the door is not mail." While his eyes were down, I studied him. He wore a thick navy coat. I noticed his belt held a cylinder, too small to be a flashlight. Wasn't pepper spray. Not the right shape for a Taser.

My pulse accelerated. It was the size of a suppressor.

Cops don't use silencers. I felt beads on my forehead.

I stammered, "I was curious."

"Curious." He raised his eyebrows.

I threw up my hands. "Officer, I'm at a loss. I came to check on my friend and you're treating me like a criminal."

"A stranger is found inside the home of a missing family. I should just take your word?"

"We can verify I'm their friend. This hostility is unnecessary."

"I'd like to look around. Please lead." I stepped toward the hall. As I passed, he stepped back, maintaining the distance.

I glanced out the window. There was no police car in sight. Maybe he parked up the block.

Maybe he wasn't a policeman. My heart slammed against my ribcage.

"Could you call another officer? We're getting nowhere."

His onyx eyes were cold as a corpse. "In due time."

We stood quietly. I was aware of my rapid breathing.

I led him into a guest bedroom. He glanced around but seemed to be studying me.

We went into Blake's room. He said, "What happened here?" He gestured with his left arm. He wore a heavy coat, but I noticed his right arm seemed odd, stiff, too large. His arm was in a cast.

It was him.

CHAPTER
THIRTEEN

Blake thought about his escape. Juan, the guard, thought he just wanted to play chess, but Blake had other ideas. So what if they were grown-ups? Blake was the toughest kid in his school. He'd fought older kids who picked on his friends.

And won every time.

His parents repeatedly told him to leave the bully enforcement to his teachers. He'd missed quite a few playground recesses and gotten in trouble at home. But the bullies always got the message.

Plus, he'd almost beat one grown-up already, making him scream by whacking his arm. He enjoyed remembering that; the only thought that made him smile. And Blake thought he might've won, had it been a fair fight. The man cheated, giving him a shot.

He could overpower Juan and take his gun. Maybe. At least he could try. What did he have to lose?

Or he could trick Juan and snatch the gun. He'd wait until Juan was distracted, playing chess. He'd shot a gun before. He tried to remember the steps. Something about a safety and chambering a round. It would probably come back to him, once he had the gun.

He was sick of moping around the room, since he couldn't stop dwelling on his parents and Aunt Susan. He couldn't believe they were dead. He cried until he thought he could cry no more but the tears kept coming.

Aunt Susan was like his mom, only younger, the coolest aunt in the world.

His father was his hero. He wanted to be just like Dad when he grew up. Dad's friends called him Riot Wyatt. Blake loved watching videos of his dad dominating in college football, crushing running backs. Mom said quarterbacks feared him. In the final seconds of a bowl game, he intercepted a pass and ran for a touchdown, winning the game. Blake decided he would play football at Boise State then become a SEAL then an ER doctor. He'd study as hard as possible in school. He'd practice football and exercise during every moment of his spare time. His dad was the best man in the world.

But he missed his mom the most. She was always there for him. Her face lit up with a beautiful smile whenever she saw him. She even knew the names of his Lego characters. Kissed his skinned knee and made soup when he was sick. Having a nurse for a mom was the best. She was funny and pretty but mostly she cared about others more than herself.

He felt guilty about the times he argued and disobeyed. When he saw her in heaven, he'd tell her he was really sorry.

He loved her so much. And now she was gone. She was the best person in the world.

He sobbed into his pillow then threw it against the wall. Finally, he dried his eyes and stared at the ceiling. He had to find a way out.

He walked to the locked door, knocking on it. The guard opened and looked at him quizzically. Blake smiled, "Juan, I'm bored. Wanna play chess?"

The guard laughed, "Sí, little *chico*. I'll get it." The man closed the door behind, locking it. Blake put his ear to the door and listened carefully. He heard the man walk down the hall then go up some stairs. He opened a door; he didn't pause long enough to unlock it.

Blake just had to run out to a street in front of the house and call for help. He could probably outrun them. He was the fastest kid in his grade.

Juan returned with a chessboard. They played for hours. Blake was an animated competitor, winning almost every time. Juan laughed often, thoroughly enjoying himself.

Blake kept sneaking peeks at the gun, wondering if he could grab it.

Blake's eyes danced with something behind them. Eyes that searched and actively interpreted rather than blankly rolling across a scene. Like his dad, they saw things others missed.

Blake took notice of Juan's muscles. They weren't as big as his dad's and Blake usually won when they wrestled. But Blake recently realized his Dad was letting him win.

Halfway through a match, Blake said, "I'm sorta tired of being inside. Could we go for a walk outside?"

"Not today. Maybe tomorrow."

"Is there a lot of room?"

"This is a very big place. Very beautiful."

"Maybe I could skateboard. Is there a street near here?

"No, you can't do that."

"Why not?"

"The boss won't let us."

"Who's the boss?" Blake moved a knight and took one of Juan's bishops.

"The man you met the other day."

"The fat guy?"

Juan frowned. "Don't say that. He gets angry."

"I already did. I called him fat."

He looked gravely concerned, sad even. "I know. But don't do it again. He wants to help you." He paused and looked into Blake's eyes, almost pleading, "Please don't."

"Okay, I won't. It wasn't very nice." Juan looked relieved.

They played in silence. Juan seemed really sad about something, lost in thought, almost like he was about to cry. Blake wondered why.

After a few minutes, Blake asked, "Any other games we could play?"

"We have Monopoly."

Blake turned on the charm and grinned. "Let's play that next!" Blake took Juan's queen with his rook. He held it up and smiled wickedly.

Juan wrung his hair with both hands. "You rascal! How'd you do that?"

"Lucky, I guess."

"Not luck! You're too smart! But it's not over yet!"

"We need more players for Monopoly. Are there others here?"

"*Sí.* Many."

"How many?"

"There are three here."

"Could they come play?" If he could get them all in the room, maybe he could run out.

"No, not today."

"Aww. Why not?" Blake moved his queen, setting up a trap. He was about to win, if Juan didn't notice.

"They're all working." Juan failed to see it and took Blake's knight.

Blake moved his queen and proudly announced, "Checkmate!"

Juan clenched his fists in defeat and groaned comically. "Aaargh! You win again!"

Blake laughed and pointed at Juan's bulging biceps. "Big muscles!"

Juan smiled broadly. "Not as big as yours! Let me see them!" Blake made a muscle and Juan squeezed it. "Wow! Big and strong! I'd hate to get in a fight with you!"

Blake wondered if he could win. Juan was probably just being nice. The biggest bully he'd fought was thirteen. And he wasn't the biggest thirteen-year-older at school. Juan was bigger. Way bigger.

Maybe tricking would be better. Probably so.

He thought about Juan's gun and handheld radio. A plan formed in his mind. He smiled.

He'd set up a trap, just like chess. Then move in for the checkmate.

CHAPTER
FOURTEEN

After noticing the cast, I quickly turned my face away so he wouldn't see my shock. I had to keep my composure. My life, and Blake's life, depended on my ability to convince him. My Glock was hanging in the foyer closet.

He'd returned to the scene of the crime, a significant risk, so he had a purpose. He seemed unsure. Otherwise, he would've already killed me. Or he was milking me for information before the execution.

We went into the garage. A door led outside. Maybe I could bolt.

He quickly moved in front of the door.

Tools hung on the wall. If I could grab a shovel, I could hit him before he got his gun. I dismissed the idea as too risky.

"Upstairs," he said. "Lead."

I walked toward the staircase, racking my brain. Maybe I could tackle him on the stairs. If I attacked from above, he couldn't unholster his gun before I nailed him.

I was much larger and probably stronger. The odds were in my favor.

I'd wait until he was on the stairs, unable to brace himself. I'd turn while speaking to him. My knee would bend, a foot pressing firmly against the vertical side of the step. Then I'd shove off, spearing him with my forehead, head butting his face. Once pinned, I'd take his gun.

I started up the stairs. Time moved slower.

I felt each foot plod. Felt awkward.

Like I was new at it. Like I'd just learned to walk up stairs.

Rehearsed thrusting off, exploding into him, fracturing his nose with my head and pinning his arms under my knees.

Halfway, three more steps.

I ran a deep breath in and out.

Two more.

I began my rotation and said, "Watch your step here."

He stood at the bottom of the stairs. He was watching me, his hand on his gun. Not a beginner.

"Watch my step?"

"The stairs are steep."

He stared, then after a long pause he spoke, softly and menacingly, "Perhaps *you* should be watching *your* step."

I hurried up. I hated not being able to see him. He'd probably shoot me in the back of the head, like Wayne. Having me lead placed him in a position of power.

He waited until I was off the landing before quickly ascending, his eyes on me. He moved like a cat, precise and confident.

We stepped into my bedroom. He looked around then motioned toward the master bath. I entered.

He hissed, "The body's just a temporary vehicle, transporting the soul."

I froze, wondering if I had heard him correctly. I slowly turned. "Excuse me?"

He said nothing. His eyes poured darkness into mine, a chill draining down my neck.

I wondered what he meant. Was it some sort of a warning? Something he said before slaying his victims?

He was probably trying to rattle me. And it worked. I looked around clumsily, awkwardly avoiding his vile stare.

He held the power. I was stuck in the small bathroom. He blocked the door. I had to end this.

I thought about crashing through the window but breaking through and getting away was improbable. Glass would slice me. Landing on my feet, unlikely.

He stepped out. We went into the upstairs spare bedroom. He spoke, his voice barely above a whisper, "Back downstairs."

I descended as he followed a few steps behind. His bizarre muttered comment clouded my thinking, probably his intention.

If I could open the coat closet, I could get my gun then blast him. But killing him would not bring Blake back. In fact, it would make it impossible.

We entered the living room. I said, "Can I leave now?"

"No." He stared, his eyes sucking hope like a parasite.

"I'm leaving."

"No, you're not."

"Then arrest me."

"You haven't answered my questions. I don't understand why you ran twenty miles instead of driving."

"I run marathons. I need to train."

He looked me up and down, weighing the chances.

"Tampering with that letter is mail fraud."

"You just said it wasn't mail. Please call for backup, arrest me or let me leave. Do something."

"I will do something. I haven't decided what yet." He fiddled with the snap on his holster, his eyes boring into me.

I had to act. I lifted a cordless phone and said, "I'm calling 911. This is ridiculous."

"Put the phone away."

I dialed and put it to my ear, keeping my eyes on him.

A female voice said, "911. What is your emergency?"

"I'm at 214 Willow Drive. A policeman is harassing me."

"Excuse me? What's your emergency?"

"Please send an officer. I don't feel safe."

"Stay on the line."

He backed to the front door then stepped out, leaving the door open. As soon as his poisonous eyes were gone, I felt an instant wave of relief.

I hung up on the dispatcher and turned the ringer off. I grabbed my pistol then crept up the stairs and flattened against a wall, peering out a window. Where had he gone? What was he doing? I had to get out before the police arrived but he couldn't know Wyatt Stryker was alive.

He could be across the street with a sniper rifle and high-powered scope, or inside a house or car.

He could be back inside our house, the front door still open.

I went into the master bath, locking the door. I crouched in the bathtub, my pistol pointing at the door.

Jefe's security guy said they didn't have wires but the assassin knew somehow. The house was obviously bugged. They might've been troubled by the lack of press about my death, as well as the disappearances of Susan and Catherine. The man came to investigate but wasn't certain enough to kill. My paranoia about photos had paid off. He didn't know what I looked like. Maybe he was convinced that I was really a friend.

If I stayed, the police would interrogate me. They would arrive in minutes. *Think, Wyatt! Think!*

I could escape out the back but I'd be on foot. If I fled before the police arrived, he'd know I wasn't a random friend. He might kill me, knowing I was fleeing the scene.

The house was wired. I had to continue the ruse. I had to convince him. If he knew I was alive, he might send Blake's ear to a local television station to cow me into silence.

I called 911 again. The same woman answered, "Officers are on the way. Please give me more information."

"My name is Brian Peterson. I came to check on my friends, Wyatt and Catherine Stryker. A policeman came into the house and was behaving oddly. He left when I called 911. I think he's an impersonator."

"Just stay put. I'll remain on the line."

"My battery's about to die."

"Tell me more about..." I turned off the phone. If he were in the house, I didn't want to betray my location by talking. I left the bathroom and put my ear on the bedroom door, gripping my gun. Hearing nothing, I stepped out. I debated about my gun then decided to keep it. Better arrested than dead.

I closed the front door then returned upstairs. I moved from window to window, searching. I saw my Leatherman and stuck it in my pocket. The multi-tool might come in handy. Little did I know how handy.

Sirens approached. I ran to the front window as two police cars pulled in the drive. I holstered my gun, pulling my jacket over.

The front door opened, "Police!"

I found two policemen in the foyer. "I'm Brian Peterson, a friend of the family. I date Catherine Stryker's sister, Susan. She's traveling and asked me to check on them. A policeman entered without knocking. He was very menacing." I told the whole story. I wanted to convince the assassin, who was certainly listening.

An officer asked, "Do you have ID?"

"No, I was jogging. I left my wallet at my house. Actually Susan's house, but I live there."

"No policeman came here today. He was an impostor."

"That's what I thought. He was acting crazy. He said something about a temporary vehicle for a soul."

"What?"

"He said, 'a body is a weak vehicle for the soul.' Or something like that."

"Sounds crazy, all right. I'd like to look around the house."

I prayed he wouldn't find the planted drugs. A few minutes later, the officer returned. "There's a ripped screen in the child's bedroom but it looks like it was torn from the inside. Everything else looks okay. I believe your story. It'd be helpful to get an official statement with a detailed description. Could you come to the station?"

"No problem."

"Thanks. We appreciate it."

"Glad to help. That guy freaked me out. I hope you catch him."

I locked the front door. Officer McCoy opened his patrol car and I climbed in, careful not to touch anything.

Once at the station, they wouldn't allow my release until they were certain I was telling the truth. Unlike the detective who gave me the runaround, they were competent professionals. Convincing them I was the fictional Brian Peterson from a fictional address would be impossible without a fictional ID.

I asked, "Have you had other cases of police impersonators?"

"Yeah, mostly to take advantage of women. Serious creeps."

"That guy fits the creepy description."

"Maybe he wanted to take advantage of you." He laughed.

I chuckled, a courtesy laugh. "Maybe so."

He guffawed and snorted. "He probably thought you were one of them types!"

We laughed harder. Actually, he laughed and I faked it.

He convulsed into a howl, encouraged by my amusement. We both practically died laughing. Laughing at a not-funny joke. Hardee-har-har.

When my aching face could grin no longer, I said, "You guys see it all!"

He smiled, pleased with his hilarious rib-buster. "You got that right. I could tell you some tales."

Well, maybe not *that* professional. But he seemed like a pretty good guy. With a pretty bad sense of humor.

"Tell me a few!"

After a fascinating adventure of Officer McCoy saving the day, I asked, "Could we swing by my house to grab my wallet?"

"Good thinking. We need your ID."

He regaled me with police heroism drama while I pretended sufficient awe. Fifteen minutes later, we arrived at Susan's house.

I walked to the front door and turned the knob. Locked.

I said, "There's a key hidden in the back."

I had no idea if there was a spare key. We walked to the back. I lifted the doormat but it was dark.

"Can you shine a light down here?" I asked.

He unsheathed his flashlight and leaned down to look. The flashlight was in the hand nearest me, his jaw unprotected. I eased into linebacker position, knees and elbows bent.

Then I exploded, throwing my weight into his mandible. My elbow connected with a crack.

His head went sideways and he crumpled, landing on his side.

He didn't move. I hoped I hadn't broken his jaw. I didn't feel real good about the assault but at least Officer McCoy had a new yarn to tell his next captive audience.

If I had gone to the station, I'd be under significant suspicion for lying once the cops knew my true identity. They'd search the house and find the drugs. I might spend days being interrogated. Our plans would be completely derailed.

I had to skedaddle. Quickly.

CHAPTER
FIFTEEN

I grabbed the top of the privacy fence and leapt into a neighbor's backyard. I landed in a bush, falling forward. An orange cat glared with orange cat hostility.

I pushed off the ground then ran to the gate. Tried to open it but there was a car blocking the other side.

I jumped the fence, landing on the hood of the sedan. The car alarm sounded, shockingly loud. I dropped to the driveway and ran into the street.

Two pedestrians paused and stared. As I ran past, I said, "My wife's having a baby!"

It didn't really make sense but it was the best I could come up with. Maybe it would delay a 911 call.

I sprinted down several streets until I couldn't hear the alarm. Searched for an older car. Newer models had alarms and keys with microchips.

I spotted an older Buick parked on the street. Twenty feet of dried weeds separated the car from a sagging ranch house.

I put on my gloves as I jogged toward the Buick. Tried the car door. Locked.

I removed my jacket and held it against the driver's side window. Smashed the window with my pistol, the coat muting the sound. Prismatic cubes rained onto the seat.

No car alarm. I pulled the lock.

I eased into the driver's seat, safety glass crunching. Removed my multi-tool. Flipped it open then placed the tool punch above the keyhole. Hammered it with the pistol grip, destroying the first lock pin. Moved an inch and crushed the second pin.

A balding man burst from the house, the flimsy door whacking the house.

"Hey!" he shouted. "You! Whatchu doing? That's my car! Thief!"

He was in front of the hood in seconds, clonking pretty fast for a guy in cowboy boots. His stained tank top heaved with indignation. His head whipped around, wildly searching for a witness. A beer sloshed in one hand, as the other dug furiously in the front pocket of his tight jeans.

Beer-thirty isn't the ideal time to swipe a car.

I stepped out, holding up my hands apologetically. "This is your car? I'm very sorry. My daughter said she left it here. Are you Mr. Biggens?"

"What? No! I don't know your daughter! I'm not Mr. Biggels or whatever!"

Still digging in his snug pocket, he stepped around and noticed the broken window. "You broke my window!"

I smiled meekly, "It was an accident. I'm really embarrassed. I'll pay for it."

He finally jerked a phone from his Wranglers and raised it triumphantly. "I'm calling the police!"

"I can pay right now. I'm so sorry!"

His blurry eyes betrayed doubt then righteous anger. "You gonna be sorry!" He stepped toward me, jabbing a finger toward my chest.

I backed up, subtly bending my knees and dropping my hips.

He advanced like a jerky ostrich, his Adam's apple bobbing.

I uncoiled, striking his chin with my forehead and wrapping both arms around the back of his thighs. I lifted his feet then drove him down.

His head and upper back struck the road with the force of our combined weight. Air escaped with a flat-tire hiss.

He curled into a fetal position. His Coors rolled, leaving a fizzy trail of pristine Rocky Mountain water.

Happy Happy Hour.

I picked up his phone, pivoted into the car and closed the door. Flipped out the flathead screwdriver, jammed it in the keyhole and turned.

It cranked.

I stomped the gas. After several blocks, I slowed, tossing his cell out the window.

As his phone left my fingers, it dawned on me. The assassin was alerted when I turned on the answering machine. Our answering machine could be checked remotely. They'd changed our code and received instant notice when the messages played. No wiring necessary, impossible to detect.

I made a mistake, a near fatal misstep.

I cruised to the mall and parked the stolen car. I shook out the glass and raised the hood of my jacket. I walked to my car then headed toward the farmhouse.

SEALs are unusual. We don't have normal adrenaline responses. You cannot make it through training if you panic or have a strong stress response. When they tie your feet and arms behind your back then throw you into a swimming pool until you are on the verge of drowning, you have to be calm. If you freak out and thrash, you're cut from training.

I'd always been able to keep my cool under pressure. I was born that way.

My hands trembled, ever so slightly.

CHAPTER
SIXTEEN

I woke up late, still adjusting from my night shift, thankful to be alive after my close call.

The women were out, gathering supplies, but Javier was in the kitchen. A pot of coffee was brewing. I poured a cup, the bitter odor inviting.

I sat at the kitchen table and said, "Every passing minute increases the chance they'll kill Blake. Or move him."

He cracked eggs into a pan. "Yeah, it's time for action. Let's discuss our options."

I launched into a synopsis of previous conversations, "Plan A is to go the authorities. We have incriminating evidence from our recordings and my testimony. Best-case scenario, they take it seriously and arrest Jefe. His interrogation leads to Blake. But, the judge might rule our recordings warrantless espionage, inadmissible and illegal, especially since we used stolen government equipment."

He scraped the scrambled eggs onto a warm tortilla. "And I'd be court-martialed. But I'm ready for a change of scenery anyway. I'd skip out to Peru. The women are beautiful in my *tierra madre*."

"Apparently, the men aren't so much. Regardless, you should avoid becoming a fugitive or getting tossed in the brig."

"I like the idea of being at large, cruising South America on my moto with a hot Latina in tow."

"Being on the lam will really help with the ladies. Try that pickup line next time you're out. 'What's your sign, beautiful? I'm a fugitive.'"

"The number one pickup line in America is 'I'm an ex-SEAL.' I read an article about it. I could combine the two, the rugged SEAL on the run, at large and in charge. Yeah, baby, I'm a wanted man!"

"Enough of your Che Guevara fantasy. Let's take this to its logical conclusion. The recording is explosive. Jefe admits to taking Blake and killing his father. They'll act on it."

He added hash browns and slid the plate across the table. "They'll probably get a warrant and start their own surveillance. But even if they arrest everyone in El Poder, they'll admit nothing."

"So, that plan's a dud. Plan B is to assassinate El Jefe. We could easily take him out with sniper fire and I'd enjoy seeing his skull emptied. But the only way that will help is if El Poder falls into disarray. Everyone runs for the hills and they release Blake, as a liability."

"Too many variables. They'd destroy evidence and that might include Blake, bringing us to Plan C, kidnapping someone."

"We could lure the assassin back to my house then snatch him."

"If you go back, he'll know something is up. No supposed friend in his right mind would return after that freak show. Plus, he might not know Blake's location. But El Jefe knows."

"The compound is impenetrable. But we know where he's going for dinner tonight."

When Susan and Catherine returned, I launched into our plan to kidnap El Jefe. I was concerned they'd balk or insist on calling the police, especially after my close call. They nodded understanding but their expressions were noncommittal.

When I finished, I asked, "What do you guys think?"

Catherine looked at Susan. Susan said, "Don't look at me! I'm not speaking first. I'm just a physical therapist!"

Catherine balled her hands then banged the table dramatically, "I'm in with both fists! Let's grab that bitch and make him talk!" Her smile was hungry, vengeful, maybe even wicked.

"A taste of his own medicine!" Susan snarled. "You take one of us, we'll snatch you right back."

Catherine grinned, "The reverse kidnap!"

I caught Javier's eye. He winked.

I was glad we had a plan to keep us busy and focused. With so much to do, we wouldn't have time to descend into a vortex of uncontrollable fears.

Catherine and Javier prepared to dine at Chateaubriand. We'd spent the day gathering equipment and disguises. El

Jefe's dinner at the French restaurant was a golden opportunity to get up close and personal. If he dined alone or with minimal protection, we'd grab him.

The assassin had seen Susan and me. Javier dining alone would be weird so Catherine volunteered.

Catherine had a fearless spirit. As a ski racer, she was known for spectacular crashes, continually pushing her limits. Her senior year, she broke her wrist then raced three more events. Guiding rafts, she confidently shepherded clients through boiling whitewater. She once jumped into an enormous rapid, repeatedly diving underwater to rescue a drowning man, his foot entrapped by a rock.

But I had concerns about Catherine's involvement, as she had zero experience. I wondered what would happen when she was in the same room with the man who ordered the abduction of her son and the murder of her husband. Would she freeze up? Become visibly nervous, gripping a menu with trembling hands? Cry uncontrollably and flee the scene? Try to claw his eyes out? I'd never seen her panic before but everything could go horribly wrong.

Her blonde hair was dyed black and cut short with long bangs nearly covering one eye. Her face was nearly as brown as Javier's due to a bronzing product and a tanning salon. I'd injected her cheeks with degradable collagen, temporarily adding ten pounds to her face.

Standing in front of a mirror, she lifted each eyelid and applied a dark contact lens over her blue iris. She carefully stroked her lashes with thick mascara. She meticulously spread dark wine lipstick on her plump lips.

She stepped into our bedroom and returned wearing a Prada cocktail dress with padded undergarments. Her figure matched her face, a voluptuous Latina.

She placed Dolce & Gabbana thick-framed rectangular glasses over her brown eyes. She looked anxious for just a moment. Then it passed.

She smiled, her first smile in days, "How do I look, darling?"

"Beautiful! You could fool me. J Lo, cry your heart out!"

She kissed me. "If you can't love different women, make the one you love different. Maybe I'll be a redhead next."

Javier strolled out wearing a dapper suit. The stunning couple drove into San Diego and caught a taxi to Chateaubriand. They each had tiny ear buds.

Susan and I followed in the SEAL van and parked near the restaurant, watching from monitors. A tiny camera was embedded in Catherine's purse. We had guns and a syringe loaded with horse tranquilizer purchased from a vet. I had no idea if the dose was right but it was the best we could do.

We were ready to blaze into the parking lot and grab Jefe. I was concerned about making such a bold move with such minimal planning, but we had no idea if we'd get another opportunity.

The maître d' led them to a table covered with crisp white linens, soft jazz crooning lazily across the dimly lit room. Exposed beam ceilings and Travertine block walls created Old World elegance. Floor to ceiling windows showcased serene ocean views.

Catherine requested a window table. She set the purse so we could view the parking area. She ordered a bottle of

Grenanche Blanc and porcini mushroom tartlets, her voice calm and steady.

The first of Jefe's men arrived in a black Land Cruiser; I recognized the vehicle from video of the compound's entrance. Four men strutted from the trucks with macho swagger, wearing blazers over silk shirts, cowboy hats and exotic animal skin boots. Most displayed thick mustaches and pistol bulges. None smiled.

My hope faltered. It would be difficult to grab him with four armed guards.

They fit in at Chateaubriand about like Honey Boo Boo at the Louvre but the maître d' didn't bat an eye. He led them to a group of four tables, one in a corner flanked by the others. Before sitting at the table, the buckaroos walked the entire restaurant, carefully studying each table. One man stepped outside and made a phone call then joined the others.

Twenty minutes later, a Range Rover led Jefe's grey Bentley limo into the parking lot, followed by a Mercedes SUV, the windows tinted like welding shields.

Four more men escorted the Jefe. He was dressed like the typical Chateaubriand diner in a natty Italian suit and Gucci loafers. He was portly with dark hair slicked back. He looked around the room and smiled, flashing enough ivory for a church organ.

Two others stayed with the vehicles and three walked the perimeter. The assassin, a wiry man who moved like a cat, was not with the entourage.

Twelve guards. Impossible. My hope crumpled. We might never get another chance.

Jefe spoke to the headwaiter by name, shaking hands with a warm smile that cloaked the malevolent beast beneath the veneer. He sat at the corner table then ordered several bottles of wine. He slowly scanned the room with eyes of fire.

Servers quietly refilled drinks and cleared plates. Jefe chatted with the beautiful waitress who smiled coyly at his attention. The narco-cowboys glared at the room and gulped expensive wine like it was Fanta.

Maybe if they got snockered, we'd have an opportunity to exploit.

Javier walked to the restroom, pocketing a saltshaker from a vacant table. He planned to survey the restaurant and the parking lot. As soon as he was gone, Jefe stood up and walked to Catherine's table. My heart lurched.

He said, "You're a beautiful woman to be dining alone." The ploy was transparent since Javier had just left.

She smiled. "Thank you, but I'm not alone. My boyfriend's taking an important call."

"More important than you? He should know better than to leave a delicate flower unattended."

She laughed, "I can fend for myself."

"You look very familiar."

My blood iced. Our house was full of pictures of Catherine. He might've seen them from surveillance images.

"I hear that a lot. I guess I have a familiar face. This is our first time here. Do you come often?" She sounded calm and cool, like a pro. I relaxed a little.

"Every Thursday and Monday nights." I smiled, *that* was beneficial information. My mind raced, trying to think of how it could be done.

"You have quite an entourage. Guys' night out?"

"They're my employees. I rotate groups." He gestured at the empty chair, "May I sit for a moment, just to enjoy your beauty?"

"Help yourself, at least until my boyfriend returns." As he sat, she continued, "So you'll bring a different bunch on Monday?"

"Yes. I have many capable workers. They deserve a reward." A different group would mean less likelihood of being recognized.

He continued, "Tell me about yourself."

"You first."

"I run the family business. We import goods from Mexico, mostly fruits and vegetables."

Next to me, Susan muttered, "And meth and cocaine."

"Are all your employees men?"

"We have a few women but mostly men. We need strong men for heavy lifting."

I had an idea. I called Javier and said, "What if she entices him to go outside to look for you? Or pretends like she wants to ditch you for him? I could pull into the parking lot and we could snatch him."

"Five men are standing guard outside. Even if we grabbed him, we'd have a hard time getting away since they have four badass vehicles. Better to be patient. We don't need a blazing gunfight with a dozen thugalicious cowboys."

"I guess I'm getting ahead of myself. He'll be back on Monday. We can make a detailed plan." I hung up and returned my attention to the video monitor.

Catherine asked, "Do you have children?"

"Yes, they live in Mexico and help with my business. My children are the most important part of my life. What about you?"

She paused for a long time then turned away. She looked like she was about to cry. My nerves shimmered, like lightning on a lake.

I could only see the back of her head but her shoulders were tense. When she turned back, tears flooded her eyes.

Things were not going well. I called Javier. "Get in there now! She's crying!"

"On it!"

I hung up, glued to the screen. Susan whispered, "Hold it together, Catherine."

Catherine wiped her eyes and recovered, "No. But I'd like to someday."

"Did I upset you?"

"No, not at all. I was touched by what you said. About your children."

Javier strolled up and made a show of pocketing his cell. Jefe stood and smiled at Javier. "I will return to my table with sadness and regret. You're a lucky man to have such a stunning woman at your side."

"Thank you. I am."

Jefe gestured toward his table and grinned, "All I have are those ugly brutes."

Javier chuckled.

Jefe returned to his seat. His men grinned in admiration at his bold move, sitting with another man's date.

When they arrived home, Javier said, "Taking him by force won't work. I inspected the Bentley limo. Bulletproof glass and armored doors. Impenetrable. Bugging his table would be a waste of time. They barely spoke, much less discussed the location of hidden hostages."

Catherine remarked, "Maybe these outings are his respite, a time to feel normal."

"Ain't nothing normal about them," Javier said. "That scene was ridonkulous, the juxtaposition of macho cowpokes with the elegance of that joint. One of those gauchos ordered escargot. After taking a few bites, he asked a server what it was. When he was told, he looked like he might go full-cowboy on the guy. I almost expected him to lasso the poor dude."

Catherine laughed, "I know, right? Then hop on the waiter's back for a victory lap around the tables."

I gazed proudly at Catherine. Given the circumstances, crying when asked about her children was more than understandable. No one mentioned her brief moment of sorrow. I didn't want to shake her confidence since she'd need to do it again in a few days. And the next time, it would be do or die.

Literally.

CHAPTER
SEVENTEEN

In my investigations about the cartels, I read about the U.S. military involvement in Mexico. Friday morning, I asked Javier, "How well do you know the commander of Operation Cartel, Admiral Landfair?"

"Pretty well. I organized his guard duty in Mexico a few weeks ago. He's top notch."

"Yeah, Senator Ripp spoke highly of him, even though he thought Operation Cartel was a counterproductive flop. If anyone knows about El Jefe, it'd be him."

"Want to speak with him? I could probably arrange it."

"Why would he meet with me? A random ex-SEAL?"

"We'd say you're a pro-military journalist writing for a major publication. I'll vouch for you and we should be good."

"What if he discovers we're lying? Would it endanger your career?"

"I'll just tell him they declined your article. He won't think twice about it."

I read all I could about Landfair, a highly decorated officer. Because of the President's concerns regarding drug smuggling, he tapped the Admiral to direct the U.S.-Mexican joint operation against the cartels. Many speculated he might be a Senate or Presidential candidate.

Javier called Landfair and he said he'd squeeze us in on his lunch hour, in two hours.

I remembered my friend who worked at the morgue. I dialed his number, "Joe, it's Wyatt Stryker."

"What's up, Riot Wyatt? Your Boise State Broncos are having another killer season!"

"Yeah. They're rolling. Can I ask a favor?"

"Depends."

"I took care of Senator Ripp in the ER. Have you seen the autopsy report?"

"Maybe. I've been sworn to secrecy under penalty of death. Who wants to know?"

"Me."

"You're gonna to be blown away. But you didn't hear it from me. You dig?

"I promise."

"He got the super-duper autopsy and the final cause of death was determined to be...drum roll, please...alcohol poisoning! That and some pain pills."

I thanked him and tried to get off the phone but he droned on about college football, Heisman candidates and who should be number one. I finally hung up in mid sentence, hoping he'd think it was a dropped call.

On the way to the base, I told Javier about my conversation with Joe. I said, "Maybe Senator Ripp's death was truly accidental."

"The timing's awfully suspicious."

"Yeah. I just don't see how he could've been murdered."

We arrived at Landfair's office. Javier saluted him and they shook hands. He was a striking man with intelligent, bright eyes.

Javier introduced me, "Admiral, this is Wyatt McDaniel, one of my best friends. As I mentioned, he's a freelance journalist working on an in-depth report about the cartels for the *LA Times*. Wyatt's a conservative, pro-military journalist. He favors a get-tough approach to the war on drugs. He aims to emphasize the benefits of your operation."

He shook my hand warmly, "Any friend of Commander Alcaraz is a friend of mine. I'm glad to assist. Please, sit."

"Thanks for agreeing to the interview, Admiral. It's an honor. As Javier said, I believe in our military. The drug problem wreaks havoc on our border. I'm planning a favorable article to balance the negativity from the liberal press. I've watched your career and was pleased when you accepted your current position." A little flattery never hurt.

"Wonderful. We need some good press. With Senator Ripp's untimely death, the media has been going crazy denouncing Operation Cartel. Mark was a close friend and we shared mutual respect. As you probably know, he was opposed to military action in Mexico. But I leave politics to the politicians. As a soldier, I do what my country asks."

"And I'm grateful. Our country should unite behind your efforts. We have to do something. Why not throw our top asset at the problem, the world's greatest armed forces?"

I was smearing it on thick, but he needed to like me and trust my motives or he wouldn't open up. I planned to wait until the end to discuss El Poder, unless he brought it up first.

I pulled a tape recorder from my bag. "First question, do you think the armed war on the narcotic gangs has been successful?"

He spoke at length, stating that Operation Cartel had freed ungoverned regions of Mexico from narco control. They'd seized large amounts of drugs and decimated supply lines. To prove his points, he spouted off a glob of data and showed us fancy charts on his laptop.

When he finished, I asked, "How much does government corruption play a role?"

"On this topic, you can quote me but I'd like to be anonymous, since I work closely with the Mexicans. Deal?"

"Deal."

"And I'll crack his kneecaps if he breaks his promise," Javier deadpanned.

The admiral smiled, "I doubt that'll be necessary."

"May I quote you as an anonymous senior official?"

"You bet. The cartels have acquired unprecedented power to corrupt and intimidate officials. Three factors account for this: preexisting corruption, weak law enforcement and the appetite for drugs in the U.S., the world's largest consumer of illicit drugs. There are decent, honest people in Mexican law enforcement, but graft is rampant. Those the gangs cannot bribe, they kill. The narcos have a saying, *plata o plomo?*' Money or lead? A grim choice.

"A major benefit of U.S. military involvement is impartiality. Mexican forces often crack down on one cartel because a rival paid them to eliminate the competition. The U.S. has no ulterior motives. We want to crush all the syndicates, restore peace to Mexico and stem the flow of drugs across the border. Mexican politicians rail about Yankee meddling but many are on cartel payrolls. The silent majority appreciates our presence."

Mexican polls demonstrated that Operation Cartel was about as popular as a bucket of Ebola vomit, but I had no plans to ask hardball questions. I just wanted to find out about El Poder.

"How much has your operation decreased drug smuggling?"

"We've destroyed hundreds of meth super labs. Cocaine is grown in South America, mostly Columbia, and the bulk of heroin comes from Asia. But Mexican cartels are the Wal-Mart of drugs, ruling the narco-universe. The Asian and South American suppliers are like Kraft Foods; they play by Wal-Mart's rules. The sum of confiscated drugs is astronomical."

"What happens to the seized drugs?"

"Most marijuana is burned where we find it but hard drugs are brought into the U.S. by armed military transport. We have warehouses along the border where the inventory is catalogued by the DEA then destroyed."

"Why bring the drugs to the U.S.?"

"When we started, confiscated drugs were stored in Mexico but large amounts went missing. We decided to transport under a strict U.S. military chain of command."

"Has the quantity of illicit drugs decreased on the black market?"

"No question. The street prices continue to rise and that means one thing. Less supply."

"Great point. Can you discuss specific cartels?"

He launched into a lengthy discussion of the various cartels and then added, "The landscape evolves quickly as competitors jockey for advantage. They mainly compete over supply routes. Production's the easy part but smuggling narcotics into the U.S. is where they really earn their money, so to speak."

Since he hadn't mentioned them, I asked, "What about El Poder Cartel and the capo known as El Jefe?"

"Wyatt, I'm surprised you know about the Jefe. He's done quite a job staying below the radar."

I smiled, "I try to be thorough."

"We haven't heard from El Poder recently. We believe El Jefe, Alfredo Rodriguez, has gone into retirement. Our intelligence indicates they've ceased operations."

"What do you know about them?"

"El Poder, or The Power, is a shadowy group. Rodriguez is from Mexico City aristocracy and has a Harvard MBA. They've never done business like the rest. The other cartels are run by the thuggiest thug of the bunch, like most third-world dictators. The most clever, bloodthirsty, backstabbing guy claws his way to the top. Certainly other capos are talented men but not nearly as educated or sophisticated.

"The Jefe created El Poder from the ground up, as opposed to climbing the ladder of an existing syndicate. They don't battle the police or terrorize innocents. Of all the cartels, we know the least about them. We believe they've diversified and moved into non-criminal activity. El Poder is, or *was*, the most intelligent act, the Goldman Sacks of the cartel world."

"Why'd they leave the business?"

"The other cartels are much more violent. We believe Jefe decided to get out while he still could. The U.S. military hasn't had a single firefight with El Poder. The Mexicans haven't in several years. As I said, I'm surprised you know about them."

"One of my sources said that they're currently based in San Diego."

"Really? I suspect that's wrong. The Jefe usually resides in San Jose del Cabo, enjoying his retirement. Where did you hear that about San Diego?"

"A informant who might've fabricated the whole thing. He's given me questionable info before. You're sure he's not based in San Diego?"

He smiled and his soft grey eyes shone, "As much as I can be. But we've been wrong before. Why should the Times care about a defunct cartel?"

"He's an intriguing character, especially since my source said they're based in the U.S. But I guess that's wrong."

"If he's even set foot in the U.S. in the last decade, I'd be surprised. Not to tell you your business, but I wouldn't mention El Poder. He's a side note in the drug war, a flash in the pan."

I changed the subject, "Do you think it's been an effective use of our manpower and resources? Is the benefit worth the cost?"

"It's a tricky situation, somewhat like the Middle East. It's unclear who the enemy is. Our efforts remain controversial but the majority of Mexicans are grateful for our presence."

As a former military person, I saw both sides. The media and a faction of congress led by Senator Ripp felt we were picking a losing fight, squandering goodwill without tangible progress. The heartland demanded intervention, to stabilize Mexico and limit the flow of drugs into the U.S. Both had valid points.

Admiral Landfair was a true believer and seemed well intentioned. We were there to find out more about the Jefe, not to debate policy. I only mentioned those issues to bolster the appearance of a valid investigation.

At the end of the interview, I said, "Thanks for your time, Admiral."

He stood and shook both of our hands. "Javier's a fine soldier. He vouches for you so I'm glad to know you."

As we walked to the car, I said to Javier, "He seems like a good guy."

"Yeah, he is. I've known him a long time."

"I thought the most persuasive argument for intervention was the increasing street prices."

"Yeah, simple economics. They're confiscating huge amounts and the price is going up, demand outstripping supply."

"What do you make of his thoughts on El Poder?"

"El Jefe is probably keeping it on the low down, pretending to be out of the business. Landfair might think it'd damage your credibility to mention a washed-up cartel."

"I'm guessing Jefe's outsmarted them. Faked right then ran left."

"That makes him a scary adversary. Brilliance trumps brutality every time. But I still can't connect the dots. Did El Poder have something to do with Ripp's death? Regardless, why take Blake and all that rigmarole? Why would they want to kill me? Maybe the guy in Mexico was targeting Ripp."

"That could be the connection. We'll find out soon. El Jefe will tell us, face to face. Or he'll die."

I swallowed hard. I was committed to action, but the gravity of what we were planning was unsettling. So many details. So little time.

So many things that could go horribly wrong.

Javier was confident but I felt a little queasy, like a horde of crazed butterflies were swarming inside.

CHAPTER
EIGHTEEN

The door leading from Blake's room was dead-bolted. He'd searched every corner of the room and there was no escape. He was in a basement. But he had a plan. He'd meticulously arranged his chess pieces.

The daytime guard was a grouch, never smiling or talking. But Blake played every evening with Juan.

Two days ago, a woman named Maria had come to Blake's room. She said the boss was her boyfriend. She asked what toys he liked.

He told her two truths and a lie.

The next day, she brought an Xbox, Legos and an Erector Set. She brushed Blake's hair, telling him how beautiful he was. He didn't really like being called beautiful, since that sounded sort of girlish, and he was old enough to brush his own hair. But she was gentle and kind, so he didn't make a fuss.

Blake was practically overjoyed to get the Erector Set, even though he never played with his own. He had ulterior motives.

He liked to take things apart, a tinkerer. Using a piece of metal from his Erector Set as a screwdriver, he removed the bathroom doorknob and turned it around, so it locked from the outside.

He stuffed a washcloth in the toilet drain, pushing it out of sight. Flushed repeatedly until water filled the bowl.

In the cabinet below the sink, he moved the toilet plunger to the rear, behind the drainpipe and spare toiletries.

The Chess Master was ready for his ultimate match.

When Juan brought his dinner, Blake asked, "Wanna play chess?"

He laughed, "We've already played three games."

Blake gave his best charming smile, "Please? I'm so bored!"

"Okay. One more. But I can't play all night."

Blake was purposely losing the match. After capturing Blake's queen, Juan beamed proudly.

Blake pointed at Juan's handheld radio and asked, "Can I check that out?"

"Sure. But don't push any buttons." Blake took the radio and pretended to talk.

He was setting the trap. The pieces were in place.

Moments later, Blake abruptly stood and announced, "I've gotta take a leak! Bad!"

He ran into the bathroom with the radio, leaving the door open. He urinated and flushed. Then he held the handle down, the water overflowing onto the floor.

"Uh-oh. Juan, we have a problem!" Blake shouted.

So far, so good. Time to win the match.

Juan rushed into the bathroom. He splashed across the tile then opened the cabinet. Blake stood behind, his hand on the doorknob.

Juan squatted and frantically removed supplies to get to the plunger. Blake stepped out and quietly closed the thick hardwood door, locking him in.

He ran from the room and flipped the deadbolt. Juan yelled and banged on the door.

Checkmate.

His pulse was bounding, but he knew what to expect from monitoring Juan's footsteps. There was a stairway at the end of the hall. He ran down the corridor then up the staircase, entering the main floor. He crept to a window and looked out into the darkness. Two men sat on a front porch.

Juan shouted for help! Loud! Blake startled and spazzed out, jumping straight up like a frightened cat.

He ducked under the window then slowly looked out. The men hadn't heard. They were talking, not paying attention.

He ran to a backdoor but it was locked with a deadbolt. He heard a loud crash.

Juan had broken the bathroom door open!

Juan had keys and would quickly unlock the second door. Blake ran to the kitchen and opened a window then pushed the screen out. He threw Juan's radio out the window.

Juan's footsteps echoed loudly as he tramped up the stairs. When he opened the door, he'd see Blake. His nerves popping like skillet grease, Blake sprinted into a laundry room.

He saw the door at the top of the stairs opening. He ducked behind a basket, barely missing Juan.

Juan yelled, "¿Dónde está el niño? ¡Él se escapó!" *Where's the boy? He ran away!*

Blake spoke Spanish fluently since he'd been in dual immersion. As he looked around for a better place to hide, he heard the other men barge into the house, "¿Que pasó?" *What happened?*

"¡El chico me engaño! ¡Me encerró en el baño!" *The boy tricked me! He locked me in the bathroom!* Juan sounded agitated, panicked.

Blake climbed inside a dryer, quietly closing the door. He heard rapid footsteps then one shouted, "¡La ventana! ¡Se escapó por la ventana! ¿Por qué fue eso desbloqueado?" *The window! He escaped through the window! Why was that unlocked?*

Blake sat in the dryer and listened for a long time. When he was sure the men were long gone, he climbed out. He considered the kitchen window but thought they would search that area carefully. He returned to the front and peeked out the window. The yard was a bustle of activity, a dozen men with flashlights combing the grounds.

He was the best in the neighborhood at hide-and-seek. He cracked the front door and slithered out on his belly. Crawled to the edge of the covered porch and dove over the rail into a thick hedgerow, almost five feet tall. He peered out.

Two men with flashlights were walking toward the house. They stopped at the porch. One said, "Vamos a buscar cerca de la casa de nuevo." *We'll search near the house again.*

They split up and walked in opposite directions, scouring the shrubbery around the house, where Blake was hidden. A guard walked toward him, poking a shovel handle into the hedge. He slowly worked his way toward Blake. There was no way to escape without being seen; he was trapped.

Most humans would shut down or panic. But Blake wasn't like most humans. He was an unusual boy.

He was still a kid, his logic occasionally grandiose and childish. But instead of cracking into fragmented, panicked rumination under stress, his thoughts settled, healed. Like his father, he was born that way. His brain automatically changed gears under extreme pressure, shifting into high, humming like a Ferrari.

On his hands and knees, he tried to make himself as small as possible. He felt around until he found a large rock. The man moved closer.

When the man looked the opposite direction, Blake flung the stone away from the guard.

He ducked down flat as it sailed an arc toward the far end of the hedgerow. The stone clattered through the sturdy bush with a big commotion, the branches rattling in a flurry of leaves and snapping twigs. It landed with a thud.

The man spun and ran past Blake. He furiously searched the area where the rock landed, jamming the shovel into the shrubbery. He struck something then dove into the hedge, flailing and searching.

Blake punched through the bush and sprinted across the yard.

He jumped behind a tree then looked back. The man was still combing the bushes. The guard jerked his head out and spoke into his radio. The other man ran around the house. Several more raced toward them.

Blake lay on his belly, scanning the yard. It was not what he expected. Not at all. Juan told him it was a large place, but it was enormous. There was a mansion up on a hill, some smaller houses and a garage. A huge wall and a metal fence encircled the property. At each corner, from tall poles, spotlights cut across the yard, brightly illuminating everything in their path.

He'd planned to run to a street in front of the house, like in his neighborhood. He had to rethink the plan.

A spotlight gradually swept toward Blake. As it neared, he pivoted around the tree, keeping himself in the trunk's shadow. The area all around him exploded in white light, but he stayed hidden. The light moved on.

There was no way he could get over the wall, so he ran toward the garage. He would hide in a car. Maybe he could sneak a ride out.

He sprinted from tree to tree until he made it to the garage. He tried a door. Locked. He circled the outside, searching for a window.

He heard voices. Flashlight beams shone past a garage corner.

He frantically searched for a place to hide. He ran to a tree and jumped, grabbing a branch and pulling himself up.

Men came around the corner. He kept climbing, staying on the opposite side of the trunk. They shone lights into the tree but kept moving.

He waited for a few minutes, the Chess Master considering his next move. Maybe he could sneak into the giant house. There were probably hundreds of places to hide.

He heard dogs yapping in the distance. He remembered something he'd seen on TV about search dogs. He peeked from the branches. Several leashed dogs were leading men straight toward the garage from the little house. They were following his track, using his scent! If he stayed in the tree, he'd be cornered. If he climbed down, the dogs might tear him to shreds.

He decided he'd rather chance being ripped to pieces than remain a prisoner to his parents' killers. He quickly dropped down through the branches then jumped the last ten feet. He landed and rolled, his feet aching from the impact.

A man yelled, "¡Ahí está!" *There he is!* They released the dogs.

They would eat him alive!

Panicked, he sprinted across open grass. He looked over his shoulder. Four Doberman Pinschers were a hundred yards away, closing fast. He felt overwhelming terror.

He raced toward the edge of the yard until blocked by the fence. He whipped his head back and forth. There were no trees to climb. No buildings to enter. He was exposed with no protection.

The barking sounded ferocious. Horrified, he looked back. The madly yapping animals tore across the yard, the guards falling behind.

He frantically dashed along the fence, until the dogs were on his heels. One cut him off, his bared teeth dripping with saliva and menace.

He snapped at Blake's face. An involuntary shriek jumped from Blake's throat.

Another bit his pants near his ankle, jerking back. Blake fell forward, screaming and covering his face as thorny jaws snarled and chomped near his head.

He was more frightened than he'd ever been.

Through eyes flooded with terror-stricken tears, their enraged thin faces and pointy ears looked bat-like, demonic.

The Doberman held his pants and backed, dragging Blake on his belly. They yelped and snapped, prancing around him.

A guard commanded, "¡Deténgase!" *Stop!* The dogs immediately stopped barking.

The only sound was Blake's sobbing. A strong hand grabbed his collar then a gloved hand clamped over his mouth. A black bag was thrown over his head. He kicked and squirmed but the men carried him back toward the house.

He heard Juan's relieved voice, "¡Gracias a Dios!" *Thank God!*

Another said, "Tenemos que decirle Jefe lo que pasó." *We have to tell Jefe what happened.*

Juan whispered, "*¡No! ¡Por favor, no!*" He sounded frightened.

"Sí, tenemos que." *Yes, we have to.*

"Él va a matar al niño y castigarme. ¡Él dejará que Behram matar al muchacho!" *He will kill the boy and punish me. He will let Behram slay the boy!*

"Probablemente."

CHAPTER
NINETEEN

On Friday afternoon, after the meeting with Admiral Landfair, a rainstorm blew in, hard drops attacking the farmhouse.

Javier slouched on the couch, studying the slowly turning ceiling fan. I said, "What's up? You seem bummed."

He slowly pulled his eyes from the fan and looked at me, betraying pain. "You need to hear something." He pushed off the couch and trudged into the computer room.

With a sinking feeling, I followed. "What is it?"

He spoke in the dull voice of depression, "I don't like the sound of this conversation. It took place a couple of hours ago."

I glanced nervously at him but his rigid face was frozen to the screen. He hit play.

Jefe's voice asked, "What do you have to report?"

The guy with the Bronx accent said, "We have a new development. Someone checked the doc's phone messages on Wednesday. Behram went to investigate. He found a man claiming to be a family friend. Behram scared him and the man called the police. A few hours ago I spoke to our guy on the force. He says the man clobbered a responding officer and skipped out."

"Behram returned to the house? Has he gone loco? It could've been the cops or the DEA."

"As you know, Behram has his own way of doing things. Even if the police were there, they wouldn't take Behram alive. More likely he'd kill 'em all and convince the world they shot each other simultaneously. Even if they captured him, he'd never snitch. He respects you, Jefe."

"It's true. He wouldn't squeal. He knows better. Why wasn't I informed before now?"

"Behram left me a message but I didn't call until today."

"Unacceptable."

"I'm sorry. I thought he was curious about the doctor. Since I didn't have any new info, I didn't hurry."

"Who was the man?"

"Don't know yet. Said he lives with the wife's sister. But her place seems abandoned. The guy said she was traveling but I suspect the two women are holed up somewhere, scared to death. I had someone travel all the way to Idaho to tap their parent's phone, but no word. Likewise, nothing from the doctor's parents in Oregon. The grandparents know nothing."

"Has the doctor's death been in the news?"

"No. We've been monitoring closely."

"Have you found any pics of the doctor?"

"No. I've had two investigators working around the clock. Nada. However, there are a few worrisome details. Dr. Stryker played college football and he's a large man, tall and broad. The guy at the house was big. The doc was also a Navy SEAL. The policeman was knocked unconscious with one blow."

Jefe responded angrily, "Damn it! Did Behram execute the wrong man? This whole thing was completely unnecessary. We should've left the doctor alone. Why aren't you certain who was killed? It's ridiculous! I employ you to keep me from worry. You are *not* earning your money."

Silence hung heavy. Finally Jefe hissed, "I feel cheated."

The man spoke softly after the rebuke, "I'm sorry. We're working on it night and day."

"The man assassinated in the park, was he large?"

"Behram took a photo of him as he walked to the bench. He fits the description. He was about six feet three inches tall."

"That's it?" he spat. "That's your proof, a picture from afar? Your operation appears to be *dis*organized crime. Why didn't you have others on scene?"

"That's how Behram wanted it. He prefers to work alone."

"Need I remind you that Behram isn't your boss? Why wasn't I consulted? Do you have any idea what's riding on this?"

"I know. I know. We're working on it."

His voice rose, "Should I employ someone else?"

The threat apparent, the man's voice quavered, "No. Please give me a chance. We'll figure it out. Please!"

I assumed that terminating someone from El Poder's employ meant exactly that: termination.

"Why would the man flee the police?"

The man recovered but still sounded unnerved, "He probably panicked. Behram was trying to rattle him."

He asked, his voice barely above a whisper, "Tell me, is the doctor alive or not?"

"I believe Behram killed the doctor. Who'd willingly place himself in that type of danger, except the boy's father? The executed man was the right size. But we'll keep gathering info."

"I should hope so. The boy tried to escape so he's been dealt with. He's gone."

I bit my fist.

The man asked, "Gone?"

"Gone. Permanently. He's sleeping with the angels and the saints."

Tears sprang from my eyes.

Javier turned off the recording then pushed his eyes with his fingers.

Everything faded to black. I gripped my head and bent over. My soul had been taken. The maw of hell opened, swallowing my spirit. I'd never felt pain like this. My eyes flooded.

I gripped the windowsill with white knuckles and stared out. Blurrily, I saw Catherine and Susan strolling around the pond, hoods up against the pouring rain.

Thoughts of Blake flashed through my mind, searching for us in the bleachers after he hit a homerun, his dimpled grin framed by wild blonde hair. My lips trembled.

I whispered, "I can't tell her yet. I need time."

He took a few moments to respond. "However you want to handle it."

The bitter rain dripped down the windowpane. After several minutes of silence, I spoke, "I need to see his body before I believe he's gone, before I give up." I was in denial but I couldn't accept his death.

Javier sat helplessly. He said nothing but his face ached with compassion and sorrow.

Slowly, fury replaced sadness. I muttered through teeth clenched like pliers, "If nothing else, I need to hear a confession from his killer, right before I strangle him."

I wiped my eyes angrily. He opened his mouth to speak but I spoke first, "I'm done crying. It's their turn."

I would turn it on them. Fear is in the eye of the beholder.

I sat on the edge of the bed, dreading Catherine's return to the house. I doubted I could fake it. If she thought something was wrong, she'd persist until I lied by making an excuse, or until I told the truth. I wasn't willing to do either.

I walked to the den. Javier sat on the edge of a chair, gazing at a blank wall. I asked, "Can I take your bike for a spin?"

He paused then shook his head, shaking loose from the misery. "Sorry. What'd you say?"

"Could I borrow your moto? I gotta get out."

"Sure. Keys are in the ignition."

As I headed out the front door, he softly said, "It's slick out. Be careful, okay?"

I mumbled, "Right."

I climbed onto the Italian racing bike and strapped on Javier's helmet. I drove slowly into the drizzle.

As soon as I was out of sight, I twisted the throttle. Hit ninety on the curvy, wet road. Pulled onto the highway and doubled the speed limit, crouched with my helmet barely above the handlebars.

I couldn't believe Blake was dead, so I chose not to believe. I would pretend I'd never heard those horrible words. It defied rational thought but I told myself that "the angels and the saints" was a code for something besides death.

The road shone with slick grime as I drove north along the Pacific toward LA. The ocean exhaled a bitter wind and palm fronds swung wildly, like cult worshipers swaying with arms raised, anticipating blood sacrifice.

I reached one forty, passing cars like I had a death wish, the incredible power of the Ducati intoxicating. I returned to my lane as oncoming horns blared, over and over again. When I arrived at Dana Point, I hung a ferocious U-turn. I drove for mind-numbing hours.

I stopped for gas and scowled at the hapless cashier. He fumbled nervously and dropped my change on the floor.

I microwaved a pizza pocket made in the previous decade. I stood outside in the drizzle, slowly chewing the freezer-burnt rectangle, glaring at everyone and everything.

But I believed it. I had to. The angels and the saints live in heaven. Blake was gone, truly gone. Anger burned inside my gut, like I'd been force-fed an ember.

Darkness fell. I headed into San Diego and climbed onto the snarled interstate, the misnomer called rush hour. The glowing river of brake lights looked like slow flowing lava, straight from Lucifer's kingdom. I ground my teeth at the lurching hurry-up-and-wait.

I exited the interstate. Didn't want to return to the farmhouse, but I had nowhere else to go. Going to a restaurant or a bar sounded suffocating. I drove aimlessly, pitifully. Mercifully, the rain stopped.

On a whim, I headed toward Jefe's house. At each turn, I was aware of the recklessness of my actions. I had no purpose, no plan. I'd left my gun at home. The wiry assassin with a fractured arm could identify me. I knew I should abort but my fury possessed me.

I decided I didn't care. If I saw his scrawny neck, I'd strangle it until his eyeballs dropped from his skull.

I drove past gaudy mansions then pulled into the parking lot of a country club. Stopped the bike and got off. Thought for a long while then decided I'd taken my pity-party far enough. I had to chill. Time to return to the farmhouse. I might be able to face Catherine and fake it. If asked, I'd tell her the truth: I had a splitting headache. My head compressed by Javier's too-small helmet and my boiling anger increasing the pressure, my skull felt like it could re-expand rapidly, even explode.

A cart rolled by with two white-clad golfers. One barked, "Private club, pal! Members only!" They zipped down the cart path.

I decided to vent some rage on the pompous elites of Rancho Santa Fe.

I followed them on my moto, cruising out of sight on the other side of a tall berm. When I drew even with them, I cut through a gap in the berm, suddenly appearing in front of the cart. The surprised driver turned hard and the cart nearly flipped. I cut donuts into the perfectly manicured green then headed back to the parking lot.

Take that, Members Only.

I glanced in the rearview mirror, surprised to see the golf cart in hot pursuit. I stopped in a muddy spot. They barreled toward me, shouting threats and obscenities. I waited until I could see the whites of their bleached teeth, and then spun the throttle hard and slowly fishtailed, spraying the cart and both men with copious muck, like a fire hose blasting mud. They held out their hands in a hopeless attempt to stop the onslaught. Once they were sufficiently caked, I sped away.

I returned to the road, dirt clods dropping from the bike. I saw Jefe's house on a hill. I pulled forward, planning to turn around. Ahead, the gates to his compound opened and a black Escalade pulled out. Angry pain throttled me.

I abandoned my turn and followed. I wanted to kill everyone in the Cadillac. If I had a machinegun, I would've blasted with vengeful glee, cackling madly as their heads splattered like tomatoes.

I kept my distance but didn't let them out of my sight. As we moved onto busier roads, I trailed several cars behind. They entered an industrial part of Chula Vista. Homeless people milled about, the night their cloak.

The SUV pulled up to a two-story, windowless warehouse. A garage door opened; men walked on both sides of the Cadillac, looking into the windows. They waved the Escalade in. The door closed rapidly behind.

I cruised away, planning to call Javier. I stopped and pulled my cell out. The battery was dead. I groaned in frustration, blaming the shoddy phone instead of myself.

I stopped to think. A battle raged in my mind. The logical, physician side of my brain told me to return home: to grieve, discuss and decide rationally. My animalistic rage told me to press on, discover ways to hurt those who had hurt me, to kill those who'd killed me.

The sadness bred with anger, birthing hatred. The beast won.

CHAPTER
TWENTY

I drove to a nearby thrift shop. Locked Javier's helmet to the bike then purchased mismatched clothing: loose fitting slacks, steel-toed work boots, a knit hat and a mangy beige corduroy jacket, too small. I strolled from the store looking like a vagrant.

I rummaged a trash bin, removing a malt liquor bottle in a paper bag. I was already filthy, my skin streaked with mud from the golf course. I smeared mud on my clothes. My head held low, I relaxed my face like a flabby drunk. I gripped the bottle and took short strides with flat-footed, halting steps.

I plodded by liquor stores, strip clubs and a seedy pawn-shop. As I passed the only decent establishment, Magnum Lounge, I glanced inside. The popular music bar was packed with the after-work crowd. Men bellied up to the bar, gulping furiously to tolerate the grinding drudgery of their looming evening at home. The sign advertised Karaoke Night.

I approached the warehouse, the real den of iniquity. From the sidewalk across the street, I studied the building. Men in jumpsuits stood outside each door, imitating workers on break. A semi was backed against the side of the storehouse; three thugs stood by an adjacent door. After circling the block, I developed a plan.

I walked to a Korean-owned corner store. The cashier frowned slightly when I entered. He followed me around the store, mopping my wet footsteps as I selected a bag of marbles, electrical tape, a multi-tool and workman's gloves. I ignored his pesky minding. He seemed relieved when I pulled cash from my grimy pants.

I went to the pawnshop, fortified with bars on the windows. The sign on the door barked: *The day they want my gun, they'll have to bring theirs!*

I entered, heavy-metal music assaulting me. They sold boxy televisions, stereos with cassette decks, and film cameras. Drum sets next to guitars in velvet lined boxes. Random college rings and lawnmowers. A variety of killing tools hung on display, guns, throwing stars, nunchuks, knives and swords. The guy behind the counter had a face weighted with twelve pounds of piercings, his black leathers strung with enough chain to pull a semi.

I didn't have my gun, nor did I have enough cash to purchase one. I asked the man for a box of twelve gage shells. He removed the box and his absurdly perforated lips contorted into a semblance of a grin. "Goin' hunting?"

I handed him cash. "Yep."

He clacked his pierced tongue across his teeth, lizard-like. "Good hunting in San Diego, I hear."

I grunted.

He handed me the change, "They say the deer are in rut, next block over." He released a snotty chortle, his alloyed nostrils flaring.

I cast a cold stare until he stopped smiling. Then exited.

In an empty storefront, I removed my new Leatherman. Pried open four shell casings, emptying the buckshot. Carefully taped a marble over the brass cap, centered on the primer. Devoid of projectile with the marble adding weight, the shells were bottom-heavy.

I stuffed a few extras into my back pocket and dumped the rest. Swinging the bottle, I strolled along the sidewalk opposite the nondescript storehouse, carrying on a psychotic conversation between me, myself, and I. The men in jumpsuits ignored me, just another crazy wandering the mean streets.

My point of attack was the eighteen-wheeler backed against the warehouse. I crept to the cab of the semi, parked in a delivery alley flanked by walls on both sides. When the guards turned their backs, I threw two shells high over front corner of the building then quickly hurled the other two.

The first shells struck the pavement. The shells exploded, the marble functioning as a firing pin. The second round detonated in quick succession, the ominous staccato echoing through the industrial buildings.

The men startled then ran toward the gunshots. Others moved warily toward the street, crouching behind parked cars.

While they searched for unseen interlopers, I scrambled onto the hood of the cab. Crawled up the sloped air dam, leapt onto the trailer then ran crouching toward the warehouse, keeping my head below the flanking walls. I jumped, grabbing the roof edge and pulling myself up. Kicked a leg up and rolled onto the flat roof then commando-crawled until I came to a vent.

I stopped to listen but heard nothing. Satisfied my intrusion went unnoticed, I pried open the aluminum vent cover with the multi-tool pliers until I could visualize the warehouse floor.

I saw men below, seemingly oblivious to the gunshots. Forklift operators navigated a maze of shelving. Most wore blue jumpsuits.

After a few moments of observation, I realized the warehouse was a bread factory. Dough automatically dropped in pans onto a conveyer belt then moved into a tunnel oven. The bread loaves proceeded from the oven to a cooling area then to a slicing machine. Preprinted plastic bags were mechanically slipped over each loaf. A worker closed each bag with a wire tie. After watching for fifteen minutes, I saw nothing unusual.

I wondered if the factory was a money-laundering front for El Poder. Perhaps the men in the Escalade were just visiting friends. The guys loitering at the doors were probably workers on break. I'd taken an unnecessary risk. So much for my secret agent escapade.

As I was about to leave, I noticed a man, his face mottled with prison tattoos. The others gave him a wide berth. He lifted a box of bread then walked toward the back. He entered a broom closet that jutted from the rear wall. Five minutes later, he was still in the tiny closet.

Something didn't seem right. I lifted my head and looked at the edge of the roof then peered through the hole again. The entire rear wall of the factory stopped nearly twenty feet from the roof edge. A smokestack jutted from the dead space. There were no doors on the solid brick wall, inside or out.

I crawled to the huge chimney. Flipping out a screwdriver, I unbolted the flashing around the smokestack, exposing foam insulation. I cut into the foam, removing a small area. I could see about half the area but no sign of Tattoo Face.

The walls were lined with shelves, loaded floor to ceiling with crates. Two men in blue jumpsuits were working. One opened a crate with a crowbar then lifted a yellow brick stamped DEA.

With box cutters, he sliced into the yellow polymer wrap then deftly peeled it off. He placed the chalky brick into a machine that hummed then ejected the block sealed in thick white plastic. The second man lifted a bread loaf from a slicing machine then peeled two slices and cut into the center with a long knife. He shook it gently and a cube of bread slid out an inch; the man tugged it out.

He slid the plastic brick into the hollowed bread. He replaced the two slices then dropped the loaf into a bread sack, tying it closed. He placed the coke-bread inside a shipping crate. I observed them process twenty DEA bricks. They tossed the yellow wrappers into a small furnace, a six-inch pipe venting into the chimney.

The smokestack was gigantic for the small incinerator. The workspace was about twelve feet wide so the walls were two feet thick. Multiple large burners jutted from the walls.

The entire space was a furnace, a giant crematory. El Poder could incinerate the entire storage area with a push of the button, vaporizing the contents and any evidence.

The tattooed man walked from the back. I wondered what he'd been doing. His entire face was tattooed with a spider web; the nape of his neck inked with a fanged spider. He muttered to the men and they laughed. All three walked from view.

I removed more insulation to widen my view. Dipping my head into the hole, I craned my neck to see.

A battered man was restrained to a chair, his mouth duct taped. The tattooed man whispered something in his ear. The prisoner squirmed, his purpled eyes twitching.

The thug began punching the man's face in a hurricane of fists, blood spattering with each blow. He stopped and picked up a wooden mallet. The prisoner frantically shuffled his mangled bare feet, smearing blood.

I jerked my head back in revulsion. They were torturing a helpless man. He might be an innocent who refused extortion or maybe another criminal. Regardless, no one deserved that. I had to find a phone and call the police. I could make an anonymous call without endangering our mission.

As I replaced the insulation, preparing to leave, the men moved into view carrying the struggling man, still tied to the chair. They opened large steel doors at the base of the huge smokestack.

They set him inside the furnace. The goon spat in his face then slammed the door with a bitter clang.

I rolled onto my back and closed my eyes, nauseated. Who was he? What had he done? They would cremate him alive. There would be nothing left. I was helpless to save him.

Reality set in. Getting onto the roof was the easy part. As my temporary insanity drained away, I realized I was woefully unprepared. I had duct tape, marbles and a dead cell phone. No one knew my whereabouts. What had I done? What purpose did any of this serve?

They didn't seem to be on high alert, but they might be searching outside the warehouse. Throwing shells wouldn't work a second time. The empty casings taped with marbles lay in plain view on the street. Hopefully they thought it was teenagers pulling a prank or a rival cartel's warning.

In the unlikely event Blake was still alive, I wouldn't be much help after being tortured to death: *You say you aren't a pig. So why were you on the roof? Maybe this will help you remember!*

Foul smoke drifted from the chimney, like roasted meat from a cannibal BBQ.

I crept to the edge of the warehouse then peered down. I jumped onto the semi and flattened. Crawled down the middle and dove down the curved air dam, sliding to the cab's roof with a thud.

The driver's door flew open and a man scrambled out. I rolled to the opposite edge and lay flat. Twenty-foot barricades flanked both sides. The wall almost touched the passenger side, preventing escape.

I slid back to the driver's side. The man was looking down, his shaved head displaying a tattoo of the Virgin Mary with a skull face: Santa Muerte.

I'd read about her. The cartels have their own culture, including bizarre religious beliefs. Many narcos worship Santa Muerte, or Saint Death, a female grim reaper depicted as a skeletal figure dressed in robes, often with garish blonde wigs and colorful jewelry.

He was removing a pistol from an ankle holster. I slowly stood, keeping my eyes on him.

Then I jumped, pulling my knees to my chest. A split second before impact, I extended my knees, stomping down.

Two hundred and twenty pounds dropping twelve feet was considerable impact. The heavy boots were like twin anvils striking the side of his face.

He shuddered and then went limp. Blood bubbled from his oddly contorted mouth, misshapen by a shattered jaw. His sightless eyes lolled above a cratered cheek.

I hurried across the street then turned and saw another man jabbering into a hand-held radio. I bolted.

I glanced back and saw several men running toward me. Cars would not be far behind. I sprinted like my life depended on it. Because it did.

If I could make it to Magnum Lounge, I'd have safety in numbers. If the thugs entered, I'd ask someone to call the police. But it was a nearly a mile away.

I hurtled down the street. At the end of the next block, I turned and saw a man in hot pursuit, on a bicycle of all things. I never expected a member of El Poder to save the planet by commuting to work. Human powered, spandex clad and gluten free. Fueled by tofu, sprouts and meth. Any driver failing to respect the bicycle lane will receive a citation and a free bullet.

He pedaled furiously, standing on the pedals. I was fast. But his bike was faster. He was about two blocks behind but he'd catch me soon. He wouldn't be pursuing with such vigor unless he had a gun. I did not. I cursed myself for not grabbing the truck driver's gold plated pistol.

The next street was completely deserted. I considered an ambush, but saw no place to hide: no parked cars, newspaper dispensers or garbage cans. I couldn't attack from a storefront since he rode down the middle of the street.

As I rounded the next corner, I saw him, one block behind and closing fast. Panic crept in. He was gaining more rapidly than expected. I was used to being the fastest guy in the game, the linebacker tackling from behind. The hunter. Not the prey.

I'd been in a dead sprint for nearly half a mile and my lungs burned. I knew I couldn't keep the pace up.

I saw an alley about halfway down the block, on the opposite side. I raced across and glanced into the garbage-strewn corridor. About fifty feet from the entrance sat four vagrants, two white and two black. A wall sealed the end. A blind alley.

None of the nearby streetlights functioned so the alley was black as the devil's pointy shoes. The street folks probably enforced the darkness with rocks flung at bulbs, keeping their secrets dark.

I knew the man would catch me well before I got to the Magnum Lounge, so I ducked into the corridor, immediately blasted by the stench of urine and rancid food. I tramped through wet trash toward the men and pulled out a wad of cash.

I thrust the money. "If you help me hide, you can have this. My girlfriend's husband is trying to kill me." I didn't expect they'd be real thrilled about hiding me from a criminal gang, armed to the teeth.

They didn't answer. I glanced out; the bicycle careened down the middle of the street. I flattened against the wall. He looked in but we were in the dark, so he kept going. I figured he'd return when he got to the next intersection and realized that I'd vanished.

I had to hide, quickly. But I couldn't, unless they agreed to keep my location secret. If they refused to help, death would be difficult to avoid.

I desperately looked from one man to the other. The closest was a white guy with a veiny nose and bloodshot eyes, his face a riddle of creases. His trunk weaved but he maintained an upright position. He attempted to bring a wobbly bottle to his lips, but the task seemed hopelessly complex.

He bleated, "Live sis lone!" Or at least I think he said that. He probably meant, "Leave us alone." Regardless, it didn't seem like a welcome greeting.

Across the alley, the others leaned against the wall. The old guy nearest the street appeared to be mentally skewed. Missing one eye and some of his teeth. Skin like a dried raisin. He muttered incomprehensible noises, the lone eye rolling wildly. Motioned for me to come closer.

I leaned down. He sang in a very high voice, "Nuthin' beats my hobo life, stabbing white boys wit' my hobo knife."

Maybe I should take my chances with the bicycle gangsta.

A black man with long dreadlocks laughed, "Don't worry 'bout old Cy. That brother ain't stabbin' nobody."

I thrust the cash toward the dreadlocked man. "You gotta help me, please!"

"I ain't taking yo' money. Have a seat." He scooted over and made a space between him and the deranged falsetto.

The fourth man, a white derelict who looked like something pulled from a trashcan, extended long dirty fingernails. He spoke like he had a mouthful of gravel, "I'll take it."

I held out the bills. He greedily snatched the cash then grinned, exposing random teeth. He stuffed the bills down the front of his pants.

I made a mental note to wear gloves from now on whenever I handled money.

As my eyes adjusted to the severe darkness, I noticed a dumpster. I debated hiding inside but I'd be easily trapped.

I decided to go with the dreadlocked guy's plan. I sat, crowding between them. I pulled my knit hat down to my eyes. The insane singer hissed and scooted away, turning his back to us.

The guy with dreadlocks spoke, "My name's Marley, like Bob. Cy's the singin' man." He pointed at the drunk. "That's Skunk. He's stanky and always drunk as a skunk." Motioned to the man who took my money. "We call his ragady self, Raggedy Andy."

"You's way more ragady than me!"

Marley chuckled. "Sheeeeeiiit. I think the man can see for hisself, ragady ass."

Raggedy Andy gripped the edge of a stained, crusty bedspread. "You wanna hide? Get under this." I threw the fetid blanket over my head. Tried not to think about what made the stains.

"We's drinkin' men, 'specially them two white boys," Marley said. "You need a drank. Pass the bottle, Raggedy."

"Got no extra."

"Give the man a drank! He gave you mo' money than yo' beggin' self make in a month."

Raggedy sighed then rummaged around in a box. He grudgingly handed me a liter of Everclear. It became obvious why Raggedy's voice was so raspy, as 190-proof firewater would scorch the old gullet.

The narco glided up on his bike. I ducked under the blanket, peeking out. He leaned his bike on the corner and growled, "Where's the man who ran in here?"

Raggedy pretended to be asleep, snoring. The drunk skunk garbled, "Ain't seen nobody! Liv sis lone!"

The narco stood over the vagabond, his back to me. He pulled a pistol. "Lying piece of shit! I saw him run in here!"

I knew he hadn't seen me. He was bluffing. If everyone kept quiet, he might leave.

He backhanded Skunk with a vicious pistol whip. Sounded like a meat tenderizer hammering a steak. Skunk fell sideways, blood draining from a gaping laceration on his cheek.

I considered rushing him, but they were twenty feet away. He'd have plenty of time to turn and shoot.

The narco pressed the gun to the drunk's head and barked, "Where is he? You got three seconds! One, two..."

We were deeper in the dark alley. Skunk pointed at me but his hand careened and lurched, so it was unclear where he aimed. I prayed the others would remain quiet. My palms sweated.

Raggedy Andy clambered to his feet. "Ain't me. This is the guy you want." He thrust a finger at my chest, leaving no doubt.

Marley muttered under his breath, "Rat bastard!"

The narco's eyes zeroed on me. There was no possibility for escape, walls on three sides and an armed thug blocking the exit. The narco approached rapidly.

CHAPTER TWENTY-ONE

The thug closed the gap, striding toward me, his gun raised. My mind raced as I tried to think of something.

I jumped to my feet, keeping the blanket wrapped around my body with my knees bent to appear shorter. I slurred loudly, "Ain't me. It's him." I pointed back at Raggedy. A pointing battle.

The mentally unhinged man stood and shuffled toward the exit, rolling his lone eye. The thug ran in front, cutting him off. Cy tried to step around him. The narco lashed the barrel across his forehead. The ancient man fell against the wall then slowly stood, muttering something nonsensical, blood dripping down his wizened face. Tough old guy.

He quickly returned his attention to us, pointing his pistol and shouting, "Everyone on your feet! Show me your hands!"

Marley slowly stood. I stuffed a fistful of crusty blanket into my collar, holding it in place. I placed the rotgut booze on a window ledge. A glass bottle against a gun wasn't exactly ideal. But better than nothing. I raised my hands above my head, purposely trembling

"I'll kill every one of you gutter rats."

Raggedy cried, "This guy paid us to hide him!" He jabbed his finger at me enthusiastically.

"Naw! It's him!" I whined. "He gave us money to say he's one of us."

"Shut up or you all die!"

The thug told Cy, "I don't need you running out to yell for help. Trot to the back, stinky." He kicked the old man in the seat of his saggy pants, hard.

Cyclops froze then slowly rotated to face the narco. The thug pressed his pistol to the old man's bleeding forehead. I inhaled sharply.

Cy turned and slowly shuffled past us, softly singing, "Nuthin' beats the hobo life…"

The narco walked to Skunk. He flicked a lighter then held the long flame to his bloody face, looking carefully.

Skunk moaned, laughed for a few seconds then fell silent. At least he wasn't dead.

With a bizarre juxtaposition of triggered memory, I remembered Zo's hilarious drunken trick. And suddenly I had a plan.

I quietly grabbed the bottle and filled both cheeks with white lightning. Carefully returned it to the ledge and thrust my hands skyward.

Satisfied that the jaundiced drunk wasn't cracking heads at El Poder's warehouse, he stood. He knew we weren't armed or we would've already exchanged pleasantries and hot lead.

He might be planning to slay us all, but one gunshot would bring significantly less attention than five. I figured he wanted to find the culprit before offing the witnesses. As far as he knew, his target could be hidden under trash or in the dumpster. He couldn't kill anyone before he knew.

The narco stepped deeper. He swung the gun back and forth between Raggedy and myself, holding the lighter up. Since he was looking for a white guy, he ignored Marley. I was squatting, putting us at eye level.

I could tell he suspected me. He pointed the pistol at my chest and held the flame closer. My head sank deeper into the blanket, like a dragon retreating into a cave.

When the light hit my face, he would know. Unlike the others, I had all my teeth. They had dirt imbedded in their pores, not smeared on the surface. The others were scarred and bulbous and knotted and weathered. I was none of those things.

Trapped, I stepped back against the wall, my mouth burning from the pure grain alcohol.

Raggedy said, "It's him. He's the one you want!"

The narco swung the gun and yelled, "Don't say another word!"

When he turned, I crouched to spring but he quickly pivoted his gun back. He kept himself out of reach while trying to see me. Held the lighter at arm's length and leaned in.

I held my elbows out further, spreading the blanket wide across my torso. I shifted my body to the left, craning my head to my right. He was right-handed so his gun would jerk to his left, my right.

He got closer. I saw recognition in his eyes. He knew. His finger tightened on the trigger.

I sprayed the Everclear out of my mouth and the liquid erupted in blue flames when it hit the lighter, the pissed-off dragon flaming out the silly little knight.

I sent a wide spray that engulfed his head in flames. He fired his gun into the blanket, the bullet sizzling under my right armpit.

He screamed and brought both hands to his face, trying to beat away the flames. His hair and face glowed blue, like a fancy dessert aflame.

Time to put out the fire with gasoline.

I grabbed the round bottle by the neck and swung. When it struck his skull, the Everclear exploded into a hellish ball of glass and flames like a Molotov cocktail. The entire alley momentarily appeared fully bright, like midday sun.

Both hands were on his face when the bottle exploded so his pistol spun loose. The additional firewater adding fuel, the flames became yellow-red. As he fell, the burning liquid dripped from his face, spreading to his shirt.

He landed on his face then rolled onto his back. I threw the blanket over him to protect my hands and extinguish the fire. Clasped his cranium with both hands then slammed it against the concrete. Sounded like a cue ball dropping from the pool table. Pounded several more times for good measure. Maybe half a rack dropping from the table.

He might survive but he would not be bothering us any time soon.

Marley muttered, "Damn!"

That about summed it up.

I picked up his semiautomatic pistol, a Sig Sauer, and tucked it into my coat pocket, happy with his choice of guns.

Raggedy fled from the alley like *his* hair was on fire. Skunk wasn't going anywhere. Cyclops rambled out of the rear of the alley, blood on his face. He kicked the unconscious narco twice. I wondered if he'd use his hobo knife.

Marley grinned, "Man, you knocked the shit outa that dude! Bet he don't mess with you no mo.' Looks like you get the girl!"

"You guys need to get gone. He's got a bunch of friends with guns. They probably heard the gunshot. They'll be here soon."

Marley didn't look concerned. "They ain't gonna be searchin' for two brothas and a white dude, is they? Want some company?"

"I don't want to put you guys in any more danger. I'm really sorry about that."

"Ain't no thang, man." He shook his head and smiled, "We like excitement, don't we Cy?"

Cyclops grinned and nodded.

"If I can make it to the Magnum Lounge, I'll be safe."

"You got it. Let's roll on over to tha' Magnum."

I threw the narco's bike deep into the alley. I picked up a charred remnant of the narco's shirt and tied it around Cy's head to stop the bleeding.

In my SEAL days, one of my comrades had a drinking trick. He'd fill his cheeks with high-octane liquor then hold a lighter in front of his mouth, spitting flames like a human flamethrower. Remembering his drunken antics saved my life.

I owe you, Zo.

We headed toward Magnum Lounge. Cy shuffled at a snail's pace. At first, I was uncomfortable with our slow progress but then decided there was a certain genius in our plodding. The narcos would expect a man running.

A low rider turned onto the street, the headlights illuminating us. Marley and Cy flanked me, blocking their view. I pulled my hat down and turned away. The muscle car crept beside us.

"Looks like the dude's friends," said Marley. "They's looking at us mighty hard."

They'd probably heard the gunshot. I stopped and pretended to relieve my bladder on the wall. The sedan halted.

I considered bolting but they would shoot. Even if Marley and I got away, Cy couldn't run. He could barely walk. I hoped this was his normal state and not a head injury. I couldn't endanger them again.

I pulled the Sig out of my pocket and held it in front of me, thinking. They hadn't gotten out of the car. I had to keep the charade going but I had no need to take a leak. I felt like an idiot with a shy bladder.

"Y'all want yo' car cleaned?" Marley shouted. "Two dollas! Best car wash in Cali!"

Cy shrieked, "Window wash! Window wash!" They ran toward the car.

The driver punched the gas and cruised down the street. I turned around.

Cy and Marley stood in the street, holding filthy rags. Marley stuck his washcloth back in his pocket. "Works every time!" he laughed. "Nobody wants a couple ol' bums smearin' dirty rags all over they glass. And Cy's ugly ass pro'ly scared 'em off with that rollin' eyeball thang."

Cy rolled his eye crazily and chuckled.

We kept moving, four blocks to go. Marley informed me Magnum Lounge had a great dumpster for finding food. He pointed out a few other food sources and primo sleeping spots along the way. I wondered if they thought I was homeless.

Cy spoke only once, abruptly shouting, "Watch out fo' Skanky Pam!"

Marley nodded his head in agreement, "A brutha gots to be careful wit' a woman like that."

Walking with them helped me relax somewhat but I wasn't really listening. I was searching every movement and shadow. Ahead, I saw a group of people dressed for a night out, likely headed the same place I desperately hoped to reach.

Magnum Lounge was around the next corner. I figured the doorman might not let me in if I showed up with my new friends. "Thanks guys. I can take it from here. I owe you."

Marley gave me a soul grip. "Man, I gotta tell ya, that spittin' fire was a helluva trick! You laid waste to his dome like napalm! I ain't seen a bomb go off like dat since Nam!"

He erupted in hilarious laughter and turned to Cy, "Thas some crazy shit, huh, Cy?" Cy's face split into a grin and he cackled. They began laughing harder, lapsing into a spasm of uncontrolled hilarity. Marley leaned on Cy's shoulder for support then doubled over in a wild fit of giggles. Cy slapped Marley's back, gasping from the gut-busting laughter. I smiled at their contagious, uninhibited merriment, barely able to get an occasional word out between the wheezing and laughter.

After a couple of minutes, I began to feel uneasy since I wanted to get going, but didn't want to be rude.

Finally Marley caught his breath and slapped me on the back. "You deserve the lady. Stay cool, brother." They strolled away, still chortling.

I wiped the dirt and sweat from my face with my knit hat. Tossed my coat and hat into a deserted storefront then walked briskly. I heard their boisterous laughter from a block away.

Past the next corner, I was home free.

Headlights shone on the street and I heard a car rumbling slowly. Too slowly.

I didn't turn around. I thrust my hand in my pocket and gripped my new pistol.

The creeping lowrider pulled aside, cruising next to the sidewalk. I stared straight ahead. They pulled forward and I saw the hood: the same car.

I quickened my pace. Maybe they wouldn't recognize me without my coat and hat.

I turned my head slightly and noticed the front passenger door slightly ajar. I jerked my head to look.

The passenger was rotated, facing back toward me. His left hand jutted through the gap, a revolver zeroed on my face.

CHAPTER TWENTY-TWO

I ducked forward then exploded into the side with all my weight, like I was tackling the car. My shoulder struck the door, slamming it shut and leaving a large dent.

His gun clattered to the street, a crunched hand trapped in the door.

He screeched like an ensnared cat.

I grabbed his pistol and scrambled behind the trunk. The car lurched forward but I ran behind, crouching. I stood, quickly firing three rounds into the rear window, shattering the glass. Narcos dove to the floorboard.

The car accelerated as I ran behind, emptying the six-shot revolver. The bullets passed through, splintering the front windshield. Tires screeched as the driver chaotically swerved.

I dropped the empty gun and ran back, looking over my shoulder. At the end of the block, the car slammed to a halt and four men clambered out, tiny glass cubes spilling onto the street.

The passenger was doubled over, cradling his mutilated hand. Three men barreled toward me, pistols out.

I sprinted around the corner then calmly stepped into the noisy, packed bar. Karaoke had started.

No one seemed aware of the gunshots, due to thick velvet drapes insulating the windows, as well as the blare of Beyoncé and a slurry woman's horrible singing. Saw a momentary gap in the crowd and rushed through, my knees bent to keep my head below the throng. I made it to the middle of the room.

Tables backed against crimson walls decorated by oil paintings and gilt mirrors. Patrons in booths cheered the singer as they drank their senses away. The lounge was in full disco mode. Colored beams swung as strobes created a slow motion, stop frame illusion.

I pressed through a horde of thirsty people jammed against the bar. I removed my gloves. As I bumped to distract them, my fingers lightly felt pockets to determine the contents. I felt wallets and keys, but not what I wanted.

Standing behind a tall man, I peered around his head. Three narcos were fanning out, standing on their toes to see above the crowd. More would follow. I was trapped.

I saw my target: her purse agape, giggling through smeared lipstick, the strobes making her intoxicated movements bizarre. Squeezed behind her, looking away and smiling like I'd seen a buddy. Reached into her purse and felt a wallet, makeup, and then — bingo — a rectangle.

I stepped away, pocketing the cellphone then pulling on my gloves. I crouched and pushed toward the restroom.

Entered the women's bathroom, thinking they might not look there. Three of the eight stalls were occupied. I slipped into the furthest one and locked myself in, sitting on the seat with my boots against the door.

I debated my options. I could call Javier but he was probably at the farmhouse, almost an hour away. Considered the police but I would be thoroughly questioned. The warehouse would be raided. El Poder had a police mole, so we'd be marked for life. If Blake were alive, he'd be further endangered. I might even be arrested for crushing the truck driver's face. That and setting someone's head on fire.

My best option was escape. Every restaurant had a freight door. But armed men would cover the exits quickly. Assuredly, by now more had arrived.

The suspended ceiling consisted of fiberboard drop panels. A toilet flushed and a stall door banged open. The woman washed her hands and exited. As soon as she was gone, I flushed the toilet and stepped on the seat, pushing up a panel. Spread my feet against the walls of the stall, supporting myself. Thrust my shoulders through, illuminating the space with the stolen cell phone. Gripped a plumbing pipe and pulled myself up.

I straddled ceiling joists and replaced the panel. As I pushed down, an edge broke, crumbling into the stall. Light poured through the gap.

As my eyes adjusted, the space pulsed with faint light bleeding from below. Roof trestle crisscrossed the entire space, a web of two-by-fours. Plumbing and electrical conduit paralleled the joists. The back wall was impenetrable brick. I ran my gloves across the thick plywood roof to no avail.

I dialed Javier. He answered on the first ring, "Hello?"

"It's Wyatt. I'm inside Magnum Lounge in Chula Vista. I'm in a serious bind. Jefe's men are trying to finish me. I'll explain later. If I live."

"I thought something was up since you weren't answering your phone. I tracked the transceiver on my helmet. I'm at the moto."

"Yes! First luck I've had all day! I'm hiding in the ceiling space above the women's bathroom. At least three thugs are looking for me."

"Should I enter? I'm in my truck."

"Park around the corner. I'll see if I can find a way out. I'll call back."

"On my way."

I heard the restroom door open then someone entered a stall. I peered through the crack but saw nothing. I heard others exit and wash their hands. If I could get to the front of the building, I could drop through and escape, especially if the men were deeper inside the lounge.

I heard a male voice, "Hello? Janitorial services. Anyone here?"

Only one woman answered, "Yes. Almost done." The toilet flushed. She washed her hands then exited.

I heard heavy footsteps. The man opened a stall then moved to the next, rapidly going down the line. He wasn't a cleaning man.

Two women entered and the man said, "Closed for cleaning." They left.

I removed my T-shirt and wrapped it around the Sig. I crouched, peeking through the gap. The man pushed on the locked door. He looked through the door cracks then squatted, placing his hands on the floor, peering at the broken debris on the floor.

He stood, his eyes rising to the ceiling, honing in on the crack. I saw his face and my breathing quickened; I'd seen him in the warehouse, one of those carrying the man into the furnace.

He pulled a revolver and aimed directly at me. I froze and held my breath, wondering if he could possibly see me through the crack. The fissure was small and I was in the dark.

The surrounding framing pinned me in. To escape, I'd have to crawl through the trestle but he'd hear movement and shoot. He lifted a radio to his lips.

One of us was going to die.

I trained the pistol on his forehead, but hesitated. I wondered if it was necessary to end his life. Killing him wouldn't bring Blake back. Could he see me or was he merely aiming at the crack in anticipation? If I were completely still, maybe he'd leave. I became a doctor to heal people. I'd already slain more than my share in the military.

Could he hear my breathing? I closed my mouth.

His head rotated slightly and his granite eyes narrowed, as if he'd seen something. He subtly tightened his grip on the gun. Cocked the hammer with his thumb, a round revolving into the chamber. Closing one eye, he aligned the rear sight with the front sight with me.

Might as well be him.

I squeezed the bang switch. The shirt muted the discharge, but the shot was still deafening. The bullet pierced the ceiling, cracking a panel as debris flew. A red dot appeared on his forehead. He sank, his hair painting the wall with a crimson smear.

I stuffed the pistol in my belt, still wrapped in my shirt. I stepped from joist to joist as fast as I could, climbing over and under ceiling trestle. The music became louder as I crossed over to the central area. I lifted a panel slightly, looking down. People laughed and danced, lights flashing to the throbbing beat. The gunshot hadn't been heard over the ruckus, at least not by those below.

I crept forward, painfully slow, the strobes disconcerting. Sweat ran down my bare chest. When I finally arrived at the front wall, I phoned Javier. "Drive toward the entrance. I'll drop through the ceiling near the front door and run out. When you see me, pull forward and I'll jump in the truck bed."

"Copy."

I estimated the location of the exit door then moved a panel slightly. Below, a narco surveyed the pub, standing directly in front of the door. The crowd was thick with partiers. At the edge of my view, I saw another blue jumpsuit from the knees down.

I could shoot the man below, but the other would react. Shooting both was possible but meant risking innocent people, especially without a clear line of sight. A gunshot would betray my position and I'd lose the element of surprise.

They'd fill the attic with lead. If I weren't killed by the initial shots, the panels would break and drop, trapping me in plain view, a fly twitching in a spider web of diagonal beams.

Again my conscience tweaked me. Shooting them unawares from a hidden position seemed brutal. Their guns weren't even drawn, much less pointed at me. I vacillated.

The dead man would be discovered soon, if not already. The police would arrive, the men would flee, and further bloodshed could be averted. I could hunker down and wait.

But the police would find me, and El Poder's informant would leak my identity. My only option was escape.

The furthest narco stepped from view. The one below turned, exposing a green spider on his neck. He rotated back, displaying the jail tattoo, a cobweb covering his face.

My conscience was no longer an issue.

I came up with a pest extermination plan. Removed a shotgun shell from a pocket then gingerly taped a marble to the brass cap. Moved the panel back further for an unobstructed drop zone. Held the shell a few inches in front of his nose. I dropped it.

I slammed back against a trestle to avoid the blast. As it passed in front of his eyes, his head jerked down to look. It hit the floor.

The shell exploded, blowing out the back of his head. The buckshot tore through the roof, globs of brain and his fancy tattoo sailing into the night sky.

That's for the man you burnt alive, Spider Man.

Screams erupted. His corpse fell backward, away from the door. Skull fragments jutted from the hole where his face used to be. The amount of blood was impressive, creating a halo around his ruined tattoo.

The second man ran under, spinning wildly, inadvertently kicking the shell casing toward the front door. He blindly fired three shots into the crowd.

He backed to the exit, directly below. I pointed the barrel straight down. Shot him in the top of the head.

He shuddered and slowly tumbled forward, landing on Spidey's body.

I jerked the panel away so I could jump cleanly. As I dropped through the hole, a narco rushed through the front door. I landed on my feet, squatting to absorb the fall.

I stood. The thug looked momentarily confused to see a bare-chested man appear from the heavens.

I cracked him across the temple with the Sig.

He crumpled. I stepped over him.

I saw the marble-taped shell near the door. As I ran out, I scooped it up then dove into the truck bed without breaking my stride. Never leave evidence. I lay flat as Javier turned the corner and slammed on the gas.

CHAPTER TWENTY-THREE

Sirens wailed a few blocks away. Barely a minute had passed after the final carnage, so I assumed the dead man was found in the bathroom while I was still in the attic, a near miss. Javier slowed to the speed limit. The sirens approached then flashing patrol cars screamed by.

The stolen cell phone rang. I recognized Javier's number. He said, "There'll be an enormous investigation. The cops might search for my truck. We should retrieve the moto then stay at my Coronado house, so we aren't driving all the way to Alpine tonight."

"We need to ditch our phones. The woman might report her cell stolen. Her records would show my calls."

"I'll destroy mine." His phone was prepaid, so the owner was untraceable but the signal was not.

Near the Salvation Army, he stopped on an empty street. He quickly reattached the license plates he'd removed before driving to the Magnum Lounge then walked to the moto.

I wiped down the stolen cell phone and placed it under a tire. I drove over the phone, crushing it.

I plugged my prepaid phone in the truck charger. As soon as it powered up, I called Catherine.

She answered, her worry apparent in one word, "Hello."

"Honey, I'm sorry. My phone died. I had a little adventure. I'll fill you in tomorrow. Javier and I are gonna stay at his Coronado house tonight."

"We've been so worried! Why didn't you tell us where you were going?"

"It wasn't planned. I went on a little joyride that went off the rails. I apologize."

"I've got enough on my mind without you disappearing."

"Honestly, babe, I didn't do it on purpose. I'm sorry."

"I forgive you this time. But don't do it again."

"I promise."

On the bridge across the bay, I tossed the Sig into the deep shipping channel. I met Javier at the gate. He went first and the guard waved me through. At the house, I told him the entire story. As he listened, he stoked a huge fire in his fireplace. I undressed while talking, tossing the clothes into the flames.

He poked the blaze, making sure every fragment was incinerated. When I finished he said, "You're a complete idiot for getting into that situation but a genius for getting out."

I sat in my underwear. "I know. It was unbelievable stupid. I wasn't myself after hearing...well, you know."

"I've thought more about that. Maybe 'he's with the angels and saints' means he's in Mexico. Half the towns down there are named saint something or angel whatever. Jefe didn't say he was killed, he said gone."

"Yeah, I wondered if it was code, like angels meaning Los Angeles."

"Either way, we should keep looking."

"No question. It's not completely rational, but something tells me he's alive." I recognized emotions weren't logical but I couldn't give up. I also knew Javier wouldn't purposely encourage false hope, so his words made my spirits soar.

With a greatly improved mood, I laughed, "I've been thinking about that ridiculous crime scene. The first guy's dead in the women's bathroom with fiberboard and my T-shirt particles in his skull. Web Master ate buckshot, with pellets likely imbedded in his groin and chest, the ballistic angle directly below him. The third guy took one straight through his noggin and the slug probably ended up in his chest. And they might find the guy with the torched head a few blocks away. The forensic guys are gonna have their hands full."

"Riot Wyatt strikes again! Solve that, CSI! They'll probably assume it was a freakish set-up by a rival gang." He paused and raised one eyebrow, "By the way, why is my precious Ducati caked in mud?"

"My bad. I'll wash it tomorrow." I was too embarrassed to tell him I'd vandalized a golf course like a delinquent teenager so I quickly changed the subject, "What about those drugs marked DEA?"

"That's wild. There's a leak somewhere between confiscation and destruction."

"I'd guess the chink in the armor's on this side of the border. Otherwise, they'd smuggle their own drugs or at least unwrap them in Mexico. Admiral Landfair said the hard part's moving them across."

"That means corrupt American soldiers or DEA agents."

"Should we tell Landfair?"

"Not now. Let's keep searching for Blake. We'll expose El Poder once he's safely home."

"I like the optimism."

"I don't think it's necessarily misplaced." I smiled, relishing the hope we shared.

Saturday morning I awoke, thinking about the previous day. My initial emotion was regret for my poor judgment that resulted in at least three deaths and multiple injuries. But as I processed the thoughts, my remorse mostly vanished. As long as no bystanders were significantly injured, it was a day well spent, ridding the earth of El Poder's brutal hit men. They could burn in hell for all I cared.

I pushed out of bed and opened the shades. The storm had blown over, the dawn's glow firing the sky. Hungry birds massacred worms that the rain brought to the surface.

I smelled coffee. I strolled into the unbelievably tidy kitchen. I poured a cup, the bitter odor inviting. "My little misadventure puts new pressure on us," I said. "Several narcos saw me last night. El Poder will put two and two together: the guy at the warehouse was the same person the assassin confronted at my house. The curse of being tall."

"Yeah, the clock's ticking. We have to pull it off on Monday."

We spent the next two hours discussing a plan then took a taxi to San Diego, renting a Chevy Suburban and a Nissan Sentra with a fake ID and credit card. We had passports, credit cards and driver's licenses purchased at an astronomical price from a shady website specializing in counterfeit documents. Javier knew about the site as the CIA had tried unsuccessfully to infiltrate.

We drove to the farmhouse.

I told them about my previous day, omitting the recording about Blake. We made a list of supplies. I called a local pharmacy, phoning in several prescriptions for Javier. He left the house in the Suburban, going to the bank, the drug store and Coronado for more equipment.

I checked the news online. The shootout in Chula Vista made the headlines. Magnum Lounge was a well-known institution.

Chula Vista, California (AP) — Police say three people have died and three are injured after a shootout in a nightclub, Magnum Lounge, in Chula Vista. Police Sgt. Brad Williams said police have taken one man into custody but no arrests have been made after the shooting, occurring around 10 p.m. yesterday.

Club bouncer Robert Ruby gave an account, verified by police, of two different shootouts. Ruby said several men entered the club searching for someone. Enrique Mosquera, age 24, was murdered in the women's bathroom. His body was discovered and the police were called. While the police were en route, a second shootout occurred near the bar's entrance. Edward Peña, age 32, was killed by a shotgun blast to the face. Johan Nieto, age 27, was slain moments after Peña.

Two bystanders were injured in the shootout but both are expected to fully recover. One of the injured men, Jose Britos, was placed in police custody. He is considered a person of interest but the police have not been able to interview Britos as he is a patient at a San Diego area hospital with a blunt-force head injury. He is reportedly still unconscious.

One witness stated that a man jumped through the ceiling and fled moments before the arrival of police. Several others said a group of men fled through a backroom exit as police were arriving.

Williams stated the three slain men were all convicted felons. Peña was convicted of four murders in Mexico and was a fugitive from justice there. He was known as La Araña, or The Spider, and was reportedly a cartel hit man. He escaped prison in 2013 after a group of armed men posing as police delivering an inmate talked their way into a penitentiary in the southern Mexican state of Oaxaca and unleashed an attack on inmates and guards. Seven were killed in the bloody assault. Peña and twelve other inmates escaped.

Williams said the leading hypothesis was that the shootings at Magnum Lounge resulted from a revenge attack launched by one criminal gang against another.

I reclined, deep in thought. What were our chances of being arrested or discovered by El Poder? The man I jumped on from the semi only saw the bottoms of my steel-toed boots. The Bicycle Gangsta saw me briefly before getting flamed out. The guy I clobbered with the pistol was unconscious. But

Crunched Hand Man saw me up close. No question, he went straight to El Poder leadership and tattled.

Multiple people saw me drop and run from the bar. My description would be in police reports. El Poder had an informant.

The police were problematic. They certainly had a description of the getaway vehicle. Police cruisers passed us on the street and likely had dashboard video of the black four-door Ram. Javier's tags were missing but his face was probably captured on film.

Javier's rare Ducati was parked for several hours at the thrift store during the shooting. Investigators could cross-reference both vehicles, Javier probably the only person in San Diego who owned both.

Once they had his name, the detectives could obtain the guard's log from the base, determining the truck and moto returned shortly after the shooting. Javier would be a prime suspect and might be arrested when he returned to base. Even worse, he could be abducted or murdered by El Poder if they discovered the police suspicions.

We didn't have a clean getaway. We would have to avoid the police and El Poder, all while planning to snatch one of the most powerful men on earth.

CHAPTER TWENTY-FOUR

Javier was going to the base. I dialed and he answered, "Yo."

"Where are you?"

"Just left Coronado. Admiral Landfair wanted to speak with me so I got delayed. He spoke highly of my reporter friend. I got everything we need from the base. I'm headed to the bank."

"Don't go to the bank. I'm worried the police could discover your identity. I doubt they could solve the investigation this quickly but it's possible." I told him my thoughts.

He whistled softly. "You're right. If detectives asked about my whereabouts, a few friends know about the farmhouse. Hopefully, they'd keep quiet. But the police might say I'm in danger. The farmhouse could be raided."

"The Salvation Army was closed and there were probably hundreds of vehicles parked in a one mile radius, so I'm hoping we're okay. There are lots of Ram trucks in San Diego."

"The thrift store wasn't closed when you parked there, correct?"

"Right."

"The employees probably noticed my Ducati when they left since the parking lot was empty. It's an attention grabber."

"Let's discuss when you get here."

I caught a taxi to a rental car place and picked up a car then I went to a bank in San Diego, opening an account using a new ID.

After leaving the bank, I called my father's best friend. Jim was like an uncle.

"Hello?"

"Jim, it's Wyatt."

"Riot Wyatt! When're you coming to Oregon, big guy? Pam and I would love to have your family for dinner."

"Hopefully soon. Are you free? Where are you?"

"I'm at my office in Hood River. Why?"

"This is an odd request but I need you to deliver a message to Dad and you can't tell anyone, not even Pam. Once you hear the story, you'll understand. Deal?"

"Count on it. I can keep a secret."

"I know you can. I'm in trouble. I've struggled with a gambling addiction. I've stopped but I owe a chunk of change."

"You know I've had my struggles with the bottle so no judgment. I highly recommend the twelve steps for booze, gambling, whatever. This year marks twenty years of sobriety."

"Congrats and thanks. I'm embarrassed but I'll survive. I'll ask Dad for a loan but I don't want my creditors to know. They're organized crime types and they've threatened me. I need to pay immediately. Can you have Dad call this number from your cell phone?"

"Are you okay?"

"I just need the money and it'll be fine. Can you do that?"

"Sure. If you need anything, including a loan, I'm here."

"Thanks but I'll work it out with Dad. Please don't call him as I'm fairly sure they've bugged his phone."

"Really? Should you call the police?"

"No. It's my own fault. They've given me a week to pay. Can you go to Dad's office and leave your phone with him? Once I've paid, I'll call you to speak with Dad again."

"I'm heading there now. Take care."

"Thanks, Jim."

Thirty minutes later, my phone rang. "Wyatt, it's Dad." He sounded concerned but my father was nails, completely unflappable.

"Thanks for calling. I'm ashamed and embarrassed."

"Don't be. We all make mistakes. You sure you're okay?"

"Yeah. They'll leave me alone when I've settled. They said your phone is bugged and I believe them. It's fairly easy to do. I'm sorry for dragging you into this. Once I've paid, you can throw away your phones and get new lines. For now, act normal and please don't discuss with anyone but Jim. I don't want those goons to think I'm going to flee or something."

"This is a lot to take in. But I'm a decent actor." I knew he'd keep quiet. Dad knew scandalous things about his patients and detested gossip. He was a vault.

"Can I borrow some money? I'll take out a second mortgage and pay you back within six months. I make plenty. I just don't have liquidity."

"How much?"

"Three hundred thousand."

"By when?"

"They gave me a week."

"No problem. I'll sell mutual funds from my retirement account. I can send cash on Monday."

I gave him the wire info for my new account. "I really appreciate this, Dad. Can I ask one more favor?"

"Anything."

"Please don't tell Mom. You can tell her after I pay them. I don't want her to worry."

"You got it."

I felt guilty lying to Dad and Jim. I hadn't lied to my parents since I was a little kid. When he heard the real story, he'd understand. But I couldn't burden him until we knew Blake's fate.

Javier would stay at the farmhouse as much as possible. We hid his KTM dirt bike next to a single-track moto trail on the backside of his property. He carried new documents and a wad of cash in a money belt. If the police came, he'd flee into the thick woods behind the house. They'd never catch him on his moto. He knew the vast network of trails and logging roads like the back of his hand. With fake ID, he could enter

Mexico, a mere forty miles away. The rest of us would plead ignorance.

We rehearsed and planned for the body snatch, everyone contributing to the planning. I was impressed with Catherine's devious creativity. In another life, we could've been Bonnie and Clyde, partners in crime.

We contemplated every possible twist or complication. We acted out potential scenes. We critiqued each other, continually improving.

I worried about Behram being at the restaurant, as he'd seen Susan and I, up close and personal. If he were, we'd have to make a game-day decision whether to abort.

Javier used the barn as his shop. I removed everything from the barn's basement, a giant, dank room.

Susan and Catherine went to a hair and tanning salon. When she returned, Susan had jet-black hair like Catherine's but practically a crew cut. I injected collagen into her cheeks and lips, temporarily altering her face.

On Sunday, they drove to LA, going to a party lighting store, Hollywood's best special effects/costume shop and an ethnic butcher shop, purchasing cow's blood and intestines. I went to a medical supply store, Home Depot and a pet shop, buying a Burmese python and five rats. When I arrived home, I unloaded a metal stretcher and Javier helped me carry it to the basement.

We were committed. We would either grab El Jefe or we would fail spectacularly. If we failed, my entire family would probably be wiped from the face of the earth.

Blake hadn't seen Juan since he tried to escape and no one had spoken a word to him, solitary confinement. He'd been so lonely and sad. He felt guilty about Juan, his only friend. He heard them say Juan would be punished.

He was in a constant state of anxiety. His sense of day and night had evaporated. He felt hopeless as his terror mounted. He wondered when the man named Behram would come for him. His reality seemed warped.

Blake was asleep, dreaming about the monster dressed in black chasing him. Devil dogs popped in front of him at every turn, snarling and biting. He kept running and running...

He awoke as someone shook his shoulder gently. After opening his eyes, he was startled to see a man. He responded by trying to punch the man's lights out.

The man held him down and whispered, "Be quiet. We're here to rescue you." He realized it was a policeman. "The guards will return soon. We have to leave now. Follow me."

Blake climbed out of bed and dressed quickly, his spirits soaring. The policeman pulled his gun then crept to the base of the stairs. He looked around the corner then motioned for Blake to follow him. Two policemen stood at the top of the stairs.

"We'll run to the car. Climb in the trunk for safety, in case they start shooting."

They ran through darkness to a black sedan with multiple antennas. Blake climbed in the trunk, his skin tingling with excitement.

They drove for about thirty minutes then stopped. A policeman opened the trunk, leading Blake into a small house.

The policeman said, "Those people sell children to men who do bad things to kids. They'll search for you once they realize you're gone. A family in Mexico has agreed to protect you. You'll stay there until we've arrested the criminals. Once we've caught them, you can return and live with your grandparents."

Blake stared at the table. "What about my parents?"

"I'm very sorry, but your parents and aunt were killed by these people. Your father was selling drugs stolen from the hospital. He stole money from the criminals."

Blake's face contorted. He covered his eyes, hiding the tears.

"The entire trip needs to be secret. We'll cut your hair and dye it black, so you'll look Mexican. A family will take you to the secret place. When you cross into Mexico tonight, pretend to be asleep. So the border guards don't question you. It's important that everyone be fooled, or the criminals might kill your grandparents. We should arrest them soon and you'll be able to return."

"There must be a mistake." His voice shook, "My dad wouldn't do those things. He's a good person."

"Everyone is surprised, but he was. We have proof. I'm sorry. Sometimes good people do bad things."

Blake was elated to be free. But his overwhelming emotion was sadness. He'd hoped beyond hope that the bad guys had lied to him about his parents' death. But the police wouldn't lie.

From now on, he was alone. Blake was an orphan.

CHAPTER TWENTY-FIVE

On Monday, exactly one week after arriving home to find Blake missing, I went to the ambulance depot. Several paramedics were cleaning a rig. I knew a few of them.

"Yo, Doc Stryker, howzit?"

"Pretty good, Sambro. What're you guys up to?"

"Avoiding debt collectors, ex-wives and work. You?"

"I'm here to get that ambulance. Which one should I take?"

"Who'd you talk to?"

"Terry...or maybe it was Vince. I'm speaking to my son's class about being an ER doctor."

"No problem. Take number four. Keys are in it."

I climbed into the driver's seat and pulled away, driving to the farmhouse. We spent a few hours in preparation.

I carefully glued a brown beard to my face. I wore mirrored glasses and a dark curly wig.

Susan applied dark contacts, cheap blue eyeliner and orange lipstick. She glued a gold bead to an eyebrow and another to a nostril. After glopping mousse on her crew cut, each hair obstinately defied gravity. Her one-piece paramedic suit bulged over padded undergarments. She chewed a wad of gum obnoxiously.

Javier shaved his head slick and cut a short goatee. He wore a matching paramedic jumpsuit.

Ideally, I'd be the paramedic since I knew the ropes but my cover was blown so he would have to wing it. But he'd have assistance; he inserted a tiny earpiece.

I walked outside to test the mic. As he chatted with Susan, I heard every word of their conversation, crystal clear. When I spoke, he heard me but she couldn't.

Catherine walked from her room. I'd sewn a tiny clear stitch next to her eyes, pulling her eyelids into almonds. She applied heavy black mascara, enhancing the Asian appearance. I'd injected even more collagen into her face and lips, so her face was boxy. Her black hair was straightened and pulled back tightly.

She wore a preposterously expensive dress with a Chinese floral print, slit to the thigh. Rounding the sophisticated Asian-American look, she carried a small purse and wore dangling earrings and red sling-backed Jimmy Choo pumps. As before, a camera was imbedded in her handbag.

She practiced talking with a husky voice. She asked. "What do you think?"

I smiled, "You sound different and look stunning, like the beautiful daughter of a white mother and Asian father."

She kissed me and I felt like I was kissing someone else, thrilling in a strange way. I even felt a little guilty.

This time, I was confident. I knew she could handle it like a pro. Her desire to get our lost boy strengthened her resolve, making her better at everything. But I was concerned about her chat with Jefe, just four days before. I hoped she looked different enough.

Catherine left the house in the Suburban. We followed in the ambulance and parked the rig about two blocks from Chateaubriand. We watched on two monitors.

Catherine parked in the second space of Chateaubriand's lot, our predetermined location. She got out and adjusted a mini-cam on the roof of the SUV, viewing the parking lot. She spoke softly, "Here we go."

Our view was chaotic as she swung her box purse. The second monitor showed the view from her Suburban. Catherine could view either with her cell phone screen.

She requested a booth far from Jefe's corner, her back to their tables. She placed her purse on the floor, the camera lens facing Jefe's corner. She strolled to a painting above Jefe's table. While studying the painting, she replaced the saltshaker. The new shaker would pour salt. And transmit voices.

She returned to her booth. The waiter asked, "Are you ready to place an order?"

"I'm waiting on my husband. He should be here soon."

A black Cadillac Escalade parked in one of four adjacent parking spots, marked reserved. Five men exited the SUV. They were uniformly broad-shouldered with charcoal suits, sunglasses and the paranoid manner common with body-guards. They walked inside.

I said, "The cowboys have been replaced by the Men in Black."

"Looks like a new crew," replied Javier.

"Good news."

They repeated the drill, walking the restaurant, entering the restrooms and scanning every table, glowering as if servers might suddenly transform into ninjas and pull samurai swords from the black-draped dessert cart, or diners with botox might morph into gangsters with Tommy Guns blazing.

Their paranoia was not entirely misplaced.

One walked out and made a call. Fifteen minutes later the Bentley limo was escorted by two SUVs. The driver opened the limo's rear door and El Jefe stepped out, dressed to kill. Four men escorted Jefe and four stayed outside.

He sat at the same table and motioned for a waitress. Through the saltshaker, we heard him order a bottle of French Bordeaux, Le Pin, 2003. Catherine heard through her earpiece.

She flagged her waiter urgently. "I'm so sorry to rush you but my husband texted that he's not feeling well. Could you bring a bottle of your French Bordeaux, Le Pin, 2003 to go?"

"Certainly. So you will not be dining today?"

"No, I'm so disappointed. But at least we can share a nice bottle of wine. Could you bring it immediately? I need to leave at once."

He quickly returned with the bottle and check. She muttered, "It's fifteen hundred bucks!" I was grateful for Dad's loan.

She went to the restroom, entering a stall. She injected a syringe into the cork while watching Jefe's table with her phone. When the area was clear of wait staff, she exited and rounded the corner toward his table.

She spoke in her husky voice, "Le Pin, 2003?" I held my breath as Jefe looked at her with interest. Had he recognized her?

He said, "*Si, señorita*. You're new here?"

"I've been here a few months but I usually serve on Mondays. I understand you're a regular." She removed the cork and poured a sip.

He picked up the glass, "Excellent. *Gracias*." He didn't seem suspicious.

She filled his glass. "*A votre santé*."

She left the bottle and walked to her booth. She left cash, picked up the purse and exited a side door.

She said, "I'm walking down the street. Be there in a minute."

She jumped in the ambulance and quickly changed into a paramedic jumpsuit and black Reeboks. Tucking her hair under a long brown wig, she covered most of her face with huge K-Mart shades. In seconds, she was transformed.

The purse-camera was gone so we listened quietly. We didn't know if Jefe had drunk any wine. They made small talk in Spanish, but Jefe remained silent.

A waitress asked, "¿Le Pin Bordeaux?" My heart lurched.

Suddenly there was a thud. "Jefe, are you okay? Jefe?" We heard a groan then chairs shuffling.

"He passed out! Get something to drink!"

"Bring water!"

The waitress said, "We'll call an ambulance."

"No! He just fainted. Don't call."

There was a painful moan. Someone said, "He's holding his chest! Call the paramedics!"

"Hurry!"

I exited the ambulance. I wore a casual business suit with mirrored sunglasses, Miami Vice style. I hurried to the Suburban parked at Chateaubriand then waited in the driver's seat.

Minutes later, I heard their sirens. The ambulance pulled to the curb. Javier, a camera hidden in his collar, ran from the driver's seat and threw the back doors open. He and Susan unloaded the stretcher and started for the door. Catherine stayed in the back of the rig.

I watched the action on my cell. The Jefe was on his back, groaning and clutching his chest. Bodyguards knelt, wiping his face with a wet cloth. Wait staff and the other guards stood nearby. Susan took a knee then placed her stethoscope over Jefe's heart.

Javier asked, "What happened?"

A bodyguard spoke, "He collapsed. He's gripping his chest like it's paining him. He's not saying nothing."

"He's probably having a heart attack," said Susan. "He could go into full-blown cardiac arrest."

Javier grimaced, "We gotta load and go. We need to get him to the hospital as soon as possible." They lifted him onto the stretcher, buckled him down and rushed into the parking lot.

A guard ran beside them. "I have to stay with him. I'll ride with you."

"There's no room," replied Javier.

The man barked, "It's not negotiable." His tone was intimidating.

Javier paused, stumped.

I spoke into Javier's ear bud, "It'll jeopardize his life. This rig's made for two paramedics and a patient."

Javier parroted my lines, "It'll jeopardize his life. This rig is built for two paramedics and a patient, no more."

The thug demanded, "I'm going."

I said, "I'd lose my paramedic license."

"I'd lose my license," copied Javier. "We can't transport you. Follow behind and run any red lights. We're going to County General. They have excellent cardiac care." They loaded him.

Javier said, "Give me your number and I'll call you with an update, in case we lose you in traffic."

"You won't lose us."

"Just in case."

The man wrote a number. Javier turned the ambulance around. The Bentley limo pulled behind.

I was parked beside the exit. Javier pulled to the street with the limo practically touching their bumper. The four-lane road was busy. I shifted the Suburban into reverse, my foot on the gas.

Javier began slowly backing up, leaning out the window and motioning for the limo to do the same.

As soon as the limo backed enough, Javier shifted gears and the ambulance lurched forward. I jammed the gas, reversing into the space between them. Javier turned on the sirens and lights, pulling into the stopped traffic.

The limo honked furiously. I killed the motor and pretended confusion, looking around. A man screamed, "Move! It's an emergency! Move, you idiot!"

I acted like the engine wouldn't crank. Others ran over, their snarling, screaming faces practically touching the window. "Move your car! Get out of the way!" Curses flew.

I shrugged my shoulders then slapped the steering wheel.

"Put it in neutral and we'll push!"

"Now! Hurry!" Several tried to open the doors but it was locked. Men leaned over the windshield, yelling chaotically, practically foaming at the mouth. I put it in neutral and they began pushing.

Another siren shrieked toward us. Perfect timing.

The real ambulance turned off the siren as it pulled into the parking lot. As the narcos pushed the Suburban into the parking space, the ambulance pulled forward, nose-to-nose with the limo. The ambulance and the limo driver honked in honking combat. The ambulance turned the siren back on. A thug stood in front of the rig.

The ambulance driver gesticulated madly then resorted to his nuclear option, the eardrum-shattering air horn.

The loudest won. The limo backed to the side. The ambulance drove past. The limo gunned forward, thrusting into traffic amid a flurry of honking horns. The SUVs followed.

Our ambulance had a two-minute head start. They were safely gone.

As I pulled out, I saw the real ambulance driver unloading their stretcher. The first ambulance and the patient would never be accounted for but weirder things happen daily in San Diego.

I drove out of the city, turned down an empty road with a long view in either direction and saw the ambulance parked in a field. I got out of the Suburban and opened the rear door of the ambulance.

Javier said, "I searched him. He's not carrying a transmitter or cell phone. They can't track us."

The Jefe lay on the gurney, still unconscious with an oxygen mask over his chubby face. He smelled like he'd used a half-gallon of cologne. Catherine had started an IV. He was connected to a cardiac monitor.

Seeing him made my blood boil. I remembered him laughing with his crony about "the crying mama becoming a widow." I wanted to choke the life out of him.

I took a deep breath, calming myself. "Let's give him one hundred milligrams of succinylcholine."

We usually paralyze patients for intubation, as it's much easier to insert a breathing tube if the patient isn't moving. Catherine injected the paralytic.

I said, "One milligram of flumazenil."

Jefe ingested midazolam in his Bordeaux. Flumazenil reversed the sedative, clearing his drug-induced trance.

In his preposterously overpriced wine, El Jefe also ingested a thumping dose of Imitrex, used to treat migraines. At high doses Imitrex causes esophageal spasm, creating excruciating chest pain. That wasn't reversed.

The flumazenil and the succinylcholine began to work. His muscles vibrated, the tiny shivers traveling like a breeze over water. The paralytic shut down his muscles so he couldn't move nor breathe on his own. Clarity returned to his frightened eyes as the sedative was completely reversed.

I played the role of Wayne Kitt, the sacrificial lamb slain for me. But, unlike Jesus, Wayne was far from sinless.

If we got out of this mess alive, I wanted Jefe to believe Wayne was his tormenter. I'd applied red facial lesions on the drive out of town. I wore a stringy wig and dental veneers, horribly full of the cavity creeps. That wholesome meth-head look.

I shouted, "My name is Wayne and I bring the pain!"

His eyes widened then froze in paralysis. He couldn't move but his cognition and other senses were unaltered. Locked in.

"You're about to die. You'll see hell soon. Tell the devil I'm coming for him."

The oxygen monitor still displayed normal levels. "You're going to burn for your sins. But first I'll bite off your nose." I opened my mouth and slowly moved toward his face. No way to know if he believed it since he was frozen iceberg solid.

After about two minutes, his oxygen saturations began to drop. We routinely give two drugs during intubation, a paralytic and a sedative, otherwise the procedure would be excruciating painful and panic-inducing. A metal tool crushes the tongue, stretches the lips beyond capacity and probes deeply into the throat. The sedative also prevents the mental torture of being paralyzed, unable to move or breathe.

Jefe had no sedative.

I pried his mouth open with a laryngoscope, hooking the blade over his tongue and compressing it flat. Visualized his vocal cords, two delicate silver strands. I watched the monitor, his oxygen slowly dropping. His mouth was cranked wide, like a fish on a hook.

Once his oxygen level was low enough that I was sure he was unconscious, I slid the endotracheal tube between his vocal cords. Inflated a balloon on the end of the tube to secure it inside his trachea then connected an oxygen bag.

I squeezed the bag, forcing air into his lungs. His oxygen levels climbed back to normal and he regained consciousness.

"We won't kill you yet," I hissed. "We'll keep you alive so the meat don't spoil."

After five minutes of psychological terror, Catherine injected a long acting anesthetic, sending him into a deep slumber.

Javier, Susan and I carefully lifted him from the gurney while Catherine cradled his head with one arm. The rear seats on the Suburban folded flat but we left one seat up so Catherine could sit beside his head and bag him. I closed the rear door and they left.

We planned to send him deeper than Dante ever went. Wayne's ghoulish return from the grave was about to wreak havoc.

My black medicine would turn Jefe's brain upside down and inside out, uncoiling his grey matter like Lucifer's snake. As Javier trained SEALs on combat interrogation, he had the dark tools to put Jefe below the ninth circle of Hell. We would manipulate his very soul.

Then, like deranged med students in an anatomy lab, we would literally dissect him alive.

CHAPTER TWENTY-SIX

I looted the ambulance, removing drugs and supplies then returned to the hospital. Sam, nicknamed Sambro, was still there, "How was it, Doc?"

"Awesome! The kids loved the ambulance. Tell your boss thanks!"

They'd eventually notice the missing drugs but I'd left enough for the ambulance to be functional. I'd be in serious trouble for stealing controlled meds. But that was the least of my worries.

I walked down the block, climbed into the rental car and headed to the farmhouse. When I arrived, I entered the barn and descended into the cellar. The giant subterranean room had only one entrance, a rickety stairway at one end.

The basement was dank and creepy. Mice scattered and flies buzzed angrily at our intrusion. Cobwebs loaded with fly carcasses veiled the ceiling. The stench of rodent urine permeated the air.

Catherine stood behind Jefe, bagging air into his lungs. She said, "He moved a little so I gave him more versed."

"Sounds good. He'll wake up soon and we'll kick off the party."

I took the oxygen bag from Catherine. She clicked several pictures of his face while he still looked asleep. She remarked, "He looks sort of peaceful."

"He won't be peaceful for long."

She left to print the photos, a key piece of misinformation. We planned to fake them out like David Copperfield.

Two powerful strobe lights hung a few feet above his face, inspired by the chaos of Karaoke Night. Javier secured stereo headphones to Jefe's ears, wrapping tape around his head. The drugs began to wear off. When he breathed on his own, I withdrew the tube and growled, "Yo, Jefe, welcome to the fiesta!"

Javier turned on the strobes, blindingly flickering in his face. He tried to turn away, but Catherine had immobilized his head with restraints used for neck injuries. He attempted to raise his hands but stopped short, his handcuffs clanging against the metal rails of the bed. He closed his eyes tightly, attempting to stop the visual onslaught. But it was hopeless. These strobes could penetrate a hippo's eyelids.

I wore loose fitting clothes since I weighed eighty pounds more than Wayne but we were about the same height. I'd treated lots of gangbangers and even more wannabes in the ER, so I could talk the gangsta talk. Like a schoolyard bully, my alter ego would mock Jefe, mercilessly ridiculing everything about him. Wayne was obviously an idiot, so the cruel insults would cut even deeper. We would destroy his pride, primarily through fear, the ultimate humiliation for a man used to striking terror in others.

Channeling Wayne's ghost, I said, "Señor Jefe the Hefty, you be needin' some music to go wit' da' disco lighting! Maybe a little mariachi? Cha-cha-cha, perhaps? A shimmy little salsa number? Just sit back and relax, I'm sure you'll enjoy our fine selection of melodies."

Javier hit play, cranking a continually replaying Black Flag punk anthem at a brain-boiling volume. Jefe jerked his legs, but solid bar leg irons connected to a heavy chain snaking through the bed frame, the chain locked to the barn's support beams.

"Pride-and-ego down" is a term used by the U.S. military to describe a remarkably effective technique to encourage cooperation. Interrogators attack the source's sense of personal worth through humiliation. The source will usually reveal information in an involuntary attempt to redeem his pride and justify his actions. The technique works particularly well on people with inflated egos and, voilà, Jefe fit the bill perfectly.

We were mocking him, not being lighthearted. Our expressions were menacing. There could be no doubt in his mind. We planned to hurt him. Badly.

After a few minutes, Javier killed the music so Jefe could hear. I said, "Yo, man. You like the tunes, huh? You clattering your legs like you be wantin' to dance. Want some more?"

"No!"

"I think you's just confused from the stressful day and stuff. You was sick as a bitch at the restaurant. I'd complain about the food!"

Javier interjected, "I bet the waiters don't wash their hands after they do their business."

"But you be dancing like America's Got Talent. Or Mexico's Got Talent. Anyway, we wanna see you bouncing like a jumping bean from Jalisco!"

Javier held his nose, "Damn, Jefe, you need to lay off the perfume."

"Yeah, he be smellin' like a grandma. But whatever, it's time to get this party *started!*"

Javier turned it back on and Jefe writhed and twitched. We left the barn. A video camera allowed us to watch him from the farmhouse.

Catherine had a final task for the evening. She put on her nursing scrubs. I clipped her stiches, returning her eyes to normal. She scrawled "Get Well Soon" in bright red marker on a large poster then attached the photos of Jefe, resting peacefully in the hospital bed.

Catherine and Susan took the poster and Jefe's clothes then headed to Saint Vincent's Hospital, on a mission to create a magician's illusion.

Javier and I returned to the cellar. I threw a breaker to halt the music and lights. I flipped another, activating multiple black lights. The black lights made our light-colored clothes glow eerily.

We stood on either side, saying nothing. His eyes darted back and forth. We slowly circled. I put my face close to his.

I softly rubbed his plump cheek then breathed heavily in his ear. He trembled, closing his eyes tightly.

Javier lifted an axe and held it above his head. We stood quietly. After minutes of silence, Jefe slowly opened his eyes.

He screamed.

We left, leaving the music and lights off. As I bolted the door at the top of the stairs, he cursed and screamed for help. We were priming him for the interrogation. Breaking him was the key to finding Blake.

He would talk, eventually.

When they returned, Catherine told us about her visit to the hospital. "Susan waited in the car and I went to the Intensive Care Unit. With fifty patients there, I had plenty of choices. I wandered around like I was window-shopping until I found a perfect Jefe impersonator, Hubert Chavez. He's in kidney failure, bloated like the Stay Puft Marshmallow Man. His entire face is distorted and his eyes are swollen shut. He's completely unrecognizable. He could be anyone.

"And he's a homeless alcoholic, constantly in and out of the hospital. He never has visitors, so he's ideal. He's on the vent but I'm sure he'll eventually pull through. He's survived more than nine lives.

"I've worked with his nurse a few times. She's a sweetheart. I told her a few of Hubie's friends had stopped by the ER, bringing his clothes and a get-well-soon poster to hang in his room. She seemed truly overjoyed to hear Hubie actually had any friends. She pulled his clothes from the bag and was like, 'Hubie has clean clothes? A suit? Look at these shoes, so fancy! Who knew?' She hung the poster at his bedside.

"Then I went to the ER so the caller ID would match and called Jefe's bodyguard. I introduced myself as the nurse who took care of Alfredo Rodriguez in the ER. The dork said they'd been waiting at County General for hours and no one knew anything about Mr. Rodriguez. Why was he at Saint Vincent's instead of County General? Why had no one called?

"I told him I didn't know, but maybe County General was full. I said Jefe had a heart attack and almost died in the ER. He was shocked back to life but was delirious. During a lucid moment, he requested an alias since he's a well-known businessman.

"I told the man to use his alias, Hubert Chavez, as none of the hospital employees know his real name. I said it was standard procedure for famous people, and it is. Alfredo AKA Hubert was placed in the ICU in critical condition. The ICU wouldn't allow visitors for a few days, since he's on a breathing machine. The dweeb said they were on their way and hung up in a huff."

I said, "Awesome. I hope that Hubert guy doesn't change much in the coming days. If he dies or gets better, the gig'll be up. Better that he stays just right."

She smiled, "Like Goldilocks, not too hot and not too cold!"

We concocted this byzantine charade since it was imperative for Jefe's men to believe, without a doubt, that he was actually in the hospital. We hoped his photos and clothes would convince them that Hubert was, indeed, El Jefe Alfredo.

Like Catherine said, his face was so distorted, he could be anyone with brown skin and black hair. If they remained deceived, they wouldn't investigate further. If they doubted, they might go into crisis mode, destroying evidence and searching for him. With minimal investigation, they could discover that Alfredo Rodriguez was never a patient.

If they had video or photos of our rig, they might be able to track the ambulance number. If they connected the dots and spoke with the emergency medical personnel, they could link his disappearance to me. Sambro and a few other paramedics knew I took the ambulance.

I hoped the deception would hold. If not, I fervently hoped our hideout was secure.

I walked to the barn and threw the breaker, firing up the strobe-lit ear-splitting shindig. Heard a faint scream from below.

Then we went to bed, leaving Jefe alone, listening to horrendous music while pondering past sins and a dark future.

CHAPTER
TWENTY-
SEVEN

At 9 a.m., I returned to the cellar with a vial of adenosine. Adenosine is used to convert irregular heart rhythms, but gives patients a horrendous feeling of doom and impending death. The sensation is universally hated.

I slowly injected the medicine, baring Wayne's nasty teeth. He began breathing rapidly as his eyes betrayed terror. *"¡Dios mio! ¡No!"* I left.

I felt a little guilty treating a human like that, but he'd ordered the murders of many, including mine. My conscience was soothed when I remembered the man beaten and placed in the furnace. With my own ears, I heard Jefe laughing about my brains being eaten by seagulls. He mocked Catherine's sorrow, cruelly deriding a mother losing her spouse and child.

The women did not participate for strategic reasons. He'd never know of their involvement, as he was unconscious when they put him in the basement.

As much as I detested him, we wouldn't use painful torture or waterboarding. Although Jefe deserved worse and my primitive urges wanted to throttle him, that was not who I was. None of us were willing to burn him, beat him or peel off his fingernails. Physical torture would make us no better than him.

Waterboarding can cause permanent brain damage or death. Information gained by waterboarding is notoriously unreliable, as a person under incredible duress will say anything to make the torture stop. Jefe might tell us Blake was in his house when Blake was actually dead. Or say Blake had been killed when he was actually alive and well in LA. He would tell us whatever he thought would make it stop.

We had one shot to retrieve Blake, so we needed actionable, concrete facts. Putting a gun to his head and demanding information would not work with a brilliant criminal like Jefe.

We needed him to be mentally exhausted and psychologically wounded before launching our questions. We couldn't let him know what we wanted until the last minute, so he wouldn't have time to invent answers. We would patiently break down his defenses through sleep deprivation, drugs and psychological stress.

We would freak him out like he'd never been freaked.

I became a witch doctor, treating him with dark medicine. With each little push of the syringe, I was able to manipulate his emotions and cognition: one minute anxious, the next drowsy, the next confused, the next terrified. The drugs muddled his thinking and made the illusions harder to comprehend; made them more believable. Just as a tranquilizer would kick in and he felt warm and comfortable, it would be reversed, his harsh reality slapping him across the face.

I injected him with narcotics then reversed them. Infused small doses of anesthetic, just enough to create delirium. Filled his IV with an epinephrine drip, to give him hours of the pleasant sensation of thirty caffeine pills. With every stunt, I used a different sorcerer's broth.

As several drugs had amnestic effects, we'd use those during his interrogation to ascertain if his story was consistent, as he'd have no memory of what was said before.

I slowly walked down the stairs, ready to turn up the fear volume. I wore a creepy clown mask and pointed a pistol loaded with a blank at the side of his head. I cracked the hammer.

Jefe clenched his quivering eyelids, his breathing erratic. After several minutes, I pulled the trigger, firing the blank with a deafening roar. Jefe screamed and then hyperventilated. I left him panting and sweating.

Javier killed a diamondback in his barn years before but kept the rattle. He crept into the basement and circled behind Jefe, unseen. Wearing a leather mask with viper slits for eyes and heavy gloves, I asked, "You know what a rattlesnake's venom does when them fangs sink into human meat?"

He didn't answer.

I cackled, "Me neither! But we's about to find out!"

I held up a writhing bag then dumped a squirming three-foot python on his chest. He screamed as it slithered around his neck then dropped onto the floor. Javier randomly shook the rattle.

Jefe began to weep. Every few minutes, I picked up the snake, returning it to Jefe's chest. By the end, he was sobbing in earnest.

We wore black executioner hoods and carried flaming torches. We placed firewood around him and a gasoline-soaked cloth over his nose. I poured water from a gasoline can onto the bed and firewood.

Javier said, "Don't worry, we won't let you die. Once your arms and legs have burned off, we'll put it out."

I laughed spitefully, "Yo, I wanna eat me some chargrilled Jefe!"

He screamed, "What do you want from me? Did the Zetas send you? Whatever they're paying, I'll pay double! Triple!"

We touched the torches to wadded-up newspaper around his bed. He flailed and screamed until the newspaper burned out harmlessly.

We randomly activated his headphones, the strobes and the black lights. We watched him on video; as soon as he started to doze we'd give him a new dose of supersonic, ear-bleeding punk rock. We'd purchased a recording of Halloween effects, so occasionally he got a blaring earful of screams, evil cackles or monstrous roars.

When I went to the pet shop, I selected the skinniest and ugliest rats. Then made them look worse with an electric beard trimmer. I descended into the cellar, carrying five rats in a cloth bag. I pushed a little dose of wacked-out into his IV then held up the filthy bag. "Yo, meet your amigos, the badass swamp rats. They ain't been fed in days and you they only food. They'll eat your soft parts first."

I bared my disgusting teeth, imitating a rat gnawing. I grabbed the feistiest, mangiest rat by the nape. I dangled it over his eyes as it squirmed and squeaked angrily.

The horror in his voice was more than I had heard so far. "Not rats. Anything but rats! Please, I beg you. I hate rats! No! I'll pay ten million dollars if you release me. Please!" He was absolutely, completely terrified.

"Quit yo' begging! That whiney shit be makin' me sick!"

I emptied the bag on the ground, their claws scratching the concrete floor. We placed water and food under his bed, so they'd return often. He shrieked for hours like we were pulling off his fingernails.

Exploiting phobias is a common interrogation tactic. The CIA used these irrational fears, famously placing harmless caterpillars on a senior Al Qaeda member known to have insect phobias. Jefe had revealed a phobia, supplying a powerful weapon for our arsenal.

None of our psychological torture would permanently damage him. Eventually, he'd realize the whole thing was a fabricated nightmare. But the more we could frighten and confuse him, the better. We wanted him terrified and desperate.

At midnight, our day's work was done. We left Jefe to his rats, pulsatile strobes and screeching rock and roll. We went to bed and slept soundly.

I dreamed about Blake, a happy dream.

The next morning, I awoke like a kid on Christmas morning, eager to discover the truth. I went to the barn and threw the breaker, giving Jefe a short respite from the cacophony before our final assault. We prepared for the ultimate mind-screw.

Javier and I entered the basement wearing scrubs and surgical masks. I pointed a spotlight in his face. Jefe awoke with a start then blinked rapidly, adjusting to the brightness. In his IV, I injected a hundred milligrams of haze and fifty of confusion.

Javier said, "My colleague here, Dr. Love, is a hopeless romantic."

I released his head so he could see us then lifted my surgical mask and smiled, displaying my horrid dentition and meth scabs. "Yo, true dat. And we know the way to your heart."

Javier turned off the lights so we were in complete darkness. I wondered if he'd really believe the scenario after all the false alarms. After prolonged silence, Jefe asked timidly, "The way to my heart?"

I screamed, "Right through your sternum!" I ripped the cord on a chainsaw, the motor roaring to life.

Javier fired the strobe lights. I waved the saw wildly under the strobes like a flickering horror movie, revving the motor full-bore as I brought it to his chest. He screamed shrilly and flailed as the saw hovered an inch from his chest. After he writhed for about a minute, I touched the chainless saw to his skin.

I killed the engine and cackled obnoxiously, "Just kidding ol' buddy, ol' pal. We's fancy surgeons, way mo' sophisticated than that!"

Javier turned off the strobes and returned the spotlight to his face then picked up rusty table scissors.

I gripped a scalpel and applied shaving cream to his chest and abdomen. "Jefe, we really is gonna do some surgery but we ain't using no saw."

"Well, maybe on his ribs."

"Yo, how much you think we'll get for his kidneys and heart? They be sayin' the black market's hella-good. We'll get mad stacks of Benjamins!"

Jefe whimpered, "Whatever you can get, I promise to pay more. Double! Please don't cut me. Please!" He seemed convinced, thanks to sleep deprivation and black medicine.

Javier said, "We won't sell your heart because Satan lives there. Wouldn't be fair to the person receiving it."

"But his kidneys ain't evil is they?"

"I guess not. Good point."

"Please, I beg you. Ten times what you can get!"

"Your begging be makin' me wanna hurl. Shut up 'fore I puke on your face. Yo, maybe we can sell his eyeballs. Whatchu think 'bout dat?"

Javier looked into his eyes. "Those'll fetch a good price. He has beautiful eyes."

I shaved the hair from his abdomen. He squirmed and the blade nicked his skin, a drop of blood running down his side.

I shouted, "Stop moving or we'll do it wit no anesthesia, beeotch!" He lay still and began to weep.

"Damn! Stop all that cryin'! You sound like a slapped hoe! We's about to put a little somethin'-somethin' inside. You know what this is, yo?" I held a three-inch metal cylinder to his face.

He whispered, "No."

"It's a lil' ol' freaky-ass remote control bomb with a tracking thingamabob. If your bitch ass double-crosses us... Kaboom!...Your stanky shit and guts'll be sprayed all over the dinner guests, poopie hanging from they fancy hair."

Javier mumbled, "Dude, that's gross."

"You'll slowly die and it'll hurt worser than a toothache. I've had a few of thems. Ain't no fun, believe me. One time I had this abscess in this tooth right here..."

Javier broke in, "Enough about your teeth."

I threw my hands up. "You wanna be in charge of this operation, Doctor Kildork?"

"No, but we haven't got all day."

"Patience, my dear. Anyway, as I was saying before I was so rudely interrupted, we's gonna insert it in your intetesta... whatchu call it?"

"Intestines."

"Yeah, thems. We'll stick it away from your heart and brains and all the important stuff. So it'll kill you, but not so fast, yo." I wiped betadine on his abdomen with a surgical sponge.

"Please! No. I'll do anything." He released a pitiful sob.

"I thought I done told you to shut up." I injected lidocaine multiple times, numbing the entire abdomen, his skin blanching.

Javier left to get supplies from the oven. He returned, quietly setting the warm pail on a stool next to me, out of Jefe's view.

I held a scalpel to Jefe's face. "This'll pain you some but if you move, I might accidentally cut something important, so I'd be still if I was you."

He whimpered.

"But, thankgodfully, I ain't you!" I sliced into his abdomen, but only skin deep. A thin white line fell open, exposing pink rapidly turning red. Padded the blood with gauze then dropped the bloody bandage on Jefe's nose. Sneaked my hand into the pail, soaking my glove in cow's blood.

"Can you clean up some of this mess? He's bleeding like a stuck pig! Oinkity-oink!"

I smeared warm blood on Jefe's face. He screamed.

"Now, now, precious. No reason for all that drama! It's just a flesh wound. Put on your big panties."

I held out my hand, "Scissor-wizzors, *por favor mi amigo.* Yo, check it out! I be speaking Mexican!"

Javier smacked the scissors into my palm. I pantomimed cutting his abdomen open. I pressed hard on his abdomen and massaged his entrails, pinching and kneading.

"Can you hold the hole open?"

Javier showed a surgical clamp to Jefe then pretended to pull the wound open. I stealthily pulled the warmed cow's intestines from the pail then dramatically lifted them from his belly. He screamed shrilly.

I spat, "I thought I told you to shut up! How can we shut this prissy thang up?"

"Stick his guts in his mouth."

"Word." I slopped a portion of the bloody intestines on his face, laying a loop across his closed mouth. "Don't chomp holes in that or you'll get all germified as stanky shit leaks from yo' guts."

The steaming viscera lay across his mouth. He pushed them out with his tongue.

"Yo, Alfredo Sauce, we want them guts to stay there so you'll zip it. Move them again and we'll leave you open then release the rats for some good eatin'! They's from the sewer so they'll feel right at home, since you's just a steamin' pile of shit."

I lay a loop over his mouth but he clenched his teeth tight.

"The doctor says, open wide!" I pulled up my mask and imitated a rat again.

Jefe finally complied, his mouth opening. I stuffed them in then poured a jumbo cup of blood onto his abdomen, dripping onto the floor.

"Damn, he's bleeding a lot! Wonder if I hit an artery."

"I hope he doesn't bleed to death."

"Lucifer lives in his heart, so he can't die unless we stab him with a crucifix."

"Interesting, I thought that was Dracula. Learn something new every day! Speaking of vampires, I'm starving."

"Me too! Let's grab some eats. I be hungrier than a hostage! Oopsie, no offense hostage…just kidding, mucho offense intended, dipshit."

Javier slapped me a bloody high five, spraying Jefe.

I whispered in Jefe's ear. "If your guts ain't in your mouth when we get back, you's a rat feast. That ain't a threat. It's a promise. My furry babies is hungry as we is. They just love chitlins."

We left for nearly an hour. When we returned, his jaw was strained wide, sweat running down his face.

"Good job, pretty. I knew you could do it." I patted his forehead. "Time to insert the little bomba. Say hello to your little friend!" I showed him the cylinder.

"Clamp, puhleez." Javier slapped a clamp in my hand. I dropped it on the floor with a clatter. "Damn, the gravity creeps got that."

"Should we clean it?"

"Hell naw! The floor's cleaner than the inside of this creevil dude."

I pushed on his abdomen for about fifteen minutes, asking Javier for a variety of surgical instruments. I mimicked suturing the bomb into place.

Javier asked, "What's that thing floating in there?"

"Hell if I know whatzit! Maybe his liver or gall-whatcham-callit? Whatchu think I is, a real doctor?"

"Should I get the surgery book?"

"Naw. Whatever it is, he probably don't need it." I threw a bloody wad of intestine against the ceiling. It stuck momentarily then dropped onto Jefe's blubbery chest.

"Sheeeiiit! Sorry about that *Señor* Jefe. Nobody be wanting they kidney layin' on they man boobs." I gingerly set the wad on his forehead.

"But anyway, time to return them noodles to the wormhole."

"His guts have slobber all over them."

"True dat. Has you been brushing yo' teeth? We don't want to put dirty guts back inside."

"Yes...No!"

"Which is it, yuck mouth?"

"Not since I've been here."

"Okay. Brush them teefes."

Javier squirted shaving cream into his mouth then shoved a surgical brush inside, jamming it around. "That should do it." He replaced the intestines back in Jefe's mouth.

I mimicked returning the guts into his belly then finally took the last loop from his mouth. I quietly deposited them into the pail. Closed the incision with loud pops from a skin stapler. His abdomen had a railroad track of staples from stem to stern.

"Well, congratulations! You're the proud pregnant mama of a little baby grenade!"

"We'll smoke cigars when you give birth!"

"Yo, I hear that childbirth is the most painful thing a person can endure. Let's crank some music! To celebrate the bundle of joy on the way!"

He clenched his eyes tightly when I started the manic punk. He was ready, ripe for the harvest.

They had taken a toll: effects, drugs, and rock and roll.

CHAPTER TWENTY-EIGHT

Blake didn't blame the woman for seeming sad when she looked at him. He felt sorry for himself and was strangely comforted knowing she did too, validating his self-pity. He felt like he would never smile again. Instead, he would probably spread grief to all, like a contagious disease.

Blake rode in the car with a Mexican family: the woman, her husband and their baby. Blake didn't like his short haircut and black color job, but he understood they were avoiding the bad guys.

The man said the border guards wouldn't be suspicious of a family, and they were crossing from Arizona because the criminals were in California. After entering Mexico, others would take Blake the rest of the way.

When they stopped at the border, Blake pretended to be asleep even though the baby cried bloody-murder, his mother frantically trying to stop the high-pitched wail. The guard waved them through quickly, probably to escape the nerve-shattering shriek. As they drove away, Blake plunged his fingers into his ears, jealous of the guard.

At a gas station, they saw two men standing by a truck, a freak with a busted face and a cowboy. When she saw the men, the woman seemed upset and whispered something to her husband.

He muttered, "¡Cállate, mujer! No es de tu incumbencia." *Be quiet, woman! It's none of your concern.*

She crossed her arms and looked away, mumbling under her breath.

The cowboy strolled up and smiled broadly at Blake. "Hello, *amigo!* I'm Gabriel, like the angel. What's your name?"

"Blake Stryker."

The cowboy spoke animatedly, his eyes dancing below his ten-gallon hat, "We have a long journey ahead but you'll like your home, a beautiful mansion beside the ocean."

"My home's in San Diego."

Undaunted, he continued, "They'll treat you like a little prince. You can have anything you want."

"What I want is to see my parents and Aunt Susan."

His smile faded. "I'm sorry."

"I'm more sorry."

"Do you like ice cream?"

Blake mumbled, "I'm not hungry."

"When you're hungry, we'll stop for ice cream, a triple scoop!"

Gabriel opened the rear door of a four-door pickup and motioned for Blake to get in. "You like video games?"

"Sometimes."

"Here you go." He smiled proudly and handed Blake a PlayStation.

The freak didn't talk to Blake. The man made Blake nervous because he seemed nervous, constantly searching for something or someone. From the back seat, Blake had ample time to study the creepola tattoo on the man's shaved scalp, a skull-faced Virgin Mary. His jaw was wired shut so he mumbled. His entire face was bruised and swollen, especially his eyes.

Blake's boredom and curiosity finally made him ask, "What happened to your face?"

The man grumbled, "I broke my jaw."

Gabriel laughed, "You mean a *gringo* broke it for you!"

The freak looked out the window, annoyed. Gabe looked at Blake in the rear view mirror and said, "Some guy tried to steal his semi truck. The thief jumped off and smashed his face with his boots."

Blake said, "I bet that hurt. I'm sorry that happened."

The man ignored him.

Blake asked timidly, "Did they catch him?"

"No. He got away," said Gabe. "But people are looking for him. He killed several men that night."

They traveled through the night, only stopping for gas and restroom breaks. The men drank beer, tossing empties out the window. The freak dribbled beer down his shirt because he couldn't open his mouth. Gabe laughed and asked if he needed a baby's bottle. The freak glared.

Blake didn't sleep well due to bumpy roads and their smelly cigarette smoke. He wondered about them. They didn't seem very police-like, especially the tattooed man.

When the sun came up, they stopped for breakfast at a café. The matronly waitress smiled and rubbed Blake's face like he was a baby, making him uncomfortable. She carried on about how handsome he was and piled a mountain of whipped cream on his Mexican chocolate pancakes. He eventually warmed up to her, since he missed being loved on by his mama.

His mood improved after a huge breakfast and the affectionate waitress. Walking to the truck, Blake noticed the model: a Lincoln Mark LT. Blake wondered if LT stood for Large Truck. He thought about his dad kidding Javier about his big truck, saying he was "compensating for something." He didn't exactly get the joke, but thinking about their laughter made him chuckle.

Gabriel grinned, "What's funny, *amigo*?"

"My dad's best friend drives a big truck like yours. They always laugh about it. His name is Javier and he speaks Spanish like you guys. You'd like him."

The tattooed freak exchanged a look with Gabriel.

Gabe continued, "I know a man named Javier who lives in San Diego. What's his last name?"

"Alcaraz. He's a Navy SEAL."

"Yeah, that's him! Where does he live?"

"He lives on Coronado Island, on the SEAL base. But he has another house in the country, in Alpine."

"He's a really nice guy."

Blake grinned excitedly. "How do you know Javier?"

"I have a cousin who lives in Alpine. I think they're neighbors. What street in Alpine?"

"I don't know. I might remember if you said it. It's in a little canyon on a stream. The name is something creek or stream, I think."

Gabriel searched the web with his phone. "It looks like there's only one street near Alpine with creek in the name. Is it Clear Creek Road?"

"Yeah, that's it!"

CHAPTER TWENTY-NINE

El Jefe hadn't eaten or drank since his sip of Bordeaux. After two sleepless nights listening to Black Flag in a nonstop nightmare, he was ready to talk.

I was shocked at some of the things he told us. During our first interrogation, I wore the leather mask with slits for eyes and Javier wore the clown mask. We began with a heavy dose of a powerful amnestic, to loosen his tongue and erase his memory of the interrogation. We fired questions rapidly, so he wouldn't have time to invent answers. We used every interrogation trick in the SEALs' black book.

We repeated the process while he was completely sober, albeit sleep deprived and severely rattled. We were able to compare answers. The third time, Jefe repeated his testimony in front of a video camera.

Either he was an amazing liar or told the truth. The tale was mind-boggling with international ramifications.

We returned to the farmhouse. Catherine and Susan looked at us expectantly. I said, "First of all, Jefe says Blake's alive and well in Mexico! And I believe him. He was so drugged up, he has to be telling the truth."

They hugged, tears of joy streaming down their beautiful faces. I smiled but felt a little uneasy since we were still a long way from getting him back. A long way.

After they recovered enough to listen, I said, "It'll make the most sense if I start from the beginning. This whole thing started when I surprised Behram at the Ripp's place in Mexico. He'd moved their TV to wire a camera. He knew their plans since he'd already placed surveillance equipment inside their San Diego home. He'd planned to kill them both in a fake robbery the day after we left. Since Tijuana is crime-infested, the police would think it was a random act of violence.

"When I confronted Behram, he initially tried to flee. But then decided to kill me since I could provide his description, once he eventually assassinated Mark."

"You should've let him go."

"You're right. But if I did, Beth would be dead."

She didn't respond but I knew she'd rather Beth Ripp be dead than Blake. And so did I.

"Since I'd seen him, his plan was ruined. Police would want to know why a guy was sneaking around inside their house, the day before a supposedly random home-invasion robbery. He assumed we would go home after leaving the Ripp's house, but we went to a hotel instead. He had my cell phone and I'd stuck a return address label on the back in case I lost it. So he knew where to go. He entered our house, planning to kill me."

Catherine said, "I don't get it. Seems like a lot of effort to erase one witness."

"He thought it'd be easy. He was going to make it look like a street crime."

"But why take Blake?"

"After Blake broke his arm, Behram wanted to kill him. He couldn't sit around and wait for us to come home since he was badly injured, so the kidnap was an improvised plan to kill both Blake and me. After Behram thought he'd killed me at the park, he assassinated Mark." I told them the details.

"But why? Mark was against all that military stuff in Mexico. Seems like the cartels would like him."

"There's more to it than that. As they say, hindsight is 20-20. Jefe's reasons for killing Mark make complete sense in the rear-view mirror." I told them. They were as surprised as I was.

"I didn't realize the fake policeman at our house was also the Mexican thief. In Mexico, I stood on a patio above him. He wore a Mexican get-up with a thick mustache and a cowboy hat. Then he stood behind me with his gun, so we never saw each other very well. At our house, I was disguised with a blonde wig and beard so neither of us recognized the other."

Catherine said, "We've got to get him! Somehow, some way!"

"I've already got an idea." I told them my plan. After I was done, I asked Catherine, "What do you think? It's risky and won't really help get Blake back."

"Count me in. I could never live with myself if we let him get away with all this. The Strykers strike back!"

"I agree. It's worth the risk, if nothing else, to prevent him from killing again."

Javier chimed in, "We not only own Jefe, but also the others. He told us how to download a video implicating the other conspirators in Ripp's assassination."

Susan asked, "Why'd he tell you about the video? Can we see it?"

"He didn't want to be the only fall guy if we released his confession," said Javier. "Plus he was so drugged up and freaked out, he was just spilling his guts. I'm about to upload the video of the confession and Jefe's recordings to encrypted cloud storage. We can watch while I upload."

The four of us gathered around and watched the recordings. Jefe had told the truth about his conspirators. We were completely flabbergasted.

We released his hands and gave him food. There was a hose for cleaning and drinking. He remained in rigid-bar leg irons connected to a heavy shipyard chain wrapped around a support beam, giving him a ten-foot radius to move.

We tore out the rickety wooden steps leading to the basement then used a ladder. Javier called me Wayne within earshot of Jefe.

The cellar was a dungeon with slab flooring, no windows, concrete walls and one metal trap door at the top of the stairs, dead bolted from the outside. He would be in the cellar for a long time. We knew how to restrain a prisoner.

We cleared the cellar of metal. We removed the hospital bed, leaving the mattress. We had a final conversation with Jefe.

Javier said, "Listen geek, you'll be here in the dungeon until it's clear you've told the truth. If you're double crossing us, we'll be back. We won't be nearly as nice next time. If you're leading us into a trap and we die, you'll stay here until the food runs out. We'll release twenty sewer rats. The rats will also run out of food in about ten days. If we don't return, you'll be their food.

"You'll want to be certain that we find the money and my friend's son. We'll release you when we return, keeping your videotaped confession for insurance. If something happens to us and we don't type the abort code, it'll be automatically emailed. We have to type the code every two weeks until we all die of old age."

"I understand. I've told the truth."

"For your sake, I hope so." I wanted to believe him, but had nagging doubts.

"What about the...explosive inside me?"

I was semi-surprised he fell for that, as it was kind of hokey. A patient's abdomen can't be cut open without causing excruciating pain, thus the need for general anesthesia. But he wasn't a medical professional. Unless selling drugs counts.

"It'll explode if the abort code isn't entered," said Javier. "When we return we'll enter the code and you can have it removed. If you remove it without the code, you'll kill everyone in the room."

"Yo, we got a video of you spilling yo guts and we'll spill them for reals if you be tricking."

The Harvard grad seemed to believe, the line of staples on his belly closing a real wound. He might realize how unlikely it was, once rested and able to think clearly. He was about to have plenty of time to sleep.

That and fret about rats.

There was one loose end to deal with before leaving for Mexico: Behram. It didn't further our goal of finding Blake but we couldn't allow Lucifer's spawn to roam freely in the world. I said, "Yo Alfred, we want a recording of that Behram cat to include with your confession. If you's crossing us, we want him to suffer like yo' punk-ass."

"It will be difficult. I don't know where he lives, what he does in his spare time, if he's married, *nada*. He doesn't use a cell phone and he usually travels by public transportation so we can't track him. My men have tried to tail him but he always slips. After our last attempt, he left me a message saying he'd disappear if we tried again. Now I leave him alone. Do you plan to kill him?"

"As it turns out, it's none of your business. If you'd rather, we'll get the music party going and invite some rats to dance on your face!"

"I contact him by calling a number, entering an access code and leaving a message."

We drove to St Vincent's. Catherine wore her nursing clothes. We waited in the rental car, watching the action through the lens in Catherine's scrub top.

There was a new nurse taking care of Hubert, but Catherine knew her. She asked if she could observe as she was considering working in the ICU. The nurse said she'd be delighted.

Catherine called the number, entered the access code then held a speaker to the mouthpiece, playing Jefe's recorded voice, "As you know, I'm at St Vincent's Hospital in the ICU under an alias, Hubert Chavez. Please come immediately. I have something to discuss." Caller ID would show the call came from the ICU.

We waited, hoping Behram would come.

The nurse said to Catherine, "I'm glad you're interested in the ICU but I'd never come in on a day off!"

"I know, right? I'm a dork. I'm just kicking around the idea. I'd like to bone up on my critical care skills."

"You look so different, I hardly recognize you." In this case, different meant worse.

"I donated my hair to charity, Locks of Love. They make wigs for children with cancer."

"You're a saint! I'll give to the parking lot Santa with the bell thingy but only because I feel guilty."

"I'm working on a blog about walking in other people's shoes. I'm pretending to be Hispanic. See, I have brown contacts!"

"*Señorita* Stryker! You're too much! If it weren't for your cute dimples, I wouldn't believe it was you."

"I caught mono and Wyatt prescribed prednisone. As a lovely side effect, my face blew up like a puffer fish!"

"Maybe he's trying to keep guys away from your hot self."

"I don't feel so hot but I'd rather be swollen than suffer mono. It's brutal! I've missed a lot of work."

"How's Doctor Wyatt?"

"We've both had a rough time recently. His best friend was diagnosed with terminal cancer. Wyatt went to Australia to see him."

"No wonder he gave you the puffy pills. He's keeping you honest while he's gone!"

They both laughed. They chatted until a buzzer sounded, "Mr. Chavez has a visitor."

"Okay. Send him in."

The nurse muttered conspiratorially, "It's so weird. I've had this patient for over a month, a homeless guy who's in the hospital more than not. No one ever visits him. A few days ago, he started getting a non-stop stream. They sit in the waiting room twenty-four hours a day! They almost seem like bodyguards, not homeless types. We had a cute poster with some pics of Hubert. His first visitor said Hubert wouldn't want his photos displayed. He removed the poster and took his clothes.

"All sorts of conspiracy theories are flying around, like he's under a witness protection program or something. Or maybe old Hubie won the lottery or inherited money so his family's come out of the woodwork. I've tried to pry but they're tight lipped. Strange people."

"Can I act like his primary nurse? To get the feel of it?"

"Sure, be my guest. I'm tired of dealing with those weirdos. I'll be here if you have questions."

Behram was escorted back. He wore a blazer over a silk shirt and wire-rimmed glasses, his hair neatly slicked back. His arm was in a cast.

Behind his back, the nurse raised her eyebrows comically. He politely asked, "May I see Hubert Chavez?"

Catherine smiled, "Of course. It's hospital policy that all visitors to the ICU wear protective gear before entering a room. I'll be right back."

She ducked into Hubert's room, putting on a mask and gloves. With her back turned, she removed a tiny canister from her pocket then sprinkled powder inside Behram's mask, gloves and surgical cap.

She exited and handed the gear to Behram. "We don't want to make him worse with our germs. His immune system's not working well."

She assisted by stretching a glove over his cast and tying the mask behind his head. He followed her into the room.

Monitors beeped monotonously. Hubert's chest heaved in response to the ventilator. His eyes were swollen shut, tubes protruding from his bloated, jaundiced face.

"May I talk with him privately?"

"I'm sorry but he's under heavy sedation since he's on the ventilator."

"I thought I'd be able to speak with him."

"He can't talk. He might be able to hear you if you want to wish him well."

"Is it possible to decrease the sedation?"

"I'll ask the other nurse. I'm in training."

They exited and Catherine asked, "This gentleman wants to speak with the patient. Could we lessen his sedation?"

"Not today. He's too unstable. If you leave your number, he can contact you once he's better. Or we can give him a message."

He paused then said, "Please tell him Jorge stopped by."

He removed his mask. Catherine held a biohazard bag at arm's length. He dropped the items in the plastic bag. She pulled the string taught.

He combed his fingers through jet-black hair then nodded courteously, "Thank you for your assistance." He strolled gracefully away.

The nurse made a silly face. "See, I told you! Why's ol' Hubie getting visitors like that? That guy looks like a fine art collector. Or maybe Mafia! He was dashing in a mysterious sort of way."

Catherine giggled. "There's always something going on around here."

When the nurse went to the restroom, Catherine quickly left the ICU. She took an employee elevator to the ER. In the locker room, she removed her scrubs and placed them in the bag then took a long shower. She put on new scrubs then exited though a back door, carrying the plastic biohazard bag. Behram would never escape, thanks to the TCDD powder.

Behram sat in his car, thinking. The meeting left him unsettled. The man looked nothing like Jefe. Certainly he was bloated beyond recognition, but Behram wasn't convinced. If he were so sick, how did he call? He sounded normal on the voice message.

He called the hospital and asked to speak with Hubert Chavez's nurse. When she answered, he said, "Hello, this is Jorge Gonzalez. I just visited Hubert and I believe I left my glasses."

"Oh no! I'll go look for them." A minute later, she returned to the phone, "I can't find them. The other nurse might've put them somewhere but she's gone. I'll keep an eye out for them. You can check back later. My name's Heather Swanson."

"What's the other nurse's name?"

"Her name's Catherine Stryker. She normally works in the ER."

With effort, he controlled his voice, "Do you have her cell number?"

"I don't, but you could call the ER. They probably have it."

"Thanks. I meant to inquire about Hubert's health. Do you think he'll be discharged soon?"

"I doubt it. He's been in the hospital for almost two months this time, but you probably know how often he's admitted. He has to stop drinking if he's going to live much longer. If he makes it out, you should really try to talk him into laying off the booze."

"I will. Thank you for your help. I was impressed with the top-notch care he's receiving. I'll call back to see if my glasses have turned up."

"Sounds good. Have a wonderful day!"

He called the ER but the secretary told him that she could not give out personal information. He asked when she would be working again, but the bitch refused to tell him.

He would find out. Catherine Stryker would soon regret her meddling.

CHAPTER
THIRTY

We prepared for the end game. Retrieving Blake would be as difficult as the most complex SEAL missions. We were done with San Diego, never to return. We'd humiliated one of the most ruthless criminals on the planet. He'd ordered a man burned alive for far-lesser offenses. We had a vicious wildcat by the tail.

Even if we killed him, once we attempted to free Blake, El Poder would hunt us down. We'd live in fear, until they killed us, one by one.

Admiral Landfair made Jefe sound mild-mannered but he was every bit as bloodthirsty as the other capos, just stealthier. I'd seen an article in the Mexican press: El Poder beheaded a crusading police chief and his entire family, including a child in diapers, and then delivered their heads to relatives. He would execute Blake without remorse.

Our capture was the only way to ensure Jefe's freedom, so he might be leading us into a trap. Even if they only captured one person, they'd employ torture, discovering the password to eliminate the uploaded video.

Deep down, I didn't really believe Blake was still alive. We heard him say Blake was gone, with the angels. What was more likely, he lied to his intelligence chief or he lied to us while chained in a basement? He was probably buying time by sending us on a complicated journey. I assumed he lied so we wouldn't kill him. Blake was a liability, kidnapped on a lark to lure me to my death.

But I had to find out.

We left Wayne's beer cans, the duffel bag and his pants, all covered in his prints. We made calls and sent multiple texts between Wayne's cell and Javier's, creating the illusion of collusion.

We pulled up the ladder and dead bolted the trap door hatch. We left enough food and water to keep him alive for a month. If we weren't finished in a month, then *we* were finished.

Late that afternoon, Javier left to button up his affairs in San Diego and we packed. After loading the car, Catherine and I strolled around the pond.

I was proud of our day's work. We had gotten a filmed confession from Jefe and had successfully tricked Behram, delivering a permanent, devastating gift.

As we returned toward the farmhouse, I froze. A man was lurking beside the house, gripping a pistol.

He hadn't noticed us. We were two hundred yards away.

I said, "Get down!"

We dropped flat in the tall grass. Catherine whispered, "Susan's inside the house!"

"So's my gun."

The man moved past the windows, peering inside. Another man crouched behind a tree with an automatic pointed at the door.

"We need to call Javier but I left my phone inside."

"Me too."

"Stay here. If they head this way, run into the woods." Catherine was a triathlete. They wouldn't catch her.

I crawled to get a better view and spotted three more men. They wore street clothes and appeared Hispanic. Not cops. We were up against at least five armed members of El Poder.

We had no weapons and killing a man with bare hands isn't easy. The television neck-twist trick never works, unless the victim is already incapacitated. I picked up an apple-sized rock as I crawled back to Catherine.

"We need to lure them away from the house to protect Susan. Stroll around the far side of the pond like you don't see them. I'll stay here. When they get to me, run. I'll ambush from behind."

She crawled down to the water's edge then stood with her back to the men, like she'd been sitting out of view. She calmly walked around the pond. One man saw her and got the attention of the others. Two narcos stealthily ran straight toward us. The sun was in their eyes, my advantage.

My heart sank as I realized three were staying behind. I'd hoped they would all chase her, so I could attack from the rear, take a gun and pick off a few as I retreated to the house.

But I'd be surrounded, men on both sides. Regardless, I had to divert attention from Catherine, allowing her escape.

As they neared, I flattened. When they were nearly to me, they abruptly took off running, passing on my right. Catherine was on the move.

Run, baby, run!

I sprinted after the closest thug, planning to club him in the back of the head with the rock. But a man at the house yelled a warning.

My prey heard the shouting and skidded to a stop. He began a turn.

I was still too far away. So I braced in a pitcher's stance and threw the rock. As soon as it left my hand, I raced the stone.

The rock arrived first, striking him in the mouth. His head flew back in a cloud of red and teeth, followed by the rest of his body.

Strike 'em Stryker strikes again.

A champion long jumper can clear twenty feet. I'd settle for ten. In a dead sprint, my boots left the earth, ten feet from the man's chest.

They landed six inches above the dirt, then, as ribs and sternum shattered, settled three inches. I pitched forward, ducking into a roll.

Gunfire erupted. The nearest thug was firing a semiautomatic pistol while running toward me. He was about thirty yards away. Handguns are inaccurate, indoor weapons, the average kill-range less than twelve feet.

But he'd be in range within seconds.

I flipped the dead man, searching for his gun. Frantically scanned the tall grass.

The man halved the distance, his bullets striking dangerously near. The others ran toward me. At a hundred yards, their AK-47s were still out of range. But not for long.

I bolted. The barn was on my right, between the farmhouse and the pond, but the men coming down were closer to the barn and would cut me off. A grove of trees stood on my left.

I ran away from the barn, toward the trees. They angled to meet me. The man behind continued to shoot, bullets whizzing past. The others were two hundred feet away but closing fast. I entered the grove on the far end, furthest from the barn.

I doubled back through the trees, moving toward the barn. Near the opposite end, I stopped and crouched. They hadn't seen me through the dense growth and raced toward the far end, the wrong end.

When the narco behind me entered the thicket, I sprinted, exiting the grove at full speed. The others yelled and switched direction.

Suckers.

They might be decent street soldiers but allowing my escape was totally amateur. A SEAL team would've spread out and prevented exit.

Gunfire chased but I was too far away. I entered the barn and deadlocked the door. The stout door had a steel core but an automatic rifle would blow the hinges in seconds.

The barn was sturdy and tight, pitch-black. I flipped on the lights and searched for a weapon. Tools hung on a pegboard.

The walls were decorated with rusty signs, ancient farm tools and vintage weapons. Considered an antique double-barreled shotgun but there were no shells. Doubted it functioned anyway.

The best option was a yard tool. He had a few axes, a mallet and machete. I lifted an axe.

Time to get medieval.

Jefe's muffled yells came through the thick basement door. He'd probably heard the gunshots and thought he was being rescued.

Footsteps announced the first man's arrival. I doubted he could hear Jefe through the thick walls.

Susan would've heard the gunfire. I wondered if she would hide or attempt to help. My pistol was hidden under my mattress but I wasn't sure she knew how to shoot. Better to call Javier and hide, both for her safety and ours. A hostage would be a game changer.

They were probably circling the barn, but there was just one entrance and no windows. I pulled a decrepit bear trap from the wall and lay it on the floor. Stomped on the corroded springs to pry them apart, but the rusty teeth barely opened.

I remembered Javier saying it required a special clamp to open. I placed the antique foot trap in a workbench vice and spun until the jaws fell open. Latched the trap open and set it on the floor near the door but couldn't find any camouflage. I hoped they wouldn't see it when they rushed in, as their eyes would be adjusting to the dark. It was bright out and I briefly wondered why they chose to attack during the day.

Human eyes take nearly a half hour to fully adapt from bright sunlight to complete darkness. In the first five seconds of adjustment, the pupils dilate, increasing the amount of light that reaches the retina. But the pupil doesn't really do much compared to the rods and cones of the retina. The rods are the dominant photoreceptors, detecting contrast. The cones provide color sensitivity. Over thirty minutes, the retina gets busy and the eye becomes up to one million times more sensitive.

The knob rattled then the metal door thumped as a man repeatedly threw his weight against it. The hinges began to separate from the wooden frame.

I opened the hatch to the basement and dropped the axe and the ladder onto the floor below, since we'd removed the stairs. When the metal clanged, Jefe stopped yelling. Probably didn't want to choose sides prematurely.

I grabbed a machete from the wall pegs. Through the separated hinges, I saw the largest man slam his shoulder into the door. The hinges almost broke free. I turned off the lights then quietly unlocked the door and turned the knob.

He took several steps back and got a running start. Right before he struck, I yanked the door open. He stumbled forward, off-balance and leaning sideways.

I slammed the door, clipping his legs. As I flipped the deadbolt, he tumbled into the bear trap, his hand landing on the trigger plate. The jaws snapped, crushing his arm and face. He couldn't scream; his mouth clamped by a hundred pounds per square inch of serrated metal teeth.

Gunfire erupted, denting the metal door. They backed up, hosing down the plank walls. I crouched behind the door. Javier's antique collection pinged and dropped from the wall under the onslaught.

I searched for the trapped man's pistol. Either it was knocked away into the darkness or was imbedded in the twisted wreckage of human flesh and rusted metal.

A narco did what the first should've done: shot the hinges. I ducked under the workbench, behind the door. He yelled for the others to hold their fire. He kicked the door down. It landed on the trapped man, blocking a clean entrance.

The man slowly came through, his AK scanning the dark room. He pushed the door with a leg and startled when he saw his *compadre* trapped like a mouse.

I used his momentary distraction to my advantage. I swung from under the workbench, chopping his patellar tendon below the kneecap. Probably got the lateral collateral and anterior cruciate ligaments also, based on what happened next.

The narco pulled the trigger and spun toward me but his leg folded sideways and backward. Not a normal, healthy movement. Not in the least bit.

As he fell, I swung a vicious uppercut, catching him squarely in the throat. Javier kept his tools sharp; the blade crunched through his cartilaginous larynx and then sliced the soft jugular veins and carotid arteries. I left the machete in his neck as he toppled onto his back.

The others fired through the doorway since the two corpses and the fallen door blocked their way. I scrambled on elbows and knees toward the basement trap door. Their eyes had just barely started adjusting, so the two thugs shot blindly into the dark. Bullets peppered the wall above me.

As they clambered inside, I grabbed the edge of the trap door and swung down into the basement, landing on my feet. Scooped up the axe then rushed into the dark.

The first man though the door chased me into the abyss, expecting a floor. He stepped into blackness and tumbled, careening facedown. Landed twelve feet later on the metal ladder with a clang and a painful grunt. His pistol clattered free.

I was thankful for the slow adjustment of human eyes.

I couldn't see him from where I stood. Gripping the axe like Paul Bunyan, I focused on his groans and moved closer. I finally saw him on his knees, struggling to stand, cradling a deformed wrist.

I've always enjoyed splitting wood. I had the technique down. Took three long strides then swung over my head. As the blade sunk, his skull burst like a dropped watermelon.

I saw the lone survivor's head silhouetted in the open hatch and quickly stepped away. Jefe remained silent.

I had to lure the man down. If he captured Susan or Catherine, it would be game over. Nor could I allow him to flee since more would return. They'd find Jefe and our plans would be destroyed.

I thought hard, wondering how I could entice him. Any sane man would leave or at least wait for backup, knowing I had a gun and plenty of hiding places.

An idea struck.

I ran to Jefe and whispered, "Be very quiet. There are many robbers here. Don't make a sound."

He nodded silently.

As I walked away, he began shouting in Spanish, "I am Alfredo Rodriquez, El Jefe de El Poder! Rescue me! I've been kidnapped!"

I grinned. That should do the trick.

I crept around the lit area below the trapdoor and swept with my foot, searching for the pistol. I was wide open.

The man peered down into the basement, his eyes slowly adjusting. The rods and cones of his retinae whirring like a tiny engine.

My shoe hit the pistol with a loud clatter. He jerked his machinegun straight at me.

But he didn't shoot. Probably worried he might accidently hit El Jefe.

I kicked the pistol into the dark as I ran away. I slowly picked up the gun, keeping my eyes on the man.

He jerked out of sight.

I walked back toward Jefe, glad to have a pistol. The farm tool weapons were giving me a Friday the Thirteenth complex.

Jefe was still yelling. I pressed the gun to his forehead and spat, "I thought I told you to be quiet, yo!" He fell silent.

"I'll let them take you. Ain't no way for us to win. We gots to escape."

He nodded.

I announced, "You can have Jefe. I'm leaving through a tunnel. If you come down before I'm gone, I'll kill you both!"

"How do I know it's him?"

Jefe shouted in Spanish, rattling off random words. I assumed they were some kind of code. He ended with, "Come now! That's an order!"

"Okay. I'm coming Jefe."

Jefe commanded, "Do not let me down!"

"Jump down in five minutes. Jefe will confirm I'm gone. There's a ladder down here so you can both climb out. I'll leave the keys to his restraints." I rattled my car keys and dropped them out of Jefe's reach.

The man would come. If he rescued Jefe, he'd be rich beyond belief. If he didn't, he'd die an excruciating death. Plus, he had a significant advantage: a machinegun versus my pistol.

I blindfolded Jefe with a torn sheet from his bed and whispered, "That's so you can't tell him where the tunnel is."

They both had to know it could be a trap. But Jefe had nothing to lose. And the other guy had no choice.

I moved the strobe light so it faced the man's landing zone. I tossed the sheet to the wall beside the light switch then stomped to a far corner. Removed my shoes then padded quietly back. I threw the sheet over my body, twenty feet behind Jefe. To shoot me, he'd have to shoot directly toward Jefe.

After several minutes, Jefe called, "He's gone. Come, *mi amigo*."

"Are you sure?"

"Yes! Come for me! You'll be rewarded generously." Jefe wasn't sure, but he knew the disposable man was his only hope.

The narco dropped down, sweeping the vast room with his machinegun. By now, his eyes had mostly adjusted to the dark. He was fifty feet away, forty feet outside the average kill-range for a pistol. I had to kill him on the first shot. If he were just wounded, he'd spray me with his entire magazine.

"Over here, *mi amigo*," beckoned Jefe.

The man turned toward Jefe and walked cautiously. When he was close enough, I hit the switch and the strobes fired, flashing into his face.

Like a deer caught in the headlights, he stared. A moment too late, he recognized the trap. He quickly looked away but his pupils had already constricted down to pinholes, ruining his vision. His retinal engines kicked into overdrive, throwing a rod. Actually, throwing several million rods.

He began firing wildly, hosing down the cellar walls, everywhere except toward Jefe. Except toward me.

Slowly and carefully, I took aim at his blinking torso, holding steady with both hands. Then popped off five shots.

He convulsed and the AK dropped from his hands.

I strode over, finishing him with a shot to the dome.

Jefe groaned.

I exited the barn with his AK-47, searching the yard and the house. Convinced there were no more bad guys, I yelled, "All clear! Safe to come out!"

Catherine and Susan crept from the forest behind the house. Once they saw I was alone and not being forced to yell, they ran.

As we embraced, Catherine said, "I ran to the house when they entered the barn. Susan called Javier. He'll be here soon. I couldn't find your pistol so we hid."

I smiled, "You did the right thing."

I called Javier and briefly told him what'd happened. I asked, "How'd they find us?"

"Probably got my name from the cops after the Magnum Lounge shootout. A dark SUV passed as I was pulling out of the driveway, so they probably saw me. I can't believe I didn't notice a tail. I was so careful. No way I would've missed someone following me from Coronado all the way to the farmhouse."

"Maybe they slowly pieced it together by following you part way, then waiting."

"Yeah. Or they could've used multiple cars to follow me, switching off."

"We'll check their phones. Maybe they didn't call for backup. If they knew Jefe was here, they would've sent a lot more men. I think this was about revenge for Magnum Lounge, not Jefe."

When Javier arrived, we started in the basement. When he saw the guy with an axe lying next to his partially missing head, he chuckled then whispered so Jefe couldn't hear, "I thought Wyatt Earp was a gunslinger, not an axe-murderer."

"I prefer think of myself an axe-self-defender."

"We threatened Jefe with that same axe. Watch this." He dragged the body over then removed Jefe's blindfold. Javier brandished the axe covered with bloody hair. Jefe stared at the man's half-head and the brains on his shirt.

Javier swung the axe at Jefe's head but stopped short. Jefe flinched and screamed.

"What a fraidy cat! Yo, the others look even worser."

Javier added, "Now you know we ain't playing. If we don't find the kid, you get the axe, but we'll start with your feet."

Jefe mumbled, "I understand."

We searched the men, finding two cell phones. Neither had been used in hours. We found their Escalade hidden on a side road. There were three more phones in the SUV but they hadn't been used recently. We sent texts to their recent contacts saying they were following their target into Mexico.

We placed the bodies inside the Cadillac. I drove to the edge of the muddy pond. Rolled down the windows and gunned it. The Escalade slowly sank.

I held the gas down, bouncing along the bottom. Once I was thirty feet deep, I swam out the open window.

Javier left, driving to a truck stop near the border. He eavesdropped on truckers until he found one pulling an all-nighter, headed to Mexico City. He sent a few more texts from their phones then placed them in a plastic bag. He wedged the bag inside the semi's bumper. GPS tracking would follow them on a long journey south.

CHAPTER THIRTY-ONE

Blake was sick of the smelly cigarette smoke, the bumpy roads and the Large Truck. They had been driving for nearly three days.

He wondered how the men had been able to stay awake. He decided it had something to do with whatever they kept snorting. Immediately after snorting, they became loud and animated, bright-eyed and bushy-tailed.

The men obviously assumed Blake couldn't speak Spanish and he never corrected them. But the more he heard, the less he understood.

Gabriel the cowboy did most of the talking. The tattooed freak's jaw was wired shut and speaking appeared difficult.

Gabe asked about their friends who were injured in "the Magnum Lounge incident." Tattoo said three of them, including Tattoo, had come to Mexico for surgery. He said they were staying out of the U.S. until everything blew over.

Tattoo asked about the boss. Gabriel said he was in the hospital after a heart attack.

They talked about money, guns, soccer and women. They cursed a lot. Blake knew those words from his friend Santiago. They called women *putas*. Blake didn't think that was very nice.

As the days wore on, they appeared increasingly sloppy, chaotic. One would talk rapidly while the other stared blankly. Sometimes they laughed uncontrollably. At others, they argued furiously. Occasionally their conversations didn't even make sense.

After one argument, they pulled over and took turns shooting at their empty beer bottles with revolvers. Tattoo's gun was made of gold. Blake wondered how much it cost.

Gabriel won the contest but Tattoo said it was because one of his eyes was swollen shut.

Gabriel asked Blake, "You want to shoot, *amigo*?"

Blake felt butterflies, or maybe moths, since their guns looked much more powerful than the .22 he'd shot with his dad. Trying to appear confident, he said, "I've shot a gun a bunch of times."

Gabriel, his breath smelling of stale beer and yesterday's food, stood behind, holding Blake's hands to steady the pistol. When Blake pulled the trigger, the gun slammed his palm, hurting. The noise nearly rendered him deaf, his ears ringing loudly.

But he wasn't about to show weakness. After a few shots, Gabe let him shoot by himself. He held the gun shakily and pulled the trigger with a bang, missing wildly as the gun nearly flew from his hand.

He took a deep breath and steadied the gun, hitting the bottle on his second shot.

Gabe cheered and threw his cowboy hat high in the air. He poured brown liquid in a small glass. *"¡Bueno amigo!* Boys grow up fast in Mexico. Drink."

Blake sipped nervously. It tasted horrible.

"One big swallow, like this." Gabe tossed it back. He filled the shot glass to the brim then handed it to Blake.

Blake didn't like the idea of drinking after him since his breath smelled so bad. Nor did he want to drink the nasty crap. But he did, bottoms up.

The tequila scalded his throat like boiling water. Tears sprang in his eyes. He broke into an uncontrollable coughing spell and flung the glass like it had stung his hand.

Both men laughed. Gabe put his cowboy hat on Blake's head.

Blake smiled weakly.

They hit the road again. Blake felt pleasant, warm. He decided those guys were pretty cool after all. He felt relaxed but noticed he was much worse at PlayStation. He tried to read a comic book but the story was blurry and confusing.

Gabriel was driving. Sometimes he drove excruciatingly slow. Other times, especially after snorting whatever, he drove like a redneck. That's what his dad called people who drove like Gabe, tailgating and passing around corners. Blake didn't care, since he was comfortably numb. He decided Gabe was a Rednexican. He smiled at the new word he'd created.

As darkness fell, Blake attempted to sleep with intermittent success, his warm comfort replaced by sweaty nausea. He eventually drifted off.

Blake awoke to loud voices and sat up. Gabe was looking in his rear view mirror at a vehicle trailing them on the dirt road.

Tattoo held a hunting knife under Gabriel's nose, powder on the business end. Gabriel sniffed then jolted, like he'd been electrocuted. He started talking louder and more rapidly.

They seemed nervous and kept mentioning Los Zetas. Blake wondered if they were talking about a fraternity.

Gabe slowed and the headlights got closer.

Blake asked, "What's happening?"

Gabriel shouted, nearly a scream, "Many banditos on this road! Robbers are following us!"

Blake wondered why Gabe was shouting. He seemed agitated, the bright-eyes replaced by flickering forty-watt bulbs. His bushy-tail bristled.

Blake rotated in the seat and saw only the bandits' glowing headlights and the ground in front illuminated, a moving half-acre, brightly lit.

When he turned back, he was surprised to be nose-to-nose with Tattoo, sweat dripping from his bruised scowl, a soggy, mottled collage.

Tattoo climbed over the seat, landing next to Blake. He reached under the seat and pulled out an automatic. Jammed a curved magazine in the slot.

Blake felt fear creep up the little hairs on the back of his neck.

He wasn't sure who frightened him more, the bandits or the increasingly crazed men in the Large Truck.

Tattoo rolled down the window, the swirl of dust stinging Blake's eyes. Tattoo leaned out and threw the gun in the back, then climbed out the window into the truck bed.

Blake turned and saw him crawling toward the tailgate. The glowing half-acre chased, slowly gaining on them.

Gabriel suddenly screamed, "Get down! Get on the floor, *you little shit!*"

Blake startled then dropped to the floor. His flight or fight instincts kicked in.

Blake saw Tattoo's gold plated revolver under the seat.

Gabe slowed until the bandits' headlights filled the cab. Blake heard the tailgate drop, immediately followed by a barrage of machinegun fire. It lasted forever.

Blake covered his ears, icy fear controlling him.

Gabriel slammed on the brakes and jumped out with his pistol drawn. Blake heard shouting and cattle bleating.

He suddenly felt like he was going to vomit. He threw the door open and leaned out, puking. He stepped out and continued to hurl, his hands on his knees.

He didn't want to look. But he did.

He saw an old man cowering beside a cattle truck. Steam billowed from the hood, the windshield obliterated. The kneeling man pled, his gnarled, arthritic hands trembling above his frayed cowboy hat.

Gabriel, like the angel, shot the elderly man in the face.

Shards of his thin scull flew back and the man toppled. His straw hat fell off, exposing his balding scalp.

Something shifted in Blake. As soon as he resigned himself to the futility of the situation, he realized he had nothing to lose. He no longer felt helpless, action replacing fear.

Tattoo and Gabe slowly walked around the cattle truck with their guns trained, their backs to Blake.

Blake became forward movement. He reached under the seat and wrapped his little fingers around Tattoo's pistol. He quietly ran into the brush, away from the road, keeping his head low as he disappeared into the night.

We had to leave immediately, since our hideout was compromised. I'd planned to attend Senator Ripp's funeral the following day. I told Beth I would go and felt bad about missing it. But going was out of the question. She would understand, eventually.

Javier and I had concluded there was nothing we could do about Jefe. We had no place to move him and neither of us was willing to execute a prisoner. We could only hope that everyone who knew about the farmhouse was dead.

But our new situation added time pressure. The texts could only fool them for so long. With every man from the raid missing, El Poder would eventually become suspicious.

The women stocked up on supplies then met us at the dock to load our whitewashed sailboat, christened Ketchum Alive, after Catherine's hometown of Ketchum, Idaho. The 60-footer, purchased with false identification and Dad's loan, had a powerful outboard motor and four cabins below deck.

The four of us pulled into the San Diego Bay then sailed around Coronado. We would spend the night a few miles from Coronado, our last night in the U.S. for a long time, maybe ever.

From the deck, I called my father's friend, Jim. I asked him to have Dad call from Jim's phone. Thirty minutes later, my phone rang.

"Wyatt, it's your father."

"Dad, we're okay, but my family has gone into hiding. I'll tell you the entire story soon but it's best you don't know, for your own safety."

"Did you pay off your debt?"

"I'm debt free. I'll send an email soon. Write this down." I gave him an encrypted email address. "Check this at least once a week. We're safe and have done nothing wrong. I hate not telling you the story but you'll understand soon. For everyone's safety, please don't tell anyone, including mom or Jim. Can you promise that?"

"You have my word."

"You may hear that we were killed, but that's part of our deception. If anyone asks about me, say you know nothing. It's imperative, even if it's the FBI. Can you promise?"

"Yes. I promise."

"I love you, Dad. You're my hero."

When he finally answered, his voice cracked, "I love you, too."

"Don't worry about us."

"Can't promise that."

"We'll be fine. It might be a few weeks, but you'll hear from me. Give mom a kiss."

"Same to Catherine..." His voice choked off.

I ached as I imagined my stoic father strangled by emotion. After an excruciating pause, he composed himself enough to stammer, "Give the little slugger a hug from Grandpa and Grandma."

"I will." I hung up, my eyes stinging, brimming.

I crushed the phone underfoot then kicked the fragments into the black water.

Before dawn, we pushed the inflatable Zodiac from the sailboat. It floated through surface fog then landed on the water with a hollow slap.

We boarded and headed toward the beach. The raft quietly bounced over dark swell, intermittently swallowed by dank fog, the ghost whales ingesting and then wetly regurgitating us like Jonah. Our uncertain mission loomed ahead: Godforsaken Ninevah.

Two hundred yards from shore Javier dropped into the chilly water and swam, lugging a dry bag. We were about to steal a grip of incredibly expensive gear from the Navy.

Or go to jail. For a long time.

On shore, he dried off and changed into his uniform. I saw the seaweed littered beach through the lens on his shirt. He inserted an ear bud.

The lowest stars began to decay as the morning sun crawled above the horizon. A truck pulled up and his soldiers congregated on the beach, ready for the training day.

He nonchalantly strolled up, "Good morning gentlemen. The only easy day was yesterday."

Several laughed as others shouted the battle cry of the SEALs, "Hooyah!"

"Where've you been, Commander? We've been missing you!"

"You didn't hear? I've been in the hospital with a ruptured appendix. But don't worry, I'm back and ready to beat you guys into submission."

"Good luck with that, geezer!"

"What happened to your hair, baldy?"

"I had chemotherapy for my appy."

Confused silence hung until a soldier spoke hesitantly, "I thought chemo was for cancer."

"That's what you get for thinking. Okay, did you wimps get everything we need? Firepower?"

"M4 automatics with under-barrel grenade launchers and an RPG launcher with three rockets."

"Explosives?"

"Got a case of C-4, blasting caps, timers and remotes."

"Grenades?"

"Every flavor. Smoke grenades, hand grenades, flash-bang grenades and impact grenades."

A joker launched into a dead ringer imitation from Forrest Gump, "Dey's uh, shrimp-kabobs, shrimp salad, shrimp stew, shrimp burger, coconut shrimp, shrimp sandwich. That... that's about it."

"Did you get the drones?"

"Got 'em. We're stoked to give those a whirl."

Another interjected, "What sort of drones?"

"Hold your horses, cowboy," Javier said. "We'll go over everything in detail later. What else?"

"Kevlar vests, diving equipment, a few hand held underwater propulsion units and the super-duper goggles."

"Good. We have a slight change of plans. I have to meet with Admiral Landfair this morning. We'll have our fun this afternoon. Sorry about that, but when the Admiral comes a calling…you know how it is. Let's meet in classroom C at thirteen hundred."

"Should someone guard the truck?"

"I want the entire team at the meeting. I'll call a grunt after inventorying the gear. I might drive to the depot to add a few toys. You sissies grab some grub and plenty of coffee. You'll need it."

A soldier tossed him the keys then they left. Javier said, "Coast is clear."

I pulled the Zodiac ashore. He backed the truck to the water's edge. We loaded the equipment into the raft. I wore SEAL issued exercise clothes, black shorts and a brown T-shirt.

As I placed the crate of plastic explosives in the Zodiac, a group of SEALs jogged along the beach, headed our way. I said, "We've got company."

"Quick, throw that stuff back inside!"

I lifted the crate of C-4 and the rocket propelled grenade launcher but didn't have time to move the rest. The ten SEALs approached then veered around the truck. Javier shouted, "Hooyah!"

The group responded in kind then kept going but the leader stayed behind. After greeting Javier, he asked, "What're you doing?"

"My team's training today."

"You got that Zodiac loaded down."

"Just seeing how much we could fit."

"Looks like too much. The weight limits are written plain as day on the side. Not much room for your men."

"They're bringing more rafts."

"Why are you two unloading the truck? Where are your grunts?"

"We need the exercise."

The man had a confused look on his face. Or was it a skeptical look? Concerned? If he pried much further, he could discover that I wasn't an active SEAL.

Finally, he said, "Have a good one. Hooyah!"

As soon as he was out of earshot, I asked, "Think he bought it?"

"Who knows? Lets hurry!"

We finished loading then I pulled the raft offshore. He moved the truck, hiding it in an alley. He locked it, keeping the keys. He swam to the raft and we headed to the sailboat, two miles out.

We loaded the gear and the Zodiac onto the sailboat then headed away from land, veering south. I asked, "What happens if the military finds out you did this?"

"They'll find out. For sure. The military investigates the hell out of any weapons theft. They'll leave no stone unturned. They'll be seriously spooked, thinking I'm selling to criminals or terrorists. Assuming they never catch me, I'll probably be convicted in absentia. But we'll be off the coast of Mexico before anyone discovers it."

CHAPTER THIRTY-TWO

Past Tijuana, the terrain became desolate and inhospitable. The rugged Mexican peninsula of Baja California is a mountain-ridged desert, separating the wild Pacific Ocean from the sheltered Sea of Cortez. Over eighty percent of the harsh Pacific coast is uninhabited, the bulk of Baja tourism existing on the protected Sea of Cortez, between Baja and mainland Mexico.

The outside coast is rugged and rocky with only a few isolated ports with very few people living between. Like a cactus apple, the tough dry husk was protecting the succulent fruit: the sparkling waters of the Sea of Cortez, the Baja of tourist brochures.

We busied ourselves with chores and reading, retreating into our skulls, not the healthiest place to reside. Very few words were spoken, the atmosphere glum and vaguely morose.

Catherine seemed lost, except when she had the wheel. She was an excellent navigator, a skill she'd inherited from her parents. She'd spent summers as a raft guide and could read water like a pro.

The prevailing northern winds and seas pushed us rapidly south, the wind at our backs. We saw several grey whale pods, as we trespassed on their breeding grounds. We avoided the shore. We took shifts, sailing night and day. Javier and I spent much of our time planning our mission.

In the only bright spot, I noticed Javier and Susan exchanging smiles often. They spent a lot of time playing cards and talking.

After significant trauma, survivors often develop deep emotional bonds. If they were falling for each other, I hoped it would be a normal courtship, not a fast paced torrent of disaster-induced infatuation. I felt protective of them both. Susan was family and Javier was my best friend.

On a moonless night, Catherine and I lay on the deck. I asked, "Do you think Javier and Susan are more than friends?"

"I've wondered. They seem to really enjoy one another's company."

"What do you think about it?"

"I'd be happy for them. Javier's an amazing person."

"Yeah. He's the best guy I know. But after what we've been though, none of us are exactly rational. I don't want them to get hurt or rush into something."

"They're grown ups. What happens, happens."

"We're all in this together for awhile. I don't want bad feelings if they fall in love then break up."

"Me, neither. But what are we gonna do, discourage their friendship?"

"True. I guess it'll play out. I suppose a fling isn't the worst that could happen. But I'd rather they stay friends than have the drama of a stress-induced obsession that ends poorly."

"Don't worry about it. Love's a good thing."

She went to bed, leaving me alone. I was slightly surprised at her openness. I thought she might want to shield her little sis from potential heartbreak. But I knew she was right. Love is a good thing.

As I looked at the moonlit horizon I thought about my biggest failure: Zo's demise. Javier and I planned the mission and his bizarre death haunted us both.

There's a difference between covert and clandestine. Clandestine missions are generally conducted with diplomatic approval, or at least not outright disapproval. But if something gets in the press, the nation claims to be transgressed and angry at the U.S. True covert missions are conducted in sovereign nations without the knowledge of their government; the U.S. government denies any association. Operators use equipment non-attributable to the U.S.

The CIA and the SEALs often work in concert to carry out covert missions. The controversial cooperation between the military and the CIA became commonplace after September 11. Before, the SEALs were under direct command of the Navy, and all military actions had to be approved through that chain of command. After 9-11, SEALs often worked with the CIA ground branch and, in certain circumstances, were under the direct leadership of the CIA.

In our only true covert operation, we lost Zo.

Alonzo, nicknamed Zo, was one of my favorites, the jokester of our team. He was a barroom magician and taught me the fire-breathing trick that saved my life in the alleyway.

He and his gregarious wife were from Mississippi and had colorful, Southern personalities. They lived on base, so we were all close friends. I often carried his son on my shoulders, his gleeful laugh contagious.

The CIA wanted an Iranian nuclear scientist dead. They felt killing the scientist would set Iran back at least three years in their pursuit of the bomb so they declared him an enemy combatant. The CIA provided intel on the scientist and outlined our goals: kill the man and escape with no evidence of U.S. involvement. The U.S. would deny involvement, no matter what. We planned to block the scientist's car with a truck then have men on motorcycles place a magnetic bomb on his car.

Zo and Javier were the best motorcyclists on our team. Javier's brown skin would blend in with the Iranians but Zo was African-American and had very dark skin. We weren't sure it was wise to have him on a covert mission in a country where there were so few black people. But we also knew he was the best man on our team for the job. And Zo really wanted to do it.

Javier and I discussed it at length. It felt vaguely racist to deny him the mission based on his skin color. We decided Zo could wear motorcycle leathers and a helmet shield.

When date arrived, it was a blistering day. Most motorcyclists in Tehran were riding in T-shirts since it was hotter than the King of Hell in pantyhose. We made a last minute decision to dress as locals, thinking black skin would be less conspicuous than full leathers.

I was in the truck that blocked the car, along with four others. Two were white, the rest Hispanic. The Caucasians dyed our hair black and applied skin dye.

Javier and Zo planted the bombs and raced away. The explosives were triggered, killing the scientist.

Those of us in the truck walked away in the chaotic aftermath, blending into the crowds. A few blocks away, a taxi driven by a SEAL picked us up. Javier and Zo were to reconvene several miles from the scene.

The Iranian government radio quickly broadcast that the scientist, a national hero, was slain by foreigners on motorcycles and one of the assassins had black skin. As Zo raced away, people yelled and pointed. Cars swerved toward him; bystanders threw rocks and bottles. Javier and Zo were separated in the confusion.

A car nailed Zo, knocking him over. He was stripped, beaten and killed by a mob. His body was paraded in the streets and shown on national television. The U.S. government denied involvement.

Javier and I were instructed to tell his widow he died in Kuwait during a training exercise. She and her young children would never know his final, heroic actions.

She knew we were lying. The hurt in her eyes told me. It was last time I ever saw her.

I stood abruptly and walked the deck, to shake the bleak thoughts loose. A chain of peaks in the distance crowned Baja's west coast. Detached mountains and hills backed the coast, dotted with numerous islands. The area was parched, fresh water limited to a few small springs forming oases and small creeks.

Javier walked up. I gestured toward the mountain range, "That's the Sierra de San Pedro Mártir."

"Yeah, the mountains of Saint Peter the Martyr."

"I was just thinking about Zo. He was a martyr."

"Yeah, I guess he died for what he believed."

"He taught me that flame-throwing stunt I used in the alley."

"He was one of a kind. Remember when he blew flames like ten feet? In that tourist bar in Munich?"

I chuckled, "Yeah, the Hofbräuhaus. That freaked the hell out of those uptight Germans!"

"And Zo was wearing that goofy Bavarian hat from the gift shop! I couldn't stop laughing, even as they were tossing us out." His smile faded as he continued, "I really miss that guy. I still feel sorta responsible."

"Me too. But we did our best. We tried to keep our team safe."

"Yeah, all we can do is learn from our failures."

"But we can't fail this time. Blake's life hangs in the balance."

"We won't."

I hoped he was right.

Behram studied himself in the mirror. Painful boils had erupted on his forehead and around his mouth. The pustules began shortly after his visit to see Jefe in the hospital. Didn't seem like a coincidence.

When he discovered Catherine Stryker was playing games, he deduced Jefe was kidnapped from the restaurant. They had to control Jefe to get the access code to call Behram.

Behram had Wyatt Stryker's cell phone, the log showing multiple calls to Javier Alcaraz. On the day he'd killed Dr. Stryker on the park bench, a man left a message: "Yo Doctor J, this be Wayne Kitt. Javier's my homie and we got plans. I'm gonna help but I need a little something-something in return. You gots to hook me up with an Oxycontin prescription. Call me, yo."

Speaking with his police contact, Behram learned that Wayne was a local thug who'd do anything for money. The mole said Javier, a Navy SEAL, drove the getaway car after the Chula Vista shootout. The police believed Javier had gone into hiding.

The boy told Jefe's men that Javier had a second home. They had a street name but no address. They spent several days scouting the road without luck. But El Poder's men had eventually followed Javier's crew into Mexico.

Behram concluded that Wayne, Javier, Catherine and Susan had kidnapped Jefe then killed him after interrogation, likely at Javier's rural home. They abducted Jefe to get information about the child. Jefe was now dead and Behram was the only person affiliated with El Poder who knew.

Jefe sent the boy to his compound in Mexico. Jefe had implied that Behram could kill the child after assassinating the senator.

But Jefe pretended he meant the *next* operation. Jefe wanted Behram to assassinate the meddling Mexican President, and said the blonde boy would be his prize.

But with Jefe dead, Behram would get his reward sooner. He knew exactly where the miserable posse was headed. He would travel to Mexico and await their arrival.

CHAPTER THIRTY-THREE

Nearly three days later after leaving San Diego, we arrived in San Carlos, a tiny fishing village. But Jefe had turned it into a meth empire. Most of the locals were on El Poder's payroll, showering fishermen with cash to keep an eye out for unwanted visitors. Jefe said his strong house, Blake's supposed location, was ten miles south of town in a secluded bay protected by rocky cliffs and harrowing waves. The Ketchum Alive moored several miles out.

"I think the best time to strike is around 4 a.m.," Javier said. "Even the night shift guards will hit a lull then. There's a chance we'll get lucky and figure out where he is tonight. If so, we grab him and head out. Let's take the surveillance equipment and weapons."

At 3 a.m., Javier and I inflated the Zodiac and headed toward the bay. The nearly moonless night was dark as tar. The motor was practically silent and we ran without lights, navigating with electronics. The boat rose and fell with the breathing of the ocean.

We'd carefully studied the satellite imagery. Sandstone cliffs guarded the southern end, sweeping the edge of the cove. On the other side, the bay had a long fingerlike rock jetty that rose about thirty feet above the water's edge. The jetty stopped a quarter mile from the cliffs, creating the bay's entrance. Inside the jetty, the bay opened up, about two miles in diameter. The water was nearly still inside the protected bay. But outside the jetty, the waves were huge.

While Javier steered from the rear, I scanned with binoculars utilizing thermal imaging and light amplification technology. Thermal imaging gathers infrared light and creates a picture according to temperature patterns. Light amplification takes all ambient light such as moonlight, starlight and infrared, converting it into electrical energy then back into light, allowing sight in near total darkness.

Just as Jefe said, a sentry post overlooked the inlet into the bay, perched on the cliff, eighty feet above the water. We planned to avoid detection by traveling along the cliffs, directly below the guard tower.

The south swell was coming strong, forming devastating curlers, the water forced upward by shallows along the jetty. We paused three hundred yards from the bay's inlet. We could be spotted with night optics, but we gambled the guards weren't on high alert. Hopefully they were playing cards or sleeping.

On the other hand, the Jefe ran a pitiless organization. Sleeping on the job might be a capital offense.

As we neared the cliff, I said, "I don't like the looks of this. Check out that churn." I handed him my binoculars. Thick waves collided with the sandstone wall, spray soaring above the cliff. Salt water flowed back down, creating a boiling cauldron at the cliff's edge. Jefe had chosen a very difficult place to arrive by sea.

"Yeah. Maybe we should reconsider. Just the water coming down the cliff could sink us."

"Let's get a little closer."

We approached the edge. We were under a waterfall thundering down on our heads, water striking like wet hammers. I reflexively hunched, as if the position of my body could lessen the onslaught.

Javier yelled over the roar of the waves, "This could sink a freightliner!" The overhead waves pounded the wall, the collisions forming whirlpools in the chaotic whitewater. The Zodiac lurched like a toy boat in a kiddy pool.

A huge wave struck and the boat tipped, nearly flipping. We jumped to the high side, weighing it down until the boat finally dropped flat.

"Let's go back out!"

"Retreat!"

Javier rotated the boat away from the cliff and we battled toward the open ocean. When we were out of the combat zone, Javier said, "Let's launch the drone to see the guardhouse. If they're snoozing, we can enter by the jetty."

As the waves bounced us, he opened the case, carefully removing the tiny dragonfly. The box doubled as the controller. He flipped up the view screen and gripped the joystick.

In the trough between waves, he launched the DragonFlyer. We watched it skim the surface then move up the cliff, soaring above the tower. Several spotlights on the roof sat beside a large object covered by a tarp.

"Looks like heavy weaponry," Javier said. "That's probably a Soviet-made KPV heavy machinegun. If they know we're here, it'll be impossible to enter the bay. Or exit. That gun will rain metal, a thousand rounds a minute. We wouldn't have a chance."

He swept the drone lower and peered in the windows. Two guards were inside but they weren't actively monitoring the ocean.

He asked, "Do dragonflies live in Baja?"

"Do I look like a bug specialist?"

"Can't linger then. A big weird insect might attract attention."

"Could we take out the guardhouse before entering the bay?"

"We can't approach the cliffs with the Zodiac. Swimming would be suicidal. We could beach the raft a few miles down and hoof it. But if they radioed during the attack, soldiers at the compound would arrange a meet and greet. Even if we killed them silently, it'd take half an hour to return to the Zodiac and another twenty to return to the bay. That's a lot of radio silence. Normal radio procedure is to make contact every fifteen minutes."

"Maybe we could swim in then escape on foot back to the Zodiac, since Blake can't swim that far. But they probably have dirt bikes and ATVs. And Blake will slow us down. There's nowhere to hide in this scrub."

"We have to escape by water. Once we're under, they can't find us. There's almost no chance we can retrieve Blake completely unnoticed. We shouldn't attempt that. Our best bet is to create a diversion and escape in the chaos."

"What about the heavy machinegun?"

"We won't be able to escape if this guard shack is operational. We'll have to take it out before or after we raid the compound."

"If we destroy it on the way in, we'll lose the element of surprise. We should demolish it on the way out. But how?"

"The Switchblade."

He brought the drone overhead but the boat rocked violently, making a soft landing impossible. He dove the drone, striking the raft's floor. "Ouch!" He held it up, a wing broken in half. "Penalty. Guess we won't be using this anymore."

I grimaced, "There goes our recon."

"We'll make do. Let's hug the opposite shore and ride a wave into the bay. No need to Titanic the raft on the cliffs."

"I hope they aren't watching when we enter. If so, it was nice knowing you."

The raft accelerated, matching the speed of the waves to stay in a trough. A wall of water loomed in front with another chasing from behind.

After clearing the mouth of the bay, he veered away from the watchtower into quiet waters. With binoculars, I studied the tower but couldn't see the roof. They might be preparing the big daddy, ready to send a metal storm.

We safely cruised across the cove. A half-mile from shore, we put on masks, flippers and oxygen tanks. We used closed-circuit rebreathers, so no telltale bubbles escaped. We swam twenty feet below, the maximum depth to safely use pure oxygen rebreathers.

I followed a navigation board with GPS, as the depths were pitch black. I kicked the flippers, soaring through the cool water. Surfaced eighty feet from shore. Treading water, I raised my binoculars.

The entire area was well lit. Two guards patrolled the beach, AKs slung over their shoulders. A mammoth three-story adobe house squatted in a grove of trees. A tower jutted twenty feet above the roof. Smaller buildings surrounded the house.

I spotted two sentries on the roof. Assumed there were more inside the tower. I dove again. We swam together and stopped near the shore. I ascended but didn't break the surface, a shallow water peek. Through the mask, I visualized the shore as if my head were above the surface.

When the guards were patrolling the opposite side of the beach, I crept onto the sand. I ran crouching then lay next to a tall coconut tree. Removed two cameras disguised as rocks from my pack and placed them on either side of the tree. I pressed a button on my goggles, checking the view from the wide-angle lenses, a nearly complete view of the compound. I slipped into the water, using my honing beacon to find Javier. We swam to the Zodiac.

As we neared the bay's exit, I said, "What's the plan if they spot us leaving?"

"We gun the engine until they shoot then we dive. We might be able to swim to the sailboat."

I didn't say anything but I knew that swimming in those waves would be impossible. Might as well swim up a white water river.

I felt anxious as we approached, but we exited unseen then entered the onslaught of breaking waves. Javier turned north, hugging the rocky jetty. I threw a signal booster onto the jetty, disguised as a rock.

We turned toward the sailboat. I said, "Humor me. I need to air out my thoughts. I've been in the healing profession longer than I was in the military. Do you feel weird about killing people before they even shoot at us?"

"In war, the rules of engagement are different than law-enforcement and self-protection, where you shoot only when obviously threatened. They're a known threat, an armed enemy."

"But soldiers choose to fight. These are poor people trying to feed their families."

"Bullshit. The narcos join voluntarily. They sell illegal poison for profit, enforced by violence. Many started in the military. The Mexican Army pays a living wage. If they stayed in the Army, they'd live decently. But most joined fully intending to use their newly acquired, taxpayer-funded skills to make bank. These aren't simple fisherman forced to carry a gun. They consciously chose greed over honesty, power over weakness, and violence over peace. Anyone carrying a gun, holding your son hostage and enforcing the sale of poison through violence is fair game. They'll kill us in a heartbeat. In this case, turning the other cheek means giving them time to slice your throat. The angels are on our side."

"I struggle with the lack of black and white."

"Stryker, there's plenty of gray in my career. But this ain't gray. Killing an unarmed nuclear scientist was gray. Killing an armed narco, not so much. They're part of El Poder and they took Blake."

"You're right."

"We're about to demonstrate the true meaning of not-gray fury and not-gray vengeance."

"Hooyah!"

We arrived at the Ketchum Alive. Catherine embraced me. "Thank God you're back! What'd you find out?"

"For the bad news: like Jefe said, a guardhouse overlooks the bay with a big ass machinegun. The good news is we left two cameras. We should be able to see most of what's going on."

"Any sign of Blake?"

"No. But tomorrow's the big day!" I kissed the top of her head.

We took turns monitoring the cameras. When I awoke the next morning, Catherine was glued to the screen like a Secret Service agent studying the crowd. While she kept constant vigil on the live feed, Javier and I replayed the recordings, analyzing the layout, guard patterns and operations.

The main house was divided into three areas. Barracks with an industrial kitchen and dining area were on the south. The north side held family apartments. El Jefe's quarters were located in the center and Maria, his girlfriend, stayed there. Jefe said Maria had taken a special interest in Blake. But Jefe wasn't certain where Blake slept. Everything he said about Blake was suspiciously vague.

Jefe said the compound was the water shipment point for a meth superlab about twenty miles inland. We saw men cruising the bay in ski-dos and motorboats. A large boathouse jutted into the water, big enough to hold at least a dozen boats. Motorcycles, four wheeled ATVs and pickup trucks were haphazardly parked. An oversized garage was connected to a storage warehouse.

Ten guards were on duty in pairs, in the cliff top guardhouse, the roof, the roof's watchtower and the warehouse. The final pair patrolled the beach. They wore street clothes and carried AK-47's, nicknamed *cuerno de chivo* or goat's horn due to the curved magazine. They rotated every eight hours, so there were about thirty guards on the premises.

By the end of the day, we'd seen several children playing soccer. A few toddlers in saggy diapers wandered freely. Some children stayed in the smaller houses but others in the main house.

No sign of Blake. The tension mounted as the day drained to night. My hope eroded toward despair. Seconds felt like minutes, minutes like hours, and hours like death. Cold, fetid death.

When we could hold our eyes open no longer, we went to bed. "You really think he's here? Was Alfredo lying?" Catherine asked timidly.

I wanted to dodge the question but didn't, "Yeah, he could've lied. His best hope for survival was to convince us that Blake is alive. If not, he knew we'd turn him over to the police. Or kill him."

"This whole thing could be a ruse? A wild goose chase?" Panic simmered beneath the surface.

"It could be."

"Then you and Javier are risking your lives for nothing?"

"We gotta find out."

"Is it better to face the truth?" She asked morosely. "Or hope and be wrong?"

"I won't, *I can't*, give up hope until we find him or know for certain he's dead."

Her maimed heart thumped next to mine. Then she began to weep softly.

CHAPTER
THIRTY-
FOUR

Behram drove the dirt road toward El Jefe's compound, a few miles away. His swollen hands ached from the gruesome pustules and boils. He glanced in the rearview mirror, his face horrifying him, a miscreated oozing freak.

When he first broke out in sores, Behram deduced he was poisoned. Originally, he thought Nurse Stryker's motivation for the meeting was to photograph him, but he remembered his skin tingling where the mask and gloves touched. As a master of the dark arts, he quickly concluded it was dioxin.

TCDD dioxin is a toxic chemical that causes chloracne, a severe eruption of blackheads, cysts and pustules. In a 2004 assassination attempt, Ukrainian President Viktor Yushchenko ingested dioxin. The perpetrators, suspected to be KGB agents, were never caught. The previously handsome man survived but was transformed into something difficult to look at, something grotesque, his face and neck covered in angry weeping pustules.

Chloracne usually erupts within a few days of contact and lasts for decades, depending on the level of exposure. There's no known cure. Skin exposure, ingestion or inhalation of dioxins inevitably causes the acne-like pestilence. Behram was exposed via both skin and inhalation.

Behram was humiliated when the child wounded him. When he realized Nurse Stryker tricked him, his anguish grew to overpowering venom. His hatred for the woman and her son was beyond any emotion he'd ever felt.

He would torture them for years, turning them into hideous creatures like himself.

He had a masterful plan for terrifying vengeance. He would have an insider put dioxin in the boy's food at El Jefe's compound. When the boy ate his next meal, he would ingest a massive dose, unbeknownst to his current hosts. He would break out in purple bumps and then they would begin to ooze.

When the silly team arrived to snatch the boy, the cute blondie would resemble the disgusting lepers from the Christian Bible. And, if they successfully rescued the boil-ridden little boy, Behram would lie in wait.

Then unleash his horrors.

We continued the vigil, feeling increasingly like a funeral wake. We avoided eye contact. The oppressive unspoken hung like stench.

At lunch, Catherine smiled sadly as she handed me a peanut butter and honey sandwich, Blake's favorite. I chewed slowly with a dry mouth. It stuck in my throat like hot tar flung on a wall.

I was overcome with a need to move. A crawly sensation crept up my knees, anxious restlessness. I stood abruptly.

"I'm going for a swim. To burn off some steam."

I dove off the deck into the cool ocean. I pummeled the water, swimming like a drowning man. Swam as fast as possible, a sprint.

Swam like a shark was chasing. I was escaping, channeling anxiety into my arms and legs.

His memories haunted me: riding bikes and climbing trees. He loved Legos and break dancing. He commanded the Crime Investigation Club, riding bikes around our crime-free hood, searching for suspicious characters. He'd breathlessly report, "We saw a burglar drive by twice! In a red truck!"

But Blake's absolute favorite was snow skiing. He had Catherine's mountain genes and never tired of sending his gravity-fed planks blazing. We spent every Christmas and Spring Break in Sun Valley, staying with Catherine's parents. Blake and the gals zoomed at unbelievable speed as I struggled to keep up. I placated my ego, reminding myself that Susan and Catherine raced competitively. But I had no such excuse with fearless Blake. "Mama's boy" took on a whole new meaning when they ripped together.

We'd discussed moving to the Rockies; my in-laws knew several doctors in Ketchum. I loved the ocean, but mountains were a close second. And I was outvoted two to one in our family.

Or it used to be two to one.

We were no longer three. It was time to face the inevitable truth. No sign of him for over a day.

We heard El Jefe say Blake was gone. He was dead. He was with the angels and the saints. Like Zo's widow, I'd never even gotten a chance to see his body.

I lashed out, fighting the ocean with each stroke. My anxiety transformed into aggression. I'd never really hated before. But hate burned inside me, burned a hole in me. I wanted to hurt, maim and kill.

I swam like I was chasing the shark.

After nearly two hours, I returned to the boat. As I approached, I heard screaming. I lifted my head but couldn't hear the words.

I was frightened. I shouldn't have left the boat. Quickened my pace. More shouts, a woman's scream.

The shark was in the shallow water. And the lifeguard was missing.

My arms and legs ached as I sprinted in panic, the sea trapping me like a watery tomb. The boat seemed no closer.

Time slowed.

Finally I heard Catherine, "Wyatt! Come back! Wyatt!" She didn't sound fearful but jubilant.

I yelled, "What?"

"We saw him! He's alive!"

I stopped swimming and sunk, cheering underwater with bubbles pouring from my mouth, my inner Fourth of July erupting.

When I arrived at the boat, they were below deck staring at the screen, entranced. Catherine said, "Come see! He's on the beach!"

Several children played on the sand in front of the main house. Javier zoomed in on one with lighter skin. His hair was cut short and dyed black.

Blake. Our son.

I couldn't believe my eyes. Catherine gripped my hand. Our tears flowed freely.

We watched, mesmerized. Blake seemed withdrawn. He knew Spanish but kept to himself. The other boys invited him to play but he appeared wistful and disinterested, unlike the Blake of the school playground, the gregarious kid leading the pack.

He scribbled aimlessly in the sand with a stick. He often drew when he was upset.

A boy returned with a soccer ball. Blake dropped his stick and ran to join. It seemed they all wanted Blake on their team.

We watched for hours. Blake scored almost all the goals, the others children giving him high fives. A woman called the group. Boys walked beside him, talking and laughing. One put his arm around Blake.

Catherine began to sob. I put my arms around her. The relief and the horror and the anxiety and the love and everything came out in one emotional blast.

Blake was alive.

CHAPTER THIRTY-FIVE

I was curious why Jefe kept him alive. During interrogation he said, "The doctor's son was a beautiful boy, a little angel. When I decided to let him live, I was concerned others would see mercy as weakness so I pretended to kill him. Trusted men took him to my house in Mexico to live with my girlfriend. Maria's unable to have children of her own." At the time, the story seemed dubious, a thinly veiled sympathy plea. But he'd told the truth. Hopefully the rest of what he'd said was true.

After dark, it was time. Each hour increased the chance that we'd be spotted or Blake would be moved.

At 2 a.m., we were ready. Susan hugged us. "Please be careful. I love you both!"

Catherine hugged Javier and kissed his cheek. "Thank you! Thank you! Thank you!"

Javier would be a fugitive with a felony record and a dis-
honorable discharge. He'd completely destroyed his career for
Blake. For us.

But he just smiled and said, "Don't mention it. We all want
him back."

Then Catherine embraced me. "When Blake made that
birthday card that said, 'Daddy's are a little boy's best friend',
I was secretly jealous. But you are. You're his best friend, his
daddy and his hero." She held me like it was our last time.
"And my hero."

We were headed to war. We believed in the mission, like
soldiers battling Hitler, but Catherine was a potential if not
likely widow.

As we pulled out, the two sisters linked arms, beautiful
in spite of terrible haircuts, dye jobs and collagen injections.
Their good looks were marred, but they were pure, their
beauty radiating from within. They waved goodbye until the
darkness separated us.

The Ketchum Alive sailed into deeper water. When we had
Blake, they would meet us at sea. Stealth, not strength, was
the key to our mission. We planned to enter the same way,
hugging the jetty far from the lookout.

I felt uneasy as we approached the ominous guardhouse
perched on the cliffs. We were unable to monitor them without
the DragonFlier. Even if we were able to penetrate the compound and find Blake, escaping past the heavy machinegun
would be impossible. They had giant spotlights and probably
infrared binoculars. The entrance to the cove was a quarter
mile wide.

The gun had a range of several miles.

We passed unnoticed, then veered north. We stopped a mile from shore then placed the diver propulsion vehicle in the water. The torpedo-like scooter had a quiet electrical motor. We wore diving gear, night optical masks and full body armor. Javier strapped two assault rifles to his back in shoot-through waterproof bags. I gripped the handlebars and he held my legs as we soared below the surface.

Using a shallow water peek, we saw the two guards on the other end of the beach. Javier swam in. I remained in the surf zone, providing cover. He stashed the guns in brush then we returned to the Zodiac. We carried a crate to shore then buried the equipment in a shallow hole. Fifteen feet out, we sank the propulsion unit.

We swam to the boat shed and carefully surfaced inside the shed, looking for any narcos or surveillance cameras. Water slapped the wharf pilings as small waves rolled through. We studied the shed, packed with multiple speedboats, jet skis, and two spectacular yachts but no guards. Javier swam down to connect his oxygen and flippers to a support pole.

We placed enough C-4 to light it up like the Dia de los Muertos. We planned to wait until we were back in the water before detonating the shelter. Hopefully, they'd presume a land assault and not cover the beach, our escape route. Javier would use his stored diving gear to return to the Zodiac.

We headed toward our buried equipment, pausing occasionally so Javier could use my oxygen. Using a shallow water peek, I saw two guards approaching then turn back, the outer reach of their patrol.

We kicked into the shallows and stood, creeping behind them. I struck the closest guard's temple with my pistol grip. He crumpled.

As the second spun, Javier landed a blow on his forehead.

He staggered but didn't fall. One knee buckled, his toe wedged in the sand as he tried to regain his footing.

I stomped his lower leg. I felt both his tibia and fibula break cleanly.

Javier covered the man's mouth to silence his scream while pressing his pistol to the man's forehead, "Si hablas, te mataré." *If you speak, I'll kill you.*

I pulled two spring-loaded syringes from my belt, designed to inject epinephrine for severe allergic reactions. I'd replaced the epi with a sedative.

With a push of the button, the needle punctured clothes, skin and muscle, injecting each man with enough anesthetic to put down a bull moose, crazed by the rut.

We bound and gagged them then hid their bodies in brush. I sank their weapons but kept their radios. I retrieved the propulsion unit, dragging it up onto the beach.

Javier opened the crate. I placed plastic explosives with blasting caps in my backpack. Connected a Blake-sized, full-faced breathing mask to my oxygen.

We bucked on our Kevlar helmets, with GPS transceivers and indwelling mics for communication.

Javier clipped grenades to his vest. He placed three RPG rockets in his pack. Javier carried our RPG launcher but my M4 assault rifle had an under-barrel grenade launcher. Rifle-launched grenades explode on impact, with more accuracy but less power than traditional hand grenades. The RPG was an anti-tank weapon, by far the most powerful and accurate.

We stayed in the shadows as we moved toward the magnificent adobe house, wearing panoramic goggles that increased our field of vision, identical to those used in Operation Neptune Spear, the mission that killed Bin Laden. They doubled our peripheral vision to 180 degrees.

On the beach side, there was a large stone patio with outdoor furniture and tables. Two men guarded the entrance. We knew they circled the building every fifteen minutes.

We crept around the corner from the guards and made a plan.

Outdoor stairs led to a balcony that circled the second floor. Javier squatted beneath the stairs. I stuck a guard's handheld radio in the sand, standing upright.

I crept up the stairs and lay on the balcony, viewing the area below. I said, "They're coming your way toward the northwest corner."

"Copy."

The guards rounded the corner, stopping when they saw the stolen radio. I stepped onto the balcony rail.

One bent to pick it up.

I jumped, landing on his shoulders. He collapsed on his face. I rolled away.

Javier struck the second guard's skull with his rifle butt. He went down.

The first man groaned, reaching for his AK. I grabbed his wrist and jerked back, reversing the ER procedure for fixing a dislocated shoulder. The round humeral head was yanked from the curved socket: the egg snatched from the nest.

His head tilted back in agony, his neck exposed. Javier chopped his throat with the edge of a rigid hand, cracking his larynx, rendering him speechless.

We tranquilized and bound them with zip-ties. Javier kept their radios and we each took a set of keys.

We walked to the beach entrance. I unlocked the solid door. We stood in a grand foyer with beautiful Brazilian Walnut flooring and wall panels. We scanned the room, back to back.

Confident it was clear, Javier exited and crept away from the house, into the shadows. Normally, soldiers stay with their partner during combat, but in this case he planned to create a diversion so we could escape.

I locked the door and placed a plastic explosive on the ceiling, pushing the putty into a corner then inserting a remotely activated blasting cap. I wedged additional C-4 above the side doors that accessed both wings. I hoped to avoid those areas since many people slept there, making them difficult to search.

I assumed Blake slept near Maria, so I planned to search the central part of the house first, Jefe's personal quarters. And I had a secondary mission in Jefe's bedroom.

I started on the ground floor, an enormous living area. The furniture and paintings were priceless. Giant pillars soared to the ceiling.

I crept up the sweeping mahogany staircase, open to the third floor, circling a large atrium. Placed explosives under the top step.

On the second floor, a huge dining area abutted a panoramic window, facing the bay. I walked down a short hall then came to a closed door then snaked an optical cable under the door, viewing through my goggles. Saw an adult in one bed and a child in the other.

Javier radioed, "Someone keeps asking for Jorge on the guards' radio. They'll be suspicious soon."

I stepped inside, closing the door behind. The boy's face was buried in a pillow. I removed two syringes then placed my hand over the woman's mouth, simultaneously firing a needle into her shoulder. Her eyes opened in fear. I pointed my pistol and held my finger up, a hush signal.

Her eyes glazed. She drifted away.

I nudged the child but he didn't move. I tugged the pillow and his face rotated into view.

Not Blake.

The boy awoke suddenly. He yelped but I slammed the pillow over his face. He clawed at my gloves. I injected a pediatric dose into the child's thigh, holding the pillow until he relaxed.

I stepped to the door. Hearing nothing, I slid the fiber optic cable into the hall. Clear. I stepped out.

I approached another door but couldn't insert the cable beneath the door, blocked by carpet. I cracked the door and peeked inside an entertainment room with a large flat screen television, a pool table and couches.

Javier radioed, "There's a bunch of radio chatter. They're agitated that guards aren't answering."

I crept up the stairs, reaching the third floor. Stuck explosives below the suspended staircase.

Engraved double doors led to the master suite on the ocean view side. I slid the cable into the foyer of a cavernous room, the size of a basketball court. Floor to ceiling windows covered one wall. Unable to see the bed, I assumed it was on the inside wall, facing the windows.

As I opened the door, a loud beep sounded.

I paused and waited. Hearing no reaction, I entered the foyer and saw a canopy bed against the wall opposite the windows.

A beautiful woman slept alone.

I covered her mouth and injected her arm. Her large black eyes opened then faded.

A Monet hung beside the bed. I holstered my pistol and removed the painting, revealing a safe. I punched in the code, holding my breath.

I suddenly felt panic as Jefe could have tricked us with an alarm, ensuring our capture. Had I stupidly risked everything for money?

The door clicked and opened, exposing stacks of bundled bonds and jewels. I exhaled.

I raked bundles of untraceable bonds banded with currency straps into my rucksack, each holding one hundred $10,000 U.S. bearer bonds, over twenty million dollars. There was also a significant amount of banded cash.

I began removing jewels from their stands. Carefully lifted a necklace, diamonds the size of quarters.

Behind me, a croak, "Hey!"

I dropped the necklace and spun.

She leaned on the bed's edge, a pistol pointed at my chest. I wore a bullet resistant vest so I'd probably survive. But a gunshot would certainly complicate matters. She was ten feet away.

I softly said, "Me alegro de que estés aquí. Alfredo me envió para estas cosas." *I'm glad you're here. Alfredo sent me for these things.*

She raised the pistol and pointed it at my face.

I swallowed hard, lacking bulletproof skin.

"Usted es un ladrón." *You're a thief.*

"Alfredo envía su amor." *Alfredo sends his love.*

"¿Qué?" *What?*

My earpiece sounded, "Hurry! Men are on the beach with flashlights, calling for the guards."

"*Ladrón, un ladrón en mi casa...*" Her words became a garble. She was losing the battle with the Sandman. Her breathing grew heavy. The gun drooped.

I lunged forward and lashed out with an open palm, sending the gun airborne. It struck the wall then clattered to the floor.

She lurched for the gun but fell, sprawling on hands and knees. I placed her in a headlock, covering her mouth.

I withdrew a pediatric syringe from my cargo pants and injected. I didn't want to kill her with an overdose but I didn't need any more surprises. I waited until she lay still then moved to the door.

I listened by the doors, still quiet. I removed the Monet from the frame then rolled the painting and placed it in a steel canister. I finished emptying the safe.

The door beeped loudly when I exited. I hoped the sound was a warning for bedroom occupants, not triggering an alarm elsewhere.

On the opposite side of the landing were two closed doors. I cracked one, sliding the cable in: two adults in one bed, no children.

I was surprised so many people were inside Jefe's quarters. I figured only his mistress slept there. The people were attractive and the rooms quite nice. I assumed they were guests or high-ranking members of El Poder.

I tried the next door, a child's room. Soccer posters decorated the wall. The floor was covered with Legos and other toys. A video game console with a gamer chair faced a large TV. A personal computer sat on a desk, littered with a child's drawings.

I saw the sleeping child, the brightly colored blankets heaving with each breath.

Legos.

CHAPTER THIRTY-SIX

I stepped inside and walked to the bed.

It was Blake.

I lifted my goggles and placed my hand over his mouth. His eyes flew open. He immediately bit my hand and flailed with impressive strength. He made more noise than the rest combined.

I whispered, "Blake, it's Dad."

He stopped fighting but kept his jaw clenched, luckily just chomping the palm of my thick glove.

I held my finger to my mouth. He released the glove and broke into a wide grin. "Daddy! You're alive!" We hugged.

"I love you, Blake. This is the happiest moment of my life."

"Me too! I thought you were dead!"

"We have to get out, buddy. I'll explain everything soon, but we have to hurry. Put these on." I handed him black tights, a balaclava, shoes and gloves.

He excitedly pulled on the pants, "I look like a SEAL! Awesome!"

"Hold out your hand." I clamped a GPS transmitter on his wrist, locking it shut.

"I have Blake," I radioed. "When I blow the window, get busy." Javier knew my GPS location.

"Copy. I'm in position to cover you. Exit from the north window. It's in my line of sight. Nothing but sand below. No guards are near. Yet."

The third floor was suboptimal for exiting but we couldn't waste time. I affixed a small explosive to the weakest spot of the metal-barred window.

A picture drawn by Blake hung beside the window, "When I was happy." It showed three smiling figures, labeled Mom, Dad and me. Below hung a drawing of a weeping boy, Now, I'm alone. An orphan. I grimaced.

"Get in the tub."

"Okay, Dad."

I placed his mattress against the wall between the bedroom and bathroom then entered the restroom. I strapped a bullet resistant vest and a chest harness to his little body.

"Listen carefully. There will be explosions then we'll run to the bedroom window. I'll connect us together. We'll slide down a rope to the sand. We'll go to the water. We may run or we might crawl. I'll be with you the whole way. If I say run, run as fast as possible. If I say drop, lay down. I might lie on top of you. Here's a radio. If I get hurt or something, call mom or..."

Blake interrupted, "Mom's alive?"

"Yes, she's nearby. On a boat with Susan."

"Aunt Susan's alive too?" His smile nearly cracked his face.

"Yes. I know you're excited, but please be quiet. We have to leave as soon as possible."

"Okay."

"You can also radio Javier. He's on the beach."

"Yesssssss!" He clenched a triumphant fist.

"Push this button to talk. No matter what happens, get as far away as possible." I pointed to the north. "Run that way until you get to the ocean, where there are big waves. Mom can't pick you up in the flat water, so keep running until you see the waves. You know where I'm talking about?"

"Yeah, I know. A man took me on a four-wheeler and I saw those waves. Who're we hiding from? Is the bad man here?"

"These are all bad men."

He looked confused. "I thought they were protecting me."

I climbed into the bathtub and lay on top of him. "They lied to you. These are the same bad guys who took you from our house. I'll explain later. When we get to the water, I'll connect us with rope again. I'll grab a machine to pull us through the water. Take a deep breath before we go under. We'll zoom along the bottom then come up to breathe. Once we're away from shore, we'll wear oxygen masks to breathe, just like snorkeling. Understand?"

He nodded silently. Then smiled and kissed my helmet.

I radioed, "Ready?"

"Ready."

I turned my face down and pressed the remote.

The explosion ripped a hole in the silence, debris slamming the bathroom wall. A rock punched through the sheetrock and shattered the bathroom mirror.

Before the debris stopped falling, Javier detonated multiple explosions. The sound of gunfire erupted from the yard in front of the house, away from the water. Javier had placed blasting caps on sequential fuses there to imitate the sound of machinegun fire. Blasting caps are the size of bullets, placed inside larger charges to detonate them. Instead, we used them as decoys.

I hurried into the bedroom, the barred widow gone, Blake's sad drawing annihilated. Good riddance to both.

Alarms sounded and floodlights popped to life. Men shouted.

I shoved the bed frame against the cratered wall then looped a rope around the desk. I connected Blake's harness to mine with a carabiner.

"Hold on tight, but if you let go, this'll hold us together."

He faced me, arms hugging my neck and legs around my waist. I backed, gripping the rope.

"Don't jump!" Javier radioed. "Two guards are on the roof, directly above the window. They're leaning out, looking at the hole. Get down!"

I told Blake, "Down!"

I lay over him, my eyes glued to the window. I unhooked, in case someone swung down from above.

Javier opened fire, a barrage across the rooftop. I heard screams of pain.

A body dropped past the window.

He said, "I got 'em both. One fell onto the sand. The other's still on the roof, but I'm pretty sure he's dead."

Suddenly, the ominous staccato of a heavy machinegun chopped the air, the rooftop tower returning fire with a surface-mounted antiaircraft gun. Tracer bullets flew straight toward Javier.

The one-inch bullets would shred him. A hit would leave a football-sized wound.

I unclipped a hand grenade and leaned out. I held it until the last second then tossed it over my head onto the roof. The grenade exploded and shrapnel flew from the roof edge.

The antiaircraft gun paused. I wondered if it was destroyed. No such luck.

It started up again, a savage barrage, spraying metal like a water hose toward Javier. A coconut tree trembled under the onslaught then dropped vertically to the sand and fell over.

I clipped Blake to my harness then tossed a second grenade onto to the roof.

When it exploded, I fast-roped down. On the sand, I lay on Blake and unclipped him. "Cover your face."

I pulled the remote from my belt and triggered the explosives I'd placed with sequential blasts accompanied by breaking glass, falling debris and shouting. The rooftop artillery stopped firing. The sirens stopped abruptly and the floodlights went dark, the power out.

I lifted my face from the sand and saw Javier in full sprint. He dove, finding refuge behind a Jeep. Relief washed over me.

He knelt behind the vehicle. Then abruptly stood with the rocket-propelled grenade launcher on his shoulder.

The tables had turned.

The RPG launched in a cloud of grey smoke, enveloping Javier. The missile burst from the cloud, cutting the air as it whistled toward the rooftop.

The guard tower erupted in hellish brilliance, like a Chinese firecracker. Glass and metal shattered outward, followed by flames and superheated smoke.

I watched the burning tower lean. It reached an angle of no return then slowly toppled like a tree in a forest fire. A burning body fell.

A door flew open ten feet from us.

Men began charging out in full battle gear. There were at least ten of them in helmets and Kevlar vests.

I scrambled for my automatic rifle, but it was strapped to my back. I pulled my pistol, shooting the leader's leg, the only obvious unprotected area. More ran out. I felt panic.

Javier trained his M4 and released withering fire, giving them the whole nine yards, nine yards being the length of a WW II machinegun belt.

Since the doorway was clogged with bodies, the others wisely decided not to exit. Javier ran across the front of the house, spraying windows. Sporadic return fire crackled from the building. I lost sight of him in the shadows.

"Run!"

Blake jumped up and ran parallel to the cove. I followed.

"Down!"

Blake dropped.

I lay beside, searching with binoculars. The entire southern side was on fire where Javier placed thermite incendiary explosives. The wall cratered as the roof bucked. The burning thermite reached five thousand degrees Fahrenheit, melting a hole to the center of the earth, dumping boiling metal on Lucifer and the newly arrived El Poder damned.

Jefe's quarters still stood but the stairway and exits were obliterated, my explosives surgically gutting the core. The sleeping beauties were safe but unable to leave anytime soon.

Javier said, "Stryker, it's time to make your push to the beach. Check out the ATV on the front driveway."

Javier cruised the four-wheeler, spraying machinegun fire at the building's front.

My heart sank, wondering why he was blatantly exposing himself.

Narcos trained every gun on him, bullets pinging off the metal. No armor could resist the withering assault. He looked like a moving sparkler.

Javier burst into flames.

I was dumbfounded.

I zoomed in. His clothes were engulfed in fire but the ATV kept moving. Every gun punished his carcass.

As the clothing burned off, I realized the driver was a five-gallon gas can wrapped in a blanket with a narco's helmet on top.

Bullets blew the tires and it finally rolled to a stop, but guards continued to waste ammo on the flaming decoy. Javier had sent the ATV on a joyride. With a sloshing driver and his sidekick: a blasting cap chain.

I grabbed Blake's hand. We raced toward the beach.

In the distance Javier yelled, "¡La venganza de los Zetas!" *The vengeance of the Zetas.* After several bursts of gunfire, he repeated the taunt.

We were in full sprint when two brilliant white flashes cast our shadows as elongated, running phantoms.

Javier had provoked with taunts then sucker-punched with flash-bang grenades. The flash activated all photoreceptor cells in their eyes, causing temporary complete blindness. Complete deafness and severe vertigo followed, the concussion sloshing their inner ear fluids.

He clamored to the south side, drawing attention away from us.

We ran in silence. Blake stumbled on the uneven sand under the weight of his vest. The gunfire became distant. Flashes intermittently lit our escape. We reached the water's edge seemingly unnoticed. Javier was hogging the spotlight.

I scooped up the propulsion unit and we splashed into waist-deep water. I clipped a cable to Blake's harness.

"Grab my belt. Take a deep breath." We submerged and I squeezed the throttle.

We soared below the surface. After thirty seconds, we surfaced. As Blake caught his breath, I placed the full-faced mask over his head.

"You can breathe underwater with this, like snorkeling. We won't come up for awhile. If you're having trouble breathing, squeeze my leg and I'll surface."

He flashed thumbs up and we sank. My little Aquaman had snorkeled since age four.

I glanced back several times. He seemed fine. The GPS led us to the Zodiac. When we surfaced, I radioed, "We're at the raft."

"I'm in the water, two hundred yards offshore. About to blow the boathouse."

The boat shed lit up then transformed into a mushroom cloud, like a nuclear explosion. Seconds later, the noise reached us with a muffled boom.

We floated away from the Zodiac, keeping distance. If the raft were spotted, we could escape underwater.

Vehicles raced along both sides of the cove and further inland. Twenty minutes later, Javier surfaced.

Blake said, "Hey Javier! ¿Como estas? Thanks for rescuing me!"

Javier slapped him a wet high five. "Anytime! Good to see you, amigo! You swim like a SEAL. I wonder if a ten-year-old can join."

"I'm ten and a *half.*"

"In that case, we can use you for sure."

Blake grinned. I noticed a large red bump on his forehead. It almost looked like a boil.

Javier said, "Nice work, Riot Wyatt!"

"Likewise. But you put the fear of God in me a few times. Especially that four-wheeler stunt."

We climbed into the raft, cranked the silent motor then headed toward the inlet. Through binoculars, I saw several narcos manning the heavy gun on the guardhouse roof, scanning the mouth of the bay. Three spotlights roved, illuminating the cove.

There was no escape. An RPG would be futile since the guardhouse was too far away and the rise and fall of the ocean made accuracy impossible. Their gun had a lethal reach far surpassing the RPG. I hoped Javier's plan was feasible, if not, this was all for naught.

Trucks and motorcycles surrounded the sentry post. Dozens of guards swarmed the tower.

Javier removed a tube, holding a Switchblade drone. The two-foot drone had a nose-mounted camera and an electric motor. He held the tube against the hull of the Zodiac.

"What's that?" Blake asked.

Javier said, "Hopefully our ticket out of here."

"It's a rocket to blow up that tower."

"Again, hopefully."

He launched the Switchblade and small wings unfolded. Javier watched the viewer, steering it toward the guardhouse. Precision was key as the warhead was not very powerful, about like a grenade. The explosion wouldn't destroy the gun, so we needed to kill the men on the rooftop then make it through the gauntlet before they were replaced. If we struck too early, they'd have time to reach out and touch us.

He said, "The drone's circling above the roof until the last second."

I gunned toward the exit. Saltwater slapped our faces as we bounced over the swells. A searchlight moved toward us.

I grimaced.

It swept across us without stopping.

I relaxed.

It reversed then honed on us.

Moments later, all three spotlights were blinding us. The gun swiveled and fired, a line of bullets bubbling toward us like frenzied piranha.

I yelled, "It's the last second!"

"Yep."

He dove the little warhead into the roof, laying waste with a brilliant flash. The crack echoed across the water.

Men sprawled at unnatural angles on the roof. Others dropped silently, colliding with rocks and splashing into watery graves.

One spotlight was blown out and the others were unmanned. One swung up, spotlighting the stars. The other remained on us. I veered the Zodiac out of the beam and hugged the edge beside the jetty.

Gunfire randomly erupted from the tower and the ground below. But we were cloaked in darkness. We entered the big waves and angled north, water splashing over the bow.

Several hundred yards out, I called Catherine on the sat phone, triumphantly declaring, "We've got Blake!"

"Thank God! Is everyone Okay?"

"Yeah. I think we made a clean get away. We destroyed the boathouse and the tower. Come get us! We'll meet you about a mile out. Keep your lights off. It's slow going in these waves. See you soon! I love you."

"I love you too. Tell Blake I love him."

I hung up. "Your mom says she loves you."

"I can't wait to see her!"

We had survived. The boathouse demolition destroyed their marine craft, except maybe a random ski-doo or fishing boat that would be no threat. They had plenty of land vehicles but we wouldn't be on land anytime soon. In fact, it was unlikely we'd touch Mexican soil ever again, since we'd broken a hundred laws and made even more enemies.

We'd cruise to the big boat and be out of reach in no time. The ocean's a fairly big place to get lost. I smiled, thinking about Catherine and Susan spoiling Blake on the sailboat. He deserved a little pampering. I gazed at the stars and relaxed.

I said, "You know what I can't wait to do? Nail Jefe and his accomplices to the wall!"

"It'll be the biggest news story of the decade. They murdered Senator Ripp so their unholy alliance could remain."

"Wonder what Admiral Landfair will think."

I steered, facing away from the bay. Javier sat on the bow, looking back at me. His smile faded.

He pointed over my head. "We've got company."

I turned and saw a large ship, coming fast from the south. I had a sinking feeling. "Maybe it's a fisherman, or a vacation boat."

"Possibly, but it could be more of Blake's recent housemates."

Blake asked, "What?"

"The bad guys."

Blake shouted, "Gun it!"

"We are."

My hopes were in tatters. The Zodiac was no match for a drug runner's launch.

CHAPTER THIRTY-SEVEN

Javier looked with binoculars. "Stryker, that's definitely a military ship. Looks like a fast attack boat and she's coming like a bat out of hell. It's hugging the shore, headed for us, two miles away and traveling at forty knots. Our max speed is twenty in these waves. They'll catch us in ten minutes."

"Maybe it's the Mexican Coast Guard. Or the police."

"We don't want to chat with them either. We just left a pile of bodies on Mexican soil."

"We could ditch the raft and swim to shore. Then hang out underwater until the coast is clear."

"They'll take the Zodiac. We'd have to surface when the oxygen runs out and they'll still be around. We're toast in the water. That boat will have radar and spotlights. We have to go onshore and take our chances."

I called Catherine, "Change of plans. There's a military ship coming from the south, likely a cartel boat that was called when we attacked. Or they might be corrupt police or military, in the service of El Poder."

"Can you outrun it?"

"No way. We'll go ashore and figure it out from there. I'll call when we have a plan. Return to San Isabel del Cristo." San Isabel was a tourist town, twenty miles north of San Carlos.

"Okay. Please stay safe, Wyatt."

"We will." A vacant promise.

After hanging up, I said, "Let's unload then send the Zodiac to sea. Hopefully they'll follow."

"Good idea."

"Good idea, Dad." Blake nodded in earnest agreement, blonde roots peeking beneath the jet-black hair. My little blondie was still in there.

The bump on his forehead seemed larger. It seemed fluid filled, like a pustule. What was it? A tropical disease? Made me think of Behram and the dioxin.

We continued away from the gunboat, angling toward the shore. I said, "That ship was probably anchored nearby to escort drug boats and provide protection from a water assault. I bet ol' Jefe led us into a trap. If we'd taken ten more minutes, the ship would've been in the mouth of the cove, trapping us."

Javier nodded grimly. "He knew we'd exit by water. If this ends poorly, I hope the rats eat him."

Blake said, "Gross!"

"Just kidding." Behind Blake's back, he silently mouthed, "Not really."

We anchored outside the shore break. The attack boat had halved the distance, coming fast. Blake helped us unload.

I hid the propulsion unit and our scuba equipment in brush, in case we retreated to the water. It wouldn't get us far, but better than nothing.

Blake and Javier swam in with the last load, Blake heroically struggling in the chop.

I duct taped the throttle open and secured the steering pole so the raft angled away from the land. Lit a delay fuse on a signal flare. Sent it.

We hauled the equipment to a sheltered area a hundred feet from shore.

Minutes later and a mile away, a flare soared above the Zodiac. The military boat altered course, heading toward it.

Motorcycles whined in the distance. I climbed a dune to look. At least ten vehicles zoomed toward us around the bay.

We had a solid understanding of the terrain from studying the satellite imagery. The road north to San Isabel traversed flat desert crisscrossed by undeveloped roads, the shoreline sheer cliffs. The primary road wound through the mountains looming between San Carlos and San Isabel.

There were scattered trees, mostly pine. Palm trees were isolated to rare fresh water. The long spiky leaves of Yucca plants pointed skyward like raised bayonets.

A pickup truck roared toward us, a roof-mounted spotlight swiveling through the scrub brush and cactus. I honed in the binoculars as they passed. They wore helmets and bullet resistant vests.

The element of surprise was gone. They were ready for war.

The narcos probably had infrared, but the area was vast and varied. Being caught at night seemed unlikely. We had to cover as much distance as possible before dawn. The search would focus on the shoreline. They would be forced to use trails and roads for motorized travel since the off-road terrain was uneven and rocky.

Motorcycles approached. We dropped flat, hunkered behind rocks. Four sped past, heading north on a trail curving through Pinyon pines. The bulk of the vehicles were still coming around the bay.

We were surrounded.

"We should've destroyed the Zodiac with timed explosives," I said. "The abandoned raft means we're on land. We need wheels."

"Eliminating a truck full of men will be tough. We could use grenades or explosives, but we'd destroy the truck. Plus every narco would respond to the attack."

"Motos?"

"Easier said than done. We could ambush, but we can't pick 'em off with a single shot since they're wearing vests. A machinegun barrage would probably destroy the motos."

"Let's knock them off with my rappelling cord by stringing it across the trail."

"That thick cord will be pretty easy to see."

We discussed further and came up with a plan. He hurried to the water's edge.

Blake and I walked to the moto trail. I said, "Dig a little ditch between these trees."

Blake furiously plowed a trench with a sharp stick. I threw the rope over a branch. Secured it to a pine on the other side. Lay the cord in the ditch and Blake covered it with dirt and sand.

Javier radioed, "I'm out of the water."

"Go ahead. We're ready."

I told Blake, "Hide behind that rock. Lie down and don't peek. Don't come out until I call."

"Okay, Dad."

About a hundred yards to the south, a detonation cracked the darkness, Javier's remotely activated flash-bang grenade. Shouting men and vehicles raced toward the explosion. A second combustion lit the night.

Javier ran up, dripping wet. We heard the high-pitched whine of the four motos returning toward the explosions.

Javier triggered a blasting cap chain. Soldiers opened fire and a firefight raged: El Poder against the ghosts.

We lay flat as the first two motos approached, the riders standing on their foot pegs. Their back tires slid in the turn as they kept going.

Salvos continued in the distance.

The last two motos neared, racing to fight Ghost Armageddon. When the leader was very near, I yanked the line taut. Javier looped the end around the trunk.

The rope clotheslined his helmet. His head jackknifed back and he tumbled. The riderless moto spun off the trail.

The last narco slammed on both brakes, but his front wheel struck the downed rider. He vaulted over the handlebars. He struck a stout tree, his neck snapping like a brittle stick.

Keeping the others distracted, Javier triggered a new salvo from the poltergeist.

El Poder laid down thunder like ghost busters.

I felt the second rider's pulse, none. Javier put the first out of his misery with a silenced pistol shoved under his helmet. We drug the bodies into the brush.

I called for Blake. He ran up. "What happened? How'd you get motorcycles?"

Javier said, "Some guys dropped off them."

"Some guys dropped them off?"

"Something like that. Hop on!"

A motorcycle was an extension of Javier's body, so he carried Blake. We traveled the trail a few hundred yards then turned onto a dirt road. Blake sat behind, hugging Javier's back.

I took the lead. Javier trailed behind, in case of an ambush. At least one pickup full of goons was past our location. A nasty surprise could be hidden around any curve.

We kept the lights off, navigating with night optics that automatically adjusted the amplification, brightness control and infrared illuminator. Due to thermal imaging, warm bodies stood out, bright against a dull backdrop. We had the vision of owls but in a monochrome of glowing green.

The attack boat would cruise the coast, investigating the vacant shoreline. I hoped that we could ride twenty miles then return to the water where the cliffs ended. Tourist and fishing boats crowded San Isabel's shoreline, so we'd blend in.

For a few miles, the road was flat and straight. We began climbing a winding pass, the road twisting with harrowing drops. The road narrowed to one lane. A fist-sized tarantula scurried across the road.

We passed through an impressive notch cut into the mountain, rocky cliffs rising on both sides. A terrain trap.

I radioed Javier, "Think we could close the road with explosives? This notch would be impassable if we blocked the road."

"Blowing holes in the road won't work."

"We could scale the cliff and wedge C-4 into cracks. Bring down a ton of rocks."

"We don't have many explosives left and we've got a pretty good head start. Stopping might give them time to catch up. Or set roadblocks ahead."

We kept moving. The neglected road was strewn with boulders and gullies. I slowed to dodge obstacles. The surface was washboard, the bars pounding my arms like a jackhammer.

We sped past an oasis, an island of lush jungle in a sea of thirsty scrub. Abandoned home sites were tucked among the palms.

A huge snake slithered across the road, ominously entering an overgrown cemetery. I wasn't really superstitious, but that had to be some sort of terrible omen.

Worse than a black cat. Definitely terrible.

We reached the top of the mesa and stopped. I lifted my binoculars and swept the ocean, seeing nothing. I searched the valley behind, no pursuing vehicles.

We continued along the plateau then started down the other side. Near the bottom of the descent, I rounded a corner. Two pickups blocked the road; a cliff wall rose on one side with a sheer drop on the other. I was close, too close.

I slowed. The gunmen didn't react. Probably thought I was one of them.

I hooked a U-turn then radioed, "Roadblock. Turn around."

"Copy."

As I sped away, I heard shouting and looked back. The trucks gave chase, spinning gravel. Bullets struck the road, kicking up dust. But the shots were wildly off the mark due to the lurching of the trucks as they navigated the rocky, pot-holed road.

"I'm taking fire from two pickups in hot pursuit. Both have guys in the back."

"They'll never catch us. Two wheels are better than four."

The uneven road made moto travel far superior. I stood on my foot pegs and twisted the throttle, dodging and weaving as I quickly left them behind. I saw Javier in the distance.

He radioed, "When we get a solid lead, let's pull over and hope they drive past."

"Roger that."

Minutes later, Javier said, "Bad news. I just crested the hill. Six trucks are coming toward us, about five miles away. I'm gonna to peel off the road. Keep going past. I'll hide Blake."

"Should we both hide?"

"Let's trap them. Go to that oasis. Use the grenade launcher to take out the first truck. I'll follow and hit the second with an RPG. Maybe the wrecks will block the convoy and we can hightail it out of here."

"Copy."

I crested and saw the half dozen vehicles roaring toward us on the plains below. The guys following had probably called them.

I passed Javier, hidden behind a large boulder. Blake weaved through cactus, sprinting toward a large pine.

I arrived at the oasis, thick with palms and low bushes, a twenty-acre jungle rising from the brittle desert. I hid the moto and loaded an impact grenade. I'd strike when they were close but it was a gamble. Being near would increase my chances of hitting the truck and finishing off survivors in the ensuing chaos. But if I missed with the single shot device, I'd be significantly outnumbered. Even if I destroyed the truck and killed them all, the second truck would be right behind. I was counting on Javier and his RPG.

"Stryker, the two trucks passed. I'll follow."

"I'm in the oasis."

"They should be there in five."

I searched for a hiding place. Snaking vines choked wooden buildings, the creep devouring long abandoned homes. Plastic bags and loose garbage scattered the roadside, hurled by locals from passing vehicles. The smell of death permeated the air. A maggot-ridden cow reclined, her swollen tongue protruding, the stench her parting gift. A cloud of flies scattered, buzzing.

Gravestones were strewn across a neglected cemetery. Vines conquered tombstones, long fingers wrenching them toward the departed below. Clusters of pale flowers suspended on the thin dark stalks of scattered yucca plants looked like ghosts hovering above swords, phantoms haunting the city of the dead.

A makeshift shrine erected to Santa Muerte loomed on the edge of the overgrown graveyard. Melted candles and pocket change littered the altar, offerings to the leering skull with long blonde hair.

I ducked behind a rock, below a dead palm. A breeze shook the dry fronds like a death rattle.

Two trucks came into view, dust billowing. The second trailed behind to stay out of the leader's dust.

I loaded the grenade then shouldered the M4. I reached in front of the magazine, resting my itchy finger on the launcher's trigger.

The truck grew closer. I'd wait for the whites of their eyes.

When the lead truck was forty feet away, I pulled the trigger, sending the grenade over the boulder, sailing toward their windshield.

The grenade exploded on impact. Shrapnel and shattered glass flew.

I gripped a grenade, pulling the pin.

The pickup rolled slowly past with smoke billowing from the cab. I tossed the steel pineapple into the truck bed.

Four soldiers jumped out.

The explosion rocked the truck, killing the two in the back. I fired a salvo and dropped one survivor but the others ducked behind the truck.

The second pickup slammed to a halt in a cloud of dust, five men in the back and two in the cab. I sprinted into the oasis.

Javier must be a running a bit tardy.

Ten against one at close range. If Javier didn't show up soon, my only chance of survival was escape. No way I could defeat them with those odds.

Run, Wyatt. Run for your life.

CHAPTER THIRTY-EIGHT

I swerved behind a clump of palms and continued running, my boots tangling with dried palm fronds, skeletal hands reaching to add a dweller to the cemetery.

As I sprinted, a narco pointed out my location, "¡Ahí ésta!" They cut the oasis to shreds with Kalashnikovs. Bullets buzzed past, one grazing my helmet.

I dropped a smoke grenade for visual cover. Heard footsteps tramp into the sanctuary. Hooked behind a tree as one man emerged from the smokescreen, running toward me. I unloaded a magazine, the suppressor decreasing the noise and the barrel's flare. A frag struck his exposed neck. Blood squirted in a solid stream. He dropped.

The man wore infrared goggles, tracking body heat. The smokescreen was useless.

I ran deeper into the tangle, replacing a mag on the fly. I ducked behind a gravestone and crouched facing the road, scanning for soldiers. Tried to control my breathing.

Gunfire erupted on my right. Angry metal hornets buzzed past. One struck my helmet and my head exploded in pain. Both my hearing and goggles went black. Felt like a rabid bat flew into one ear and out the other, gnawing through and short-circuiting my brain.

I rolled and sprinted further into the trees. A slug found my shoulder blade, knocking me on my face. An involuntary groan escaped my lips. Wasn't sure if it penetrated my vest.

I crawled as bullets chopped the vegetation, diced leaves raining down.

I pushed off then ran, crouching. I shoved the destroyed goggles onto my helmet. I had no idea where they were without night vision.

But they knew my location, exactly.

Once my hearing returned, I radioed, "I'm trapped in the oasis with ten men in pursuit. Where are you?"

Silence. My radio was also damaged. I was blind, deaf and mute.

Fleeing was the only option. I was the fastest linebacker in the conference. I could outrun them. But the race would stop at the end of the oasis, the finish line finishing me.

I blindly sprinted through the woods. Palm fronds tore at my face. I tripped on a yucca plant and fell. Spotted a clearing a few hundred feet ahead, maybe a spring or a pond. I barreled toward it.

A branch caught my shoulder, knocking me sideways.

The other trucks had probably arrived. The convoy carried dozens of soldiers equipped with AKs, infrared goggles and bullet resistant armor. They would fan out and find me. Then shred me like the chopped salad covering my shoulders.

For all I knew, Javier was already dead. Maybe he crashed. Maybe they pulverized him with an RPG. Maybe he had a flat tire. Maybe a sniper blew off his head. Maybe he ran out of gas.

Maybe I was screwed.

I wondered what would happen to Blake, stranded alone in the desert. I chased the thought away. Focused on not dying.

I arrived at the source of the oasis, a murky pond about two hundred feet across. Thick underbrush and overhanging palms surrounded the pool, a footpath weaving through the snarl. I heard a million insects, telling me to leave.

I crept into the water, careful to avoid stirring the surface, and then sank to the bottom. Their infrared goggles couldn't see me under water, sensing only the surface temperature.

I fished in my pack for my dive mask, equipped with night vision. The water was too dirty for visibility but I could use them near the surface. I could hold my breath for three minutes; triple the average human.

As I swam along the soft bottom, I remembered the enormous viper slithering into the nearby graveyard. I wondered if gators lived in Baja. Didn't like either thought all that much.

I rose for a surface peek. No soldiers. Took a breath then sank below the surface, barely. I slowly turned to visualize the periphery.

A minute later, two soldiers came into view, running on the slender footpath about a hundred feet away. I swam underwater, gripping my M4.

I neared the edge, twenty feet from the narcos. They ran past. I kicked into the shallows and stood, aiming at the closest guy's unprotected neck.

I unloaded, obliterating his cervical spine. He toppled.

As the second spun, I fired a burst into his side. He was wearing standard armor with a front and back plate, his flank vulnerable. He fell sideways, his body suspended in vines.

I sank and replaced the magazine.

Two more ran along the same path, coming in and out of view as they passed through the thick vegetation. They arrived at the downed narcos. One knelt to assess. The other stood sentry, scanning.

I glided under the surface, a hunting crocodile.

The man hanging in the vines was still alive, talking to the soldier. He'd tell them I was in the pond. The soldier listened but shrugged his shoulders like he couldn't understand. The man was probably incoherent or unable to force air from his punctured lungs.

I trained my gun on their backs, protected by armored vests and helmets. Moved into shallow waters near the edge, four feet deep. The second soldier knelt to listen, confident that nobody was near since his infrared goggles would spot any living thing.

Unless the living thing lurked underwater.

One turned and scanned the pond, but the dark waters hid me. In daylight, my presence would be obvious. The other turned toward the water.

I trained the gun on his goggles, the only place lacking armor, my barrel an inch below the surface. But the M4 wasn't constructed for underwater shooting. The gas powered recoil system might be destroyed. Regardless, I couldn't surface with them watching the pond.

I took my chances and pulled the trigger, bullets jumping like metallic flying fish from the burbling water.

His goggles shattered, blood pouring from his eye sockets.

Shifted my aim to the second man's goggles and fired. His AK pinwheeled from his hands, spinning like a drum major's baton. Both were dead.

I kicked into deeper water and checked the gun. The recoil system was destroyed, rendering it useless. Let it sink.

I had my Glock, but it wasn't suppressed so it would betray my location, both with sound and flame. Not to mention, a pistol versus machineguns was like bringing a knife to a gunfight. More accurately, like bringing one knife to fight five guns. Or, if the convoy had arrived, dozens.

I rose for a peek, slowly rotating. A lone soldier walked the trail, opposite the dead narcos.

I swam below the surface, wondering why the man was alone: a rookie move. Some of their tactics were fairly rinky-dink. About half seemed like trained soldiers but the rest were yahoos with guns.

He circled the water's edge. If he arrived at the bodies, he'd know the men were shot in the face from the pond and he'd radio the others. They would storm down and surround the water, trapping me.

I swam as fast as I could, attempting to cut him off. Needed to come up for air but couldn't risk a ripple. I thrust forward, my lungs aching.

I swam under overhanging palms then slowly surfaced, taking a breath. He was fifty feet away. He had infrared, so I needed to avoid direct line of sight. I crept from the water and crossed the trail, crouching behind thick underbrush. I kept my pistol holstered since I needed to kill him silently.

I waited. Twigs cracked as he neared. I heard his breath.

He strode into view on the water's edge, looking across the pond. He was a hulk, one of the biggest Mexicans I'd ever seen. He was shorter than me but probably heavier.

I rushed forward, crouched.

Hearing movement, he swung around.

I uncoiled, striking his flank with my helmet and wrapping his waist. It was like tackling an offensive lineman. But I had the element of surprise. Leveraging my weight, I churned my feet, keeping him off balance.

He splashed into the water, dropping his gun as he sank.

My boot hooked under an exposed root at the pond's edge. My foot trapped, pain shot up my leg as I toppled facedown into the murk.

He spun and leapt onto my back, pushing my head facedown in the soft mud, his knees pinning my arms to my side. He wrapped my throat with both hands from behind, choking the life out of me. His was grip astonishingly strong: a python crushing prey.

I jerked wildly but he remained in control. My throat was being crushed. The pain was horrible. I felt lightheaded, on the verge. My brain was not getting nearly enough blood. My tongue protruded into the mud under the intense pressure.

In the SEALs, we learned how to correctly choke from behind. Ball the digits tight and press the knuckles against the airway, protecting the fingers.

Obviously he missed that lesson, so his fingers were fair game.

I kicked my foot free. Using the soft mud and his buoyancy to my advantage, I slowly worked my hands up to my neck.

I grabbed the lowest appendage, a pinky, and snapped it. Like breaking a sturdy pencil.

I twisted and jerked the broken digit, but his clutch held fast. His fingers dug even deeper into my windpipe, threatening to break the cartilaginous rings. He wasn't the sneaky Boston Strangler who had the luxury of scurrying away from a combative woman due to an injury. He could tolerate pain knowing one of us would die.

Having failed with the pinkie, I jumped to his index finger, closest to my jaw. With my thumb, I applied sideways pressure to the bottom joint while pulling in the opposite direction, dislocating it.

Lacking two digits on his right hand, his grip weakened considerably. But he was still on my back, pressing my face into the mud. My three minutes had passed. I felt desperate for air.

I pulled his loose pointer finger into my mouth and bit down, crunching the fingernail like a peanut.

I ground through skin and muscle.

Injuring fingernails has been a popular torture method for centuries, because it hurts like hell. Lots of pain-sensitive nerve endings on the nail bed. Maybe worse than hell.

He jerked back and I rotated under him, onto my back. I sank deeper and took him with me, his head barely below the surface. He tried to pull his finger free but I held fast, granulating the bone with my molars. He screamed underwater, air boiling from his mouth.

As he yanked back again, I bent my knees and placed my feet against the bottom then bucked hard, throwing him off. Wrapped his knee with an arm and rotated off the bottom, spinning him down. I stood in the waist-deep water, wrenching his back and neck, his face sinking in the mud.

My mask full of muddy water, I yanked it onto my helmet.

He smashed my nose with his free foot, breaking loose.

I saw nothing but white and toppled back, nearly falling. My vision returned.

He floundered under the muddy water, trying to stand. I took a deep breath, crouching.

His helmet broke the water's surface, facing me.

I exploded into him, my helmet striking his face. Full on. I wrapped his arms in a bear hug, kicking into deeper water.

We sank. His legs flailed helplessly.

I tightened my arms, squeezing the air from his chest. He thrashed mightily but I held on. I scissored my legs, sending us into a tight spin, the crocodile disorienting his prey.

As we spun deeper, his struggle weakened. After two minutes, he inhaled water then went limp, unconscious. Game over.

I kicked to the surface and took a deep breath, keeping his head below. We sank again.

When I was nearly out of breath, I checked his pulse. He was dead, his lungs and stomach probably full of water. I surfaced and removed his ammo then delivered his waterlogged body to the bottom.

I found his AK-47 in the shallows then swam into deeper water. I pinched my crooked nose to stop the flow of blood, and then rose to the surface. After several minutes of observation, the area seemed deserted.

I had to escape before the oasis was crawling with narcos. And I couldn't delay, even for a moment, since Javier might be outnumbered four-to-one. Or fifty-to-one if the convoy had arrived. I swam to shore and slowly rose. Took a few steps forward and listened.

Nothing.

I ran about twenty feet then crouched behind a palm. I scanned the forest with binoculars.

The horrible sound of gunfire erupted, slightly behind and to my left.

I dropped and kicked around the tree to face the attack.

More machineguns announced their presence from my right.

I flattened. A bullet grazed my helmet.

They had flanked me, unnoticed. Bullets whined, the Reaper whistling like he was calling a dog.

A salvo struck the palm tree inches from my nose. I instinctively recoiled and kicked back a foot. Half my boot was blown off and probably most of my foot.

I pushed forward. Several shots bounced, punching into my back.

I yelled, "¡Yo me rindo! ¡Me rindo!" *I surrender! I surrender!*

"¡De pie, con las manos en alto!" *Stand with your hands up!*

I lifted my hands and stood. I was buying time, gambling that they'd interrogate me. But would never let me live.

"¡Saca su casco!" *Remove your helmet!*

I dropped my helmet. I faced three narcos, the air thick with fury and the promise of blood.

From behind, a rifle butt struck the side of my head, a nauseating electric ache dropping me to my knees. Hot blood spurted from my ear, dripping down.

A boot kicked between my shoulders, knocking me flat. A gun barrel rammed the back of my neck.

He growled in my ear, warm breath on my bloody face, "Usted va a morir, pero primero usted rogar por la muerte." *You will die, but first you'll plead for death.*

He grabbed my hair and cranked my head back, straining my neck. He muttered, "Usted va a sufrir más de lo que nunca creyó posible." *You will suffer more than you ever thought possible.*

It was over. My bloody face sank into the dirt, a shallow grave.

CHAPTER THIRTY-NINE

The thug's boot pressed hard on my back, making it difficult to breathe. His breath smelled like the bloated cow. The others stepped forward, guns trained.

One knelt and spit in my face. Then stood, pulling back to kick my face.

I jerked and his jackboot only landed a glancing blow.

The man gripping my hair slammed my face into the rocky ground. Pain exploded from my broken nose. He pushed the barrel down on my neck with all his weight.

Hello, Javier? It's about time for some serious heroics.

As if on queue, gunfire erupted.

Señor Stanky Breath loosed his grip. His body slumped onto my back, his warm blood mixing with mine.

Blood brothers in the cemetery.

Shouts, bullets and boots flew chaotically. By the sound of his gunfire, I knew Javier was about thirty feet behind. I stayed under the corpse. Peeking out, I saw three men crouched, shooting over me at Javier.

I pushed up with my elbows and removed a grenade. Pulled the pin and counted, holding it to the last moment. Thrust my arm from beneath my blood brother. Rolled the grenade toward the narcos. I jerked back under the human shield.

The grenade detonated. The deafening explosion dropped two narcos in a flash of blood and pain.

The lone survivor attempted to run but one leg was mutilated, dragging behind. He hopped on one foot. Javier marched forward, peppering the thugs on the ground. He removed the spent mag as he continued toward the injured man.

The man lost his balance and fell against a palm trunk, wrapping it with both arms. Javier hammered him to the tree with hot nails.

I sat up and spat a mouthful of blood. "Better late than never."

"You all right?" he asked.

"Maybe. By my count, there are no survivors from the two trucks. What about the convoy?"

"I took care of them. What're your injuries?"

I touched the side of my head and felt a gaping scalp laceration, my hair matted with warm blood that trickled over my broken nose.

"Took a shot to the cranium but the helmet saved me. Another got me in the back. Did it pierce my vest?" I removed my vest.

He inspected my back. "You've got a bruise the side of a coconut, but you're not wearing a bullet."

"So I'll live a few more hours. Thank God and the Navy for Kevlar."

"Gotta get moving."

"I'm not sure I have a foot." I gingerly inspected. My foot was intact, only missing the heel of my boot.

As we ran toward the road, I asked, "What's up with the convoy?"

"I didn't want the trucks to see me following, so I lagged. I thought you'd attack further from your position. After you launched the grenade, I gunned it. But they'd already chased you into the tangle."

"I waited until they were close. Didn't want to miss. I should've told you my plan."

"Should've told you mine. I figured our odds'd be grim if the convoy stopped at the wrecked trucks. So I went to greet them. I hid around a bend, where we passed through that notch with cliffs on both sides. I took out the lead truck with an RPG. The others were blocked since the road was so narrow. Two motos got around the wreckage and chased me. I hid. Then I subtracted them."

"Strong work."

"Your radio was silent."

"My electronics quit working after I took a brain bullet."

"Makes sense. When I got back, I entered the jungle and located the narcos. But I was perplexed about your location. Since I wasn't finding you with infrared or GPS, I thought you might've escaped the oasis. I didn't want to start shooting until I knew where you were."

"I was hanging out in the puddle."

"No wonder."

"I took out five while lurking like the Tick-Tock Croc. One of nearly choked me to death and busted my nose. The recoil system blew on my M4, but I got an AK."

"Your folks didn't name you Wyatt Earp for nothing! You're a badass gunslinger!"

"Well, I feel like an ass. And pretty bad, to boot. "

"I guess that counts as badass. When the firefight broke out, I crept up and wasted that guy on top of you."

"He whacked my head, thus the new hairdo. As I said, better late than never."

We arrived at the cemetery. He pointed at a neglected grave, "How's that for freaky?"

"For sure. I hid behind a tombstone during a firefight, like something out of a weird movie. You see that shrine to Santa Muerte?"

"Yeah. Them some creepy fellas."

He pulled his bike from the brush and said, "The convoy might move the destroyed pickup. But I bought some time. They'll have to push the truck a hundred feet before they have room to get around. A front wheel was blown off and it's got a broken axle. It'll be a serious chore."

I wore my snorkel mask, equipped with night vision. My helmet's radio was nonfunctional but we still had Blake's handheld radio.

We drove to Blake, using the GPS tracker I'd placed on his wrist. He was anxiously drawing in the dirt with a stick. He often drew when he was upset.

"Hey buddy! Let's get going!"

He ran and hugged me. "Dad! You guys were gone a long time! I was worried."

"It took a little longer than we thought."

"What happened to your face?"

"Got in a fight."

"Your nose is crooked. You okay?"

"Yeah. You should see the other guy!"

He smiled and his eyes lit up. He thought I was invincible, and we were going to be all right.

The bump on his face was purple. I couldn't tell if it was a boil or a raised bruise.

"What happened to your head?"

He rubbed the bump. "Maybe I hit my head when we slid down that rope."

He climbed on with Javier. I took the lead. Blood trickled down my face but we couldn't waste time bandaging.

We arrived at the bottom, where the trucks had been parked. Then headed down a flat, straight road. An ocean breeze blew dust and obscured our visibility so I slowed. As we approached road kill, buzzards scattered.

An abandoned building sat near the edge of the road. Cactus stood sentry, surrounded by sagebrush. I watched warily as it would be a perfect spot for an ambush. Nothing moved as I passed.

Low clouds filtered across the moonless sky. A skinny dog ran along the road. The hum of our motos grew monotonous and I relaxed a little thinking about Catherine and Susan. I wanted to call them, but I didn't really have anything to say and didn't want to stop. If the trucks were El Poder's final stand, we'd be in San Isabel in an hour or so.

I was jealous of Javier, riding with Blake, being hugged from behind. I wondered if Blake was scared, happy or anxious. Probably all of the above.

I eagerly anticipated the joyful reunion of Blake and his mama, seeing Catherine's beautiful smile again. He'd be in heaven. I smiled, thinking of the three blonds commiserating over their black hair. One more hour and we'd be a happy fivesome.

We droned on until I saw the glow of a village. I stopped and waited for Javier. "Should we drive into town?"

"Let's scout it out. If it's quiet, we'll keep trucking."

At the top of the next hill, I scaled a palm tree. Saw lights along the road, near the pueblo. I increased the power in the binoculars, holding my hands as steady as possible.

My sprits dropped at the grim sight. Five trucks squatted on a bridge over a dry river-channel, armed men loitering on both sides. Several motorcycles and ATVs were in the group, plus men on horseback. Machineguns were mounted on two truck beds.

I climbed down and relayed the news, "We can't win a direct battle. Our last RPG might destroy a truck or two. But not thirty men armed to the teeth."

"We can't double back. The convoy will eventually get past the demolished truck. Gotta bypass the roadblock on foot. The off-road terrain is too rocky for motos. Local police might join the hunt soon."

"Yeah, the narcos could say we kidnapped a child."

"The local cops are probably corrupt anyhow. They could call in a heli from Cabo. They'll have police dogs."

"It's freaking hard to avoid a dog. We'll have to double back a lot."

Dogs determine the direction of a target by the strength of the scent, so doubling back creates false trails.

"They have Blake's scent from his room."

Blake said, "Big dogs chased me when I ran away from the house in San Diego. I was really scared."

"You're a brave guy."

"We should get moving."

We hid the motos. Javier said, "Blake, take off your socks and T-shirt."

"Why?"

"We're gonna create a false trail."

Blake removed his shirt and socks. Javier tied the clothes in knots with beef jerky inside. He placed them along the roadside. "Wild animals will drag them off. Good luck finding the real trail, doggies."

I said to Javier, "You're smarter than you look."

"You're not. That's pretty bad, considering."

We picked our way through the sagebrush. Blake rode my shoulders to avoid leaving his scent. We zig-zagged and doubled back. Javier walked about fifty feet in front, keeping an eye out.

I asked, "Blake, what happened after you got kidnapped?"

He told me all about his capture and attempts to escape. I smiled; it's hard to keep lighting in a cage.

Then he said, "One night, policemen came to save me. They said the bad guy killed you all. I cried for a long time about that. I cried every day." His voice cracked and he began to cry.

I lifted him from my shoulders and hugged him. "I love you, Blake."

He sobbed, "I love you, too."

My eyes stung. I wondered if he'd ever be the same after so much mental trauma.

We resumed hiking and he continued, "A family took me across the border then two guys drove the rest of the way. They got drunk and I think they were using drugs. One night, they killed an old man. They thought he was a robber. I took a gold gun and ran into the desert.

"They searched and yelled for me. But I kept running from their flashlights. I was really close to them a few times and even pointed the gun at them. But they never saw me. I thought about sneaking back to the truck and driving off. Except for one little problem, I don't really know how to drive. We were in the middle of nowhere so I was worried that I might die of hunger if they drove off. When the sun started coming up, I decided to go with them. I walked back and said I was hiding from the robbers. But I really hid from them. I kept the gun under my shirt, in case they tried to shoot anybody else.

"The next day we finally reached the beach house. They told me I was supposed to act like I was Maria's kid, the lady who lived there. But I'd seen her at the first house, so I was sort of confused and suspicious. They gave me tons of toys and everything. Maria was nice, but it was weird how she wanted me to be her son or whatever."

"What did you do with the gun?" I remembered the truck driver at the warehouse with the gold-plated gun.

"I kept it hidden in my room at the beach house. I guess it's still there."

I wasn't sure what to say about that. I didn't like the idea of Blake having a pistol at his age. But his actions were incredibly brave and shrewd. So I said nothing.

He continued, "I couldn't stop thinking about you guys. I was so lonely."

"We've been looking for you every minute of every day," I said. "We'd never give up."

"I know, but I thought you were dead. I didn't think anyone was looking for me. Except the bad guy. I wish I'd hit him in the head instead of his arm."

"You were very brave to help Susan. I'm so, so proud of you. You're a wonderful son."

He smiled, the pure innocent smile of a child.

Javier stopped and waited for us to catch him. He said, "We need a vehicle to get to San Isabel."

"Maybe we can steal one."

"Gonna be difficult."

"We could have Blake lay in the street, like he's injured. When the driver stops, we can commandeer the vehicle."

"I like it."

Blake said, "I'm a good tricker!"

CHAPTER
FORTY

We returned to the road, a mile past the pueblo. As we waited for daylight, I removed suture materials from my first aid kit. Javier held his reflective goggles like a mirror. My face was swollen about like Hubert, Jefe's hospital imposter. Both eyes were shiners from my broken nose, my skin rusty with dried blood.

I placed my thumbs on my crooked nose and steeled myself.

Then straightened it with a nauseating pop.

The pain was toxic. Sweat ran down my forehead. After a few minutes, it settled to a dull roar.

I studied the three-inch scalp laceration. My skull gleamed white under the football-shaped wound, like a milky, blind eye inside red-rimmed eyelids.

I washed it with drinking water, flushing out dirt and a few pebbles. I held the needle in a clamp and hooked the skin edge, bringing my scalp together. It hurt, but not like the nose. I placed six stiches, satisfied with the closure.

I smeared my blood on Blake's face and dripped it on his shirt. He practiced his stunt, ready for his Oscar-worthy trickery.

At dawn, a brightly colored delivery truck wound toward the town. Blake ran and lay in the street with legs and arms sprawled, just like we'd practiced.

The truck stopped and a middle-aged man ran to Blake. He knelt. "¿Que paso, niño?" *What happened, little boy?*

Blake moaned and his eyelids fluttered. Javier crept up, touching his pistol to the back of the man's head.

Javier said, "Si nos conduce a San Isabel, yo te lo pagaré tres mil dólares. Si te niegas, te vamos a matar." *If you'll drive us to San Isabel, I'll pay three thousand U.S. dollars. If you refuse, we'll kill you.*

He was rattled but not hysterical. "No problem, but there are several roadblocks in the next two towns."

The man walked to his truck, Javier close behind. He unlatched the rear door, sliding it up with a rattle. Crates held snacks, soda cans and beer bottles. Blankets padded the merchandise.

Blake and I knelt in the rear of the cargo hold.

In Spanish, Javier said, "I need a blanket to hide beside you. You try any funny stuff, we die together." He held up his pistol.

The man nodded, "*¡Si, Señor! Comprendo.*" His forehead glistened.

The truck hooked a U-turn and headed north. I pulled a blanket over us, Blake in my arms.

I heard Javier speaking on his mic, "Is there another road?"

"There is one. But I'm sure there's a blockade."

"Take it. You passed those roadblocks once this morning. They'll wonder why you turned around."

"*Si, Señor.*"

"Why the roadblocks?"

"They're looking for men traveling with a boy, but didn't say why."

Quiet minutes passed. Then the man said, "Here's the other road."

The truck slowed and turned. We bumped along the unimproved road.

"I'm coming to a roadblock. But I know these men, from my pueblo."

"Get us through and I've got ten thousand dollars for you. If not, I have a bullet."

"*Comprendo.*"

The truck slowed to a stop. I reached for my pistol and whispered, "If the back opens, don't move. Breathe quietly."

"Okay, Dad. Thanks for coming for me." He kissed my cheek.

A voice spoke, "*¿Qué tal, amigo? ¿Has visto algo inusual?*" *What's up, amigo? Have you seen anything unusual?*

"Like what?"

"There was an attack on Jefe's place in San Carlos. The Zetas kidnapped El Jefe's son."

The man paused. If he were transporting Jefe's child, he'd face a death far worse than a bullet. I anxiously wondered if he was giving a signal.

"I haven't seen anything."

"All right. I'll go tell them to move the truck."

Not good. The narco could've yelled to the men instead of walking back.

A minute passed.

"I'll go talk to them."

Javier growled, "Stay in the truck, or die."

Silence.

I heard the driver's door fly open. The man yelled, "They're in the truck!"

Javier could've killed him but his death would serve no purpose. He muttered, "Hold on! Here we go!"

Javier jumped up into the driver's seat and threw the truck into gear. I held Blake tightly as the truck lurched forward.

Gunshots thumped the truck. I yanked Blake under me and lay on top of him. We crashed into something metal. Slowed but didn't stop.

The truck rocked as we drove over something. There were screams and shouts.

Bullets pierced both sides. They fired conventional weapons, not machineguns. Small dots of light illuminated the cargo space as rounds penetrated above us. A shotgun unloaded, two giant holes appearing in the side. Soda cans, potato chip bags and bottles exploded and spilled.

They weren't concerned with Blake's life. They knew he wasn't Jefe's son.

"I punched though the roadblock." He paused, breathing heavily, and then continued, "I'm hit!"

Bullets raked the rear door then faded. Blake and I were thrown about as Javier barreled along the pockmarked road.

A soup of broken glass, beer, soft drink and floating corn chips sloshed over our boots.

I asked Javier, "You okay?"

"Not sure. A round penetrated...the vest...into my left chest. Not breathing too well." He groaned. "Need to pull over."

Left chest.

"How many vehicles?"

He grunted, "A truck and three motos. I smashed the truck and ran over a bike."

A few minutes passed then Javier whispered, "Two motorcycles are chasing." His voice sounded different, a burdensome hiss, his breathing increasingly labored.

I heard motorcycles approaching from behind. I crawled toward the door, lying facedown.

"Can't breathe." Javier gasped. "About to...pass out. I need..."

The motorcycle din drowned his voice. The truck slowed and drifted off the road, bumping wildly.

I unhooked the door and peered behind the gun sight. One moto was close behind and closing fast. He wasn't wearing a helmet.

I unloaded, flames flying from the barrel of the AK.

The bullets struck his arm, his handlebar twisting abruptly. He cartwheeled over the bars, Superman-style. His bare head crunched the bumper.

The other slammed on the brakes and skidded, putting his foot down to execute a U-turn. I riddled him and he toppled, one leg pinned below the bike. The truck rolled to a stop.

"Javier? I got both of them. You there?"

Silence.

"Stay hidden. I'll check on Javier."

I slid the door up and jumped out. As I ran backwards toward the front of the truck, I held the trigger down, spraying both men.

Javier slumped face down on the seat. Blood spattered the dash and steering wheel. I grabbed his legs and pulled him gently from the truck.

He appeared dead. His vacant eyes bulged, his skin purple. His neck veins popped, trachea pushed to the right. Blood pooled from his lips, dribbling down.

I turned him over, blood draining from his mouth and nose. I threw him on his back and unzipped his vest then ripped open his sticky undershirt. The bullet entered the left side of his chest, above his heart.

Foamy blood poured from the wound.

"Javier, talk to me!" He wasn't breathing. I felt his neck for a pulse.

None.

Blake ran up, disobeying my orders. Seeing Javier, he cried, "Is he dead, Daddy? No! Don't die, Javi!" He released a loud sob, tears flooding.

Javier's mouth hung open but no breath escaped.

I continued searching for a pulse. Jerked my pack open, removing a syringe. Punctured his skin with the needle, a few inches below the collarbone. Air hissed out like a punctured tire.

I pushed a hemostatic cylinder into the wound; powdered coagulant sealed the wound.

Still no pulse.

I grabbed a scalpel to slice open his chest but stopped, knowing it would never work. Without cardiac bypass equipment, he wouldn't survive open-heart surgery in the middle of rural Mexico. Flaying him like a butchered cow was pointless.

He was dead.

CHAPTER FORTY- ONE

I flung the scalpel then jammed my fingers into his carotid, desperately seeking that tiny thump, the subtle nudge that would signal life occupying his cooling body.

Time slowed. CPR would be futile.

"Daddy, save him! Javi can't die." Blake's voice echoed.

I noticed the scar above Javier's left eye and remembered the story of his childhood downhill bike race, planting his head against a parked car. His parted lips exposed a chipped front tooth. I'd wondered about that tooth for years but never asked. I observed the faint crow's feet at the edges of his eyes from a perpetual smile, from a smile I'd never see again.

Blake's cries seemed distant, my surroundings dreamlike, faint.

In addition to more severe, unknown injuries, Javier had a tension pneumothorax. His injured lung acted as a one-way valve. Air leaked out of his lung into his chest cavity, collapsing his lung. The air pumped into the space around his lung under increasingly high pressure, crumpling his heart and lungs. His trachea was pushed aside under the pressure. His heart couldn't pump and his lungs were unable to expand, leading to his rapid death.

The needle relieved the pressure, releasing his heart from the pressurized tomb. But it didn't beat and his lungs didn't breathe. I assumed he had other injuries, maybe a severed aorta or a bullet through his heart.

I struck his chest with my fist. No pulse. I struck it again, harder. Began chest compressions. Blake cried louder.

Struck it a third time and searched for a pulse.

I felt a faint beat.

He inhaled.

I exhaled.

He moaned. The cold purple was chased away by warm crimson. He slowly opened his eyes, unfocused.

Blake yelled, a mix of a sob and a cheer, "Daddy, you saved him!"

"Can you hear me?"

He opened his mouth noiselessly. He groaned, closing his eyes again. A minute passed then he opened his eyes and whispered, "I owe you, Riot."

"You don't owe me anything. I love you, bro."

A faint smirk crossed his face. "Do I get a kiss, Loverboy?"

"I love you both!" Blake kissed Javier's cheek. Javier attempted to sit then quickly lay back down.

"Stay still. Just rest for a few. You're okay."

"If you say so."

"One more thing. It'll hurt, but will be over soon."

I stitched the needle to his chest. He winced as the needle entered his skin. I tied it, securing the needle in place.

When a tension pneumothorax is treated with needle decompression, the patient will usually breathe almost instantly. He did not, because his heart was in ventricular fibrillation. The electrical system of his heart, housed in the cardiac muscle, malfunctioned due to a lack of oxygen and blood flow. Instead of beating, it quivered in spasm, like a convict strapped to an electric chair.

V fib is a rare complication of a tension pneumothorax that would be immediately apparent on a cardiac monitor in the ER, rapidly treated with defibrillation paddles. Striking him with my fist was an attempt to jumpstart his heart, a low-tech substitute.

It worked. But he wasn't out of the woods.

I pulled him to a seated position and searched for the exit wound, finding none. The bullet could be lodged in his heart or aorta. If it moved or the clot broke, he'd die instantly. I needed to get him to safety, soon.

I bandaged the wound, wrapping his thorax, and then helped him with his Kevlar vest. I said, "Gotta keep moving. We can't take the truck. Every narco from here to Tijuana will be searching for it. More'll be here soon. Those motos might still function but I razed them pretty good. Can you move? If not, we could hide you and then return."

"Let's see if I can stand."

I hooked my hands under his armpits and lifted. He stood. Blake steadied Javier's waist with both hands, a childish attempt to help.

"Hurts like a summabitch. But I can probably manage a moto."

I inspected the bikes. One was fine but the other leaked gas and radiator fluid. I took the cap off and peered inside the bullet-ridden tank. There was gasoline below the puncture, so it would probably run. I bandaged the hole with tape. The radiator was ruined but it would run a little while before overheating. We still had about ten miles to go.

We undressed one body and Javier put the narco's shirt over his vest. I was too big.

Javier's mumbled, "Let's put the bikes in the back and drive the truck. I can rest a little. Until we have company."

Javier asking for rest concerned me. He was one of the toughest men on earth. I wondered if he was dying. He might have an injured vessel, slowly bleeding to death internally.

I loaded the bikes. They climbed in.

Javier spoke, barely more than a whisper, "Blake you sit there and I'll guard the rear."

I put the truck into gear. The windshield gone, dust and air poured in like a polluted river. My eyes stung.

Towering cliffs loomed along the Pacific until San Isabel. If Javier were uninjured, we could ditch the truck and hike to the water. We were only a few miles from the ocean and could rappel down the cliffs, one of us holding Blake.

The potential for dogs, helicopters and the attack boat would complicate a run to the water. They knew we were heading to San Isabel. The driver of the hijacked food truck surely told them.

There was only one road through the next pass. A final stand with a concentration of armed men seemed a forgone conclusion.

I dialed the sat phone. Catherine answered, "Hello?"

"We're on our way."

"Yes! Is everyone okay?"

I downplayed Javier's injuries. "Javier and I have new scars, but we'll live. Unfortunately, they know we're headed for San Isabel. Head into deep water until you hear from us."

"All right. Give Blake a kiss."

We turned onto the main road then started up a winding pass. The road was as bad as the rest, rutted with potholes. My back ached from my gunshot injury, my neck stiff. I quickly became more aware of my fatigue. I blinked a few times to clear my head. Tried to think of a plan, but nothing came to mind. We'd just have to take challenges as they arose.

Through Javier's mic, I heard Blake ask timidly, "You okay, Javi?"

"Yeah, I'm fine. You?"

"I'm so happy. It's like the best birthday ever. I found out my parents are alive."

"Awesome."

"Wanna thumb wrestle?"

"No, you stay there. I'm going to rest a bit."

"Okay. Me, too. We can thumb wrestle on the boat."

"Good idea."

There was so much left unsaid. Blake was worried about Javier. He felt helpless, seeing Javier in pain. Like me, he probably felt guilty about Javier's injuries. Childlike, he wanted to help without knowing how.

Javier's voice betrayed an attempt to disguise pain and exhaustion. And possibly impending doom.

When Javier and I were in BUD/S training, we encouraged each other. We made a pact that we'd do whatever we could to help each other make it. During Hell Week we got four hours of sleep for the entire week, four one-hour naps. Instructors made us exercise non-stop. Over eighty percent that were accepted into BUD/S failed. They either dropped out or were cut.

They split us into teams for competition. We swam, ran and competed on the obstacle course. We raced with heavy logs on our shoulders. We paddled in rafts. The winning team got to rest for a few minutes.

When we won, I remember looking at the other guys' faces. Most were barely surviving, their faces betraying strain, fatigue and doubt. Javier was tired but far from defeated. I gained strength from his unbreakable spirit.

But today, he sounded broken.

He knew he was facing the Reaper and thought his injuries created a burden for us. Believed he'd failed us.

"Have you been to Legoland?" Blake asked.

"Not yet. Is it fun?"

"It's so much fun! We have to go when we get back to San Diego! There's a ride where you squirt each other with water cannons, just like SEAL stuff. You'd be really good at it."

He mumbled, "Sounds great."

"We can all go! My dad wins prizes every time on the basketball toss! I have a bunch of cool stuffed animals we won there."

"I can't wait."

"It'll be fun."

"Yeah."

"Yeah."

Awkward silence followed. I imagined Blake wondering what Javier thought and trying to cheer him. Javi humored him, but needed to rest, probably ached to rest. My eyes stung.

We'd never return to San Diego, none of us: no Legoland, no basketball toss and no cuddly stuffed doggies. We'd be lucky if any of us thumb wrestled again. The whole thing was a Shakespearean tragedy, a tragic comedy. To be so close, yet so far. I thought about Zo's death, the last time I had seen Javier so low.

The sunlight crested the hills, illuminating the distant ocean. A horsefly struck me in the cheek, stinging.

We started down the hill. A thin cat scampered, holding a squirming lizard in its mouth.

I struck a pothole hard and winced. Each jolt probably felt like a knife to Javier, with dirty metal hovering near his heart.

A huge roadblock loomed in the distance.

I felt weak. I wanted to be done. They had taken the fight out of me.

I said, "There's a multi-vehicle roadblock at the bottom of this pass."

"I'm so sick of roadblocks, I could puke."

"Others are probably coming from behind. We have to engage, unless we hoof it. Could you go on foot?"

"Not sure. I doubt we could outrun them. I can barely walk."

I stopped and raised binoculars. They saw us and leapt into action, one man shouting orders. Narcos jumped to their feet and shouldered their guns, others racing to meet us.

"Motos and ATVs are charging us."

He mumbled, "Time for Custer's last stand."

"Or the shootout at okay Corral. That's where my namesake got his reputation. I like that ending better than Custer's."

"That's the spirit, Wyatt Earp."

CHAPTER FORTY-TWO

Three motorcycles rounded a corner, a hundred yards ahead. They pulled to the side of the road then knelt behind their motos, firing with Kalashnikovs.

I stomped the gas and returned fire through the vacant windshield cavity. Spent cartridges ejected, bouncing around the cab like popcorn.

At the last instant, I ducked down. The AK's hot barrel touched the passenger seat, melting the foam.

Their bullets thumped the hood and whistled through the empty cockpit, the last remnants of glass blown away. As we passed, Javier opened fire from the rear.

"I got two," he said. "One hid behind a rock."

I rounded a corner and a four-wheeled ATV sped toward us, kamikaze style. The driver gripped the handlebars and the passenger leaned around, flames leaping from his barrel.

Sparks flew off the hood. The radiator spewed boiling steam.

Boulders lined the road so there was no room for the ATV to exit. I dropped below the dashboard and punched the accelerator.

With a sickening crunch, I plowed headlong into the ATV.

The four-wheeler slid under the bumper, trapping the driver. The passenger toppled back, falling under. I counter steered aggressively, struggling to stay on the road. Held the pedal down, my rear tires spinning.

With a screech, the ATV slid out of the way. The truck tires bounced over a body. A staccato of gunfire signaled Javier finishing them.

I barreled toward the roadblock, at least seven vehicles with about thirty men. As I navigated tight curves, they came in and out of view.

I radioed, "We can't get through. Can't bulldoze through that many."

"Stop before the last turn and we'll unload the bikes. We can booby trap the truck with frag bombs and send it. Then try to get past on motos. I still have one RPG and several grenades."

"One moto's still behind, the guy that hid behind a rock."

We stopped at the last curve. I ran to unload the motos.

Javier winced as he rolled them to me. I grabbed two cameras and two frag bombs. They'd kill anyone in a fifty-foot radius.

I fixed them to the top of the cab and under the rear bumper with adhesive backing. Javier placed a blasting cap chain in the passenger seat. We swapped guns, since my stolen AK lacked a launcher.

"This might be the first time innocent civilians send a truck loaded with explosives into a crowd of terrorists."

He smiled weakly, "Car bomb coming atcha, bitches."

"Blake, hide in those bushes. When we come back, run to the motorcycles."

Javier sat on the rear bumper. I placed a heavy rock near the gas pedal.

I slowly turned the corner. Soldiers opened fire. One truck had a heavy machinegun mounted on the bed.

I fired a smoke grenade through the empty windshield, landing in front of the blockade. Javier tossed another smoke grenade into the back of the truck, and then stepped off the bumper. He lay down a ferocious onslaught as he marched, peering around the truck's passenger side. Smoke filtered up, clouding the view.

I slowly drove forward, ducking below the dash. Bullets peppered the truck as I accelerated.

Their truck-mounted machinegun released a sinister staccato, pulverizing our hood and shredding a front tire. The truck listed sideways, dropped on one rim. Foam stuffing floated from shredded seat cushions.

I shoved the rock against the gas pedal. Activated two smoke grenades and left them in the cab. Triggered the blasting cap chain, the staccato rattling.

As I entered the fog, I jumped, rolling into the bushes.

The truck collided with the front vehicles, white clouds pouring from the cab. The blasting cap chain banged away, the noise amplified by the cab.

The narcos furiously returned fire from all sides. The heavy machinegun shot through the truck, bullets exiting the cargo hold. The blasting caps went silent.

I ran up the hazy road.

I slowed to watch the action on my handheld video monitor. Soldiers moved toward the truck's cab, filling it with lead. One ducked beside the passenger window and fired blindly inside. Soldiers circled behind, riddling the back.

The firing slowed. Others stood to look. From both sides, men marched through the dense dust and smoke clouds with guns trained, closing in. Looked like they were approaching through milk.

I lay flat on the road.

A soldier opened the rear door and unloaded into the cargo hold. More came from behind other vehicles.

I pressed the button.

The explosions were deafening. Razor edged shrapnel flew in every direction, slicing muscle and bone. Men screamed. Then some fell silent and others wailed.

I sprinted up the road. As I rounded the bend, Javier was perched on his moto, helping Blake climb on. His automatic was on his back, the RPG launcher propped on the motorcycle.

I heard the buzzing of a two-stroke engine then the trailing moto came around a curve. The man had his AK cradled in one arm.

He slowed and trained the barrel on Javier and Blake, only yards away.

In full sprint, I fired a burst.

The gas tank exploded and the man toppled backward. His bike skidded out, both the man and the bike engulfed in fire.

The burning man crawled, leaving a flaming trail. He slowed. Then stopped.

I jumped onto my moto. We drove toward the roadblock but stopped before the curve. Javier got off, shouldering the RPG.

The smoke had mostly cleared. At least ten men survived the dual blasts. Two were on the truck with the mounted machinegun. They saw us and yelled.

Javier fired his final RPG with devastating accuracy. The rocket struck the cab with the mounted gun and detonated. Smoldering bodies flew like rag dolls.

Javier dropped his RPG launcher and jumped on his bike.

I radioed, "Tell Blake to close his eyes. The ground's strewn with body parts."

We accelerated then stopped behind the burned-out delivery truck. I heard groans and frantic voices.

Avoiding bloody chunks, I looked under the truck and saw a few men moving among the wreckage. Rolled a smoke grenade between the tires.

I removed a hand grenade from my vest and Javier did the same. I whispered, "One, two, three!"

We flung our grenades and ducked.

After they exploded, we weaved through the smoky tangle. The wreckage would slow any narcos coming from behind.

We exited the other side and sped away. Not a single shot was fired.

There were probably survivors. But after five sequential explosions, we had taken the fight out of them.

CHAPTER FORTY-THREE

Behram followed their progress via radio reports of the fighting. The group arrived by water and would leave the same way. The women were on a boat somewhere, planning to retrieve them. The truck driver said they were headed to San Isabel, the closest water access.

El Poder's men tried military force, against a team led by Alcaraz. The pathetic rubes were no match for an experienced SEAL Commander with advanced weapons and technology. So, many of the unworthy men died. They should've quietly waited on the beach, the group's obvious destination.

So Behram would have to do it for them.

When he went to the compound to poison the boy with dioxin, the ignorant peasants were horrified at his appearance, thinking he had an infectious disease. They brought Maria to see him. But she knew of his desire to kill the child;

the double-crossing Jefe had told her. He doubted Jefe ever intended to let him slay the boy.

Maria told the guards to kill him if he returned, so he left in humiliation. The following day, he stopped a guard on his way to the compound. He planned to offer the man a fortune to perform the deed, but he fled from Behram's sickening appearance, worried he would catch whatever it was.

Behram lurked in the hills, watching the compound from a distance with binoculars. One night, he stole a radio from a guard's car.

When the fireworks started, he only observed. Once the gunboat arrived, he thought they'd be killed, but was pleasantly surprised when the carnage began marching north.

He drove to San Isabel. Sailboats and fishing craft crowded near the shore. Eager fishermen and smiling families wandered the beach, basking in the morning sun. The Mexicans were intolerable with their happy-go-lucky ways. After Jefe's betrayal and his subsequent maltreatment at the compound, his contempt for the useless Hispanics grew. He ached to murder them all, mowing them down with a machinegun. He'd love to watch the feckless beachcombers scream with fear, scurrying like a frightened covey of bobble headed quail. Especially the children. He detested the snotty little cretins.

He climbed a small hill and tried scanning with binoculars but one eye was swollen shut. He drooled copiously since he couldn't close his boil-infested lips, saliva dripping onto his shirt. He was a sniveling, grotesque creature. His hatred burned like hellfire.

The monster's prey would arrive soon.

We headed north on a long flat stretch. Javier's bike weaved a bit. I considered asking him if I should carry Blake but then I saw the town.

I said, "Let's ditch the bikes and walk. This is the closest spot to the water."

"Sounds good."

We pushed the bikes behind rocks and placed a few small branches around them. The camouflage was inadequate because of the scarce vegetation.

We started toward the water. Javier appeared weak, his temporary burst of strength exhausted. Blake walked beside him, studying Javier's face with concern.

I considered our final step, connecting with the sailboat. Lookouts might scan the beach so I didn't want the boat near shore.

I called Catherine, "We're south of San Isabel. We'll enter the water there, either swimming or in a boat. Track us via GPS. Javier's injured, a gunshot wound to his left chest."

She inhaled sharply, but didn't say anything.

"I'll need medical supplies in Javier's cabin. Set up for an IV and a chest tube."

"I will. See you soon."

After mere feet, Javier was panting like he'd sprinted a mile. The air was cool but sweat dripped from his nose.

"Let's stop and rest."

"No...gotta keep moving."

Moments later, he tripped and fell into my back.

"Let me carry your pack and weapons."

"You need to be ready for action."

Blake said, "I'll carry them. I'm strong. You need to rest, Javi."

I placed his ammo and grenades into my pack. He kept a pistol.

I emptied the chamber on his assault rifle then showed Blake how to carry it, propped on his shoulder. He attempted to contain a proud smile, but failed.

We started again. Javier lagged, shuffling like an elderly man.

He stumbled.

Blake looked at me, questioning. I ignored him, for lack of anything to say.

A minute later Javier stopped and panted, hands on knees. Coughed up a mouthful of blood.

"Sit down. Let me look you over."

"Dad's a doctor."

I felt his pulse, racing at 140 beats per minute. I didn't like it. Takes considerable blood loss to increase the heart rate that much. His pulse was weak, signifying low blood pressure. Much worse and he'd lose consciousness. Probably had internal bleeding, along with everything else.

I pulled his eyelid down, observing his conjunctiva: ghostly, signifying profound anemia. I inspected the needle in his chest. It still functioned properly, air flowing out with each breath.

"Is he gonna be okay?"

"Yeah, he'll be fine."

Javier mumbled, "Tell the children the truth."

"If you're well enough to quote Bob Marley, then I am telling the truth." I wished it more than believed it.

He lay on his back and closed his eyes, laboring to breathe. Blake wiped sweat from Javi's forehead.

The beach was still two miles away, over uneven territory. The motorcycles would soon be discovered. We'd be trapped between narcos waiting at the shore and others marching toward the ocean. We had to keep moving.

I helped Javier to his feet and shouldered my gun. A minute later, he crumpled to his knees and fell sideways, unconscious.

I knelt. His face was wet but he was breathing. I lifted his legs, the blood running to his head. Blake helped by holding his feet.

He slowly opened his eyes and turned sideways, blood running from his mouth. He whispered, "Whoa."

"You passed out."

His skin white as dried bone, he offered a smile of singular bleakness. "I need to chill out for a bit." His eyes closed.

The blood in his mouth came from a continually bleeding lung.

We could ditch the guns and hope for the best. A firefight would be almost impossible to win with no vehicles or bombs.

I announced my plan. "I'm going to carry you to the water."

Between breaths he said, "Naw, Stryker...I can walk...just need to rest."

"We gotta keep going. When they find those bikes, we're done for. They'll send everyone to the beach."

He whispered, blood bubbling from the corner of his mouth, "Funny, ain't it? How life can just slip away? After so much effort...along comes a banana peel."

"It's not slipping! You'll be fine. We're almost there. I'll carry you."

His eyes knitted. "As you wish. Carry on my wayward son."

He sat up then abruptly lay back down.

I hoisted him, using a fireman's carry. His body laying across my upper back, I held one arm and one leg.

Blake put on Javier's backpack and shouldered the gun. He looked ridiculous with the giant gun and pack, but was clearly pleased with himself for helping.

Each step became an effort. Javier seemed to be unconscious most of the time. He mumbled occasionally but I remained silent, trying to let him rest. We approached a road paralleling the beach.

I set Javier down. Small houses lined the road. Typical Baja dwellings, some with unpainted cinder blocks and others like peacocks, bright and proud. The raked-dirt yards were decorated with plastic trinkets and enclosed with low fences. There were no empty lots on our side of the road, so we had to walk through someone's yard. I wanted to avoid the road so we could hide if necessary.

I decided to ditch the M4, attempting to pass as wandering tourists. If the locals knew about the raid and the fighting, they probably thought the attackers were a rival cartel. I stripped down to my T-shirt and cut the legs off my pants. Combat boots and black cut offs were odd, but tourists here weren't known for their high fashion.

I helped Javier remove his vest and dressed him in the narco's shirt.

"I can walk. I'm feeling better. But, once we're on the boat, I plan to sleep the clock around twice. At least."

We left the automatics, helmets and vests in the weeds but kept our pistols. I slung my pack over one shoulder like a duffel bag. I held hands with Blake, hopefully seeming like a father and son with a Mexican guide.

I found a footpath between houses. People watched from their yards. A toothless elderly woman smiled and waved. Blake and I returned the wave then followed the path down to the ocean.

We paused in a grove, overlooking the water. Boats crowded near the beach. People fished from the shore. A small boat was stored under a palm tree.

I said, "Lookouts will be searching for two men and a boy, so let's split up."

"I'll go first and check out that skiff."

"Good. Blake, let's see if you'll fit in my pack."

I stuffed my last grenade and ammo into Javier's pack then buried the first aid kit, snorkel mask and handheld radio. I lifted Jefe's treasures from the bottom of my rucksack, noticing multiple bullet holes in the moneybag.

My heart sank. The oasis shootout had destroyed the stolen bonds and cash.

Javier took off his pants. His boxers could pass for shorts. He strolled down to the beach then knelt beside the boat, dropping his pack. He wrapped the pants around his pistol, to muffle the noise.

He shot the padlock chaining the boat to the tree, then immediately dropped the gun into tall weeds.

The closest fisherman spun, looking around. Javier also glanced around then shrugged his shoulders and strolled toward the water. The man returned to fishing.

Blake climbed into the rucksack, balling up. I managed to close it, the zipper straining.

I carried him down to the beach. Then tipped the boat, finding one paddle underneath. I drug the skiff to the water and pushed off.

Javier treaded water about a hundred feet out. When we got there, he clutched the boat, panting.

I pulled him into the boat. He lay in the bottom, eyes closed.

"You okay?"

"That swim was brutal…thought I was goin' under…don't have much gas left."

"Just a few more minutes, we're almost there."

I unzipped the pack and Blake crawled out. He lay next to Javier. "You're my hero, Javi. You can rest now."

I paddled out. The Ketchum Alive came into view.

I called, "Pull between us and the shore, to block the view." They veered toward the beach and hovered one hundred feet away.

I told Javier, "Sit up once we get out. Anyone watching will still see one man. Leave your shirt behind."

Blake and I swam to the sailboat. Catherine was waiting on us and embraced Blake, kissing his cheeks furiously. They both began to cry.

But she knew Blake had to get out of sight quickly so she tore herself away. Through tears she said, "Get below with

Susan. I'll be down soon!" She kissed him once more then Susan took Blake's hand, leading him below deck.

I told Catherine, "Pull forward. Lookouts will see someone remaining in the boat."

I went below. Susan had Blake in a bear hug, crying joyfully. He looked embarrassed but was beaming nevertheless. I hugged them both then quickly gathered supplies.

We pulled alongside the skiff. Javier climbed in. Catherine blanched at his ghostly pale face.

I crawled onto the rowboat, carrying a hat, a foam buoy the size of a football and a wetsuit packed with towels. Draped Javier's shirt on the wetsuit then shoved the buoy into the collar. I drove a thin fishing knife through the suit into the buoy then placed the floppy hat on the buoy. Propped up the scarecrow then swam back.

I hugged Catherine, knowing she ached to hold Blake. But we needed a lookout and she was our best captain. I had to tend to Javier. She pointed the sailboat toward deep water.

Behram lowered his binoculars. They were exactly where he knew they'd be. He would win, as always.

He walked to his motorboat, limping from weeping sores on his feet. He'd bought the boat that morning.

He transferred supplies from his vehicle into the boat, his aching hands gingerly lifting the scuba equipment and underwater propulsion device they'd left on the beach, near Jefe's compound. The gear was easy enough to find since dead narcos marked the spot they came ashore. The equipment was labeled *U.S. Navy*, confirming his suspicions that Alcaraz was the ringleader of the foolish little band. There was a certain delightful irony in using their own equipment to destroy them.

It would be simple to attach a bomb to the underside of their sailboat, killing them instantly. But that would be too quick, too merciful. He wanted them as permanent captives to his painful whims, at least the women and the boy.

He'd lay in wait and strike when they least expected. He'd deliver maximal emotional pain by allowing them to believe they'd succeeded. Then cruelly dash their hopes.

Waiting had another benefit. They would become complacent. He climbed into his boat and steered toward them.

He licked his teeth with a misshapen tongue. The drooling creature was eager to feed.

CHAPTER FORTY-FOUR

Javier lay on the bed in his cabin, my supplies on the bedside table. Catherine had covered the bed with a plastic sheet, anticipating blood. Lots of blood.

If the round deeply penetrated his thorax, he'd need major surgery quickly. If the bullet were wedged into his heart or aorta, he'd likely die almost instantly if I touched the slug.

I administered pain meds and IV fluids then listened to his heart and lungs. His left lung was dim, probably full of blood.

I had surgical skills but a deep chest bullet would require a thoracic surgeon and cardiac bypass equipment. If he needed emergency surgery, the nearest major hospital was Cabo San Lucas, almost two days by boat. I didn't like the idea of staying in Mexico, El Poder territory, but San Diego was at least four days away.

I injected topical anesthetic then sponged his brown skin. Sliced between his ribs with a scalpel, the skin falling open, revealing yellow tissue below. Placed a curved hemostat into the cavity, punching through muscle. Then pierced the pleura, the thin wrap enveloping the lung. He grimaced.

Blood pooled from the wound, ran onto the plastic tarp then dripped to the floor.

I plunged my index finger into the hole, making sure the tunnel was clear. Then fed the plastic chest tube into the opening.

With my foot, I slid a bucket under the tube sputtering with blood and air like a water hose. I fixed the tube to his skin with sutures.

Normally, the tube would connect to mechanical suction. I improvised by attaching a large syringe then repeatedly withdrew blood and dumped it into the pail. When his wound ran dry, there was over a liter and a half of tomato soup in the bucket and more on the floor.

A two-liter blood loss would be fatal.

I cut a fingertip off a latex glove then secured it to the end, creating a flutter valve that allowed air to escape but not reenter. Injected additional morphine until he was barely breathing. Then hung a second liter of fluid. I was thankful I'd brought more than enough medical supplies, anticipating bloodshed. I still had several bags of IV fluid to spare.

Took a deep breath. The next few moments might be his last.

But I had to keep going.

I removed the bandage from the bullet wound. After numbing, I cut into the bullet wound then pried it open with hemostats.

Catherine opened the door. I turned and nearly fell, my foot gliding sideways on the blood-slicked floor. She instinctively reached for me.

I muttered, "This floor is slick as bat shit!"

She stared at the pail full of clots and the red floor. "Is everything okay?"

"Yeah." I didn't want to alarm Javier.

"There's a motorboat headed straight toward us, about a mile away."

"Veer off. If they adjust course, they're following. If so, I could scuba underneath and take them out. But if it's El Poder, the big gunboat will be coming. There's no way we can escape that thing."

"I'll adjust course. And pray."

Under new time pressure, I returned to the wound, digging with the hemostats. Felt a crunch. Picked out rib splinters then pushed deeper until feeling a click.

I smiled.

The slug was less than an inch below the shattered rib. I grasped the bullet and dropped it in a metal trash can with a satisfying clatter.

A pulmonary vein poured blood. I clipped hemostats on either side of the vein then tied it off. The bleeding stopped. Irrigated the wound then closed it.

"You'll be fine now. I got the bullet."

His lips upturned with a faint smile. He wouldn't need further surgery. An infection was still possible, but I breathed easier.

I went above deck. Catherine said, "They didn't change course."

I held up binoculars. It looked like a sport boat but it was stopped a half-mile away. I wasn't sure. The lone occupant never looked our way, seeming uninterested. I couldn't make out his features.

"Javier will live. But Blake's dying, dying for a hug from his mama. I'll take the wheel."

She lightly kissed me and bound downstairs.

Behram stopped the motorboat, far enough away to avoid suspicion and their prying eyes. He dropped the propulsion device and scuba gear into the ocean then slipped into the water.

He traveled below the surface, propelled by the device. The dive mask didn't seal over his knotty forehead, so water entered, causing poor visibility. The mouthpiece was nearly impossible to keep in his warped mouth. The saltwater stung his open sores like wasps. He seethed as his rage reached a boiling point.

He eventually made it to the craft and looked up at the hull. He imagined the gleeful crew inside, so happy and so joyful.

He ached to slaughter them now, but he resisted, anticipating a better reward.

The boat cast a shadow, fish disappearing as they entered the dark shaft then reappearing on the other side. He swam toward the surface.

His right arm badly injured by the boy, he could only use his left to swim. So he slowly spun as he ascended the columnar shadow, like someone whisked from earth in a dark tornado.

He quietly attached a magnetic beacon to the metal hull.

No matter where they went, he'd find them.

He returned to the propulsion device then turned away, returning to his motorboat. He navigated by GPS, but the water in his mask made it hard to see the monitor. Frustrated, he pushed it against his face and a boil ruptured, splattering pus against the lens and into his eyes.

CHAPTER FORTY-FIVE

We traveled until I couldn't see any other boats. We would sail far from land then refuel on the mainland, in Puerto Vallarta, the closest significant city past Baja. Cabo was too close to San Carlos.

I went below deck. Blake, Catherine and Susan snuggled blissfully in bed. Catherine read Harry Potter aloud.

I was surprised she wasn't asking about his adventure. But mama knew best. She instinctively knew Blake needed to veg and decompress. I squeezed in to hear what was going down at Hogwarts.

Javier was asleep. He'd probably stay in bed for days.

That night, Susan boiled lobster and I made margaritas. I brought one to Javier and held a straw to his mouth. He slurped it down.

The following morning, we replaced the white sails with blue and switched the flag from American to Canadian. We painted the boat blue and orange, Boise State colors. Susan drew *The Bronco* with a marker then Blake painstakingly filled the block letters with blue paint. We sank the old sails.

I dreaded returning to Mexican soil but we had to refuel and purchase supplies. Puerto Vallarta was the closest tourist town, so we'd blend in.

Absent light pollution, the stars displayed a magnificent glitter. We cleared the boat of all weapons since officials might search the boat and Mexico had strict firearm laws. We dumped them overboard.

Good riddance.

The Bronco approached Puerto Vallarta to the sounds of seagulls and boat horns, the universal sounds of a waterfront. Palms swayed in the breeze, high-rise hotels in the distance.

Behram chased the boat's GPS signal from the shore, racing along in his truck, purchased in Tijuana with plates stolen in Ensenada. After leaving the beacon on their sailboat, he followed to the end of Baja, hoping they would stop in Cabo. He knew they'd embark to refuel, or ditch the boat and travel by land.

But they kept going.

Panicked, he drove north several hours and caught a car ferry from La Paz to mainland Mexico. He landed in Mazatlán, far north of the sailboat's GPS location.

The boat was docked in Puerto Vallarta, a five hours drive from Mazatlán. He traveled at a ferocious pace. If they left the boat behind, they'd be beyond his reach.

Several times, he almost lost control of the vehicle, but the flesh prize was all he had to live for. Their escape was too much for him to consider.

His felt an anxious gnawing in his gut, knowing they could already be gone.

We each had three passports with different names and nationalities, along with companion birth certificates, driver's licenses and ID cards. The passports were perfect forgeries, appearing well used with multiple stamps. Our primary passports were Canadian, matching our flag.

We pulled into the marina and a port authority official checked our papers and told us where to dock. Susan handled the refueling then went into town to buy rations.

I caught a taxi to the airport, wearing a full beard with a blonde wig and thick black-rimmed glasses. I walked to an airport café.

Sunburned Americans loitered. I noticed a friendly man with a Southern accent. I asked, "Where y'all from?"

"Heading back to Atlanta. Way too soon. We love it down here. You?"

I had a pretty convincing Southern accent. "Nice to meet a fellow Southerner! I grew up in Chattanooga but live in Dallas. This is my first trip here. I'm on business but gotta bring the family next time. My kids would love it. Where'd y'all stay?"

After a few minutes of small talk, I pulled out my laptop and conspicuously made a commotion of not being able to turn it on. "Could I borrow your computer? I need to send an email to my wife. Mine got a wicked virus. Guess it's modern-day Montezuma's Revenge."

He laughed, "Montezuma will get you somehow! No problem." He gave me his laptop.

I lay my computer bag over my right hand and the keyboard. While he was speaking with friends, I attached a thumb drive. Hit a few buttons to upload, and then a few more keystrokes to hide my work.

He'd never know.

I returned his computer. "Thanks! Y'all take care."

"Glad to help. Maybe we'll see you next year!"

In three days, the email would be sent from Atlanta. The message would go from his computer to cloud storage. The FBI would receive notice of an encrypted message from the cloud, not the man's computer. The secure cloud would authenticate the recipient, decrypt the message and display it back via a secure browser session. After the FBI download the email, it would be automatically deleted from server memory.

Even if the NSA or FBI could eventually beat that, we'd be long gone.

I caught a taxi back to the port. We would spend the night then disembark in the morning. We were on our way to a new life. It would take a few weeks to reach our next destination, Peru.

The email sent to the San Diego's FBI office detailed information gleaned from El Jefe's interrogation.

To Whom It May Concern,

If you are reading this, I am dead. This email was automatically sent, as the cancellation code was not entered.

Alfredo Rodriquez, El Jefe, ordered the murder of Senator Mark Ripp. Mr. Rodriguez is the leader of the Mexican drug cartel, El Poder. His primary assassin is Anwar Gupta, known as Behram.

Behram killed the Senator with VX gas. Then placed a tube into his throat, pouring vodka mixed with crushed pills. The paramedics performed CPR, pumping alcohol and narcotics into his bloodstream.

The senator was assassinated in collaboration with U.S. Navy Admiral George Landfair, the commander of Operation Cartel. Under the admiral's direction, the military decimated rival cartels, leaving El Poder alone.

The military confiscated drugs from El Poder warehouses in Mexico, as well as from genuine raids on other cartels. The drugs were taken across the border on U.S. military vehicles. Corrupt soldiers guarded several depots. They replaced large quantities of meth, cocaine and heroin with counterfeits. They removed the narcotics from the base in garbage trucks. El Poder sold the drugs to American crime syndicates for street level distribution.

The military seemingly destroyed enormous amounts, bolstering the illusion of success in the war on drugs. But the bulk entered the U.S. black market. The well-documented rising street price was touted as evidence of decreasing supply. In reality, the prices were due to El Poder's near monopoly and huge profit margins.

Senator Ripp was outspoken in his opposition to Operation Cartel. He was preparing to call for a congressional vote on a bill he authored, requiring the removal of all U.S. forces from Mexico and the demilitarization of the border.

Rodriguez and Landfair grew concerned that Sen. Ripp was garnering the needed votes. The admiral did not want to lose his influential position and El Poder did not want to lose the game-changing aid from the U.S. Military, so they made the decision to assassinate Senator Ripp.

Rodriguez had the most powerful military on earth doing his bidding, annihilating his competition. When the other cartels were decimated, El Poder would become an all-mighty monopoly. El Jefe felt safer living in the U.S., out of the reach of other cartels.

El Poder paid Landfair ten million dollars annually. The admiral planned to eventually retire and write a book about his military triumphs. He would make big money giving speeches and being on talk shows, therefore having a plausible reason for his enormous wealth. He would launder his money by purchasing his own book, driving it to number one on the bestseller list.

Admiral Landfair is considered a strong candidate for higher office. His millions could fund an election campaign. Interestingly, Senator Ripp could have been his main competitor. Both men have been touted as presidential candidates.

Landfair supplied top-secret, untraceable ViXen gas, created by CIA labs for clandestine assassinations. VX gas is created at the moment of use by a mixing atomizer then rapidly degrades, impossible to detect. He had access to ViXen, ostensibly and ironically to use against corrupt Mexican politicians and police officers working for the cartels.

Behram has murdered countless, including innocents and children. Senator Ripp's doctor, Wyatt Stryker, discovered Behram placing surveillance in Ripp's beach home in Mexico. Dr. Stryker and his entire family were murdered.

A video of Behram is attached but he was recently poisoned by enemies and will undoubtedly have boils covering his face and hands.

I am Wayne Kitt. If you are reading this, I am dead.

El Jefe is confined at 322 Clear Creek Road, Alpine, California, imprisoned in the basement of the barn. Norma Johnson owns the house but knows nothing. Mrs. Johnson lives in Alabama. Her brother is Javier Alcaraz, the former CO of SEAL Team 3. Commander Alcaraz and Dr. Stryker were friends in the SEALs. When Dr. Stryker's family went missing, Javier investigated.

He discovered that the likely culprit was Rodriguez and enlisted my help. We captured him and uncovered this. El Poder eventually killed Cdr. Alcaraz.

Jefe produced the evidence included, as protection against betrayal by Adm. Landfair or Behram.

Admiral Landfair will be found in shock, his pious arrogance deflated.

Behram will be found sniveling, covered in bumps somewhere.

Sincerely,

The Ghost of Wayne Kitt

Attachment one: Video of Anwar Gupta, known as Behram.

His face was shown clearly on the screen, recorded by Catherine in the hospital. "I thought I would be able to speak with him."

Attachment two: Video of Admiral Landfair and Alfredo Rodriguez discussing the murder of the Senator.

The Admiral and Jefe are sitting in a limo. Both faces are shown.

Jefe said, "Nice to see you."

Landfair replied, "Can't say the same. Why do we need to meet? I prefer alternative communications."

"I need assurance."

"Are you recording this?"

"Don't cross me and you won't need to worry. If you do, you'll need to worry about more than a video."

"That a threat?"

"*Tranquillo, amigo.* We're friends."

"My friends don't threaten me."

"My friends don't forsake me...so let's stay friends. Shall we discuss Senator Ripp?"

"For God's sake! Are you recording this? I'm walking!"

Jefe stared out the window. Landfair glared at the side of his head. After a pregnant pause, Jefe spoke quietly, "You may leave."

"I really hate you."

"But you love my pesos, dear Admiral. On the other hand, I rather cherish the company of a red-faced Yanqui soldier."

"Whatever."

"Whatever?"

"He's gathering support in the Senate. We need to terminate him."

"Risky. If we're discovered, the game is up."

"It's up if the bill passes. He's calling for the removal of all U.S. personnel from Mexico within six months."

"I employ the world's best assassin. No question, he can kill the Senator."

"Will the death seem natural?"

"Much more difficult, but if anyone can do it, he can."

"We should act soon."

"Can you offer assistance?"

"Good question."

"Thank you." Jefe smirked. "Would you answer the good question?"

"Smart ass." The Admiral shook his head irritably then continued, "I have access to VX gas that degrades quickly, impossible to detect."

"I will discuss with Behram."

Attachment three: Banking records showing payments to Behram and Admiral Landfair.

Jefe's records were kept in encrypted cloud storage, coerced in a drug-induced fog. Under the influence, Jefe sang like a bluebird, telling us about Landfair's involvement, their military scheme and how Behram killed Ripp.

There were several reasons for our email deception. We wanted to create doubt within El Poder about our identities. El Jefe might think his kidnapping was a ruse to get money, and his tormentor was Wayne. If they thought we were dead or at least uncertain, much better. We did not want the fury of El Poder directed at us, or our unsuspecting parents.

Nor did we want the FBI searching for us, so we created a plausible evidence chain. Wayne disappeared the same week Ripp died. His personal items would be found in Javier's house. His cell demonstrated communications between Wayne and Javier, our false electronic trail. Jefe might provide a description of Wayne, covered in meth sores. Beth Ripp would confirm I surprised Behram in Rosarito.

FBI investigators might piece together the true chain of events, but our crimes were committed bringing El Poder to justice. Not to mention, we delivered the case of the decade on a silver platter. Hopefully they would leave us alone.

We considered several plans to kill or capture Behram. Like Hitler or Bin Laden, I'd kill him without remorse. But death seemed too quick and painless.

The TCDD was perfect. Javier had access to military grade dioxin. Behram would no longer be a chameleon, moving freely with murderous intent. His face would be plastered on broadcasts, worldwide. Once the other arrests became public, he'd disappear, probably spending the rest of his life in isolation, cowering like Al-Qaeda terrorists, maybe in a burka.

The boils were a disadvantage but if Bin Laden could remain free for years during a multi-billion dollar hunt, so could Behram.

I would probably have nightmares, waking up with a foul, lumpy-bumpy man lurking at the foot of our bed.

CHAPTER FORTY- SIX

Behram arrived in Puerto Vallarta in a state of severe anxiety. As he parked the truck near the port, he saw the sailboat moored. With binoculars, he saw the large man, Wayne Kitt, exit a taxi and walk down the dock before disappearing below deck. Behram's relief was instantaneous. They hadn't escaped.

The boat was repainted and renamed, a silly attempt to avoid detection. Under the same circumstances, Behram would've purchased a different boat or, even better, changed his mode of travel. Pathetic amateurs.

But to err is human. Their error meant he'd feast on those humans.

He eagerly anticipated his brutal ambush. If they disembarked, he would sacrifice the occupants of a moored yacht, an elderly British couple, and then follow the sailboat into deserted waters. If they stayed in port, he would attack, feeding Kali with new blood just like history's finest serial killer.

He would climb aboard in the dead of night, killing the men with his silenced pistol and restraining the others. Once they were in deep waters, the fun would begin with his straight razor and blowtorch. He'd force-feed them dioxin and break the child's bones.

From radio reports, he knew the little gang had stolen an enormous haul from Jefe's safe. Drug trafficking was a cash-only business and they kept huge sums in secure vaults.

He finally understood why Wayne Kitt, a self-centered deadbeat, joined them. But the tall mercenary hitched his wagon to the wrong train.

His stolen money would soon be Behram's.

And Kitt's dismembered body would be bobbing in the ocean, hungry fish picking at his entrails.

They must have physically tormented El Jefe to get the code to the safe. But they were novices. They had no idea how to inflict maximal pain.

He would gladly teach them.

He considered the ramifications of taking El Poder's money. When they realized Jefe was dead, Tincho the Torturer would become the reining capo. Tincho was Jefe's eldest son but far more blood thirsty and ruthless. He would never stop searching for the little crew on the sailboat but Tincho would hunt in vain. The men would be dead and the women and boy chained in a rural basement.

El Poder would never know the untraceable cash passed into Berhram's hands. He concluded there was no significant risk. The money was his for the taking.

And that was fortunate because his career as an assassin was over. He bore the mark of Cain. He'd never be able to disguise himself and move like a wraith of the night, a murderous spirit appearing just long enough to separate souls from their bodies before vanishing.

He regretted losing his prestigious career but felt solace knowing he would forever be an exceedingly wealthy man. And his horrible appearance had a benefit: it would create a terrifying serial killer.

He would murder again, at least for sport. After each grisly murder, he would return home to spend time with the sailboat occupants, his permanent slaves of misery. His anticipation grew.

He lowered his binoculars and noticed his left arm was hot and swollen. He grimaced to see the open lesions had become infected. His right was permanently crippled from severe nerve damage. Performing his lethal duties with two wounded arms would be difficult if not impossible.

He sat in the truck. As he awaited darkness, he felt feverish. Shortly after, he developed shaking chills and felt nauseated.

He stepped from his truck and buckled. Sweat dripped from his patchy hair, chunks missing where boils sprouted from his scalp. He weaved like a drunken man, delirious with fever and blinded by hatred.

He screamed in frustration, saliva flying from his deformed mouth. Several bystanders spun in shock and then hurried away. Car doors slammed as they escaped the insane beast with the communicable disease.

Struggling, he drove toward a medical clinic. Sweat, nausea, chills and bitter bile wreaked havoc on his ability to drive.

Eventually he arrived and parked outside, waiting for it to close since the ignorant rubes would probably deny him service. When the staff vacated, he slowly walked forward, stopping to rest twice.

He broke a window and climbed in. He searched the storeroom and found what he was looking for. He gathered supplies but his failing strength made it difficult. When he eventually made it to the truck, he vomited all over his clothes and the steering wheel.

He drove away from the city into a forested area, parking in the shade under a tree. His arms shook from the angry bacteria swimming inside his body. Trembling, he wrapped a piece of rubber around his bicep then slapped his veins. Carefully stabbed a quivering purple vessel with a needle, like threading a writhing bloodworm onto a fishing hook. A red trickle ran down his knotted forearm.

He connected tubing then hung a vial of IV antibiotics from a tree limb. He reclined in the truck bed, the healing fluid battling the germs intent on killing the killer.

The stench of vomit, sweat and disease made his nausea worse. He tried to sleep but couldn't stop worrying about the little crew. If they left the sailboat, he would never find them.

CHAPTER FORTY-SEVEN

I swam around the moving boat as Blake tried to hit me with a Nerf football. I zinged it back, pegging him with an ocean soaked spray and a squeal of laughter.

We were moving south. The waters were warm and the fish were biting. Shallow bays held emerald water, glowing like a magic potion.

We purposely silenced all electronic communications so we were unable to check the news. We didn't know if our email had even reached the FBI. If not, Jefe might already be rat food.

That afternoon, we pulled into a beautiful deserted cove surrounded by Costa Rican rainforest. Iguanas soaked up the sun on the beach. As we swam, schools of colorful fish parted. A sea turtle loped lazily past while crabs scurried along the bottom. We saw toucans, a sloth, bright parrots and chattering spider monkeys. Blake was enthralled with each new discovery, especially the monkeys.

Javier was strong enough to swim a few minutes but fatigued quickly. He was resting on the beach so Blake and I joined him.

I reclined and thought about how fortunate we were. Our take from the safe was thirty two million in cash and bonds. Four million was shredded by the gunfire in the oasis, but the rest intact. Plus we had the jewelry.

But all that paled in comparison to having my family whole again.

Javier said, "Soon, I'll be wearing a necklace with quarter-sized ice, straight from Jefe's vault. Them rocks'll blind anyone who dares look my way. Who cares if it's a woman's necklace? From now on, nobody tells me what to do. I might start a campfire with thousand dollar bills."

I laughed, "I'm gonna get me some grillz and three carat studs for each ear, pimping in a full-length fur like Joe Namath. What about you Blake?"

"A Boise State tattoo on my chest!"

"Attaboy!" *We were home free!* I couldn't stop smiling. The nightmare was over.

I glanced at the horizon and saw low clouds stalking, the gusty wind pushing them intermittently. The clouds paused as if waiting and then rushed forward, like a patient cat on the hunt. Shafts from the low sun fired through, spotlighting the storm's march toward land.

Behram would feed the ravenous goddess Kali with the flesh of his tormenters. He'd recovered from his frustrating infection but the delay had unforeseen benefits. Crossing into new territory meant they probably jettisoned weapons due to risk of search. In addition, his prey was lulled into complacency. They were far from the chaos of San Carlos.

The deserted bay was perfect as forest animals would be the only witnesses to their screams.

Behram hid in the jungle as they frolicked, oblivious to the horror awaiting. The moment had come to exact his revenge, possessed by the spirit of the ancient serial killer. He would soon disgorge the men's souls from their fleshly vessels. The others would beg for the same.

As the sun dipped below the horizon, a storm blew across the ocean. The intermittent wind gusts would be beneficial, hiding any noise. Dense fog filled the bay, the night as dark as his intentions.

At 3 a.m., he swam through the shallows wearing infrared goggles. He carried a suppressed pistol with a laser sight, restraints and torture instruments. He had two Tasers, a handheld probe and a pistol. The gun fired two dart-like electrodes, propelled by compressed air, the skin barbs connected to the pistol by conductive wire. But he preferred the probe if the victim was within reach.

He climbed aboard. The laser sight of his automatic pistol sliced the rolling fog like a thin light saber. He walked the deck, considering the layout below. Concluded there were four cabins, a galley and a restroom.

He approached the stairs but his right hand jerked in spasm, a recurring frustration due to nerve damage. His pistol dropped, striking the deck with a thud.

He picked it up, quietly cursing as he slid back into the water, enshrouded by mist.

Someone came up the stairs, a woman. Catherine Stryker sleepily strolled the deck in a robe, looking around. Appearing satisfied she sat near the edge, gazing at the ocean. She hugged herself as a gust swept the water, her hair coming to life in a swirl.

Behram's disfigured mouth curved into the semblance of a smile. He swam below her with his Taser pistol and made a small splash.

Her hands gripped the rail above him.

He splashed again and she peered down.

He fired the darts.

She convulsed and slumped, still twitching.

He grabbed the rail, pulling himself up. He continued the Taser shock as he bound her convulsing body with thick zip ties and a gag. Then he pulled her into the cockpit and stood behind as she recovered.

When clarity returned, he spoke over the wind, "Nurse Stryker, your sins will be paid with pain."

He grabbed a fistful of hair, twisting her head to view his angry pockmarked face. "You and your son will soon look like me, the beginning of your life of misery."

Her eyes widened as she screamed silently.

Behram crept down the stairs, clutching his pistol. Below deck, the cabin was pitch dark, his vision through the goggles a greenish pall.

The last cabin door was partially open, the others closed. He concluded Nurse Stryker left her door open; the boy shared her room and the others slept alone. He would kill the men. And the rest would be child's play.

He slowly opened the first door: a vacant bathroom. He moved to the next and saw Susan sleeping, stunningly beautiful.

He studied the tiny room. Luggage was stored beneath her bed. A bedside table held a reading lamp.

He would deal with her later. He couldn't risk waking the more lethal adversaries. He took another long look. Maybe he wouldn't poison her with dioxin but keep her as a plaything.

He debated whether to kill the men immediately or keep them alive for a bit of fun. Wayne Kitt was just a mercenary, hired help. He decided to murder Wayne, but keep their friend alive for a few days unless forced to kill him. Behram would derive pleasure as Javier helplessly witnessed his savage wrath.

He opened the door across the hall and saw a man snoring facedown. He trained the laser dot of his pistol on the Hispanic man, Javier. Then raised his other hand and fired Taser darts into Javier's neck.

Javier convulsed violently, releasing a groan as his body arched. Behram quickly stuffed a cloth into his mouth then paused, listening. The wind howled as it buffeted the boat, concealing all noise. Nobody stirred. He gripped his pistol, listening for several minutes.

Satisfied Javier's grunting didn't wake anyone, Behram returned to his bedside. He looped a nylon rope through Javier's mouth and tied it behind his head, stretching his mouth like a sadistic horse bridle. Then connected the cord to his vibrating arms and pulled them behind his back. He whipped the rope around Javier's ankles, hogtieing him.

A single rope connected his head, arms and feet. Javier's neck and spine arched cruelly. The rope cut in and blood trickled from his cheek.

He reloaded the Taser gun and stuffed it in his pack.

His next victim would not be spared.

The hall was vacant. He looped rope around Javier's door handle then stretched it tight across the hall and tied it to Susan's door, ensuring that neither could be opened. He didn't want to confront Susan until he'd killed Wayne. His pulse quickened, his work almost done.

Wayne was in the final cabin, across from Catherine's room. He cracked the door but found the boy instead, fast asleep. Finding the child was a surprise, but he felt a surge of perverse satisfaction. He anticipated coating his tender skin with dioxin and fracturing his limbs.

Behram would never understand loose American women. Her husband's body barely cold, Catherine slept with Wayne.

He mentally chastised himself for not looking in the other room first. With the door partially open, Wayne could've heard him.

But he had not. The cabin was silent, except quiet snoring from Wayne's room.

Time to free Wayne's soul and set sail with his bounty.

The greenish vision illuminating, he pushed Wayne's door completely open. His semiautomatic pointed at the bed. Like the other cabins, there was barely space for a bed and a small table.

Wayne lay on his side, his back to Behram.

Standing in the doorway, he aimed the laser at Wayne's hair. He pulled the pistol's trigger rapidly, pumping bullets in swift sequence down his body, from head to neck to spine. Blood spurted, soaking through the sheets.

Wayne wasn't breathing. The shot to the skull base killed him instantly. His blood dripped from the bed, tiny rivulets crossing the floor.

Pleasure boiled through his veins and he broke into a painful grin.

After so many setbacks and costly mistakes, his revenge on the Stryker family was complete. His crippled arm and disgusting boils would be avenged a thousand times over. He would spend the remainder of his life tormenting his tormentors.

Behram would do unto them worse than they had done unto him, his version of the Golden Rule.

He stepped forward to inspect the dead body.

CHAPTER FORTY-EIGHT

I could barely see the intruder in the darkness. The man trained his laser sight on the bed then emptied bullets with a suppressed pistol. I held my breath, praying he wouldn't look behind the door. He held a gun and I had a reading lamp: an unequal match.

The man stepped forward and yanked the blankets back, sending my wig flying. Punctured IV bags rolled off a stack of pillows and clothes and dropped from the mattress. I'd hurriedly grabbed whatever I could find to make the decoy. The medical supplies had been stored under our bed.

I stepped from behind the door, swinging the lamp at his head.

He ducked, but not fast enough.

I landed a fairly solid blow. Blood sprayed, peppering the wall. The intruder grunted and fell to his knees, his upper body on the mattress.

I swung again but he rolled. The lamp ruptured an IV bag. I released it and grabbed his gun with both hands, attempting to wrench it from his grip.

Quick as light, he lashed my throat with a vicious blow, gagging me.

As we wrestled for control, I attempted to yell but only a weak croak escaped my injured throat. "Javier! Help! There's a robber on board!"

Susan screamed and a door rattled.

With snakelike reflexes, he stabbed fingers into both eyes with his free hand, blinding me. The pain was excruciating.

I finally overpowered him, ripping the gun from his grip.

He held my arm with both hands and worked a finger into the trigger guard, behind the trigger to prevent me from squeezing.

Between the darkness and my wounded eyes, he was a faint blur. I tried to raise the gun but he held fast. With my free hand, I attempted to wrench loose his grip.

He head butted me in the face, his thick cranium striking hard. It felt like a bowling ball dropped from a balcony.

I stumbled back, crashing into the wall. One eye lost vision, instantly swollen shut. The other was blurry.

But I still held the pistol. I raised it but couldn't see him.

A heavy boot struck my hand and the gun sailed away, striking the wall. I was sure at least one bone in my hand was broken.

Ignoring the pain, I blindly searched on my hands and knees.

Suddenly I felt a horrible electric shock. My muscles seized and I collapsed face down, twitching bizarrely. I couldn't breathe and released a prolonged groan.

The man pushed a hand-held Taser into my back, the shock continuous.

I felt the pistol's hot silencer pressed against my skull.

The battle was over. He had won.

My life was about to end. I wondered why we parked the boat near shore. Simply moving the boat a mile from land would've prevented this. After everything we'd been through, we would die at the hands of Costa Rican bandits, common criminals.

"I can't get out!" Susan screamed. "Javier! Wyatt!"

I assumed Javier and Catherine were already dead. Blake and Susan were goners, unless Blake could escape and swim to shore.

Yes, Blake would swim. I would go to my death believing Blake escaped.

But my hope was thwarted, knowing there were probably multiple thieves on board. Even if he got away, Blake couldn't survive the thick jungle. We were miles from the nearest town.

My brain told my muscles to move. But they didn't respond in a meaningful way. They moved but only little jerks.

He knelt on my back, pinning me. He took off his pack and lay it on the floor then removed something.

He flipped me over and placed a foot on my chest, the gun on my forehead.

My vision cleared a bit. I saw an inhuman creature, a monster. The man who was about to end my life had some sort of horrible disease.

The creepy mouth hissed, "Your precious cargo will become my slaves. But I won't kill them. They will live with unending pain and misery."

I wondered what sort of crazed bandit had boarded, maybe some weird Central American cult. Seemed like a freakish nightmare.

"My name is Behram."

I was confused. Behram the assassin? It made no sense. How did he find us?

He held a hunting knife to my uninjured eye. "Would you rather be blind or dead?"

I lay silent, my thoughts racing.

"Answer me or I will slowly cut out your eyeballs. Then kill you."

The sharp point pressed down, the eyeball pushed deep into my skull. The knife pierced my clenched eyelid.

The pain was unbearable. I grunted involuntarily. A scream was not far behind.

He kept pushing. Blood flowed like tears.

Ignoring the agony, I focused. Behram had outsmarted us all. It seemed impossible that he could trail us from San Diego to Costa Rica.

But he had. He snuck on our boat without anyone noticing, in a remote place where we no one would hear our screams.

He'd already killed Javier and Catherine.

I was next.

Susan would never escape. Nor would Blake.

His blade dug deeper into my eye.

It was over.

CHAPTER FORTY-NINE

I heard a faint buzzing sound and the knife clattered to the floor, the pistol no longer pressed to my skull.

Behram dropped to his knees and then fell over, shaking violently beside me.

"Daddy, are you okay?"

The lights came on.

Through blurry vision I saw Blake standing with one hand on the light switch, the other holding a Taser pistol.

Behram stopped seizing.

My faculties slowly returning, I said, "Hold the trigger down. Keep shocking him." The Taser darts were still embedded in his skin. Pulling the trigger would send 50,000 volts, disrupting his nervous system.

Blake squeezed.

Behram convulsed.

Aching all over, I tried to stand but couldn't. "Give me the gun. See if there's a rope in his pack." I took the Taser from Blake and kept the voltage flowing.

Behram flopped like a grounded fish.

His backpack lay open on the floor. Blake withdrew plastic restraints and handed them to me.

I yanked Behram's shuddering, lumpy hands behind his back and zipped them tight. "See if there are more."

Blake reached into the pack and withdrew a small blow-torch and a long straight razor. I grimaced. He found more restraints.

I released the trigger and pulled Behram's feet onto the bed, connecting his ankles through the bedframe.

He was quiet, his brain short-circuited.

I made another attempt to stand but my knees buckled.

"Where are the others?"

"Mom's tied up on the deck and Susan's in her room. I think Javier's in his cabin but I don't know for sure. I haven't heard him."

I yelled, "Blake and I are alright! We've restrained the intruder!"

Susan cheered then began laughing deliriously. I assumed Catherine could not hear me above the wind. Javier was conspicuously silent.

I asked, "What happened?"

"When you yelled, I woke up and saw you fighting. I went to Javier's room, but I couldn't open the door. Ran up the stairs and found Mom. She had tape on her face. I pulled it off and told her. She cried then told me to help you. I think she was worried about me coming down here. But I was the only one who could help you.

"I found a hammer and snuck down. The man was holding a gun to your head. I thought the hammer might just hurt him and he'd shoot you. His backpack was lying open behind him. I saw that gun thing. So I aimed and pulled the trigger."

"You saved my life! That's the man who kidnapped you."

"Really? What's wrong with his face?"

Behram lifted his head and bellowed, spit flying from his floppy mouth like an enraged elephant seal.

We both startled.

I gave him another shock. He instantly changed from an enraged seal to a salted slug, quivering.

My legs felt stronger. "Let's check on the others."

I placed the weapons in Behram's pack and threw it over my shoulder. Then steadied myself by holding the wall. My pulse raced as I imagined Javier's fate.

I cut the rope between the doors with Behram's knife. Susan jerked her door open and hugged Blake.

I entered Javier's room and turned on the lights, instantly relieved. He was soaked in sweat from his awkward position, his mouth stretched in a gruesome smile. I cut the rope behind his head.

He collapsed flat on his face and mumbled into his pillow, "Thanks, bro. I thought we were dead."

"Thank Blake. He saved us all."

Susan cried, "Oh my God! Where's Catherine?"

Blake said, "She's fine. She's up on deck." Susan and Blake stomped upstairs.

While I was cutting the ropes from Javier's wrists and ankles, I heard Blake shout from the top of the stairs, "Everyone's okay! The bad guy's tied up."

I told Javier, "It's Behram. Make sure he's secured. Give him a shock with the Taser to keep him down."

I climbed the stairs with monumental effort. I cut Catherine's restraints and the four of us embraced.

Susan sobbed, "I was so worried. I stopped yelling when I heard the commotion, hoping the thief might not realize I was here."

"That wasn't a thief. It's Behram."

Her face blanched. She put a hand over her mouth.

"He's horrible!" Catherine said. "His face is mutilated."

I grimaced, "He looks worse than any photos of dioxin poison I've ever seen."

Catherine shuddered, "He's the most evil person alive."

Blake said excitedly, "I never saw his face when he kidnapped me since he wore a mask. Why is his face like that?"

"His enemies poisoned him."

Blake made a distasteful face, "Nasty!"

I whispered in her ear so Blake couldn't hear, "I think we overdid the dose."

"What happened to your face? Your eye's bleeding."

"Behram tried to gouge my eyeballs out."

Blake cried, "Your eye is gone!"

"No, it's still there. Just swollen."

Susan whispered, "How did you overpower him? Without a gun?"

"I awoke when Javier groaned and heard someone in the hall. The door was half open so I peeked out and saw an intruder. I quickly grabbed stuff from under the bed to make a dummy. I threw pillows, clothes and IV bags under the sheets then stuffed a shirt into the wig I wore to the Puerto Vallarta airport. I hid behind the door and made snoring noises. He opened the door and shot up my bed.

"I thought he'd realize it was fakery, but with colorblind night vision he probably thought the IV fluid was blood. I hadn't intended that but it probably bought me a little time. He seemed to be gloating in his victory until I clubbed him with the lamp. We fought until he tasered me. He was about to cut my eye out when Blake tasered Behram with his own gun. Blake saved us all!"

Catherine and Susan were speechless. They kissed his cheeks and hugged him. He looked proud and happy. Mostly happy.

"I'm going to check on Javier and Behram. You guys stay here."

Javier was still very weak from his near-fatal bloodletting in Baja. He barely had enough energy to snorkel. The hogtie business left him exhausted and pale. He sat against the wall, staring at Behram.

He said, "I wrapped him up a little more." Behram was gagged. Each hand was restrained to the frame and his torso wrapped with the rope.

"Strong work." I emptied Behram's backpack onto the floor. My good eye was barely a slit so I cocked my head to view his vile instruments.

Javier said, "I should hogtie him to return the favor."

"Let's cover his hate face." I placed a pillowcase over his head, covering his parasitic eyes.

"How'd he find us?"

"There must be a GPS tracer on the boat. I'll search. He probably hid one underwater." I gathered snorkel gear.

I snorkeled using a flashlight and found the tracer in less than five minutes. I removed it and crushed it on deck.

I asked, "What should we do with him?"

Catherine turned to Susan, "Will you take Blake to the other end of the boat? We need to talk." They left.

"We could leave him on the beach and call the local police." I said. "The Costa Ricans would be happy to take credit for capturing the guy who murdered an American senator."

Catherine's voice shook, "We'll never rest while he's alive! I'm sure he'll murder again, even if it's a prison guard or fellow prisoner. We should kill him."

I shifted uncomfortably, "I don't like the idea of killing him while he's helpless."

Javier looked awkward but said nothing.

She began to cry, somewhat pitifully. "I think he deserves to die. Don't you?"

"Yes, but…"

She sobbed, "Do what you think is best."

She walked away and crumpled on the deck, hugging her knees and rocking, her soft cries haunting.

I felt horrible. I didn't really know what was right. Didn't feel right leaving him alive nor killing him.

I whispered to Javier, "What do you think?"

"I don't know. I'd love to shoot him but executing a prisoner doesn't seem right."

"It's morally gray."

"At best."

"I don't want Blake to think we're cold-blooded killers."

"If we restrain him to a tree, there's no way he could escape. We can wrap him with ropes and the anchor chain."

"The Costa Ricans hate the Mexican cartels. They'll do the right thing."

Javier abruptly grabbed the boat rail, his face sweaty and pale. He slumped down, leaning against the rail.

"You feeling okay? Will you be able to help?"

"No problem. I feel fine."

"Liar."

"Just got a little light headed. You can't take him to shore by yourself. I'll help."

I sat next to Catherine and put my arms around her.

She asked timidly, "What are you going to do?"

"We don't feel right about killing him. I'll bind him so tightly, there's no way he'll escape."

She wiped tears. "I guess you're right. I'm just so scared!"

"He'll spend the rest of his life in prison."

"Susan can stay with Blake in his room. Maybe he'll go to sleep. I don't want Blake to see him again."

Javier had Behram's pistol, the only gun on the boat. We inflated the Zodiac then went downstairs and tasered him again: refried brains.

I pulled the darts from his skin and removed the ropes, but left his hands and feet restrained with the plastic ties. I pulled the pillowcase from his head.

I placed the darts in my suitcase as a victory souvenir.

As we lifted him from the bed, he suddenly lurched and bent at the waist. Still very weak, Javier dropped Behram's feet.

He kicked off the deck and twisted free of my grip. He rolled across the floor, stopping against the wall.

I booted him in the nose, like kicking a field goal.

Blood poured from his crushed nose. Kicked him again for good measure, a kidney shot.

He groaned as my boot struck his flank.

"I'll kick you to death if you try any more funny stuff."

We carried him up the stairs, wearing headlamps. Thick fog poured over the deck. The wind had shifted directions, angling away from shore.

Catherine observed with a look of disgust, her mouth twitching.

From the rear of the sailboat, we lowered the raft into the sea. Wind churned the dark waters. Looked like boiling tar.

Javier and I carried Behram down the ladder and placed him in the Zodiac.

I climbed the ladder to get supplies. I gathered the rope, winding it into a coil.

From the raft, Javier shouted over the wind, "I can help."

"I got it. Stay there." Ignoring me, he began climbing the ladder awkwardly since he had Behram's pistol in one hand.

As he transferred the pistol between hands, Behram suddenly lurched forward and yanked Javier's leg.

Falling, Javier's chin struck the ladder. He plunged into the chaotic water between the raft and the boat.

I dropped the rope and ran to the edge, but fog and swollen eyes obscured my view.

Behram reached over the raft's edge and clutched Javier's neck, pressing the straight razor to his throat. He jerked Javier side to side, keeping him unbalanced in the water.

Nearly unconscious from the blow, Javier raised Behram's pistol from the water, shakily attempting to shoot behind him.

Behram easily ripped it from his hand then aimed the laser sight at me.

I ducked below the rails. I immediately knew he'd picked up his razor when we dropped him. He'd used it cut his plastic restraints.

I could leap over the edge and try to land on Behram, but he'd have time to get shots off.

Behram announced, "I will skin the pelt from this seal, starting with his scalp."

I frantically searched the deck for a weapon, prying my best eye open with my fingers. I saw none, because we had none.

I considered running downstairs to get the Taser. Maybe I could swim under and come up behind them.

But I had no time. Javier would be dead before I reached the stairs.

CHAPTER
FIFTY

The boat pivoted. I turned and saw Catherine at the wheel, looking past me at the Zodiac. I assumed she was frantically trying to leave or something.

I shouted over the wind, "We can't leave Javier!"

She didn't reply. She was probably unhinged, abandoning Javier to save her family. She seemed intently focused on getting the wheel in exactly the right place.

Behram spat, "If you're too cowardly to watch, you can listen to his pathetic screams! Then I'll toss his scalp to you!"

Javier made a painful noise.

Catherine bolted from the cabin and ran to the rear of the boat, looking down at the raft. A strong gust struck and her hair whipped her face.

I yelled, "Get down! He's got a gun!"

Ignoring me, she shouted, "Take me instead!"

He laughed horribly. "The poisonous nurse."

I lifted my hands and slowly stood.

He pivoted the gun from Catherine to me, the laser on my chest. "Whose soul shall I free first?"

Blood was running down Javier's face. Behram held the razor to his carotid.

The fog rolled through in pulses, causing whiteout conditions. Watching both of us carefully, he swung the pistol back and forth, the red laser cleaving the sea smoke.

When it cleared a little, I noticed that her pivot brought the anchor, suspended on a rod jutting from the rear of the boat, directly over the Zodiac.

Directly over Behram.

Behram was so focused on us, he hadn't noticed.

He shouted at Catherine, "Your son will be next! I'll carve him thinly! Starting with his fingers and little piggies!"

He swung the gun toward me.

Catherine released the hundred-pound anchor, the chain rattling.

Behram startled and looked up.

The deadweight apex landed on his mouth with a brutal crunch, spraying teeth and blood.

He toppled back, his gun dropping into the water. The anchor bounced from the raft and splashed, barely missing Javier.

Behram twitched on the floor of the Zodiac. Half his nose and everything below was obliterated. His mandible was shattered and gaping, like a weird deep-sea fish with an unhinged jaw and enormous mouth.

Javier swam forward then slowly climbed the ladder, his blood-soaked face registering disbelief.

I silently watched Behram squirm.

A gale rippled the waters, the raft shuddering. The Zodiac leaked air, punctured by the anchor. Everything seemed kind of hazy and slow motion. The fog of war combined with the fog of fog.

Javier mumbled, "I'll get the knife."

He quietly backed away. Catherine followed him below deck.

Alone with the dying beast, I studied his face.

The sinister drain of his eyes was gone, replaced by horrible fear, the first time I'd seen them show anything but hatred or contempt.

His jaw muscles contracted and a piece of bone twitched. Blood and broken teeth bubbled from the preposterous yawn. Then his partially tethered tongue parted the red sea. Like the staff of Moses, transformed into a serpent.

I thought I might vomit.

The raft listed but didn't sink. A strong gust twisted the Zodiac. A warped edge jutted skyward, acting as a sail.

It began moving with increasing speed, farther and farther.

By the time Javier returned, the raft was distant, rotating away from the shore in a slow death spiral.

EPILOGUE

Nearly a week later, we entered the waters of Peru, sandy beaches interrupted by rocky points and prominent headlands. After days of numbness, our spirits soared as we saw the Andes paralleling the coast.

My eyes were healing but faint shiners remained.

Blake was oblivious to the horror we'd witnessed and his laughter was contagious. Relief and happiness slowly replaced our war-weary shock.

We pulled into a deserted Peruvian cove, about a half-mile from a luxury resort Javier visited years before. We exited the boat, carrying duffel bags and a suitcase with a hidden compartment, loaded with cash, bearer bonds, jewelry, the Monet and our alternate documents.

I returned to the sailboat and steered away from land. We'd purchased the boat under an alias but abandoning it might raise unwanted attention.

I lay an oil soaked chain of sheets on the stairs, leading to gasoline-drenched cabins. About a mile out, I lit the long wick and dove overboard, swimming toward shore.

The craft continued on its final, fatal journey.

Blake gave me a high five when I stepped onto the warm sand. We strolled the pristine beach to the resort.

About thirty minutes later, we saw the faint glow of the boat as flames erupted.

As soon as we were in our room, I connected to the Internet and devoured the news.

El Jefe had been apprehended and was being held without bail in San Diego.

The following day, Admiral Landfair was arrested. The news was plastered with perp-walk photos of Landfair, hands cuffed behind his back as military police escorted him from his office.

The FBI would not have risked arresting Landfair unless confident of the evidence. I assumed Jefe had corroborated the admiral's guilt under interrogation, no honor among thieves. Or narcos.

Their arrests had been front-page international news for weeks. The trials were months away but they'd already been convicted in the eyes of the world.

Javier's uncle was a lawyer in Lima. He deposited the money in anonymous numbered accounts in a Swiss bank's local branch. He mailed my parents an untraceable cashier's check for the borrowed money.

The jewelry was worth several million, plus we had the priceless Monet. At about ten million per adult, none of us would need to work again.

Ever.

A week later, the five of us boarded a plane to London.

When we arrived, I called my dad's friend from an airport payphone. Like before, I asked Jim to take his cell to my father's office.

When I called back, he answered, "Wyatt, it's your father. How are you?"

"Better than I've been in months. I've got quite a story for you. Are you sitting down?"

Over the next hour, I told the story and he listened, occasionally asking clarifying questions. When I apologized for lying about the gambling fiasco, he responded, "Don't say you're sorry. You did the right thing. I'm very proud of you."

I almost lost it. Even at my age, my father's unwavering support and acceptance meant so much. After a long awkward silence, I eventually regained my composure.

I requested that he and Mom travel to tell my in-laws and Javier's parents, face-to-face. Everyone needed to be sworn to secrecy as they were likely under surveillance. I gave him secure encrypted email addresses for each of us as well as contact info of a PI buddy, an ex-SEAL, who could sweep for bugs.

Finally I said, "Dad, we won't be coming back to the U.S. for a long time. Find a time in the next few months to meet us in Paris or London. I'll email details."

"We'll be there. You just say when. Send my love to Catherine and Blake."

"Tell Mom I love her. Can't wait to see you both!"

I hung up and smiled. He didn't seem even slightly rattled. It was almost like we were discussing the weather. But then again, I'd really never seen him get riled or anxious. Dad was rock solid.

We flew to Geneva then boarded a train to the Italian Alps. I'd visited South Tirol in college and fell in love with the region. We would spend the Christmas holidays in the quaint Alpine village, plus many more.

The spectacular area would be our new home.

South Tirol was Austrian until awarded to the Italians after WW II. The remote area was unbelievably beautiful. The village was a quintessential European town, surrounded by the Dolomites, rising like canine teeth. The area had an international flair, as native Tyroleans spoke German but lived in Italy. A few random Canadians would blend in with no problem. We rented a slope-side chalet, planning to ski as much as possible.

Javier and Susan would spend the holidays with us then head their separate ways. I was still uncertain if they were romantically involved. If so, they were keeping it on the lowdown. I was glad they were taking it slow, rather than latching ferociously to each other. If meant to be, it would happen in due time.

Javier planned to visit South America in the spring, making good on his idea to travel the continent on motorcycle, Che style.

I smiled, thinking about him chilling on a Brazilian beach wearing a glittering, gaudy diamond necklace from Jefe's safe: Debonair Javier.

The evening we arrived, we went for a walk on the cobblestone roads. The glowing mountains surrounded the town, illuminated with Christmas lights. We strolled past the medieval castle guarding the villa then arrived at the ancient town square, anchored by a beautiful gothic church. The town felt mysterious but inviting.

Catherine snuggled into my side. Blake threw snowballs at Javier and he returned the favor.

I felt relaxed and jubilant.

We awoke early our first morning in the Alps. After breakfast, we stepped out and clicked into our skis. We skied down to the lift and rode to the top of the mountain.

The view was expansive, glaciated mountains in all directions. Blake said, "I bet I can beat you to the bottom!"

He took off before I had a chance to answer.

Several weeks later, I unlocked a secret compartment in the suitcase. I gingerly lifted the handwritten Father's Day card that I'd taken from our house the day Behram surprised me.

I opened the card and studied Blake's drawing, titled, *The Warrior's Arrow*. Two ancient bow fighters were labeled *Dad* and *Blake*. The fighter representing Blake was handing me an arrow, like a warrior's helper. Lightning bolts raged in the background.

I read the Psalm on the cover, *"Like an arrow in the hand of a warrior, so are the sons of those who have been shaken. Hurl lightning bolts and scatter them. Shoot your arrows and rout them."*

When I read it weeks earlier at the house, I felt like I was a father without a son, a warrior without arrows. Now the card had new significance.

I thought about it, turning the card over in my hands. Rifled around and found the Taser darts Blake fired at Behram.

I carefully glued the inch-long darts to the card, on Blake's bow and in his hand. I smiled at my handiwork, at the rich symbolism. Blake fired the lightning bolts that brought our mortal enemy to his knees.

Blake shot the warrior's arrow.

ACKNOWLEDGMENT:

I would like to thank my technical advisor, SEAL commander Steve Vanlandingham, for his critical advice on the battle scenes and military info in *Caged Lightning*. Commanding Officer Vanlandingham was in charge of SEAL Team Three and led several high profile missions in Iraq and Afghanistan. Since elementary school, we've goaded each other into a variety of hazardous activities, like leaping more than 100 feet from a waterfall, raining fireworks down on a police station, breaking ice for our annual New Year's Day lake swim and writing a book together

THE AUTHOR

Dr. Brent Russell is an Emergency Physician and author (a memoir of his residency, *Miracles and Mayhem in the ER*, was published in 2013). Dr. Russell received inspiration for *Caged Lightning's* main character, Wyatt Stryker, from a fellow EM resident who served as a Green Beret. Dr. Russell grew up in the South, lived in Mexico and Paraguay as a young man, and then settled in Portland, Oregon for the first half of his career. He currently practices in Sun Valley, Idaho. Dr. Russell is an avid traveler, mountain biker and skier. He's the best break-dancer on his block (if you exclude his son). The sequel to *Caged Lightning* is forthcoming.

A strategic publisher empowering authors to strengthen their brand.

Visit Elevate Publishing for our latest offerings.
www.elevatepub.com

NO TREES WERE HARMED
IN THE MAKING OF THIS BOOK

OK, so a few did need to make
the ultimate sacrifice.

In order to steward our environment,
we are partnering with *Plant With Purpose*, to plant
a tree for every tree that paid the price for the printing of
this book.

⟹ PLANT W TH PURPOSE

www.plantwithpurpose.org

go to www.elevatepub.com/about to learn more

CPSIA information can be obtained at www.ICGtesting.com
Printed in the USA
LVOW08s1404100716

495760LV00007B/718/P

9 781943 425372